MW01482031

At Risk

Passion and Peril at Sea

By

Jackie Ullerich

Brighton Publishing LLC
501 W. Ray Rd. Suite 4
Chandler, AZ 85225
BrightonPublishing.com

At Risk

Passion and Peril at Sea

By

Jackie Ullerich

Brighton Publishing LLC
501 W. Ray Road, Suite 4
Chandler, AZ 85225
BrightonPublishing.com

Printed in the United States of America

Cover Design by
Patricia McNaught-Foster

Copyright©2011

First Edition

ISBN 13: 978-1-936587-29-2

ISBN 10: 1-936-58729-7

ᴄᴡ*Acknowledgements* ᴄᴘ

First, I owe a world of thanks to my husband Conrad for his dedication in assisting me along the slippery path to publication. Not only has he put in hours in typing my manuscripts, he has served as researcher, consultant and sometimes editor. Conrad, you're tops in my book! (Pun intended.)

To my precious daughter Nicole, your loving support and unwavering faith in me as a writer have fueled my determination to reach my goals. Bless you.

I would like to recognize Fran Pardi, an exceptional editor, from whom I learned so much. What a pleasure to work with you!

Last, but certainly not least, kudos to my dynamo of an agent, Anita Melograna of Crosswind Agency. Always accessible, creative and persevering in her zeal to provide the best representation, she also brought me into the wonderful world of Brighton Publishing.

Thanks to all!
Jackie Ullerich

ᴄᴡ*Dedication* ᴄᴘ

To My Loved Ones:

Conrad
Nicole
and Sanjay

❧ *Prologue* ❧

Late for dinner, Ben Redford hurried past boutiques and shops that led to the ship's main dining room, only to pause before the open doors. Where was everyone?

An unnatural hush, a dearth of people seated at tables, fed his anxiety. Surely it was only rumor that the ship was being placed under quarantine. Various sources had spread the word of an outbreak of Legionnaires' disease, or food poisoning, even that a woman who'd come aboard at the last port suffered a highly contagious fatal disease. Baseless rumors, for God's sake. Or so he hoped.

When Ben entered the room, he caught sight of Julio, who served his table. He was able to establish eye contact, his questioning look spurring the waiter to approach.

"Good evening, Señor. Would you like to be seated? I think you are the first to arrive." Julio's demeanor was serious, with no trace of his skittish good humor.

"Tell me what's going on." Ben kept his tone quiet, confidential. "Why aren't we moving?"

The waiter hesitated, and then said, "It's crazy around here. All these rumors, you know? Now they say there's a woman overboard." He raised both hands. "Lost, gone, we've heard."

"Oh my God." His words came out in gasps as he felt his throat close off. This was fact, not rumor. He thought about his wife. Recovering from a sinus infection, Patty elected to spend the evening in their cabin. At least, she'd been there minutes ago.

It crossed his mind it could be any woman from the ship, with hundreds at risk. He shook his head as he felt his face turn hot, then cold. A chill now coursed through his body. No, not *any* woman.

Ben turned from Julio and, at a half-run, left the dining room.

❧ *Chapter One* ❧

Pacific Palisades, California

Tracy Bradshaw stood before sliding glass doors in the master bedroom suite to look out onto the veranda. She groaned. The infamous June gloom had made a preemptive strike against the merry month of May.

In the dim morning light, the patio furniture appeared faded and uninviting, the deck drippy and sodden from mist off the ocean. With the sky overcast, the water had turned a murky gray, dankness seeping through glass barriers to envelop her.

It wasn't only the weather that rankled. She had slept fitfully after one interminable dream in which she'd presided over a group of women who viewed her with loathing and disgust. How dare she abandon her husband, the good life, *them?*

Whatever the implications of her dream, Tracy couldn't dwell on this now. She checked the time and then her bedroom mirror. She was groomed to perfection—her mother-in-law Ann Bradshaw's standards of perfection—except for a missing name tag. Big deal. She'd simply have to muddle through today's board meeting minus name identification. She'd looked for the damned thing, to no avail. Sorry about that, Ann.

In any event, it was countdown time. In fifteen minutes, not a minute before or after, her mother-in-law, name tag prominently displayed, would arrive at the front door. If it's Tuesday, it must be Assistance League. Next week, Westside Women's Club and Allied Arts. She winced. Ann was still working on her to perform for Allied Art's fall fund-raiser.

She blocked the thought, concentrating instead on the ever changing skyscape beyond their veranda. Brighter out now, the breaking clouds showcased tiny patches of blue, with the ocean taking on luster.

It took time and effort to find this dream home, high on a bluff overlooking the Pacific Ocean. Plus a little dumb luck. The sellers were divorcing, the husband under pressure to make a deal in order to accept a job offer back East.

At the time, it seemed everything had gone their way.

She thought ahead to late evening, to the possibility of a spectacular sunset, with bursts of fiery orange and gold, deepening into crimson streaks, only to soften into peachy coral, low on the horizon. Could she walk away from this? Tracy felt a welling-up in her eyes. Could she walk away from Peter?

The sounds of a door closing, of footsteps, broke into her reverie. Tracy looked at her watch. Surely not Ann.

She left the bedroom to peer over the railing at the top of the stairs. It was Peter. He set down his briefcase and took the steps, two at a time. What on earth?

"Surprised you, did I?"

"Good heavens, yes."

His fine brown hair was a bit mussed and his tie askew for well-groomed Peter. He appeared flushed, energized.

Peter stood before her and placed both hands on her shoulders, as if to steady her. "We need to talk." He looked past her into the bedroom. "The sitting room is as good a place as any."

"Now I'm really curious," Tracy said as Peter led her to the sofa. "What's going on?"

When they were seated, he said, "I have good news and bad news. The good news—the really exciting news—is that I've been asked to consider a run for state assemblyman from our district. In fact, I have a luncheon meeting today with the chairman of the selection committee."

"Oh. Wow. I need to catch my breath."

"Pretty exciting, eh?" He paused. "Or maybe not. You seem dubious."

"No, I'm thrilled for you. I was just thinking about what the job might entail."

"Think I'm in over my head?"

"Not at all. You have the law background, you're attractive and articulate. And you're the kind of man people place their trust in."

"Hey, I like that. It would make great campaign copy." He laughed, then sobered.

Something was off, Tracy thought, as she looked into his eyes, hazel darkening into brown, the fine lines of his forehead deepening.

"And the bad news?"

He reached for her hand. "I'm so sorry, but I'm going to have to back out of the cruise. An important case has been rescheduled for next week and I'll be flying up to Sacramento in the same time frame to discuss campaign strategy. If I commit, that is. But I want you to go. I insist that you go."

Tracy shook her head. "You can't be serious. First of all, I have no intention of taking a cruise by myself. Secondly, we planned this trip as a get-away for the two of us." When he didn't respond, she said, "We'll set another date. I'll phone our travel agent this afternoon."

Peter released her hand. "I think a separation would do us some good."

She swallowed hard. "What do you mean?"

He bowed his head for a moment, and then looked her in the eye. "You've seemed distant, on a different plane lately. Certainly self-absorbed." He held up his hand. "I'm not criticizing. It takes two to connect. Oh, hell, I don't know what I'm saying. I simply think a change of pace would do you a world of good. When you return, we could go off somewhere for a long weekend."

"Only a long weekend?"

He shrugged. "If I run for office, we'd be hard pressed to get away." He patted her hand, and then rose. "I know you're disappointed, and God knows I'd love for us to be together, but I'm sure you understand this is an important step in our lives."

"You say *our* lives, but Peter—" She started at the sound of the doorbell and quickly got to her feet.

They moved together out of the bedroom and to the top of the stairs. Janet, their housekeeper, was already at the front door. Peter brushed his lips against her cheek. "We'll talk more this evening."

Downstairs he greeted his mother, waved to Tracy, then ducked out the door.

"Isn't this exciting?" Ann called from below. "I heard the news from Peter Sr. minutes before I left home."

On the thin side, Tracy's mother-in-law made a fine appearance, her graying hair smartly coiffed; clothes, shoes, jewelry were understated, yet elegant.

At Ann's side now, Tracy noted imperfections as well—the loose skin under her chin, pronounced lines from her nostrils to the edges of her mouth. Surely she could afford a face lift. Tracy looked away, nonplussed, as her mother-in-law stared at her intently.

"I suppose this is all a bit much to grasp," Ann said.

"Yes. If you don't mind, I think I'll skip the board meeting. You can fill me in if there's something I need to know."

Ann nodded. "You know, I'm not much in the mood either. Why don't we sit and chat for a moment?"

The 'chat' took place over coffee in the breakfast alcove in the kitchen. Ann seemed enthralled with the new kitchen curtains and commented on the hanging plants of philodendron and ivy, the African violets that filled the window box. The woman was not into horticulture, nor did she ever miss a board meeting, all of which raised a red flag. What was coming, Tracy wondered?

As if on cue, Ann placed her cup firmly on her saucer. "Now," she said, "I'm sure you're disappointed that Peter has to miss the cruise."

So she knew about that. Tracy studied her nails, then making her tone light, said, "Peter thinks I should go on without him."

"Will you?"

"I don't really want to. No. Why would I?"

"Do you mind if I speak frankly?"

"Please do."

"Sometimes it's good for a husband and wife to be apart for a while. Not a long while, mind you," she said with a twinkle. "What I'm trying to say is that a brief separation might be good for both of you."

Tracy gave a little snort. "What is this, a conspiracy, you and Peter in cahoots? He said the same thing."

Ann shook her head. "Believe me, Tracy, I've never discussed you with Peter. Now with Jenny, that was another matter. At any rate, I can't help but think the trip would bring back that sparkle in your eyes, serve as a pepper-upper." She paused. "You've seemed preoccupied, a bit down lately. Furthermore, when Peter and his advisors move forward with the campaign, you'll have to hunker down for the duration."

"*If*, Peter decides to run. He said we'd talk about it this evening."

"Oh. I didn't think there was any doubt."

Tracy felt the warmth suffuse her face. High color was her Scottish father's depiction of Tracy with her dander up. "I thought it was customary for husbands or wives to consult with their spouses before entering the political arena."

"Well, yes, I suppose so." Ann gave a small cough. "I expect the two of you will work it out." She paused to sip her coffee. "Why did you and Peter decide on the Mexican Riviera? I'm sure it's a lovely trip but personally, I've always fancied the Caribbean."

Tracy shrugged. "It started out as a toss-up between the two places, though I may have tilted the board toward Mexico because of my interest in Mexico's history and culture. However, Peter was all for this trip. He thought the itinerary was excellent. Also, I wanted to make notes on the areas we visited as background for a writing project. But now that's beside the point. I'm not going. Period."

Tracy looked on as her mother-in-law checked her watch, and then pushed back her chair. 'Writing project' apparently failed to engender any curiosity.

"I'd better be on my way. It's one thing to play hooky from a meeting, but I don't dare miss my hair appointment."

"I'll walk with you to the front door," Tracy said.

Only steps outside the kitchen, Ann turned and placed her hand on Tracy's arm. "When I think of the contrast between you and Jenny, it simply astounds me. She was a selfish, shallow woman, immature beyond belief. Obviously, I'm glad she's out of Peter's life. *And* that he found you." She raised her eyebrows as if to underscore her remark. "You're a lovely young woman, Tracy, and so right for Peter. Well." She took a breath and flashed a smile. "Talk to you tomorrow. I'll see myself out."

Tracy returned her proffered kiss, adding that yes, they would talk tomorrow.

With Ann out the door and on her way, Tracy wandered aimlessly back into the kitchen and then into the family room. Oh yes, she knew all about Jenny, the total bitch—at least from her mother-in-law's perspective. Peter had apprised her of their doomed marriage, taking care not to disparage his ex-wife. But he was devastated over the failure of his marriage, blaming himself for his 'error in judgment', for his shortsightedness in teaming up with a woman whose character flaws should have been obvious to him in their courtship.

Tracy couldn't have cared less about the long-departed Jenny, but it disturbed her that Peter should be so hard on himself. Could he withstand a second marital failure? It was a question she pushed back into the recesses of her mind, unwilling to contemplate the consequences of leaving him. And now on the horizon were Peter's political aspirations. Oh, God.

She stood before her desk, taking solace from the portrait of her parents, taken on their twenty-fifth wedding anniversary. She had her mother's nose, which was more aquiline than straight, but mostly she resembled her father. On the tall side for a woman, she had inherited John McDermott's smoky blue eyes, vibrant coloring, and brownish-black hair. Her face was too long to be labeled a perfect oval, but she was blessed with high cheekbones, courtesy of her mother.

Sophia, her dear, darling mother died of a heart attack only a few months after this picture was taken.

She thought back to the time Peter had introduced her to his parents, of how taken she'd been with them and of how warmly accepting they were of her, of Tracy McDermott. Later, when they learned of her background, that she was half-Jewish, she sensed a small but discernible withdrawal on Ann's part. Was she being super sensitive? Probably. But she encountered the same subtle distancing from others as well.

Be that as it may, this was not the time to dwell on *that*.

Tracy left the family room for their bedroom, with the thought of changing out of her suit and into more casual attire. But once inside the room, a sudden radiance of sunshine drew her to the veranda.

She stared out at the ocean, her beloved ocean, and thought about the Mexican waters off the Sea of Cortez, the bustling Old Town of Puerto Vallarta, of Zihuatanejo's quaintness. Of Acapulco's glamour.

With Ann, she had been adamant over her decision to stay home. Less so, with Peter. At any rate, she'd convinced herself she could not, would not, take the cruise by herself.

And then she thought about her husband's decision to alter their lives without consulting her—never mind he'd said *if* I commit, *if* I run for office. Because that was crap. And, damn it, Ann knew before she did about Peter's presumptive run for office, his backing out of the cruise.

Suddenly she wanted to go. And why not? Neither her husband nor her mother-in-law would object since they regarded a cruise as a cure-all for what ailed her. Depressed, moody, preoccupied? She knew better. Try bored, stagnated, and distressed over the lack of challenge in her life, and Peter's unwillingness to confront these issues.

Aside from sightseeing, she'd make time for writing and relaxation, a break from the constraints imposed upon her.

And for reflecting on whether or not she wanted to end her marriage.

❧ *Chapter Two* ☙

Phoenix, Arizona

Joanne Watkins had convinced herself that stepping out of her marriage was not an option; yet at times she wondered what life would be like without Jack Watkins. The thought would bubble up from out of a cauldron of repression only to dissipate into fragmented images, too indistinct to pursue. Like now, for God's sake, when she should be focused on happy and exciting events to come.

Blame these incursions on stress—*good* stress, but stress nonetheless. Ah, but relief was close at hand.

And as Joanne stood at the kitchen sink in her Phoenix home, she eyed the bottle of vodka on the counter. She'd had cocktails before dinner, but that was then, and in view of tomorrow's events, a celebratory nightcap was definitely in order.

She filled her glass half full with ice, poured in vodka, and as she removed one ice cube, then another, she contemplated the next ten days.

It was not that she was unused to travel, having toured the U.S. and abroad as a military wife. But she'd never enjoyed the constant moves, all the packing and unpacking, plus setting up new households. Joanne thought about friends she'd made, and then lost with each move, about the difficulty of adjusting to foreign cultures or of having to endure stateside regions that were distasteful to her.

This time, however, was different. Hallelujah. She and Jack were about to embark on a Mexican Riviera cruise, with no conditions thrust upon them other than to take pleasure in each day. Moreover, Jack had insisted on booking a cabin with a balcony, and though she protested the added expense, secretly she was pleased with this added luxury.

Her husband, recently retired as an Air Force Lt. Colonel, seemed at loose ends, disinterested in attending to his coin collection and no longer pouring over his precious books on history and economics. She hoped this break might lessen his restlessness and provide some space before starting a second career if, indeed, he chose to do so.

Joanne tasted her drink, and then took another sip, thinking back to when they'd signed up for the cruise. At first she'd been only cautiously excited as she planned ahead, mindful of real and imagined complications that might cause them to cancel the trip. Gradually she'd relaxed, allowing herself to take pleasure in planning her wardrobe, in making decisions regarding shore excursions. Now that the trip was a day off, she felt confident nothing would go wrong, even feeling a sense of joyful anticipation.

Joyful? Joanne puckered her lips, as she used her finger to swirl the ice in her drink. No sense in getting carried away. On the downside, she worried about fitting in, whether people would seek her out or simply ignore her.

Enough of that. With her free hand, she opened the patio doors and stepped out into the desert night. The air was fragrant, and even in the dark she could detect cacti, towering saguaros and palm trees in silhouette that yielded to a glittering ceiling of stars. She inhaled the night, enjoying the quiet, the solitude.

Except that in the absence of distractions, maybe it was too quiet. She sipped her drink, resisting then giving in to troubling thoughts that crept into her mind like little demons in gleeful play, jabbing at her temples.

Ha! Substitute Jack for demons. Joanne raised her glass and drank deeply. Well, for gosh sakes, it was only a phone call—a *long* call Jack had taken two days ago behind the closed doors of their den.

Later, he explained that a fellow officer he'd worked with in the finance office on base had called to chat, to update Jack on news from the workplace.

For a full hour, and in private? That didn't sound right to her. Had a woman been on the line? Joanne let out a soft giggle. Wrong assumption. Not even close. Jack as a ladies' man prompted another giggle.

Still, after the phone call, her husband had perked up—a lot. Which was good, of course. Then why couldn't she shake her uneasiness over the clandestine nature of the call?

Joanne raised her glass again. Why, why, why? Who cared? Jeez, it was warm for a May night. Nature could take a flying leap. She had better things to do than stare at the stars.

As Joanne reentered the kitchen, she was surprised to see Jack. "I thought you'd gone to bed," she said.

He smiled. "I see you're having—what, a nightcap? Maybe I'll join you. We can toast the start of an adventure."

"Oh, Jack, that sounds like fun. Would you like me to fix you a scotch and soda?" At his nod, she found what she needed and busied herself at the sink, mixing his drink. When she was finished, she poured a little more vodka into her glass. To keep Jack company.

She joined her husband at the breakfast table. "I know I won't sleep tonight with all we have ahead of us." She stared into her drink, forming images in her head. "Imagine being able to sit out on our balcony and follow the path of the moon on the water, or to drink coffee in the morning sunshine." She smiled and looked up. "And what is that song '—down Acapulco way'?"

"Waxing poetic, are you?" He raised his eyebrows, his gaze falling briefly on her drink.

She would not let him spoil her mood. "I hope the band on board ship is good. We haven't danced in a while."

He raised his glass in a salute. "We'll show them. We always do."

Joanne nodded in return, but what now occupied her thoughts reached beyond dancing, beyond sightseeing. Simply put, would she be able to play bridge? Surely there would be passengers willing to make up a foursome. Call it a diversion, a time filler.

She drained her glass. Come on, Joanne, bridge was more than a means to pass the time. What was that expression she'd learned in French class? *Raison d'être?* Reason to be. Wait a minute. *Bridge* was her reason to be, the focus of her life? She felt an almost uncontrollable desire to laugh but quelled it in time.

Yet what if it were true she was addicted to the game? She had broached the subject to Jack, but he had simply shrugged, as if it didn't matter. Well, so be it. She wasn't harming herself or others by playing bridge, for God's sake.

Jack barely touched his drink. "I think I'll have a tiny bit more," she said, getting to her feet. "Want me to top off your drink?"

"This is plenty. But go ahead, help yourself. We'll drink another toast."

Ah, she thought, as she filled her glass, what a great beginning to an incredible happening. They would be pampered, wined, and dined, with all their needs attended to. Forget responsibility, the humdrum of day in and day out.

Maybe she could even put Teddy out of her mind. She passed the back of her hand across her forehead, as if to erase images. Their son's latest falling out with his father had been ugly, to put it mildly. Joanne felt a tear slide down the side of her nose. Yelling, cursing, accusations, ultimatums—oh, Lord, she didn't want to think about it. What she wanted, wanted desperately, was her son back home, or at least to know where he was.

She sipped her drink, responding to small talk from Jack, while in the back of her mind she searched her memory for advice which her mother had given her, for nuggets of wisdom to help her cope with another family crisis. Not that her mother had ever come up with much, she conceded.

Much of what? She'd lost her train of thought. Oh. Advice. Now she remembered. "You stash away your troubles in a box, seal the box, and label it *LATER.*"

Jack was giving her the strangest look. Had she spoken aloud? No matter. The important thing was to box up your troubles and—whatever the rest of it was.

She raised her glass to her lips in a silent toast. Here's to putting on hold suspect phone calls. And—she glanced at Jack—here's to our son, wherever he may be.

❧ *Chapter Three* ❧

Alexandria, Virginia

Patty Redford had engaged in a frenzy of activity during the day in preparation for the cruise, all the while giving thanks for the privilege of sailing off with a man she adored.

Now, in late evening, came the best part.

"What do you think, Ben?" Patty moved her feet in one-two-three waltz rhythm, then performed a dramatic twirl, mindful that even in three inch heels, she made a doll-like appearance before her tall, lanky husband. "Do you like chiffon? Will this dress be suitable for one of our formal nights? The Captain's reception, perhaps?"

She had invaded his den, interrupting his work as she modeled selections from her wardrobe in preparation for the cruise.

Ben lay down his pen and set aside his notebook, giving her his mock put-upon expression. "Let's see now," he said. "This is the fourth, or fifth, or maybe sixth evening dress. Isn't the Mexican Riviera cruise casual?"

"Oh, you darling," she said, pushing herself up onto the edge of his desk. "I know you're teasing. Well? Come on, what do you think. Is this old lady going to make the cut?"

He leaned back in his chair and crossed his arms behind his head. "If forty-eight is old, what does that make me? Ancient at fifty? But to answer question number one, I like this dress and every dress you've trotted out for me. And your impromptu dance performances. Take them all."

Patty laughed. "And then what? Change gowns in the middle of the evening? Too much work, my love. So. Now I have to choose three out of the total, not to mention earrings, bracelets, rings, bags, shoes—oh, sweetie, you don't know the half of it."

He sat forward and placed his hand over hers. "We could always stay home," he said softly.

"I didn't hear that," she said in a sing-song tone. She was about to tease back but then her gaze strayed to his notebook. "With classes over, I thought you'd have put the university behind you."

Ben released her hand, and then placed the notebook and other papers in a bottom drawer. "This has nothing to do with the university. I'm working on a small project for the FBI. I'll finish it when we return from Mexico. Which reminds me, I'm only half packed."

He came around to help her to her feet. "You need to decide on your formal wear, plus the razzle dazzle stuff."

She nodded. "Maybe I'll throw in a few extra goodies in case there's a talent show. Now don't make that face, Ben. I'm not suggesting you try out. If you had to choose between facing an audience and jumping overboard, we both know what your choice would be."

"Sweetheart, when classes are in session, I face a huge audience several times a week. Granted, I'm not at the lectern to entertain— economics doesn't lend itself to gripping, edge-of-the-seat dynamics— but I rarely see heads nodding or eyes glazed over. At any rate, we need to be up early tomorrow morning, so we'd better get moving."

She stood on tiptoe to kiss him softly on the lips and received a hug in return. "You're not only dear, but brilliant to boot. How could I get so lucky?"

His smile, the love in his eyes were like a tonic that charged her energies, imbuing her with the desire to put his needs above hers, to take pleasure from his pleasure.

Life had not always been this euphoric. Both had been granted second chances. For her, this marriage was the antithesis of a short and dismal first trip to the altar. For Ben, who had remained single after a failed relationship, she could only hope their union fulfilled his expectations, expunging the heartbreak from the past.

Patty had to restrain a giggle. How two such disparate individuals could come together was simply beyond her. But who was she to question?

Ben had put his desk in order and as they made their way out of the den, Patty thought about the lengthy trip to Los Angeles where they would board the ship. It would be a grueling day, for sure, but worth it. She was tickled pink to be making her first trip to Mexico; moreover, it was Ben who initiated the idea. True, they had discussed the need to get away, even to embark on something frivolous. But Mexico? She had let out a whoop and holler of excitement when Ben brought home the brochure on the *Sea Star* cruise line.

Only later did it occur to her that it was out of character for Ben to opt for Mexico over Europe or Asia. Then she dismissed the thought. Why not Mexico? Why shouldn't he target the type of vacation that would delight his wife?

Now as Patty sat at her dressing table, she wanted to sing out "Hooray! Hooray!" that Ben would leave his work at home, though she did wonder why he'd cleared his desk so quickly. This, in turn, made her think about her husband's relationship with the FBI. At first, she'd thought it strange Ben would become involved with the organization, given his distinguished academic background. After all, the man was a full professor, with a PhD in economics. But he also had a degree in criminology, which could account for his interest in FBI matters.

Still, it wasn't as simple as that. What triggered the bureau's notice, she remembered, was the paper Ben published on the subject of fringe groups—hate groups.

She smiled as she reached for a tissue. Could she possibly be jealous of a big, gray entity that in present times projected a tarnished, rather than heroic image?

Not likely. On the other hand, it was Ben's dedication to these so-called projects, his peppiness, the spring in his step when he was 'consulting', whatever that meant, that gave her pause.

Of course she wasn't jealous. She was glad something other than his wife brought him alive.

Just so long as it wasn't another woman.

❧ *Chapter Four* ☙

United Airlines, Flight 602, Sacramento to Los Angeles

"Gawd, they make these seats so narrow." Shirley Goodweather wriggled her ample derriere into a more comfortable position, and then fastened her seatbelt.

Her traveling companion, Jodie Campbell, was already settled and leafing through a magazine she'd taken from the pocket in front of her.

Shirley tucked strands of golden-blond hair behind her ears, revealing four little yellow butterflies, connected by tiny clear green stones, dangling from her ears. She purchased her outfit, a yellow and green patterned sundress, to match her earrings, and then came upon a green and gold choker necklace that was a perfect match.

Her ring, however, was the *pièce de résistance*. She raised her hand to the window for the light to capture the splendor of topaz and emeralds in an ornate gold setting. So what if it was faux or fake. Who would know?

She turned to Jodie. "I swore I was going to lose pounds and pounds before the cruise, but wouldn't you know we crank out an office party for Dr. Edlemann and his fiancée and then up pops a baby shower and a wedding shower all in the same gosh darned week. Then the gang takes me out to lunch for my birthday. And, of course, it never fails that someone brings in doughnuts or cookies at least three times a week." She sighed. "I guess when you turn forty-two, the old metabolism just putt-putts along."

Jodie closed her magazine with a snap. "Shirley, you're not fat. Well, you're not thin, either. You're just right for you. Furthermore, I can tell you're going to have the time of your life. You already look radiant."

"Oh, aren't you the doll," Shirley said, squeezing her friend's hand. "You look great, too." But she didn't really, Shirley thought. Jodie looked peaked, with dark circles under her eyes. She also seemed droopy. What was that word? Lethargic. Maybe after the cruise, she'd suggest Jodie make an appointment with Dr. Edlemann for a check-up.

Shirley put all this aside now as they prepared for take-off. Once airborne, they could relax and enjoy each other's company.

Later, as they sipped Cokes, Shirley felt a glowing sense of well-being. The Mexican Riviera! It had such a romantic sound. She studied the brochure, entranced by sunset colors turning exotic structures a soft pink, captivated by stretches of sea and sand along the ports that promised fun in the sun. And oh, the ship. The *Sea Star* was to die for with its restaurants and bars, the dance floor, the show room.

She started as Jodie gave her a poke. "What are you smiling about?" she asked.

Jodie had placed the blanket they'd found on their seats around her shoulders. Shirley thought to comment, and then decided otherwise. "I was thinking happy thoughts. About the cruise, I mean." She paused. "You know, Chuck, my second husband, planned to take us on a cruise. 'Anywhere in the world you want to go, babe. Caribbean, Mexico, Europe? You name it.'" She gave a snort. "That was before I caught him and my neighbor Doreen in a nooner at our house, in our *bed,* for God's sake." Shirley noted the woman across the aisle craning her neck to get a look at her. Nosey old biddy. So okay. She had a voice that carried.

"And then there was Glen, husband jerk number one. Oh, could he sweet talk you, like clear to the moon and back. Me and a dozen other women. The only decent thing that came out of that marriage was my son, Steve. Now he's a nifty guy, the best." She shook her head. "I don't know why I'm attracted to losers. At least there was great sex. For a while. And boy, honey, do I miss that."

Jodie set down her Coke. "Maybe you'll find Mr. Right on the cruise."

"Fat chance, with my luck. What about you?"

Jodie clutched the blanket tighter to her chest. "Hank was my whole life, Shirley. When he died, I pretty much lost interest in men. But you never know."

"That's the spirit. It'll be a hoot, shopping in the ports, gambling in the casino, seeing the shows." Head back, she closed, then opened her eyes. "Can you picture all those yummy desserts? And who knows? We might even pick up on some guys who are single."

Jodie made a face. "If they're not a hundred years old."

"Oh, who needs men, anyway?" Shirley said, rolling her eyes.

17

Jodie smiled in return, then leaned her head back on the seat and closed her eyes.

Shirley looked askance at her friend. *This was supposed to be a festive, fun flight. Come on, Jodie, we're supposed to throw confetti, pump up balloons, so to speak.* Except the confetti had scattered, the balloons shriveling into faded blobs of litter.

Shirley took a deep breath. Something wasn't right with Jodie. She had tried to bury a sense of uneasiness, to ignore what was obvious: that the woman was unwell.

Jodie must have felt Shirley's gaze. She opened her eyes and sat upright.

"Are you okay?" Shirley asked.

"Good question. I'm—I'm not sure." She paused as if to gather her thoughts. "I do know I lack energy, and I'm cold a lot of the time. I probably should see a doctor."

"Why in the world haven't you?"

Jodie shrugged. "Except for my feet swelling, it's not as if I have any specific symptoms—aches, pains, headaches. Also it hasn't been long since I was made loan supervisor at the bank. It would have been awkward to ask to take time off."

"What do you bet the cruise will bring back the old pizzazz," Shirley said, giving her a comforting pat.

"Wouldn't that be wonderful?"

Yes, wouldn't it? Shirley thought. But her apprehension was building. Jodie would not expect her to play nursemaid. If it came to that. However, the picture was far from rosy. More like sad, even bleak.

Oh, hell, why did this have to happen?

❧ *Chapter Five* ☙

First Night at Sea

Her husband had been overly generous, Tracy Bradshaw thought as she settled on the sofa in her stateroom to feast her gaze on the floral display before her. Yellow and white roses, irises, anthurium, and carnations, interlaced with baby breath and backed by several varieties of greenery provided a breathtaking spring flower arrangement.

Part of her questioned this grand gesture. Was Peter making up for not seeing her off? His reasons, business related, were surely legitimate, his goodbye warm and tender. And yes, they had made love the night before. Still, some of what passed between them seemed to her forced, lacking in spontaneity.

They had talked, briefly, about Peter's possible run for office, with the word 'if' recurring a lot. Mainly, they agreed on the necessity for further discussion. Had she been too hard on Peter in assuming she had no say in the matter, for assuming his candidacy was already in the works? Probably.

Tracy examined his card for the second or third time. It read: "Relax, enjoy. I'll think of you every day. All my love, Peter." She had to smile. His message was not exactly a paean to love, a soaring declaration of devotion, but from Peter, meaningful.

Earlier Maria, her cabin attendant, brought Tracy a basket of fruit, along with what appeared to be a note or invitation.

Now she was back with the bucket of ice Tracy had ordered for the champagne her in-laws provided to celebrate first night at sea. "May I open the bottle for you?" Maria asked.

"Please do." Peter Sr. and Ann would have chosen only the best, and she might as well enjoy a glass of bubbly before dinner.

There was a loud pop as the cork trajected toward the ceiling, followed by a giggle or two from the women. But when Maria left the room, Tracy was struck by the stillness. It was as if she wandered onto a deserted stage, now bereft of laughter or pathos. What remained was the set, with its soft lighting, multiple mirrors, pale blue carpeting, with matching blue and cream bedspread and draperies.

She felt on the brink of tears. What had possessed her? She had been right in the first place that she had no business going off on her own. How could she have been so crazy to think she could pull it off?

Because, she reminded herself, she wanted adventure, a break from the predictable. And time to think. She sighed. What was that saying, be careful what you wish for? Well, good or bad, the die was cast.

She ambled over to the dresser where Maria placed the fruit basket, curious as to what the envelope contained. Aha! It was an invitation, though not one she was particularly thrilled about. A pre-dinner cocktail reception was scheduled the following evening in the library for solo travelers. She'd skip that, she thought. Though on the other hand, a depiction of rapacious singles, circling for the kill would add spice to her journalistic jottings.

She studied her reflection in the mirror above the dresser. First night at sea was always casual, and she opted for a jaunty navy blue and white top with gold buttons to wear over navy blue slacks. It was a look, complemented by shoulder length hair and subdued makeup, which raised the question of age. Did she really look all of thirty-two? Definitely not. There now. She felt better already.

With about forty minutes to go until second sitting at 8:15, Tracy resolved to enjoy her balcony, along with a glass of champagne.

Outside, she felt wind and spray and moved her chair back from the railing, close to the floor-to-ceiling glass doors that opened onto the balcony. She had expected a more balmy evening and a less choppy sea, but that would change, she knew, as they headed south. Tomorrow they would spend a full day in Cabo San Lucas.

As Tracy sipped her champagne, she became aware of voices from the adjoining balcony. She knew from the outlay of the ship the cabin next to hers was smaller by almost three hundred square feet. Here she was luxuriating in all this extra space, but Peter had insisted she sally forth as planned. As they had planned, she amended, tightening her grip on the glass.

The teary feeling was upon her once more but waned as the voices on the next balcony took on a rancorous tone. She'd had a brief glimpse of this couple earlier when they'd all left their staterooms for the life boat drill. The man, about her height, sporting a crew cut, had smiled at her, showing even white teeth that gleamed against tanned skin. She had smiled back, adding a "Hi," but the woman was unresponsive. In retrospect, she appeared—dazed? No, unfocused was more like it.

Now, Tracy listened shamelessly and was rewarded by an escalation in pitch, the words "—I didn't expect to find—" and then sounds that were muffled, too low to distinguish.

She raised her glass to her lips, only to freeze. Chimes from the intercom carried outside. It was probably something innocuous, as in greetings from the captain, but she hurried into the cabin, closing the glass doors behind her. "—sorry to announce," she heard, "that due to a medical emergency, the ship is returning to port in Los Angeles, from where we will once again set sail."

Tracy could imagine a collective groan from throughout the ship. "Not good, not good," she muttered. Was this an omen, a sign they were destined to make news as one of those so-called cruises from hell? *At least the air conditioning still functioned, the toilets hadn't overflowed, nor had they experienced engine trouble or hit a reef. Yet.*

She began to laugh. What would be, would be. So on to the next adventure. She checked her table assignment, and then said a silent prayer. Please, no loudmouths, querulous little old ladies, or droning-on-and-on bores.

There was always room service, she reminded herself as she left the room.

She hoped it would not come to that.

The Oceanic Dining Room lived up to its name, Tracy thought, admiring the muted blue-green carpeting, with chairs in similar but deeper hues, highlighted by touches of silver. Huge, glittering chandeliers brought a dazzling elegance, while wall sconces between the windows provided a more intimate glow.

Oh, good, it looked as if the Maître d' were leading her to a window table. She had requested a table for six or eight—and six it was. She wasn't the first to arrive, she realized, as one couple was already seated.

Following her escort's lead, she came around to face the twosome and was seated. Well, what do you know. The couple from next door.

The man was all smiles. "I think we're neighbors," he said. "Right, Joanne? Allow me to introduce myself. I'm Jack Watkins, Lt. Col., retired, and this is my wife, Joanne. We're from Phoenix."

"Nice to meet both of you. I'm Tracy Bradshaw, and I must say this is quite a coincidence."

Joanne looked at her husband, and then favored Tracy with a tentative smile. "Yes, I agree. A coincidence."

Jack shook his head. "Some way to start a cruise, ladies. Imagine having to return to L.A."

Joanne seemed to perk up a bit. "What do you suppose happened?"

Jack looked straight at Tracy. "Why don't we ask this lovely young lady her opinion?"

Oy vey, Tracy thought, brushing off the fact her mother would have deplored her use of the phrase. "I suppose it could be anything from someone dying to breaking a hip or leg. These things happen," she added lamely.

Joanne nodded, her faint smile an indication she'd come to the party.

"Fortunately, we stand to lose only about four hours," Jack said.

Joanne stared at her intently, as if assessing her vital statistics, her character. Suddenly she brightened, and her lips curved into a smile. "Tracy. I'll bet you're a bridge player. Are you?"

"I've played some, especially back in college, but I'd have to read up on bidding and no trump, not to fall on my face. The truth is, Joanne, I was never very good at the game."

"Oh." Joanne's expression became a polite mask, and she turned to her menu.

Tracy felt as though she'd failed some sort of test. She caught Jack's eye, and he gave her a sympathetic wink. Oh, my, bring on the old ladies, the loudmouths, and the bores.

Actually, things were looking up. A tall, nice-appearing man and a smiling petite woman were approaching their table. Her soft blond hair framed a conventionally pretty face; her eyes, a true blue, reflected delight in the moment.

They took seats next to Tracy and across from the Watkinses. One chair stood vacant across from Tracy.

"What a lovely table," the woman said, her hands aflutter. "I'm sorry we're late. It's my fault. I tend to dawdle or lose track of time. It drives my darling nuts."

"Hardly ever," he said with a wry grin, "though we didn't earn any Brownie points with the crew by showing up late for the life boat drill."

She patted his hand, then said, "I suppose we should sit boy, girl, but my husband, with his long legs, is always more comfortable at the end of the table. We're the Redfords," she continued, "Ben," she nodded toward her husband, "and I'm Patty."

After Tracy and the Watkinses introduced themselves, Patty addressed Joanne. "As a military wife, I'm sure you've had some amazing adventures, especially in foreign places. Before the cruise is over, I hope you'll share some of your experiences?"

Joanne's pale skin had taken on color. "We could give it a try," she said, with a nervous laugh. "More to the present, I was wondering if you're a bridge player, Patty."

"Yes, I play two, sometimes three times a month."

Jack was shaking his head. "Joanne, for goodness sakes, you can play bridge anytime. I'm sure these folks have better things to do."

Patty smiled at Joanne. "We could certainly get up a game sometime. Don't you think so, Ben?"

"Sure, I'd be willing."

Jack turned to Ben. "I'll venture a guess you're in the medical field. Are you Dr. Redford?"

"Yes, but I'm not an MD."

Jack nodded. "PhD. I should have known. You have that scholarly look about you. What field?"

"Economics."

"Ah." Jack's expression turned secretive, his eyes taking on a peculiar gleam. "I'm an avid student of the political process which, of course, is tied in with economic theory. I'd welcome a discussion on either subject."

Ben quirked his head, giving Jack a speculative look. "What did you have in mind?"

Their waiter appeared as well as the sommelier, to take dinner and wine orders.

"I guess now is not the time," Jack said, flashing his wide smile.

Their appetizers arrived shortly, followed by a bottle of wine for each couple. Tracy also elected to order a bottle, since it would undoubtedly serve her for several nights.

She wondered if there would be a sixth person joining their table. Strange, he or she had not yet shown. As for the others, Tracy had taken an instant liking to the Redfords. Patty, especially, perked up the table. That she appeared somewhat scatterbrained in contrast to her more sober-sided husband was not off-putting, but endearing.

Square jawed, with wavy brown hair, Ben might be considered almost handsome, Tracy mused. Like his wife, his eyes, meltingly brown, were his best feature, even behind stylish gold-rimmed glasses. She detected, however, a hint of arrogance in his demeanor, and suspected he did not suffer fools easily.

At any rate, the Redfords seemed affectionate and at ease with one another.

Not so the Watkinses. Tracy sensed tension, an undercurrent of coolness between them. Or it could be she read too much into what she surmised was a hostile exchange earlier.

Jack, she observed, had gone out of his way to engage her in conversation, as if to make up for his wife's show of indifference toward her. Apparently, not playing bridge was tantamount to being uncouth or at the very least, unenlightened.

Tracy pushed aside the chilled bowl that had contained a delicious shrimp cocktail. On second thought, she didn't think his attentiveness had anything to do with Joanne. Not that it mattered, but Jack Watkins seemed hell-bent on wanting to impress her. Was he coming on to her?

They completed their soup course and now as their waiter, Julio, placed salads in front of them, Patty turned to Tracy. "I may be off base, but do I detect a slight English accent?"

"My, but you have a good ear," Tracy said. "I was born in London, but by the time I was school age, my father had to return to the states."

"Foreign service?" Jack asked. It appeared she had the attention of the entire table.

"No. At that time, my father worked for Brown and Thompson Publishing. He met my mother while he was assigned to their London division."

"We had a tour of duty in England," Joanne said. "I take it your mother is English?"

"No, she was born in America."

"Sounds as if there's a story there," Ben said. "How did your parents meet?"

"At a fundraising event where my mother was guest of honor." At his questioning look, she continued, "My mother was a concert pianist and quite well known in European musical circles. More so there than in the United States. My father says he was captivated by her talent and charm." Tracy smiled. "Obviously enough for them to build a life together."

"And her name?" Patty asked.

"Professionally she went by the name Resnik—Sophia Resnik."

Ben nodded, while the Watkinses looked at her blankly.

Patty set down her salad fork. "Sophia Resnik! I have some of her recordings. Oh, isn't this exciting. Tracy, you must tell us about this wonderful woman. To think your mother is this accomplished performer. To think—" She stopped as all eyes focused on the woman who now took her place opposite Tracy.

"I'm Shirley Goodweather," she announced. The table was complete.

As the third round of introductions began, Tracy was glad attention had shifted from her to the newcomer. Not because she disliked talking about her mother—quite the contrary. It was what inevitably followed that she wanted to avoid, questions pertaining to her own musical aspirations.

"I'll skip the appetizer and soup. Just bring on the salad," Shirley said to the waiter who made a sudden appearance. She threw up her hands. "Honest to God. What I've been through." Her statement was directed to the table at large. "My girlfriend and I were supposed to be at another table, but then she had to bow out." She shook her head. "Curtain down. Refund the money, honey."

Ben gave Shirley a quizzical look. "Would this have something to do with our having to return to L.A.?"

"Would it ever. Oh, jeez, what a mess. I mean I come on vacation with a good friend. We're supposed to keep each other company, right? I'm supposed to have someone to shop with, to have a drink in the bar with, and to see the shows with, right?" She paused to examine the salad placed before her, then continued, "I could see it coming that Jodie wasn't well. I mean, the poor kid was practically out of it.

"So. We get back to the cabin after the lifeboat drill, and Jodie says she's feeling dizzy or nauseated. Anyway, she goes into the bathroom, and I hear this sound like a moan, then a thud. Well, my God, she's passed out on the floor and in that tiny space, it looks like she's hit her head on the edge of the basin or toilet."

"Oh, how awful." Patty shook her head, as the others murmured like sentiments.

"Sounds serious," Tracy said, "since returning to L.A. must mean they need to hospitalize her."

Shirley nodded, taking time now to taste her salad. "It's serious, all right," she said between bites. "She was disoriented when she came to, and the doctor thinks she may have a concussion. At any rate, she's down in the medical clinic and from what I could gather, they're watching her very carefully."

"It's a darn shame for both of you," Patty said, "particularly for that poor woman. Did the doctor have any ideas as to why this happened?"

"If he did, he's not confiding in me."

"What about your plans?" Joanne asked.

"What do you mean, my plans? Am I going to go on with the trip? I don't see why not."

Oh, oh, Tracy thought, *we're getting defensive and probably feeling more than a tad guilty.*

Their entrees were now being served, with conversation slacking off as they began to eat.

Whatever Shirley's feelings over her current predicament, Tracy could only assume that under less trying circumstances, she was a pleasant, good-natured individual. Tracy suppressed a snicker. If manner of dress offered a clue to personality, then the woman was definitely outgoing. The floridly patterned sun dress spoke volumes, her earrings and necklace overkill.

It was the ring that fascinated Tracy the most. Garish beyond belief was her uncharitable assessment. But then, Shirley probably thought Tracy's outfit and accessories boring and unimaginative.

Shirley now stared at Tracy, wide-eyed. "When I came to the table, did I hear all of you talking about your mother? That she was famous?"

"Yes, indeed." It was Patty who responded, who with much gusto recited the details of Tracy's background.

Thank you, Patty, was Tracy's thought. But apparently she wasn't off the hook regarding her personal life. Shirley's gaze was now glued to Tracy's diamond solitaire and wedding band.

Tracy decided to dispel any misconceptions. "My husband had to back out of the cruise at the last minute. For business reasons."

"At least you have a husband," Shirley said. "Let me guess. He's in real estate. No? How about broker, lawyer—ah, lawyer, that's it," she said, responding to Tracy's nod.

Once again, all eyes focused on Tracy. "Criminal law?" Ben asked.

"Nothing so high profile. Corporate law, trust deeds, that sort of thing."

"Big money in that," Jack said, raising his eyebrows.

"Whatever your husband does," Shirley said, "the fact remains you and I are on our own, so let's take some tours together. I'll go over the list with you. And what about the cocktail reception tomorrow evening? You're going, aren't you?"

"I'm not sure. I look at it as a gathering for singles and obviously, I'm not single."

"Never, never pass up a party," Shirley said. "Besides, you'd add class to any wingding. Incidentally, I love your hairstyle. Do you think I'd look good with the same cut and styling?"

"You look fine just the way you are. Your hair is lovely."

Shirley beamed. "Thank you. I'll take that as a huge compliment, coming from a person with your taste."

They were now on the dessert course and as Shirley began quizzing Jack about his military career, mentioning she had a son in the service, Patty gave Tracy a nudge. "I think you've acquired an ardent fan."

Tracy smiled, but she was thinking that a little of Ms. Goodweather went a very long way. Under no circumstances did she intend to team up with her or any other individual on this cruise.

The thought of room service seemed not such a bad alternative.

Tracy had given in, telling Shirley she would attend the cocktail reception for solos, but that she planned to skip the welcome aboard review in the showroom.

She simply was not in the mood for perky, chirpy smiling faces and snappy dance routines. What appealed to her now was privacy. She would cozy up to her journal, admire her flowers, and sip champagne before it went flat.

Earlier, she had peeked in at the Poseidon Lounge, a pre-dinner and post-dinner venue for dancing and drinking. Too bad she was one husband short for joining in. She had not checked out the piano bar.

Now as she approached the piano bar, she heard music that made her stop in her tracks. Oddly enough, it was the lyrical slow movement from Rachmaninoff's *First Piano Concerto*. Or was she imagining this?

She had to look in. Save for the man playing the piano, the room was unoccupied. Behind the pianist were red and black curtains in a filmy material, studded with stars and half-moons, draped to create a harem effect. But it wasn't the exotic decor that gave her pause. Something about the man, his style of playing, the way a strand of hair fell to one side of his forehead, prompted her to stand and stare.

He looked up and made eye contact. His smile, something in his gaze telegraphed recognition, as if they'd met before. He stopped playing and gestured toward one of the seats. "I'm Marc Frias. Won't you join me?"

Tracy found her voice. "Another time," she said. "I'll be back."

Outside, her heart pounding, Tracy had to stop to catch her breath. His smile, the warmth in his dark eyes brought it all back. Marc Frias was almost a clone of Michael Forteney, her first love.

She had put Michael and her year at Juilliard out of her mind. He no longer mattered; it was all in the past, as simple as that. Then why did her mouth taste like cotton? Why did she remain rooted to the spot, unable to place one foot in front of the other?

Stay far away from that piano bar, she cautioned herself. She took a deep breath. In no way, under no circumstances would she return to Marc Frias.

Shirley was delighted Tracy decided to attend the cocktail reception, stating this to Jodie as she visited her in the ship's infirmary.

"I'm glad you found someone to pal around with. I feel so guilty about deserting you."

Jodie sounded weak, but her color was better, Shirley thought. "My God, as if you could help it. Did the doctor say what caused you to faint?"

"He thinks I must be quite anemic, though that in itself wouldn't cause me to pass out. They'll get to the bottom of it." She mustered a smile. "If it weren't for the concussion, I'd be sailing off with you. Tell me about your tablemates."

"I've already told you about Tracy, what a cool, classy woman she is. Uh, let's see. There's this one couple, the Watkinses. He's retired military, and I'm hoping he can give me the lowdown on getting Steve into officers' school. But forget the wife. She's drab all over. Drab skin, drab hair, clothes that would put you to sleep. Worse, she's snooty as all get out. She said to me, 'I don't suppose you play bridge.' I don't, but I said back, 'Who cares about bridge? We're on a cruise.'

"The other couple is okay. He's a university professor." She laughed. "Just my type, huh? Well, he's nice, really, but aloof, kind of stiff. Patty, his wife, is a little harebrained but fun to be around. We've already talked about shopping together."

She looked up to see the doctor's assistant in the doorway. "Well, dear one, I'll wait a few days, then phone you at home from the ship." They were docked now, the ambulance was waiting, and it was time for goodbyes.

Shirley decided to end the evening with a nightcap. Maybe she'd have a Black Russian or a martini. God knew she was entitled after what she'd been through. She decided to bypass the Poseidon Lounge and head for the Crow's Nest on the upper deck. That's where the action was, where the singles congregated.

She was feeling cheerier by the moment and hummed along with the tune coming out of the piano bar. She knew the words "—That's why the lady is a tramp."

What about the piano bar? Maybe it was worth a look-see. She pushed her hair behind her ears (shows off the cheekbones, not to mention showcasing her earrings) and looked in. Hey, not bad. A couple of guys were seated around the piano, with plenty of room to spare.

She spotted an empty space close to the piano player. Oh, wow, the guy at the piano was gorgeous. To die for.

Once again she felt the sense of well-being that had eluded her since halfway into their flight.

She was on a roll. She knew it and Jodie knew it. This was to be the cruise of a lifetime.

❧ *Chapter Six* ☙

Reflections

The music resounds, harsh and discordant, like a child using her knuckles to thump up and down the keyboard. Up and down. Up and down.

No, no, no. What is she thinking? It's Prokofiev, his third piano concerto—wild, edgy but also contained and rhythmic. Sophia has mastered the work, amazingly so, despite her small frame. It's all in the hands, of course, the firm square palms, fingers trained to ripple, pound, or caress the keys.

Tracy has long, tapered fingers—the better to reach an octave— an inspired touch, emotional depth, and good technique. What's missing? The words repeat themselves over and over.

The music has slowed, become mournful, a dirge, the tone now blurred as if weighed down by tears. Her tears, her father's tears. They have laid Sophia to rest, and as a weeping Tracy clings to her father, John McDermott whispers to his daughter his world will never be the same.

The image dissolves into blissful silence, except for a tenuous creaking sound brought on by the swell of waves, the soothing, rolling motion of the ship.

Tracy lay very still, invoking the powers that be to allow her to be rocked back to sleep. Let it be a quiet sleep, serene, restful, *sans* dreams.

It was not to be. Tracy slipped out of bed and reached for her robe and slippers. In the dark, she groped her way to the sofa, started to turn on the light, and then changed her mind.

She breathed in the scent of attar as she settled on the sofa. She picked up the card from Peter, fingering it as she sorted her thoughts. Conversation at the dinner table had stirred up remembrances, and now she was compelled to review chapters out of her past.

Her father was still a presence in her life. He no longer lived in Pacific Palisades but had retired to the Palm Springs area. Rancho Mirage offered golf, country club ambience, and the beauty of desert

31

flora and fauna against the backdrop of the San Jacinto and Santa Rosa mountains.

She enjoyed her father's company, as did most people. Maybe it was his hearty laugh, the fact that he was outgoing, that he genuinely liked to be around people. A widower for eight years, he had charmingly eluded husband-seeking women who were drawn to his gregarious nature, his manly good looks.

She thought about her mother and father together. Like the Redfords, they could never be mistaken for brother and sister, so vast were their physical differences, as well as contrasts in personality. Her mother was the more introspective of the two and unlike her father and perhaps because of the nature of her work, Sophia could embrace solitude.

Despite their differences, the bond between them was impenetrable, a true heart-and-soul connection. Clearly, it was unthinkable to picture them apart.

And yet, the unthinkable had happened.

Tracy clasped Peter's card to her bosom, surrendering to the past as she thought through the time line. In 1993, she'd returned from Juilliard to her parent's home to pursue her musical studies in L.A. Sophia no longer performed publicly, devoting her time instead to an art gallery in the Palisades that she co-owned with a friend.

At times Sophia would sit in on her daughter's practice session. "What do you think?" Tracy asked one afternoon, rubbing her left shoulder muscle.

"I think God created Chopin not only to enhance our sensibilities, but to drive the musician into an excruciating state of frustration."

"That bad?"

"Not at all, my darling. The scherzo simply needs more work."

"Some days I feel this burst of energy, like it's all coming together, that I might become as good as you." She smiled. "Someday. At other times I ask myself, why bother? Why inflict all this pain? Hey, I could take up belly dancing or play the kazoo.

"No, seriously. What if I lack that—that indefinable quality that goes beyond mastering the craft to produce the artist?"

"Tracy, you're immensely talented. I wouldn't encourage you otherwise. But oh, the work ahead of you. How well I know this to be true."

"I've heard you play the *Paganini Rhapsody*, the Brahms *Second*. It seems so effortless."

"Before it became so effortless, as you put it, I heard Arthur Rubenstein perform the Brahms, and I despaired of ever, ever measuring up to his level of accomplishment."

Sophia patted a place beside her on the sofa. "Time to take a break. Come sit with me. Tell me how you're doing outside of your music."

Tracy already stood, stretching, rotating her shoulders, and now she joined her mother.

"What can I say? I'm happy to be home," she flexed her fingers, "and life goes on, even without Michael."

Sophia peered up at her daughter. "You seemed so happy, so well suited to one another."

"Michael is gifted, intelligent, and handsome. What more could you want? Oh, and sensitive. He broke down when we said our goodbyes."

"So to temper all this perfection, he brings conflict and chaos into his life and yours. It's what Europeans called *Sturm und Drang*."

Tracy gave a small laugh. "Nothing quite so abstract. Try blond, willowy, eyes as big as a pond, only bluer. Also known as Meredith James, first chair cello with the New York Philharmonic."

"He simply up and deserted you for a blond in the string section of a symphony orchestra?"

"Not any symphony orchestra, Mother, as you well know. But that's by way of background. Michael and Meredith—how euphonious— had plighted their troth, so to speak, a year before Michael and I met. For whatever reasons, they parted, and then Miss Wonderful reappeared on the scene.

"I sensed trouble. Frankly, the joy had gone out of our relationship. Oh, at times Michael was absolutely adoring, almost worshipful of me. Then his mood would switch from loving or playful to polite, distant. He'd become preoccupied or restless, make some excuse

33

about having to go somewhere or do something. Hours later he'd call, and once again I was the love of his life."

Tracy was quiet for a moment, and then wiped away a tear. "It all finally came to a head. Like in a B movie, we met at our favorite bistro. One look at him and I felt like a lamb being led to slaughter. Simply put, he loved me, he would always love me, but he couldn't deny his feelings for Meredith, and so he was torn, unable to choose between me and his former love." She sighed.

Sophia rolled her eyes. "There must be more?"

"Yes. He had decided to return home to St. Louis. His goal was to jump-start his professional life. He said something about finding an agent, about booking concert dates. Making this move, he told me, would allow him time to gain perspective about us, about his feelings for Meredith."

Sophia shook her head. "Sounds to me he wanted out, that he wasn't ready to commit to either of you."

"He said," Tracy choked back a sob, "we would remain in touch, that he'd call me when he was settled. It's been six months."

Sophia drew her close in a hug. "Oh, baby, it still hurts after all this time?"

"Maybe forever." Tracy smiled through her tears. "Well, probably not that long."

Sophia released her daughter. "Somebody wonderful will come your way. I can sense it, feel it." She paused. "Why so pensive?"

"I think I'd like to take a break from my music."

"I hope not too long a break. You've made significant progress in the last couple of months. However, time away from the piano might do you good." She thought a moment. "Would that time out involve travel?"

"It's a possibility." Tracy paused. "Actually, I'd say it's a certainty. I could visit London. We have friends there, even family." Sophia was shaking her head. "All right, but what about Italy, Greece, and Spain? Mom, come with me!"

Her mother laughed off the suggestion, arguing she had a business and a husband to tend to. However, she would help with the itinerary and contact friends who might provide Tracy with names of places to see outside the usual tourist haunts. And who knows? These friends might come up with introductions to people in her age group. And so they did.

One of the introductions was to Peter Bradshaw, whom she'd met at their villa in Viareggio, outside of Florence.

Now, memories came flooding back as Tracy switched on a light. Several rose petals had fallen onto the table, forming a graceful, golden extension of the formal arrangement. Peter, she recalled, had flowers delivered to her hotel room the afternoon of their first date in Viareggio.

There followed intriguing explorations of Florence, romantic dinners overlooking the Grand Canal in Venice and memorable excursions into other Mediterranean ports. Theirs was not a whirlwind or volatile courtship in the sense of devastating lows or euphoric highs, but she had been taken with Peter immediately, impressed by his intelligence, kindness, and sincerity. They had fun together and were comfortable with one another. In other words, they were compatible. Moreover, Peter was a most attractive man. And so easy to love.

They were married in the Westwood Community Church, not far from the law firm where Peter's father was a senior partner. Sophia and John gave their only child a lavish wedding and reception, and Sophia, on a note of triumph, had reminded Tracy more than once of her intuitiveness. "You see," she would crow, "I knew someone wonderful was waiting in the wings."

Tracy stood now. She could return to bed or seek out the ocean. Slowly she moved toward the windows, opened the drapes and doors and stepped outside.

She sat in the chair she'd occupied earlier. It was pleasantly cool, with occasional light as the moon played tag with the clouds. She closed her eyes, succumbing to the sounds of the sea. The somber but majestic opening chords of Rachmaninoff's *Second Piano Concerto* came to mind. For her the rhythmic eloquence of the music was in cadence with the imposing grandeur of the sea.

She remembered sitting at the piano in her parents' home several months after her mother's death, the Rachmaninoff work propped up in front of her. She could have worked on the music at home, but had felt an overpowering need to feel connected to her mother, to risk taking this emotional first step.

Tentatively, Tracy had fingered the chords, reading the music, keeping it soft. Though not her first attempt, it had been months since she'd worked on the concerto. It seemed to be coming with ease, and now with more assurance, she increased volume and tempo, caught up in the rhythmical surge of sound.

Suddenly she stopped. The fading late afternoon light had dimmed the room. But it wasn't the onset of darkness that caused her to pause. She felt a presence, as if her mother were in the room, head cocked to one side as she assessed her daughter's performance.

Tracy turned, her gaze directed to the sofa where she and her mother had chatted. For a second or two, Sophia was there, her hand raised in a beckoning gesture.

Tracy bowed her head and worked at steadying her breathing. Maybe this was too soon, after all.

She decided to head on home.

As she rose from the bench, she started. Someone stood in the shadows beyond the doorway. Now as the figure moved slowly, almost furtively into the room, Tracy held her breath, then let it out in a sigh of relief. It was her father.

"Tracy. Good to see you. How's my girl?"

"Gosh, Dad, I didn't know you were home. I hope you don't mind." She glanced over at the piano. "I felt the need to—to—" She swallowed hard. "Well, you know."

"Give the old man a hug. There. No need to explain."

"Actually, I'm on my way out. Peter and I have theater tickets for tonight, and we're going to dine out before the show." She stopped. "Dad, are you all right?" His eyes were wet, and he stared at her intently.

"I heard you at the piano. I thought for a moment it was your mother."

Tracy managed a smile. "I guess I can take that as a compliment. But I'll never be as good as Mom."

John McDermott bowed his head for a moment, and then spoke. "Tracy, I don't know what to say."

"You don't have to say anything."

"I can't talk about this now. Can we get back to this discussion

36

another time?"

"Of course."

They let it go at that. The comparison between mother and daughter did not resurface, which was fine with Tracy.

As Tracy stepped up to the railing, she realized how the men in her life had not been very supportive. First, her father seemed to imply she could not match her mother's talent; then Peter had spoken logically against her chances for recognition, quoting statistics, percentages and the like. Only with Michael had she experienced the wonderment of sharing her dreams. She thought his talent outweighed hers, but he was generous in his accolades and, she thought, moved by her playing.

"I picture you on the concert stage," he had said, "bringing the audience to its feet, enthralled by your performance and beauty." He had grinned. "Completing this scenario, we have maestro Zeus-Kowkosky, dean of conductors, eying you and growing hornier by the minute."

"And at the post performance reception," she continued, "he invites me to his hotel suite where, between sips of champagne, the word protégé pops into the conversation."

"And of course, there's a little of this," Michael said, reaching for her, fondling her breasts, "and a little of that." He had her blouse unbuttoned, her bra undone and was kissing her breasts, his tongue making her nipples rigid. She remembered feeling the wetness below and how overwhelming her desire to give of herself as their kisses and caresses intensified. What started as a joke had escalated into unrestrained passion.

Had she given a small moan as she gripped the railing?

Someone cleared his throat and at the sound, Tracy loosened her grip and in that same instance became aware of something fluttering from her hands overboard.

Was it Peter's card? Had she carried the card with her onto the balcony?

"Mrs. Bradshaw? Tracy? It's Jack Watkins."

She hadn't realized she was standing so close to the partition that divided the balconies.

"This is a surprise," Tracy said. "Can't sleep?"

"I often wake up during the night. We actually went to bed fairly early. Joanne was feeling under the weather."

"I'm sorry. Is she prone to seasickness?"

"Uh, not really." He paused. "She enjoys a cocktail or two and, well, sometimes it gets to her."

"I see," Tracy said, not seeing at all. Was he implying his wife was an alcoholic? She'd seemed quiet at the dinner table, but certainly not inebriated.

"At any rate, it should be an interesting day for us in Los Cabos. We'll see you at breakfast or somewhere along the line. Assuming Joanne makes it, of course."

"Let's count on that," Tracy said.

"You know, Tracy, it's our gain to have someone like yourself at our table."

"I'm not sure why, but thank you."

"You're young, beautiful, and you've got class. Also I've always enjoyed being around people who lead a privileged life. Which reminds me, I'd like to hear more about your mother."

What, she questioned, was there to tell that would be of interest to him? They left it at that and said goodnight. But as Tracy left the balcony for her cabin, she felt uneasy. Earlier she'd suspected the man was trying to make points with her. Now his overtures were more blatant.

Back in the cabin, Tracy, after a cursory glance at the table, searched the sofa and floor for Peter's card. It was gone, she determined, adrift at sea.

Blame it on Jack. He had startled her out of her reverie, thereby causing her to let go of the card. And of remembrances past.

Joanne was sitting up in bed when Jack entered the cabin. With the only illumination coming from the night light over the bed, she couldn't catch his expression, but he seemed surprised she was awake.

"How are you doing?" he asked. "Everything okay?"

"I guess it's obvious I'm not in a drunken stupor."

He walked around to his side of the bed and sat on its edge. "Who said anything about a drunken stupor?"

"Maybe you prefer under the weather?"

"Oh. So you followed me out to the balcony?"

"You left the door partly open, and when I awoke and saw you were gone, I decided to investigate. I don't appreciate what you said to that Tracy woman."

Jack raised his hands. "I didn't mean any harm. You know you like your cocktails, Joanne. I don't object to that. But sometimes you overdo."

She shrugged. "That's my problem." When he didn't respond, she looked over at him, then tried to look away but could not. He eyed her with such intensity, she felt locked into his gaze.

He reached now to take her hand. His voice soft, he said, "What you call your problem could become my problem, as well. Some people talk too much when they drink. We can't have that, can we?"

"I don't know what you're talking about."

He released her hand and his voice turned cold. "I think you do."

"All right, Jack. That's enough." She could hear the tremor in her voice. "I simply want to concentrate on happy events, on enjoying our cruise."

He sat motionless, then nodded and as he slid under the covers, Joanne turned off the light.

Focus on the trip, she told herself. Focus on the trip. The gentle sway of the ship, the repetitive command worked its magic as she drifted off. Once again, all was well with her world.

❧ *Chapter Seven* ❧

Los Cabos

At an outdoor café on Plaza Las Glorias, the Redfords lunched on taco salads, accompanied by chips and salsa.

They climbed the hill to Finisteria Hotel for a commanding view of the Pacific Ocean and captured on film their ship in the distance, a symbol of both haven and adventures to come. They also had taken the boat out to El Arco, an impressive rock formation that was the main tourist attraction.

Now it was enough merely to sit and dally over their meal while they watched the passing parade of locals and tourists.

And then Patty spotted Joanne and Jack Watkins. "Look, Ben, I think the Watkinses are searching for a table here. Do you want to go after them, ask if they'd care to join us?"

"It's not enough we'll be seeing them every evening for the duration of the cruise?" He paused. "On second thought—" Ben was partway out of his chair, and then sat back down. "I guess they've changed their minds. I can see they're past the restaurant now."

Patty dipped a chip into her sauce, popped it into her mouth, and then made a face as she felt her eyes tearing. "I have the feeling the Watkinses are not your favorite people."

Ben tasted his margarita, taking his time, as if gathering his thoughts. "I can't say I feel one way or the other about Joanne, though it would be nice just once, to hear her venture an opinion or show some spark.

"As for Jack, well, I guess he's okay, but there's something about the man that bothers me. I think he comes across as glib, insincere."

"You mean as if he were play acting, assuming a role?"

Ben was quiet for a moment, then nodded. "Not a bad description."

"Maybe he's compensating for his wife's shortcomings, her being so aloof, for example. Of course, people like that are usually insecure. Whatever the reason for her behavior, I sense Joanne is a troubled woman."

"All right, smarty, let's turn this around. How do you suppose the Watkinses perceive us?"

"That's easy, Ben. I'm an airhead; you're an egghead."

Ben's laughter drew attention from the table closest to them.

Lunch had been a pleasant break, and now as they waited for their check, Ben gave her a tired grin. "Do you realize how much walking we've done today?"

"Oh, my, yes. I feel like a ballerina."

Ben raised his eyebrows. "Maybe we shouldn't have had this second margarita?"

"My goodness, Ben, I'm not tipsy. I am surprised you can't make the connection. Ballerinas wear out their slippers, one pair after the other. Now look at these shoes. They're darling, yes, but not very substantial. I'm sure they'll have to be replaced soon."

"Sweetheart, what you need is sturdy over flimsy. May I suggest walking shoes?"

"We'll see. Maybe we should stick with boat excursions." She looked at her watch. "I do think we have just enough time to make it to Plaza Bonita before the ship sails."

He raised an eyebrow. "By all means before the ship sails."

Seconds out of the restaurant, Patty heard someone call her name. She turned back to see Shirley Goodweather coming toward them at a gallop.

"Wait up, you two."

Patty ignored Ben's deep sigh. "Look who's here. How's it going, Shirley? Have you been taking in all the sights?"

Shirley pulled at one strap of her sun dress, her lips twisted into a grimace. Today's colors were red, white, and blue, the blue bulging at the waist.

"I'm doing okay. Saw you on the boat out to the rock. Then I decided to check out San José del Cabo."

Patty nodded. "The older part of Los Cabos. I wish we'd had the time to explore that area. The guidebooks mention jacaranda trees and quaint pastel colored cottages. I can imagine a myriad of flowers, as well."

"Oh, yeah. Flowers and lots of trees—orange, mango, avocado. But the place is really run down and kind of dirty looking. Anyway, I was wondering where you were off to."

Ben had wandered over to a newsstand, and now as he rejoined them, Patty said, "Plaza Bonita. The Sergie Bustamente Gallery is there, and I can't wait to see his sculptures, the jewelry, and his pre-Columbian designs."

"I've heard there's some really neat resort wear shops at Plaza Bonita. Pottery, too."

"Uh, ladies. Excuse me?" Ben raised his hand. "Would you mind going on without me?" He turned to Patty. "There's something I want to check out. I'll meet you back at the ship if that's okay with you."

"All right, sweetheart. I know you're not much for shopping."

He leaned down to give her a peck on the cheek, then taking long strides, merged into a crowd of tourists.

Later, when Patty questioned his actions, Ben said he was exploring the prospect of deep sea fishing, garnering information that might be useful at other stops.

His explanation was perfectly reasonable, but something in his tone, his body language, gave her pause.

Now as she stood before her mirror, she swept the thought from her mind as she would brush aside a pesky gnat. Far better to concentrate on today's purchases, her favorite being one of the signature sun designs from the Bustamente collection. If she wore it with a gold chain, it would create a unique necklace. She held the piece of jewelry up to her chest and studied her reflection.

Ben came up behind her. He kissed the back of her neck. "It's lovely," he said. "You're lovely."

She turned to face him. What was wrong with her? How could she have doubted him, even for one minute? He was a loyal, devoted husband, a dear, dear man. And truly the love of her life.

Shirley needed a pat on the tush, a reassuring voice to tell her she looked terrific, that men would find her adorable, or better yet, sexy.

She thought about her efforts to coax Tracy into attending the singles' cocktail reception, her rallying cry that God forbid, anyone should pass up a party. Now she was having second thoughts.

She missed Jodie, her anchor, her stalwart friend who kept her grounded, who stopped her from running off at the mouth or indulging in that extra martini.

She sighed. Okay, so she was on her own, free to mess up. But so what? What was wrong with being herself? Face it; she was not a conservative person, so why pretend otherwise?

The library/card room, site of the gathering, loomed ahead, but oh, good, she'd come upon a ladies' restroom. She ducked in and saw she had the place to herself. The long mirror above the counter revealed the woman others would judge. Or admire.

Eyes narrowed, she tried to view herself as others would. The outfit she'd picked earlier at the resort shop was a tad subdued for her taste, the cream and rose colored blouson top mated with an ankle length, slitted off-white skirt. Patty loved it, bubbling over about how festive it was, how feminine it made her look.

Shirley wasn't so sure. She knew style, and something was out of sync. Like the top was way too blousy. Women had boobs. Why not show them off?

Something had been out of sync with Patty, as well. True, she'd been enthusiastic about the outfit, but she'd hurried her into making the selection, fidgeting and looking at her watch. Other than drooling over the sun goddess doohickey she'd bought at the gallery, Patty seemed preoccupied, at times barely responding when Shirley pointed out an item of clothing or jewelry that deserved a comment. Maybe she was upset over the professor's disappearing act?

Once again Shirley peered at her reflection but this time nodded in approval. Cherry colored drop earrings with a matching three-strand necklace were the perfect addition, breathing life into bland. She could liken it to berries spread over cream of wheat.

She took a deep breath, and then smoothed back her hair. *Here we go kiddo. Tummy in; smile! The world awaits.*

Fifteen minutes into the reception, Shirley sipped from a glass of Chablis (Why the heck didn't they offer an open bar?) and smiled or nodded in response to the man standing close to her. Maybe too close?

He had a pleasant, low-pitched voice that was kind of sexy and a great tan that brought out the blue of his eyes, but he was too short for her taste and did the stupid male thing of combing sparse strands over bald spots in a pitiful attempt to deny the obvious.

As for the men in the room, the lucky stiffs were outnumbered, as always, by the women.

She turned back to Ray, Roy, whatever his name, and noted he had a firm, solid build and strong masculine looking hands. He had a nice smile, too, and was asking if she'd join him after the show for a nightcap in the Crow's Nest.

Sure, she'd like that, was her response which was their cue to part and circulate. Now that she had a date—*ta da!*—she could relax. As for the other men, let them chase her. She planned to play it cool.

She looked around for Tracy, but apparently she was a no-show. Damn. Also it appeared no one was racing to the side of Ms. Cool.

Shirley eyed the three women she'd chatted with when she'd first arrived. They hadn't budged from the wine bar, nor did they appear interested in seeking out others. Some party. At least they'd been friendly. In fact, the heavyset red-headed woman wearing a copper sleeveless top over see-through harem pants had remarked on how stunning Shirley looked.

She started over to them, and then hesitated, aware now of music in the background. A piano rendition of Duke Ellington's *String of Pearls* sweetened the room. She remembered the piano was located by the entryway and turned to check it out. Well, well. It was the gorgeous guy from the piano bar. Now he played a peppy tune that made her want to cut loose and dance. "No, no," Jodie would have said, "Show some class." So okay. She would meander over, stand next to the guy and hum along.

He smiled at her and without missing a note, said, "Nice to see you again."

Oh, wow, she needed to think fast, come up with a request to keep his attention. Maybe if she could impress him? Who knows what might happen. *Jesus, Shirley, come up with something first-rate, sophisticated.* She thought for a moment. Bingo. She had it. *My Funny Valentine.*

She even remembered his name. Bending down, close enough that he couldn't miss her cologne, she said, "Marc, how about—" but suddenly he'd shifted from swing to *The Most Beautiful Girl in the World,* played in a soft 1-2-3 tempo. The way he touched the keys, as if he were making love, caused her to shiver.

She looked up to follow his gaze. Wouldn't you know, it was Tracy, and Marc was practically devouring her with his eyes.

Tracy appeared flustered, hammered in place. She stared at Marc, and then saw Shirley. She smiled, waved, and then kept going, headed presumably for the wine bar.

Marc segued into another tune she didn't recognize, still keeping the waltz rhythm. He looked at her and smiled. "What can I play for you?"

She could go after Tracy or—ah, the heck with Tracy. For now, anyway. She leaned into Marc and gave him her request.

Sweet, seductive, irreverent, *My Funny Valentine* came across to her like it was meant for her ears only.

She wished she could hold onto this moment forever.

At the dinner table, Joanne tried to tune out Shirley Goodweather. Her voice at top volume grated on her, as did her nonstop commentary about her super son's accomplishments. Call him St. Steve and be done with it. Jeez! She rubbed the back of her hand across her forehead.

Jack was attentive, but she could tell from the way he shifted his feet he was tired of acting advisor and counselor to this woman regarding her son's military career. What the hell. It wasn't her problem. Let Jack deal with it.

Most at the table had finished their entrees, waiting now for the dessert course. The thought of something rich and gooey turned her stomach. An after dinner drink would be much more to her taste.

She looked at Tracy. She'd been cordial but quiet, as if deep into her own thoughts. Had she asked her about bridge?

Shirley apparently had decided to shut up for the time being and finish her entree. In the lull in conversation, Joanne caught Tracy's eye. "Did I ask you about bridge?"

"Yes, you did, but given my lack of expertise I doubt you'd want to recruit me."

"Patty, do you play bridge? Oh, of course you do." She read the puzzlement in Patty's expression. She didn't dare look at Jack. "I guess I'm trying to process too much. With all that's going on, I mean?" She made a vague gesture with her hand.

"If you play bridge as well as you and Jack dance," Patty said, "you'd make a fabulous partner or a formidable opponent. Aren't they good, Ben?"

"Tops. Does your talent come by naturally or have you taken lessons?"

Jack shrugged. "A little of both, I suppose. I've danced for years, starting back in college."

Joanne took a sip of her wine. "Jack and I met in our senior year in college. On our first date we went dancing, and this man literally swept me off my feet, he was so good." The sudden heat in her cheeks brought her to silence. It was so unlike her to gush.

But Patty was beaming at her. "You two need to sign up for the talent show. There's a meeting for participants tomorrow afternoon."

Shirley looked up from her plate. "We're in Mazatlan tomorrow."

"I know," Patty said, "but it's only for a half day. I think we sail at 3:00. Now don't shake your head, Joanne. Jack, talk to her."

Jack held up his hand. "We'll be there."

"So, Tracy," Shirley said as she buttered her roll, "do you play the piano like your mother?"

"At one time I studied seriously." She shrugged. "I may or may not go back to it."

"About your mother," Jack said. "Is she still performing?"

"No, she passed away in 1994."

"Oh." Jack executed a little *pas de deux* with his water and wine glass, his restiveness a sign he was up to something, Joanne thought.

"I confess I'm not familiar with the name Resnik. Is it Polish?"

"I suppose so. We have relatives who divide their time between London and Warsaw. Actually, the name my mother was born with—Robinowitz—is Polish."

Jack's expression turned thoughtful. "I assume members of your family lived in Poland during the war years and suffered persecution?"

"Those were terrible times, yes."

Patty broke the silence. "Tracy, would you honor us by performing in the talent show?"

Tracy smiled. "Thank you, but I'm afraid not."

That was definite enough, Joanne concluded. Moreover, in her husband's eyes, Tracy would have stepped down from the ladder of perfection. Way down

Michael Fortenay. Marc Frias. Same initials, Tracy realized, as she tried to concentrate on the singers on stage. She sat at the back of the showroom, the better to escape, just in case.

"I can do anything better than you—" Tracy tuned out the duet from *Annie Get Your Gun* as she thought about Michael and the secret she'd kept from her family. Five days before her wedding, Michael had called. He offered no excuse for the long delay in contacting her, saying only that he couldn't get her out of his mind, and that he had to see her.

When she informed him she was about to be married, his response was a long silence. Then he asked if she were sure. She heard the regret in his tone, then words that bounced by her as if her hearing had shut off. Something about commitment, a lifelong commitment, his voice soft yet so serious.

She'd felt a momentary displacement, her vision blurring. Then everything cleared. She was on the right track, she assured him and yes, she was certain about taking this step.

She had not forgotten he'd said she would be in his heart forever, that she had only to call and he would come running.

As it turned out, several years into her marriage she was tempted to contact him. What stopped her was a photo in the Sunday Times of Michael at a post-concert party, his wife (a petite brunette) by his side.

She focused on the stage a few more minutes, and then decided to make her exit. She supposed Shirley would soon head to the Crow's Nest to meet her date. She could join in and dance with the ship's escorts or play the game of shunning the undesirables. Both ideas depressed her and as she neared the piano bar, she decided the hell with it. She wanted to know more about Marc Frias.

Two couples sat at the bar, engrossed with one another and inattentive to the medley of show tunes coming from the piano. Tracy knew the room would fill when the show ended and noted empty seats on either side of Marc.

As she approached him, he looked up, his eyes widening with recognition. She took one of the seats closest to him and as he continued playing, a waiter appeared to take her drink order. Now Marc was into what she supposed was his signature theme song, the notes soaring in a climactic rush to signal break time.

He came out from behind the piano to take a seat next to her just as the waiter brought her drink.

"It's on me," Marc said. He raised his hand to the server in a gesture of dismissal.

"No, really, that's not right. You shouldn't—"

"I see we share a taste for Cointreau, but aside from that, I don't even know your name."

"It's Tracy Bradshaw." She raised her glass to him, and then tasted her drink.

Marc gave her an appraising look. "I've had the strangest feeling I've known you—that we've met before. And believe me, that's not a line." He seemed to hesitate, and then said, "I'm also curious as to why you've tried to avoid me."

Tracy laughed. "I guess that's changed." She studied her drink for a moment, and then looked him in the eye. "That first night when I peeked in, I was taken aback, practically in a state of shock because you so closely resemble someone from my past. And that's not a line."

Marc held her gaze with an intensity that reminded her of Michael when their love was new. She reached for her drink, like an actor carrying out stage business, grateful to have a prop.

"Was this man from your past a musician?"

"He was and is a classical pianist. He's quite in demand, both on the concert stage and as a soloist with symphony orchestras. I looked in here in the first place because I recognized the slow movement from Rachmaninoff's *First Piano Concerto.*"

He smiled. "I seldom stray from pop standards or show tunes, but once in a while I sneak in something by Rachmaninoff, Gershwin, Chopin, even Debussy."

"It sounds as if you have a classical background."

"I do." He looked at her questioningly. "I can tell you know your music, Tracy. Do you play an instrument?"

"I studied piano in L.A. and at Juilliard."

"Wow. Impressive, indeed." He looked at his watch. "I have to get back to work, but I'm free during the day tomorrow. Why don't we see Mazatlan together? I'd like to get to know you, to hear about your background. Besides, I know of a great place to have lunch."

"Marc, I don't think that's such a good idea."

He stood, and then leaned down to speak softly into her ear. "9:30 in the departure lounge. See you then."

Had her spine dissolved into soggy bread? Did she have a brick for a brain? Tracy shook her head, and then reached for her drink. Marc was playing Gershwin's *A Foggy Day.* She loved Gershwin. She loved feeling so mellow.

Tomorrow she'd regret coming here and tempting the fates, but at the moment it didn't matter.

Let the chips fall where they may.

❧ *Chapter Eight* ❧

Mazatlan

Light streamed into the cabin through floor to ceiling windows. Shirley turned on her side, stretched and sighed contentedly. Apparently she'd forgotten to close the drapes, and now her eyes were beginning to ache from the glare. But that was okay. She liked to awaken to sunshine, to the promise of a new day. Moreover, she'd bet the farm that Mazatlan offered a lot more pizzazz than pokey Los Cabos.

Eyes shut against the brightness, she turned from the window onto her back and stretched her arms wide, only to make contact with— with something.

Shirley looked to her left. Oh, for God's sake, it was Roy. She propped herself into a sitting position. How could she have forgotten? More to the point, how could she have let this happen?

The answer was she'd been a horse's ass and obviously bombed out of her mind. At least she'd had the presence of mind to put on a nightgown.

Roy was still asleep. Stealthily, Shirley inched her bottom to the edge of the bed, then made contact with the floor. On tip toe she started for the bathroom. Once inside, she would brush her teeth, comb her hair, and put on a robe. Whatever Roy might think of her, she was no whore, thank you very much.

When she'd accomplished what she'd set out to do, Shirley took a deep breath and stepped down from the bathroom into the room. Roy was awake.

"Hi, beautiful," he said.

"Hi, yourself."

"Is that all you have to say?" His voice sounded more smarmy than sexy.

"What's that supposed to mean?"

"You were, shall we say, very expressive last night?"

"Look, I don't usually do this sort of thing."

50

"But you do it so well."

She felt the heat in her cheeks. He sat up now, and she observed the black mole beneath his collar bone, the fact his chest hair was gray.

"You make me feel cheap," she said.

"Shirley, come on now." He held out his arms. "Let me make it right."

"I'm sure we had a terrific time, that you were *superstud* to the max. But that was last night. Look, we're in port." She gestured toward the window. "I'm dying to see Mazatlan."

"And I'm dying to make love to you. Come here, baby. I want you to feel this erection."

"Roy, I'm not coming back to bed. We're in Mexico. I want to see Mexico."

"We can screw *and* see Mexico."

"That's it, buster. You do what you like. I'm getting dressed." She didn't wait for a reply but stomped to the closet, grabbed her clothes, shut herself in the bathroom and locked the door.

She took her time applying her makeup and arranging her hair. Maybe he'd be gone when she came out.

Roy sat in a chair, smoking a cigarette. She didn't know he smoked. At least he was dressed.

"Well, well, look at you," he said, flicking ashes on the carpet. "All dressed up and raring to go." He took a drag and expelled the smoke. "What have we cooked up for today? Wait. Don't tell me. I think I know."

Shirley decided to remain standing. "What are you rambling on about?"

"Coming on to the next chump. Should be a breeze, kiddo. You'll have him falling at your feet. You know why? Because you make promises."

"What are you talking about?"

"Last night, you were hell bent on getting a good fuck. You were even begging for it. Anytime, you said."

"Oh, brother, do you have a fertile imagination. And use an

ashtray, for heaven's sake. Better yet, take your cigarette and get the hell out of here."

He took his time, reaching for the ashtray, stubbing out the lighted end so that an acrid odor permeated the cabin.

He stood. "Guess you won't be needing my services anymore." His swagger, his smirk, as he started for the door infuriated her.

When his back was to her, his hand on the doorknob, Shirley said, "I thought I'd known some bastards in my life, but you take the cake. You are one crude jerk."

The door was open, but now Roy turned back to her. "That may well be. But you know something, Shirley? You've got a fat ass." With that, he was gone.

She had to sit down before she fell down. It could have been worse, she reasoned. It could have gone beyond verbal abuse. Oh, hell. She'd been cocky, foolish, and stupid. When would she learn? Would she ever learn?

She wiped away a tear. Jodie would understand, would grant forgiveness. She needed to call her friend, ask how she was feeling, find out if they'd found the cause of her problems. *And* 'fess up about last night. She gnawed her lower lip. On the other hand, poor, sick Jodie didn't need to be dumped on. *So deal with it, Shirley.*

If anyone asked about her 'date', she'd shrug it off—say that on a scale of one to ten he rated a measly three. No one had to know he limped in at a subzero, the creep.

So, on with the day. She'd look for Tracy, see if she wanted to team up to explore Mazatlan. She sauntered over to the closet. Dress tonight was formal, and she needed to select shoes, evening bag, and jewelry. But, that she could do later.

She ticked off her agenda: Breakfast first, then she'd put in a call to Jodie. Oh, and find Tracy.

With Roy, she'd made a horrendous mistake. Not that having sex was wrong, but she cringed at the thought of how needy she'd been. If he'd told the truth. *If, indeed.*

Well, no real harm had been done, and she was not about to make herself miserable over one degrading incident.

She snapped her fingers. There. Gone, over with, like it never happened.

The best was yet to come.

As Tracy explained to Marc, Mazatlan represented uncharted territory, unlike Acapulco and Puerto Vallarta, where she'd vacationed with her family.

Their taxi was headed for Zona Dorada, a tourist area known for its ocean view resort hotels and sandy beaches. Marc's smile was rueful. "I'm sorry I hurried us away from the historic district, but I wanted to be sure we had enough time for a leisurely lunch."

"It's a shame we're here for only a half day, but at least we saw the Pazuela Machada. I thought the boutiques and cafes were charming."

His expression turned apologetic. "We could have eaten there. I wasn't thinking."

"Then we'd have missed this fabulous place you've insisted on taking me to."

He pressed his palm to his forehead in a show of mock frustration. "You see what I do? I set myself up for a fall. What if you hate this place?"

She laughed. "Then I'll have to get even, like coming into the piano bar and demanding a full evening of polkas or church hymns."

They stopped at a signal and now as the taxi lurched forward, Tracy grabbed Marc's hand. "Sorry," she said. "I'm convinced taxi drivers in foreign countries operate under some sort of death wish."

He placed his free hand over hers, to give it a gentle squeeze, and then leaned forward to give instructions to the driver.

Back to Tracy, he said, "We're approaching Camaron Sabalo, where the resort hotels are located. That's not where we're going, however. The place I mentioned is in a more secluded setting."

And as Marc described what sounded like a romantic hideaway, Tracy felt as if she were living in a parallel universe as a reincarnated Madame Bovary. Frankly, it felt good. Too good.

Casa Bonita was everything Marc had described, except he failed to mention that the outdoor area—they selected the terrace over the elegant dining room—was redolent with the fragrance of jasmine and gardenias. Their table was cloistered on one side by a trellis of intensely red bougainvillea that nudged a fountain embellished with gold and copper carvings. An abundance of tropical greenery shielded them from the midday sun.

While Marc gave their wine order, Tracy pondered how he knew about a place that was off the main thoroughfare. Through word of mouth? Or had he brought a string of women before her. She surmised he was single, though the absence of a wedding band did not guarantee bachelor status.

As her rings caught fire in the sunlight, Tracy wondered if Marc was even faintly curious as to why she had decided to join him. She had, after all, expressed reluctance to the idea. On his part, why not seek out a married woman? How better to avoid commitment?

The waiter left, and the only other occupied table was distanced enough that voices and laughter were muted. Marc turned to her. "Would you say this is private enough? What's that saying, away from the madding crowd?"

"Marc, this is perfectly lovely. I confess I'm enjoying this break from the shipboard regimen."

"The setting becomes you. If I were a painter, I'd use the bougainvillea as background for a portrait of you." He looked at her closely. "Your coloring—dark hair, smoky eyes, your high cheekbones remind me of paintings I've admired by Sargent."

Caught off balance, she stared back at him. Was he serious? Apparently so. "I'm hardly in that league." She shook her head. "Not even close."

"Then I beg to differ."

The waiter arrived with their wine, and Tracy welcomed the interruption. The conversation was becoming far too intimate. What started as a casual outing was taking a new direction, crossing the line from innocent flirtation to—what?

Marc ordered a white wine, a Pinot Grigio that after toasting and tasting proved to be deliciously light. Now he set down his glass and gave her a sidelong look, the twinkle in his eye suggestive of a mischievous boy striving to make amends. "Am I in trouble? I'm sorry if I've made you uncomfortable."

"I didn't mean to give that impression. But Marc, I'm sure you understand I had misgivings about joining you today. I'm married. In fact, my husband and I planned this trip together." At his questioning look, she continued, "He had to cancel at the last minute. For business reasons."

"So he's a businessman. That covers a lot of territory."

"Actually, he's an attorney."

Marc tasted his wine, and then nodded as if in response to an inner voice. "I think I see the problem."

"What problem?"

"You were drawn to me because I remind you of a past love— someone, I dare say, who respected your talents . . . who was your soul mate."

"Are you implying my husband lacks these qualities?"

He shrugged. "How would I know?"

"You don't know."

"Does your husband encourage you to pursue your music? Does he ask you about your dreams, your aspirations?"

Tracy raised her hand in a gesture of exasperation. "Enough about me. Let's talk about you. You play very well, which suggests you've had excellent training. Where have you studied? Also, where is home? Do you have a family?"

He smiled. "So now you expect me to divest myself of the cloak of mystery?"

She smiled back. "Something like that."

"I grew up in San Diego, but I also lived with relatives in Mexico City when I attended the university there. I've studied piano with private teachers in San Diego and Mexico City.

"As for family, I'm divorced with no children and presently live a nomadic life."

"Do you enjoy playing piano on a ship?"

Marc pursed his lips. "Yes and no. I'd like to devote my time to the piano, to study full time at a conservatory. That's my dream. On the other hand, what I do is not so bad. Not if it brings me in touch with someone like you." With that, he signaled the waiter who hovered nearby. "Please bring another two glasses of wine, and then we'll order."

To Tracy's relief, the conversation turned to more general topics, including Marc's role in setting up and performing in the ship's talent show. "As you can understand," he said, "the entertainers on board add substance to—forgive me—amateur night. Now what about you?"

She shook her head, and he didn't pursue the matter. She sipped from her second glass of wine and listened to the soothing splash of water from the fountain and, when the breeze picked up, felt an occasional droplet on her cheek. *A symbol of purification* was her whimsical thought.

But it was the enchantment of her surroundings, the temptation of the forbidden that aroused in her a sense of vibrancy, the wonderment of being alive. She thought about the piano, of what it might mean to take it up again. Dare she risk it?

And what about Marc? He caught her gaze, and she quickly looked away. Enjoy the moment, she told herself. Enjoy this man's company for now. Soon enough she would return to the real world, and Peter.

She felt her heart skip a beat. God forgive her, but what if she did not return to Peter?

Patty sat at the rear of the showroom, absorbed in the action on stage. This was the world, albeit years ago, she'd aspired to be a part of. Never mind she was involved in a mere shipboard talent show. The theater, whatever form it took, conveyed a special mystique, invoked a magical aura.

Back home, she rarely missed an opportunity to take part in little theater productions. She never tired of that electric moment before the curtain rose, when the tension and concentration of all concerned were almost palpable. She also enjoyed the camaraderie among cast and crew.

Most of all, she loved losing herself in a role, though to her chagrin she tended to be cast as herself. *Forget high drama* was her wry thought. Bring on the comedies, with the loonies, the giddy ones. But that was okay, too.

She shifted her gaze from the stage to her right, sensing someone's presence at the end of her row of lounge seats and cocktail tables. It was hard to tell in the dark, but she thought she recognized Shirley Goodweather.

Before she raised her voice in greeting, Shirley was upon her.

"Hi, doll. Are you watching the auditions?"

"I wouldn't exactly call it an audition, Shirley. The people in charge have to exercise discretion, but they can't offend anyone who's really determined to be in the show." She laughed. "Of course, they can plead time constraints and weed out the really awful ones." She saw that Shirley wasn't listening, that she appeared to be mesmerized by something taking place on stage. "Come sit down. Are you going to try out?"

"Are you kidding?" Shirley sat in the chair next to hers, but her gaze was glued to the stage. "I could eat crackers in bed with that man any time."

"Who? Oh, are you referring to the accompanist? He is a most attractive man."

"I shouldn't be sitting here," Shirley said. "I need to press my formal for tonight. Oh, I meant to ask. Are you in the show, Patty?"

"You bet. I'm dancing the Charleston with two other passengers and two of the male dancers. Oh, look!" She clasped her hands together. "Are the Watkinses coming on stage? I love to watch them dance."

"I'm amazed she dances so well. That woman's really got a bee up her behind."

Patty nodded. "Joanne can be standoffish; however, you never know what's going on in a person's life. Which reminds me, have you heard anything about the friend you were traveling with?"

"I talked with Jodie today. I really needed to hear her voice."

Shirley paused and Patty thought she'd caught something forlorn in her tone. "Is she all right?"

"Yes, thank goodness. I don't have a lot of details because it's so damn expensive to call from the ship. Anyway, her illness turned out to be a low thyroid problem. The doctor said she was also anemic, and that a combination of factors caused her to pass out. Jeez, without medication, she could have turned into a vegetable."

"Sounds as if she's on the path to recovery." Patty turned her attention to the stage. "Look at the Watkinses. Aren't they wonderful? If I hint hard enough at dinner, maybe Jack will ask me to dance this evening. What about you, dear? How did your date turn out?"

"It wasn't really a date. In any case, he's not my type. I think I'll stick with the escort guys or hang around the piano bar. Well." She stood. "If I don't get to a laundry room to press my dress, I won't be going anywhere. See you at dinner."

Patty nodded, but continued to watch Joanne and Jack. Somehow she would finagle a dance with Jack Watkins. No question. The man was simply superb.

❧

Patty and Ben had corralled a table for two in the crowded Poseidon Lounge. They'd danced a couple of slow pieces, and Ben made a half-hearted effort with a rumba and swing number. Now he set down his Drambuie next to her champagne cocktail and nodded toward the dance floor. "Isn't it about time Prince Charming asked you to dance?"

Patty felt the warmth in her cheeks, just as she had at the dinner table. "Oh, that Shirley. Imagine blurting out that I was dying to be Jack's dance partner."

"She also said, 'You can count me in, too.'"

"I suppose she thought she was being cute." Patty looked over her shoulder. "I don't see our blond friend, but it could be she's in the piano bar. Shirley seems to have an enormous crush on the piano player."

Ben leaned sideways, placing his lips close to her ear. "Look who's coming our way."

Jack was almost upon them. "Oh, my, I hope I don't stumble or say something silly." She felt like a girl at her first prom.

Jack stood before them, flashing his wide smile. He nodded at Ben, and then extended his hand to Patty. "May I have this dance?"

"Certainly." She rose, and without a backward glance made her way with Jack onto the dance floor. The band was playing *Stompin at the*

Savoy in an easy swing rhythm.

Jack smiled his approval as she followed along, as they swung out, made turns, and then came together. She held her breath as he introduced some tricky footwork, but she could do it. He was a masterful leader.

When the music stopped, she could feel herself beaming with pleasure.

"You're a natural. You dance very well," Jack said, cocking his head as the band started up with *Moon River*. "Now this one we have to dance to. No question."

She hesitated, and then said, "I guess it will be all right. We don't want to neglect our spouses, though."

He drew her close. "Joanne was going to make a powder room stop, and if I know her, she'll be ordering another drink about now."

They danced in silence for a while, and then Jack said, "We certainly have an interesting table."

"A very nice table, I'd say. We're a diverse group, but that only adds to the fun."

He spoke into her ear. "At least we don't have any niggers sitting with us."

Patty missed a step. "Sorry," she said, avoiding eye contact. They danced on for a moment or two. "Jack, I'm afraid I'll have to sit down. My shoes must be too tight because my right foot is simply killing me."

"Oh, too bad. I'll walk you to your table."

"No need to do that. You hurry on back to Joanne. See you tomorrow."

She hadn't actually lied. Her right foot did hurt, possibly because of all the fancy footwork.

Apparently Ben noticed she was limping. "Are you all right?" he asked as he seated her.

"A minor problem," she said, "but no, I'm not all right."

Ben gave her a searching look. "What's wrong, Patty?"

"I can't believe what I just heard." And as she related the Nword incident to Ben, he nodded as if he weren't surprised.

"It's too late to change tables," she continued, "so I suppose we'll have to be cordial for the sake of maintaining harmony within the group."

"Oh, honey, don't take this so seriously. You're going to run into bigoted people wherever you go."

"I know, but I'm surprised a man with his background, with his exposure to so many people and cultures would use that word. Don't you agree?"

Ben's frown brought out the lines in his forehead as he appeared immersed in thought. He started to say something, and then hesitated. Finally, he took her hand and raised it to his lips for a kiss. "Think of it as an acting challenge," he said. "You're a good little actress, Patty, so pretend his behavior is unimportant to you. Play it cool, stay neutral. Certainly, you don't have to be his friend, but you shouldn't shut him out completely." He gave her a sheepish smile. "You said it better than I."

"What did I say?"

"You know, about maintaining harmony in the group?"

Patty's head was spinning. Ben had not commented on Jack's character or answered her question. Instead, he seemed more concerned about her response to the situation. In other words, don't rock the boat.

"I suppose you're right." She peered at him closely. He seemed relieved she would let the matter drop.

Later, when they returned to the dance floor, Patty pasted on a smile and attempted to conjure up her bubbly side. But her heart wasn't in it. Once again, she recognized inconsistencies in her husband's behavior, with the Ben she thought she knew.

His arms tightened around her, and Patty looked up into his eyes. How she loved this man. Obviously, she was overreacting, creating problems where none existed.

Except what had transpired was taking on a life of its own, becoming a too-familiar scenario.

The Watkinses swirled around them, Joanne's expression impassive, Jack smiling, engaged in his dancing. He waved to her. She did not wave back.

Shirley didn't stay long in the Crow's Nest. Roy was nowhere in sight, thank God. But the escorts, in black tie, were outnumbered by women in multi-hued sequined or beaded tops worn over chiffon or silk floor-length skirts. Shirley opted for a long-sleeved gold sequined top, with a low-cut scooped neckline, over the requisite black skirt. It was the correct uniform but so ho-hum. That she failed to stand out, she decided, was because she'd wimped out on her selection of jewelry. Gold hoop earrings and a simple gold chain necklace did not make for exciting. She'd tried to style her hair like Tracy's, but it turned out too full. All told, she felt like a bloated blob of gold.

She thought about returning to her cabin to remedy the situation, and then gave up on the idea. Maybe she was being too hard on herself. After all, she had noted several men casting admiring glances at the cleavage that showed at her neckline. So maybe simple was better?

Music from the piano bar beckoned her like the sirens in the poem she'd read in high school.

Her heart began to thump. There it was again—*My Funny Valentine*—a sure sign of a connection between herself and Marc. She stood at the entrance for a moment. The place was crowded, but fortunately there was no sign of Roy the Rat.

Shoot. The seats closest to Marc were occupied, with only a few empty places, but people were bound to leave. And if she had to step on a few toes to reach her soul mate, so be it.

Then she took a second look. The woman seated at Marc's right was leaning into him, angled in such a way that what Shirley saw was mostly back. But she recognized the dress, the hair style. It was Tracy.

Now Marc sang softly into the microphone, his gaze directed to the woman at his side. It was as if he'd shut out the rest of the room, that it was just the two of them. Shit.

✑ *Chapter Nine* ✑

At sea, mid-morning

Joanne thrust her card into the door slot, jerked open the door and stormed into the cabin. Jack sat on the sofa, hunched over papers and a notebook. She saw he was both surprised and annoyed by her appearance. He drew whatever it was he studied closer to him.

"You're back early," he said.

"I can't believe what happened." Her anger had dissipated, and she now felt close to tears.

Jack's frown lines disappeared. Apparently she'd whetted his curiosity. "You went to play bridge with Patty. Right?"

"No, it was with Myrna what's-her-name. You remember she sat at the table next to ours in the Poseidon Lounge? We made a bridge date for this morning. Believe me, it was all very definite."

Jack's expression had softened, and in his eyes she read concern over indifference. He moved his papers and notebook to the end table. "Come sit with me. Tell me why you're upset."

When Joanne settled in next to him, she said, "Myrna and I agreed to meet in the card room at 10:00. I was only a minute or two late—maybe it was 10:05—and there she sat at a table with three other women. I said, 'Myrna, I thought we were going to play together.' She said, 'Well, you weren't here and these ladies insisted I join them. Sorry.'"

Jack shook his head. "Not nice. Did you see Patty?"

"Not at first. I'd decided to stick around to see if someone who needed a partner might show. No luck there. Then Patty strutted into the room, skirts a-swirl.

"She saw me, waved hello, and then made a bee-line for a table at the back of the room. It almost seemed she was avoiding me. Anyway, I went after her and when we were face to face, she was cordial but not overly warm."

Jack patted her hand. "I take it she was not available."

"Right. Suddenly I couldn't get my breath. I felt hot all over. I had to get out of there. It was like I was back in junior high." She bowed her head. "Always the last person chosen to be on a team."

"Oh, honey, you're taking this too personally. Call it what it is— a run of bad luck."

Had she heard correctly? Had he said 'honey'? She lowered her head onto his shoulder, and he kissed her forehead.

"Think of us tonight at the talent show. You'll have so many admirers, the women will be standing in line, begging you to play bridge."

She raised her head. "You know, you can be a sweetheart."

"I'll do you one better. How about a mid-morning pick-me-up? Vodka? Gin? You name it."

She never drank before lunch, but given the circumstances... "Sounds great. I'll fix myself a vodka and tonic."

"No, no." He was on his feet. "I'll take care of everything. We'll call for some ice. Unless you want it neat?"

"Oh, don't bother with ice. What about you?"

He nodded. "Why don't you go out on our balcony? I'll do the fixin's."

Outside, Joanne pulled the two chairs and the small table out of direct sunlight. Then she stood at the railing and stared down at white froth spilling over into ripples of variegated marine hues. She cast her gaze out to the horizon. The sea beyond was glazed marble, a serene contrast to the turbulence created by the passage of the ship.

The sea, with its many faces, benign or brutal, fascinated her. She pictured waves splashing onto shore, a tranquil, sunny scene of children at play in the water. Another image came to mind of giant waves, of thunder and lightning, a ship listing against a cruel sea.

People, too, she mused, exhibited a variety of faces, not all of them kind. Witness this morning. She sighed. Other instances came to mind where she'd been left out, ignored.

She wasn't big on self-analysis, but in her gut she perceived herself as wanting, of lacking spontaneity, of having a weak personality, whatever that meant.

She clutched the railing. She always worried about fitting in.

Well, dammit, maybe she needed to reinvent herself, reach out to people, be a more loving person... She started at the sound of the door sliding open.

"Here we go." Jack stepped out onto the balcony and placed their drinks on the table. When they were seated, he raised his glass. "To us. To tonight. Let's knock 'em dead."

After they'd clinked glasses, Joanne took a healthy swig, then leaned back in her chair, breathing in the ocean air. "I'm so glad we decided on this cruise."

"I think you're feeling better already."

She giggled. "I'll drink to that. No, seriously, I'd call this morning's disappointment a wake-up call."

"How so?"

"I'm—I'm not very outgoing. It's no wonder people tend to avoid me."

He shook his head. "Now you're being melodramatic. There's nothing wrong with you."

"Thanks for the vote of confidence, but—" She paused, as he looked away. "Can't we talk about this?"

He patted her hand. "Talk is cheap. If you want to change, then change."

Maybe I will. With or without your help.

They sat quietly for a few minutes, sipping their drinks. Jack gestured beyond the railing. "Quite a sight, isn't it?"

"Oh, yes. I feel I could sit here forever."

"Not without a refill." He got to his feet.

"Oh? Well, okay."

When he returned, he carried one drink. "Cheers," he said. "Enjoy."

"You're not going to join me?"

"I'd like to, but I have something I need to finish."

When Jack was back in the cabin, Joanne moved her chair to catch the rays of the sun. She felt as if she had drifted into a world unknown to her where the gentle motion of the ship, the warmth, the lapping sound of waves conveyed a heavenly sense of peace.

She tasted her drink, and as the liquid slid down her throat, her sense of well-being was complete.

The sound of breaking glass awakened her. Oh, for God's sake, she'd dozed off and dropped the damn glass. She looked back through the window into the cabin and gave Jack a what-the-hell hands-up gesture.

In seconds, he was out on the balcony. "Sorry," she said, "I must have fallen asleep, succumbed to the elements."

He smiled and gingerly picked up glass fragments that fortunately had not shattered into tiny shards. She knew what he was thinking. Substitute drink for elements. Oh, well.

When they were inside, she said, "I think I will call for ice. Sitting in the sun made me thirsty."

He nodded but seemed engrossed in whatever it was that held his interest.

When the ice arrived, Joanne decided that water and ice could use a bit of enhancement. Namely, vodka. She reached for the bottle.

Jack once again commandeered the sofa, so she sat in the chair opposite him. Between sips she placed her glass on the counter top of their dresser.

"What are you writing?" She asked.

Without raising his head, he said, "I'm making notes in preparation for my meeting."

"What meeting?" She thought for a moment. "Does it have to do with the material I found in your suitcase?"

"Come on, Joanne. Let's not get started again." His response was barely a mutter, and still he avoided eye contact.

He was shutting her out. Her hand shook as she poured more vodka into her glass. "Jack! What meeting?"

He looked up at her. "You don't remember? I told you I planned to get together with some people in Acapulco. That's tomorrow, so I want to be sure everything is in order."

"I don't like this. I don't like this at all."

He threw down his pen. "What's your problem, Joanne? Why are you so concerned?"

"It's one thing to take a political stance. You have a right to your beliefs, and you know I support you for the most part."

"But?"

She reached again for her drink, this time maintaining a steady hand as she raised the glass to her lips. She took a sip, then another sip before setting it down.

"I caught only a glimpse at your papers when I opened your bag, but it appears you're becoming actively involved with a bunch of crazies."

"What you call a bunch of crazies are people dedicated to preserving our nation, to maintaining the highest standards of living. We have God-given rights to protect ourselves from users, to vanquish the rot in our land."

"I still don't understand why you're meeting with people in Acapulco."

He spread his hands. "We have work to do in Phoenix. Without going into detail, I'll say only that our Mexican supporters have risen to the cause. I have to talk to these people, outline some plans. In return we expect financial support."

"Oh." Her gaze strayed to the windows. How she wished they might recapture those pleasurable moments when they'd sat together on the balcony. If only she could press a button and turn back time. Presto! Just like that. She snickered, and then raised two fingers to her lips in a shushing motion.

Look at Jack, peering over his notes, copying crap into his notebook, satisfied his good little wife will keep her nose out of his business. For all he cared, she was merely a fixture in his life, an adjunct to the furniture in the room.

She sat quietly for a moment, and then freshened her drink. 'Work to do in Phoenix' sounded ominous. Was Jack getting in over his head?

She thought about that awful scene between Jack and Teddy, with their son berating his father, calling him terrible names. What if Jack had tried reasoning with Teddy by explaining his point of view? But no. She covered her ears, but she could still hear Jack shout, "Get out of my house, you little shit!"

She gulped back a sob. "I miss Teddy."

Jack closed his notebook with a snap.

"Joanne—"

"You don't miss your son?"

"I don't miss his arrogance, his disrespect." He shrugged. "I'm sure he'll show up one of these days. Besides, it's not as if we're childless. We do have a daughter and a grandson."

"How long has it been since we've heard from Laura?"

"What is your point, Joanne?"

"You don't bend, you see everything as black or white. Your children call you rigid or worse and turn away from you. And now you're getting yourself into God-knows-what."

"What do you propose to do about it?"

His tone and his expression of icy detachment were almost enough to bring on sobriety. Almost.

"What can I do? Nothing." She wanted to scream out the words, but they came out a mere whimper. Furthermore, she didn't have the energy to scream. "I'm going to take a short nap before lunch."

He nodded. "By all means, conserve your energy. We have a big night ahead of us."

"Right. A big night," Joanne muttered, as she made her way to the bed. "A big night," she repeated.

Ah, the bed felt good. A short nap, and then she'd be fine.

Tracy regarded her overdone hamburger. Bad, bad choice. Still, with all the pickles, onions, and tomato slices she'd piled on, plus gobs of mustard, it had to be edible. She tasted her Merlot. Ah, it was definitely up to standard.

At Risk – Jackie Ullerich

She sat at a table in a shaded area on the pool deck where she could observe the antics of people splashing and submerging themselves in the water. The Mariachi band belted out Latin favorites as people downed margaritas and piña coladas at their deck chairs. Against this ambience, the ocean behind her pounded out its own cadence, in counterpoint to music and laughter.

She could have rollicked in the pool or joined people at the bar, but she opted to bring her journal along to lunch, with the expectation of penning character sketches of her dinner companions. Earlier, she'd recorded her impressions of Mazatlan and Cabo San Lucas, and had touched on shipboard life.

By the time Tracy finished her burger, the Mariachis had strolled off and the pool noise abated. She rummaged through her bag and brought out her pen, only to set it down. Her bag triggered the recollection of an unsettling night.

Sleep had been difficult, her dreams ugly. She remembered how relieved she was to awaken from a nightmarish situation where she'd lost her purse and panicked over being without money, driver's license, and credit cards. Worse, she couldn't find her car, couldn't remember her own phone number.

She didn't need a course in dream interpretation to explain the obvious. What she'd failed to address in her waking hours—a course of action that would affect the rest of her life—had played out as an anxiety dream. Sadly, she was no closer in determining what to do about her marriage, her career goals, than when she'd left home.

It seemed weeks, not days ago that Ann and she had talked, yet one sentence played in her mind like a stuck record: "You're so right for Peter." Tracy remembered the warmth in Ann's eyes, but she had caught an undercurrent of steel in her mother-in-law's tone. "You're so right for Peter." Was this a blessing or a curse?

Tracy turned to face the sea, to take comfort in the continuum of its rhythm, to focus on the sound, color, vastness of this great body of water. If she tuned out her thoughts and gave in to a suspension of reality, might she start anew with fresh insights?

She had not intended to visit the piano bar last evening. After all, she and Marc had been together for most of the day and for them to continue on would serve no purpose. But she had shown up anyway. Why? Because he reminded her of Michael? Because he dared to challenge her relationship with Peter? Or was it because he was attentive, handsome and a romantic, to boot. Maybe all of the above.

Enough. All this soul-searching—or perhaps it was the wine—was making her drowsy.

The pool games started up, and Tracy turned her chair to watch, only to have her view blocked by the man standing by her table. It was Jack Watkins.

"Mind if I join you for a minute or two?" Without waiting for a response, he seated himself across from her.

He studied her for a moment, his gaze probing hers. "You know, Tracy, I'm fascinated by people and their life stories. I think of all the people at our table, you have the most diversified background."

"I remember you used the word 'privileged' in another conversation."

He smiled. "That, too, but now I'm referring to information we've shared at the dinner table. I suppose you're pretty much a world traveler. Right?"

She shrugged. "I've been to a few places."

"Poland?"

"No. Why do you ask?"

"You mentioned your mother's family in the context of the war years. From what you said, I gather they were Jewish? I mean, my God, to be in Poland when Hitler occupied the land." He shook his head.

Suddenly, Tracy felt wide awake. "I think it was you who brought up the war years. At any rate, I still do have relatives in Poland. Jewish relatives."

"Is that so? You must have had an interesting upbringing."

"Because I'm half-Jewish?"

"I would think it might be difficult to reconcile two opposing faiths."

Where was this going? Tracy struggled to maintain a pleasant expression. "I don't care to discuss such personal issues."

"I apologize if I've been out of line." He stood. "Aha. I think you're due for more company." He waved to someone behind her.

69

Tracy looked back. It was Patty Redford. She seemed to hesitate, and then raised her hand in greeting. Now she moved toward them slowly, in contrast to her usual fast clip.

"Hi, dance partner," Jack said to Patty when she was upon them. Then to Tracy, "Our Patty is an exceptional dancer. Well, you girls have a great afternoon." He favored them with a big smile, and then made a hasty retreat.

Patty sank down into the chair Jack vacated. "Are you having a great afternoon?" Missing was her usual display of lightheartedness.

"I was until Jack came along."

"Oh?"

Clearly Patty wanted more. Tracy shifted in her chair. "I can't read this man. He can be pleasant, flattering," she nodded at Patty, "but at times he comes on like he's reading from a script."

"Ben and I thought the same." Patty frowned. "Maybe he's not quite who he appears to be."

"What are you saying?"

"Please don't repeat this, Tracy. Something happened last evening—well, Ben thinks I overreacted, but—" Hands fluttering.

"It's okay, Patty. You can trust me."

"It was when we were dancing. He referred to our table and said words to the effect that 'at least we didn't have any niggers'." She'd whispered the last word.

Tracy shook her head. "Maybe he doesn't like Jews either. He went on about my mother's family in Poland, asking if they were Jewish and so forth. Not that he used a disparaging tone, but the word hypocrite comes to mind."

Patty remained silent for a moment, and then perked up. "It probably doesn't mean a thing. Ben says there are bigoted people everywhere. We'll simply ignore him."

Or maybe not, Tracy thought. Drawing him out might be advantageous. She patted her notebook. Might he be one of her more interesting characters?

"What do you bet our show will be the best?" Shirley declared over dinner. "First time around will be a warm-up. Trust me."

Patty and the Watkinses joined first seating and presently were entertaining the early diners, or so Tracy hoped. The entertaining part, that is.

"On the other hand," Ben said, with only a tinge of skepticism, "let's hope they're not worn out by the time they get to us."

Ben could be taciturn at times, Tracy observed, but with only the three of them present, he opened up and charmed them with anecdotes about university life. She also found his comments on national and world affairs stimulating and provocative.

And then Shirley jumped in and tenaciously occupied center stage for the remainder of their dinner.

"Tracy," she said, "we've hardly had a chance to talk. I know Ben won't mind if I bend your ear. You know, girl gab?" She'd smiled sweetly at Ben.

And so it began. Tracy's clothes were stunning. Did she shop in L.A., Pacific Palisades, Beverly Hills?—an ocean view home? My Gawd—eyes bulging—what was the decor, the color scheme, who was their interior decorator, what did it cost? Did Tracy and her husband entertain a lot? Of course, they had to, why wouldn't they, how could they not? And so it continued, on and on.

Ben's smile had been barely perceptible, but Tracy caught his glad-it's-you-not-me expression.

Tracy was tempted to turn the tables and interrogate Shirley, but out of consideration for Ben, she kept quiet. Now if she could only avoid her for the rest of the evening.

The turnout for the talent show was respectable, if not great. Once again, Tracy sat at the back of the showroom, the better to make an unobtrusive exit, if necessary. Plus, she'd noted Shirley hurrying to find a place down front. She'd been tempted to skip the show, but with three people at their table involved, it behooved her to attend.

Also she wanted to acknowledge Marc's contribution to the show. If she ran into him. A return visit to the piano bar was out of the question.

In any case, he deserved kudos for carrying several soloists through their numbers. Later he performed a Cole Porter medley with the orchestra. No question about it, he was good.

So was Patty. She and the Charleston were made for each other, and when the dancers stood back to allow her to demonstrate her skills, Tracy clapped and called out "Yay, Patty!" with the rest of the audience.

It was a hard act to follow, and Tracy began to fidget through a saxophone solo and a magic act. She looked at her watch. Surely the show was beginning to wind down. Where were the Watkinses?

There was a pause on stage, the conductor glancing toward the wings. Another pause, and then the conductor nodded and gave the downbeat.

In a flowing motion, the Watkinses waltzed on stage, incredibly smooth, as if gliding on ice. In minutes the music changed to a Latin rhythm. In step, in sync, they followed the beat, with Tracy tapping her foot in time to the music.

Uh-oh. Joanne appeared to hesitate, and then stood in place as Jack danced around her. Tracy held her breath, but it was okay. Joanne was back in step, in perfect rhythm.

Now they segued into a swing number. Wow. Look at them go— nose to nose, feet going a mile a minute. Jack swung her out, and then drew her in for more showy, intricate steps. He swung her out again. And she kept going! Joanne teetered backwards, clear across stage. And then fell. She didn't rise.

There were gasps and murmurs from the audience as Jack ran toward her. Two men appeared from backstage. The three of them brought her to her feet. Head bowed, with support from the men, Joanne slowly made her way off stage.

In seconds the emcee was at the mike. "It's okay, she's fine. A minor accident, folks. Weren't they great?" He led the applause.

Tracy returned to her cabin, with the idea of curling up with a book or writing in her journal. She tried both but couldn't concentrate. She stepped onto her balcony, but it was windy and besides, she didn't feel like standing or sitting. She needed to walk.

She passed only one couple in the corridor as she headed toward the stairway that led down to doors that opened onto the deck. She figured people either retired or were still at play in the casino or lounges.

Once outside, Tracy determined she didn't need the scarf she'd grabbed before setting forth. The wind had died down to a playful breeze that brushed tendrils of hair against her cheeks and caused the hem of her skirt to tickle her knees.

She thought how nice it would be to take a stroll with Peter, then end the evening with a nightcap in the Crow's Nest. Damn him, anyway. She blinked away tears as she watched a couple standing arm-in-arm at the railing. She turned to walk in the opposite direction.

Some of the deck chairs had not yet been removed for the night, and as Tracy strolled past them, something caught her eye. She slowed and looked more closely. Someone was huddled down into a chair, their face not visible. With only a dim light from the overhang above, it was hard to tell if it was a man or a woman, but she would have guessed it was the latter. She walked on past, then turned back. This person could be sick—or worse.

It definitely was a woman. Tracy tapped her on the arm. "Are you okay?"

The woman raised her head and stared at her blankly.

Tracy took in her breath. It was Joanne. "Joanne, its Tracy. Can I help you?"

"Tracy? Oh, God—" She began to sob.

Tracy moved a deck chair close to Joanne and sat down. She reached for her hand. "Please talk to me. Tell me what's wrong."

Joanne had stopped crying, but her woebegone expression aroused in Tracy a feeling of compassion. The snob, the stick of wood was human, after all.

"You were at the talent show?" Joanne spoke barely above a whisper. At Tracy's nod, she continued, "So you saw what *happened*." The last word came out a whimper.

"I saw that you and Jack did a superb job. Of course, the accident was unfortunate, but it could happen to anyone. I hope you weren't hurt. Are you all right?"

"Physically, yes. Oh, it's all so humiliating." Her voice taking on a teary tone. "After a bad start, the morning turned out to be wonderful.

For a while. Then everything fell apart." Her head bowed, it was as if she'd been talking to herself. Now she looked straight at Tracy. "Jack can be very cold. We had words and, well…" She trailed off.

And not for the first time, Tracy gathered. "It happens to all of us. My husband and I have had our moments." Speaking of husbands, where was Jack? "Joanne, don't you think you'd be more comfortable in your cabin? Why don't I walk you back there?"

"You've been very nice to me. I really appreciate—" She gasped as she looked beyond Tracy's shoulder.

Tracy turned. It was Jack. He came upon them at a half run.

"My God, Joanne. I've been looking for you everywhere."

Joanne stared up at her husband. "Did you purposely push me back so that I lost my balance?"

"Did I *what?* You know very well what the problem was. I don't have to spell it out. Come on, let's go to the cabin." She rose, as did Tracy. Only then did Jack address Tracy. "Joanne has a problem from time to time. Enough said?" His smile was perfunctory.

Joanne started to say something, and then apparently changed her mind.

When the Watkinses were out of sight, Tracy mulled what had taken place, and then decided she didn't want to think about it.

What she needed was music and warmth and a nightcap. At the piano bar.

When Tracy returned to her cabin, she saw the message light on her phone was blinking. Marc? They had agreed to meet tomorrow at Paradiso for lunch. Perhaps there'd been a change in plans and he had to remain on board, after all.

She pushed the message button and listened; then, heart thumping, she played it again. She'd heard correctly: *Be in the terminal building tomorrow morning at approximately 10:30.* As a surprise, Peter had arranged to spend the day and evening with her in Acapulco.

ᕦ *Chapter Ten* ᕤ

Acapulco: In Port

Patty toyed with her roll, ignoring the fan-shaped pats of butter and the small crystal containers of marmalade, strawberry jam, and honey that came with the breakfast provided by room service. She should have been savoring her meal and especially the view from their balcony. Acapulco Bay was an azure centerpiece, ringed by resorts, with villas perched high above the water against a backdrop of towering mountains. Small craft chugged below them, impervious, it would seem, to water-skiers darting in and out of the traffic.

Her husband, she noted, ate with gusto, putting away eggs, ham, and sweet rolls. "No appetite this morning?" Ben asked.

"I guess I'm saving up for the buffet luncheon on the tour. Ben, I wish you were coming with me. You're going to miss all the major attractions."

"Think about tonight, sweetie. La Quebrada. Dinner at La Perla. And wait 'til you see the divers with torches plunge into the water between the cliffs." He raised his eyebrows. "When they make the drop, it has to be expertly timed with the incoming waves. Or—" He made a cutting motion across his throat.

"My goodness. It should be spectacular." Patty broke off a corner of her roll and reached for the butter. "I shouldn't complain. I know how much you've looked forward to this fishing expedition."

"Speaking of which," Ben looked at his watch, "I should get going." He came around to her side of the table to give her a kiss. "You won't lack for companionship. There's bound to be someone on the tour from bridge or the talent show or," he winked, "even one of our dinner companions."

"That reminds me… I came upon Tracy yesterday when she was out on deck." She made a face. "Jack Watkins was sitting with her, but thankfully as I arrived, he was leaving. Tracy and I talked a bit and—well, I confided what Jack had said on the dance floor. Turns out he'd been questioning Tracy about her relatives in Poland."

Ben had been about to enter their cabin. Now he reclaimed his place across from her. "The Jewish connection?"

"You figured that out too? Anyway, Tracy made some comment about Jack's knowing she was half-Jewish."

"Did she say anything about his attitude? Was he unpleasant?"

"Apparently not, but the fact that he questioned her makes me uneasy."

Ben reached across the table to pat her hand, and then got to his feet. "I'm on my way."

"Ben, wait. I'm surprised you tolerate this man. In fact, you seem more attuned to him now than when we first met the Watkinses."

"Know the enemy, huh? Kidding, I'm only kidding." He threw her a kiss and left the balcony.

Patty jabbed her fork into her scrambled eggs. How could he be so indifferent, so unaffected?

She thought a moment. Call it insight or intuitiveness, but it occurred to her that Ben might engage Jack in conversation as a means of finding out more about him. The question was why? Was the title of his next scholarly text: *Portrait of a Bigot?* Or did Ben perceive Jack in a more sinister light?

Enough guesswork. She'd simply ask.

Joanne awakened with a sense of dread. What would Jack say to her? How would they get through the day after last night? She had embarrassed and humiliated them both. Worse, she'd accused Jack of causing her to fall.

To her astonishment, her husband acted as if the incident had not occurred. He was pleasant throughout breakfast, his conversation centered on aspects of their morning tour.

Now, as they prepared to leave the ship, Joanne was elated over how well the morning had gone. She pushed her concerns about Jack's afternoon meeting from her mind. In return for his courtesy to her, she would refrain from bringing up the subject. She would stay out of his business and be a loyal and loving wife.

As for Teddy, Jack was right that their son had been out of line.

Whatever Jack's faults, he had his pride.

But then, so did Teddy. She swallowed hard and wished it were already time for lunch. And a drink.

Shirley was about to board the bus for the four-hour Acapulco City Tour, when she spotted Tracy. She broke away from the line. "Tracy! Are you taking this tour? You look really spiffy. Love your outfit."

Tracy looked startled as if she'd been miles away in thought. She stared blankly at Shirley.

"I said: Are you taking this tour?"

"Oh. Hi, Shirley. No, I'm going out on my own. I know Acapulco pretty well from previous visits."

Shirley nodded. "I should have guessed. Enjoy your day." She waved goodbye and snaked her way back in line, beating out some of the slowpokes. She hoped she hadn't sacrificed a good seat. God forbid she'd have to sit in the back of the bus.

Oh good. She'd found a seat by the window. Outside, throngs of shorts-clad people boarded buses or walked into town. She wondered where Tracy was headed. Probably to a fancy dress boutique or jewelry shop that catered to the got-lots.

But. Bargaining was the name of the game. Shirley rubbed her hands together as images of jewelry, leather goods, and pottery came to mind. She hadn't brought along an extra suitcase for nothing. She'd make room for something nice for Jodie, as well.

Her thoughts turned once again to Tracy. She'd looked really gorgeous in a sleeveless, gauzy white dress with turquoise drop earrings and a silver and turquoise necklace. With her hair up, she looked like a model. Such a classy, elegant lady. No wonder Marc was always making goo-goo eyes at Tracy.

Now, if she could get Gloria to style her hair in an up-do—the thought disintegrated, shot down by the enemy.

Roy was boarding the bus.

Tracy spotted Peter before he saw her. Immediately she relaxed. He looked like the Peter she remembered from earlier times—carefree, happy, as if he were taking pleasure in the thought of their reunion. Her spirits soared.

"Peter! Here I am." His face lit up as he spied her, and in seconds she was in his arms in an embrace so tight it took her breath away.

When he released her, she laughed out of pure joy. He grasped her hands, then stepped back so they stood at arm's length. "I wish I could whip up a portrait artist to define this moment for all time. I can't take my eyes off you."

'Portrait' brought forth an image of Marc, but only fleetingly. "I can't believe you came all this way to be with me for one day. Peter, this is wonderful. I've missed you."

"Surprised you, did I? Well, hang on, my darling; I've a few more up my sleeve. But first I'm going to whisk you away to a very special shop in the downtown area. Mind taking a short walk?"

"I love to walk. You know that." Tracy took his arm. "Let's see this shop of yours."

❧

Peter had not specified what kind of merchandise was featured, but as they toured the shop, Tracy was not surprised to find display upon display of precious gems set in silver, platinum, and gold. In addition, individual tables exhibited an array of silver items, including glistening candlesticks, coffee and tea services, ornately carved boxes, and many other decorative pieces.

Peter steered her toward the jewelry display cases, and though she laughingly protested that her birthday had come and gone, in the end they selected a sapphire ring edged with diamonds.

Now, as they rode along Costura Miguel Aleman in the chauffeur-driven car Peter hired, Tracy made a wave-like motion with her right hand. "Can you see how dazzling my ring is? I'm so captivated by the darn thing, I'm missing most of the scenery."

"If you're referring to resort hotels, restaurants, and misguided drivers, you haven't missed a thing."

Tracy shook her head. "Peter, my goodness, you didn't have to do this. Having you here with me is more than enough."

He appeared to ponder her statement. "I'm glad you're happy to see me."

"Of course I am. That goes without saying." Until now, all had been contained and sealed in lightness and mirth. The bubble hadn't burst, but something in his manner gave her pause.

They needed to move on. "I'm eagerly awaiting the next surprise," she said.

He brightened. "You've noticed we're starting the climb into the hillside? There's a spectacular restaurant ahead called Coyuca 22."

"I went there once with my parents. The views are breathtaking. However, as I recall, they serve dinner only."

He squeezed her hand. "Possibly we'll dine there, but I was about to add that besides this restaurant, we'll see some lovely homes. Would you like to visit one of them? Better yet—Well, I don't want to spoil the surprise."

"For heaven's sake, I can't wait. You've got to tell me."

He pursed his lips and assumed an expression of deliberation.

"Okay, Peter, you know how you *love* to be tickled? Well, you're going to get it." Tracy pounced.

"All right, all right." He was laughing. "Back off. I'll talk." When she stopped, he peered out the window. "You know what? I think we're almost there."

The driver was slowing, and then came to a stop before a house that looked rather plain except for lush ground vegetation and bougainvillea that reminded Tracy of the intense, vibrant red flowers at Casa Bonita. Whatever the interior of the house, Tracy suspected the view would be worth the trip.

The woman who greeted them at the door introduced herself as the housekeeper. She was small and plump, with lovely, wide-spaced eyes and full lips. Her smile, however, revealed teeth that were irregular and discolored.

As they stepped inside, Tracy gasped. "I had no idea. This home would garner a spread in *Architectural Digest*."

Peter stood in place, hands on hips. He made a whistling sound.

"Makes our place look…"

"Deprived? Let's look around, see what they've done that we haven't."

The entryway was set with Mexican tiles in an abstract motif of muted blues and greens. In its center, a lighted pool showcased floating hibiscus blossoms. Ringing the pool was foliage laced with gardenias. Overhead, a black ironstone chandelier in the form of candlesticks cast a warm glow.

They moved into the living room. Tracy took in billowy white drapes tied with gold tassels that touched upon plush gold carpeting, mere footnotes to the oversized white brocade sofa with accompanying love seat and the large gold-inlaid glass cocktail table. Tapestried chairs in a combination of gold and white graced each side of the fireplace.

"All right," Tracy said with a laugh. "You've sold me. I'll take the house." Carpeting in the sitting room had now given way to white-tiled flooring in walkways leading to other rooms.

As they explored the rest of the house, Peter explained that one of the firm's clients owned this place as a vacation retreat and had graciously offered to open his home to them for the day.

"With lunch thrown in," Peter added. "The woman who let us in will serve us on the terrace."

"Oh, my," Tracy said as they stepped outside. "Isn't this fantastic?" They stood in a glassed-in portion of the terrace, furnished with green-cushioned chairs positioned around glass topped tables. Planters filled with white and yellow flowers that reminded Tracy of exotic creations she'd viewed at an orchid farm added a decorative touch, while twin fountains stationed on each side of the entryway spewed forth a medley of rushing, splashing water from shell-like openings.

Beyond the solarium was an open patio with chairs and tables arranged around a swimming pool. Palm trees served as a backing, their branches executing a graceful nodding motion. The *pièce de résistance*, however, was the unobstructed view of Acapulco Bay.

"I vote we have lunch here," Peter said. "How can you beat the view?"

Tracy agreed, and Rosa, the housekeeper, soon appeared with appetizers and wine.

As they sipped their drinks, talk was relaxed and easy. Tracy tried not to think about a similar occasion in Mazatlan. She was with her husband, and she felt the stirrings of sexual desire. More so now, she realized, than in previous weeks or even months. Intensifying these feelings was the tropical warmth, as yet soft and velvety like the down of a comforter.

Peter raised her hand to his lips. It was the tender gesture of a devoted husband, but she read a tentativeness in his manner, a hint of uncertainty in his gaze. "We have the run of the house," he said, "including the bedrooms."

Tracy's laugh was soft. "Bedrooms, plural? Sounds like an adventure in the making, my darling."

Once again he reached for her hand, only to retreat. Rosa had arrived with their salads, an attractive arrangement of pineapple, mango, cantaloupe, and watermelon slices, dressed with a creamy lemon sauce.

Tracy tasted her pineapple, nodded approvingly, and then said between bites, "Call me addlepated, but I've been so caught up in your being here, I haven't thought to ask when you're flying back. You did mention something about dinner?"

Rosa brought a second bottle of wine and now as Peter filled their glasses, he said, "We're on for dinner. Absolutely. I'll take you back to the ship, then return here to stay the night."

"Oh. I thought you said something about having the run of the house for the day only. I didn't know you had permission to stay overnight. But that's great. I only hope you don't have to be up at some ungodly hour for your flight home."

"Actually, I'll be staying tomorrow night as well."

Suddenly her mouth felt dry. "Why is that?"

"Do you recognize the name Robert Ochoa?"

She nodded. "Prominent figure in Southern California politics?"

"Yes, indeed. Anyway, he's here on family business. My"—he raised his hands—"advisors thought I should set up a meeting with him." He smiled. "I'm told his support would further my chances for election."

She moved her new ring in an up and down motion. "So fortuity kicked in to bring you to him and me in one fell swoop?"

Peter's expression turned wary. "It seemed the perfect opportunity to combine business with pleasure."

"If Señor Ochoa had not been in Acapulco at this time?"

"You're asking would I have made the trip here anyway?"

Tracy watched as Peter speared a piece of watermelon. He studied it intensely as if seeking an answer, then set down his fork. "I'm not sure."

"At least you're honest."

"God knows I've missed you, but given other circumstances, who can say?"

Tracy poked at her salad. "If the timing had been different—say if I were in Puerto Vallarta at the time Ochoa was here, would you have come to Acapulco?"

"I don't know. Probably not. Look, what's important is we're here together now."

"I know, Peter. It certainly all worked out."

They fell silent as Rosa cleared their plates, then set before them a pineapple teriyaki chicken dish with rice pilaf and zucchini slices. Tracy was grateful the portions were moderate. "It sounds as if you're fully committed to the race."

"A lot has happened since you left. Meetings, meetings, and more meetings, along with my trip to Sacramento."

"Wait a minute. When we last talked, your candidacy was still iffy. In fact, I thought we agreed to discuss the ins and outs, so to speak."

"I know this is a big step for both of us." He paused. "Tracy, I would not pursue the nomination without your blessing."

But you already have. "Maybe I need more details, Peter."

"I'll bring you up to date. But first I want to hear about you. How do you like the ship, the stops so far?" He gave her a speculative smile. "I can picture the single guys turning handsprings to catch your attention. I know I'd come after you."

She shrugged. "They're not exactly standing in line for the favor of my company, but thanks for the compliment."

Tracy tasted her chicken. It was excellent, but she knew she'd have to force herself through the remainder of the meal. "It's been a good trip," she said, "but I've felt lonely at times, particularly in the evenings."

"I know what you mean."

Tracy felt the heat rise in her cheeks. "How could you possibly have the time to feel lonely?"

"Being busy doesn't erase the fact that I've missed you." He shook his head.

She picked at her chicken. "I know I sound cranky. Maybe it's the heat. I think it's become more sultry." She fanned herself.

"We can move inside." He looked around for Rosa.

"No, I'm okay. You asked about the trip. I'll save Los Cabos and Mazatlan for later. Let me tell you about our table." Like an artist creating life with the stroke of a brush, Tracy sought the right words to effect a vivid portrait of the people with whom she dined.

Peter appeared fully absorbed in her description, responding with a chuckle, the lift of an eyebrow, a sympathetic shake of his head.

When she'd finished, Peter leaned back in his chair. "I have to give you your due. You've breathed life into what could have been stick figures. That's a gift."

Tracy felt a renewal of energy. "There's more." She had delineated her cast of characters in a lighthearted manner, emphasizing (and exaggerating somewhat) their peculiarities, while focusing also on positive qualities. She had not zeroed in on the villain of the piece, Jack the Bigot, but now—against her better judgment?—decided to add an edge to her narrative.

Peter's response was disgust. "Just your luck to be stuck with a racist." He studied her for a moment. "Do you think he might turn nasty because of your family background?"

"I don't like the fact he's brought up the subject of my Jewish relatives, but he hasn't shown any hostility." She snorted. "Yet."

"Avoid him at all costs."

She laughed. "How am I supposed to do that at dinner? Seriously, Peter, if my writing project turns out to be the basis for a novel, he'd make an interesting character. So maybe I'd better learn all I can about this man."

Peter gazed out at the bay, seemingly lost in thought, then turned to her. "I'm tempted to take you off the ship and arrange for us to go home together."

"Peter, for heaven's sake. It's not as if I'm in danger or that Jack Watkins can harm me in any way."

His grin was sheepish. "I suppose not. I guess I overreacted. Besides, I want you to enjoy this break. Before we know it, there'll be strategizing meetings, fundraising dinners, out of town trips. In all, a hefty schedule."

"I can't believe what I'm hearing. For God's sake, what happened to discussing my part in this venture? *Before* you committed, my dear?"

He bowed his head a moment, and then looked her in the eye. "You know what they say. Timing is everything. It all happened so fast—being tapped as a candidate, I mean—and then you were on your way to Mexico."

"At your insistence. No, that's not fair. I wanted to take the cruise." She paused. "It's not that I'd stand in your way, Peter. But damn it all, there are so many imponderables. Suppose you are elected. How would that impact our life? What kinds of demands would be made on our time? Our privacy? Oh, I could go on and on."

"Of course there'd be changes. Some, very exciting, I would think." He moved his wine glass in a circular motion. "I had hoped for a more enthusiastic response."

Tracy pushed back her chair. "This has been a wonderful meal, but I can't eat another bite. I hope Rosa isn't planning to bring out dessert."

He stood. "We don't need to wait for Rosa. You look flushed, Tracy. Are you feeling all right?"

"A little shaky, is all. Let's get out of the sun."

Once inside, Peter led her to the master bedroom. That it was palatial and luxuriously appointed seemed fitting. The handsome king-sized bed with its gold silken coverlet—a contrast to thick white carpeting—dominated the room.

Tracy removed her sandals and felt the comforting softness hug her feet. She looked questioningly at Peter. "I don't think I'm quite up for romance."

"Why don't we both lie down and rest for a bit. Then we'll see how we feel."

Tracy fell into a deep sleep, and when she awakened in Peter's arms, the outside light was softer, deflected by cloud cover, the room less bright, made more intimate by shadow. While she didn't feel the sexual excitement generated earlier by their reunion, she was aroused by Peter's warmth, his gentle kisses. Ultimately, it was impossible not to respond as their embraces grew more impassioned, as they kissed, touched, and caressed to bring each other to climax.

Later they dined on the terrace at Coyuca 22 and marveled at their elegant surroundings, at the city lights across Acapulco Bay. For Tracy, it had been a long day—exciting and fulfilling, but also perplexing and exhausting.

She wondered if Peter shared her sentiments. He was low-key but attentive as they dined. They talked about Mexico, world events, mutual friends, and home repairs. The latter she could do without, especially in this romantic setting, but anything to ward off a discussion of Peter's political agenda.

They arrived at the ship at 11:00, a half hour before sailing time.

"Too bad I can't sneak you aboard," Tracy said. "The plan is for a lavish sail-away party on the top deck. Not that I'm particularly in the mood for mixing with the party animals."

Peter held her close for a moment, and then released her. "We'll have our own party when you return home. Okay?" His words held promise, his tone was light, but she thought she detected a trace of sadness in his expression. He held her gaze as if memorizing her features, then kissed her gently on the lips.

She stood in place as Peter, his shoulders hunched, walked in the direction of the terminal building. "Peter!" she called out. He turned. "Have a safe trip back, my love." She threw him a kiss.

His wave was jaunty, his step brisk as he continued on his way.

Inside her cabin, Tracy debated whether or not to join in on the festivities. She stepped onto the balcony and could feel the vibration of ship's engines, revving up for departure.

Now they were moving, and the music, the vibrant voices overhead conveyed an audible tribute to the luminous array of lights that defined the shoreline. And to what lay within the city—glamour, garishness; beauty, squalor; excitement, futility.

As they sailed farther away, as the radiance dimmed, she thought of Peter bedding down for the night in Acapulco, alone in the gold and white home on the bluff. In the bed they had shared.

She moved inside and sat before flowers that now were more wilted than fresh. The card, of course, was gone.

She began to sob as if her heart would break.

The party on deck was winding down, and Shirley yawned as she set her glass on the bar. She was tempted to order a second margarita but decided to pass. They were at sea now and the hoopla over setting sail seemed like a scene out of a movie—fun, raucous, crazy—a moment to remember after the fade out.

She yawned again. God knew she'd had a full day, but what the heck? She decided to order a martini, top off the evening with some real booze.

She could imagine a conversation with Jodie:

"Tell me about Acapulco, Shirley."

"Hot and sticky but with gorgeous, expensive resort hotels and a million shops. Sophisticated but gut-wrenching." She shuddered, remembering the crippled, the blind, and the small children shabbily dressed, all with hands extended, the little guys pushing trays at you, filled with Chiclets or trinkets.

Would she tell Jodie about Roy? Probably. Her drink was now before her, and as she tasted it, she thought how she'd practically swallowed her teeth when she saw Roy board the bus.

The aisle seat was taken, thank God. Not that he'd be brazen enough to sit next to her. At any rate, if he recognized her, he gave no indication. At the various stops they managed to avoid one another, though out of the corner of her eye she caught him eyeing her.

She'd also taken the night tour to see the divers and ran into the Redfords, but there was no sign of Roy. She sighed, and then perked up. So what if she did run into the bastard? She had nothing to be ashamed of. Well, not a lot.

She took another sip of her drink. Ah. She had the solution. Why hadn't she thought of this before? Roy did not exist. He was a stranger, a nameless idiot passenger among many. Certainly not worth a second look.

Tomorrow they would be in that place that started with a Z. Weird name. She looked at her watch. She'd better call it a night and get some sleep. She'd finish her drink pronto, then hightail it to her cabin.

She smiled. Maybe with a quick detour to the piano bar?

❧ *Chapter Eleven* ☙

Zihuatanejo, Ixtapa

At the sound of the breakfast chimes, Joanne burrowed deeper into her covers. She felt Jack stir, then leave their bed to make his way to the bathroom.

In minutes he was back in the room. Feigning sleep, she remained very still, eyes tightly shut.

"Joanne." He shook her gently. "Come on. Time to get up."

Her journey from prone to sitting position was labored. "Oh, what an awful night. Bad dreams and then the rocking of the ship kept me awake for hours."

"Really? I wasn't aware of any roughness." He stepped to the window and opened the drapes. "Looks great out there now. Sunny and clear." He squinted into the light. "We're barely moving. In fact, I think we're anchored. I understand we board a tender to take us into Zihuatanejo."

Joanne watched as an energized Jack bustled about getting dressed, whistling something under his breath.

For her part, she moved at a snail's pace as she brought clothes out of her closet, then entered the bathroom. From his sidelong glances, it was evident Jack had taken note of her listlessness.

So far, so good.

At the breakfast buffet, Joanne bypassed her usual selection of melon, scrambled eggs, and an English muffin for orange slices, dry toast, and coffee.

Jack was busy unloading his tray of breakfast meats, hot cereal, and blueberry muffins. Now he placed his napkin in his lap and gave her a look of satisfaction. "Should be an interesting day if we can work our way past the unpronounceable names." This was said with a chortle.

Jack, making light of a situation? Joanne eyed her husband as he bit into his muffin. He was in good humor and in fact had been uncharacteristically cheerful since his meeting in Acapulco.

Now, between spoonfuls of cereal, he talked about Ixtapa. "It's supposed to be ultra-modern—the hotels, condos, the marina area. Then we have Zihuatanejo, which is described as a quiet little fishing village." He chuckled. "I suspect the quiet part is a misnomer, or at least will be for the duration of the ship's beach party."

Joanne nodded. "It should be a mob scene, all right."

"I only hope the buffet is decent." He looked at his watch. "Speaking of food, you'd better grab the rest of your breakfast."

Joanne pushed her plate to the side. "I don't have any appetite."

He looked at her closely. "You think you might be coming down with something?"

"I don't know. God forbid its Montezuma's Revenge. I experienced some stomach cramping this morning."

He shook his head. "I don't recommend being on the beach or on a bus, for that matter. I think we'd better stay on the ship."

"I'll stay on the ship. Now Jack, please don't interrupt. What's the sense in both of us staying behind? You'd be bored, and I certainly wouldn't be good company. Besides, I've never been fond of beach parties."

"If you're sure—"

"Absolutely. If I rest, chances are I'll be fine by this evening. I'd rather skip today and be well for Puerto Vallarta tomorrow."

He patted her hand. "That's the spirit."

Joanne accompanied Jack to the showroom where ticket holders waited for their numbers to be called for the tender. He protested her tagging along, arguing she should be resting. She'd responded she had all day to rest, plus she wanted to be out of the cabin while it was being made up.

It wasn't enough that Jack's number was called. Joanne made sure he was off the ship and had boarded the tender. Only then did she take a deep breath and head for their cabin.

The room had been made up—everything neat and tidy. She

stood in the center of the cabin, immobilized. Her breathing was shallow, and the oranges from breakfast left a sour taste in her mouth.

Move, idiot. It's your only chance. Jack's briefcase was propped against the desk chair, a study in complacency, as if daring her to invade its privacy. Joanne glanced at the door, and then made her move.

The case was locked. Of course. Why would she have thought otherwise? If Jack had taken the key with him, then she'd either have to continue with her little charade or fabricate a quick recovery. On the other hand, if the key was in the room, she'd find the damn thing.

First their closets. Stealthily, as if she were being watched, she searched pants pockets, shirt and jacket pockets, as well as Jack's toiletry kit, but came up with nothing. She didn't think he'd simply toss the key into the drawer where they kept plane tickets, passports, and items relating to their itinerary, but looked anyway—with no luck.

What next? Their dresser drawers. She examined shorts and undershirts, careful to return them to their neat piles. She even rummaged through her drawers of undergarments, hose and lingerie. Nothing.

Joanne paced the room. What had she neglected to examine? Ah. The top shelves in their closets. Had he slipped the key under the life jackets or extra bedding?

She stepped away from the closet and shook her head in exasperation. All right. One more look in the dresser drawers. Perhaps the key lay hidden in a far corner. She ran her hands over the back and into the corners of every drawer, with no success.

Damn and double damn. She started to close Jack's underwear drawer, then took a second look at his collection of rolled socks. What if one tiny key made its home deep in a fold? Carefully, she separated a pair of blue socks, and then refolded them. She did the same to a black pair.

On the third try she found the key. Her elation was tempered by the realization she'd have to return the key to the same set of socks in their precise location.

She fumbled in her first attempt to open the case. In her second try, she met with success despite damp palms, the pounding in her chest.

What she came upon first was a newspaper article on Hayden Lake, Idaho. She soon discovered this was not a travel piece but a description of a hangout for racist and anti-Semitic extremists. She recognized the names Phineas Priesthood and Aryan Nations, though she couldn't remember when or where she'd heard mention of them. The article zeroed in on skinheads, neo-Nazi white supremacists, and the followers of Christian Identity and World Church.

Church groups? She read on. Well, not her definition of church teachings. She'd grown up in a household where disparaging remarks were made about Jews and black people, where she'd been told not to associate with either group—not that she'd had any desire to pal around with Jews or Negroes. But her parents never spoke about Anglo-Saxons as the 'chosen people' or denigrated Jews as 'children of Satan.'

World Church, she read, aimed to create an all-white nation. The article also quoted from writings that advocated the killing of Jews and non-whites, the assassination of political leaders.

What the paper called 'hate groups' were listed as existing in Washington, Idaho, and Montana as a 'profile of hate' in the Northwest.

Apart from the article were pages of typed notes. Page one made reference to Phoenix as virgin territory, where the Brotherhood would establish a stronghold of men and women whose goal it was to establish a white supremacy.

She flipped to the second page, the third and fourth pages. What she read made her heart race. There were names, obviously Jewish names, with notes as to profession and standing in the community. Also listed were banks, law firms, medical clinics, corporations, schools, day care centers, and more, all to be targeted.

Joanne felt bile rise in her throat, a light-headedness, as if she had passed into an altered state of consciousness. Her gaze strayed to the corner of the dresser, to the bottle of vodka, then down to her clenched hands. *Stay with this. Use your brain; focus on the material.*

Turning back to the listing of day care centers, she saw there were two: Jewish Community Preschool and Chabad Day Care. The type blurred, and then cleared. A note pad. She had to find a note pad. But where? In her purse? In her carry-on bag?

Her purse yielded only a crumpled grocery list at the bottom of the bag. But glory be, in a zippered compartment of her carry-on bag, she found the travel diary she'd forgotten she'd packed in the last minute scramble to assemble everything for the trip.

She glanced at her watch. She didn't expect Jack to return for at least a couple more hours. Still, she felt his presence—in the room, lurking outside the door.

She set to work, copying the names of the day care centers, schools, clinics, and other places listed, scribbling furiously. She had to stop to flex her cramped fingers, and then rewrote portions that were unreadable. There was no rush, yet she felt demon-driven.

When she was finished—she had included only a sampling of individual names—she placed the material back in the briefcase and locked it. There. Now what? Oh, God, the key.

Her evening gloves lay between her jewelry case and evening bag in the bottom dresser drawer. She knew she was being ridiculous, but couldn't stop herself. Once her gloves were on, she used a towel from the bathroom to wipe the key, and then placed it back in the folds of the designated socks.

Back to the briefcase. It occupied the same space as before, propped against the leg of a chair, as if in jaunty defiance of its sinister content. She was tempted to reopen the case to make sure she'd placed Jack's papers exactly as she'd found them, and then backed away from the idea, too exhausted to pursue the task. Once again she felt lightheaded and, despite the air conditioning in the cabin, warm and sweaty.

She needed air. She removed her gloves, tossed them on the bed, and then stepped onto the balcony and up to the railing. It felt good to breathe in fresh air, to feel the sun on her face, as if she'd escaped from a closed, contaminated habitat.

She thought back to her uneasiness over Jack's lengthy phone conversation behind closed doors, to the papers she wasn't supposed to see in his suitcase. Now that her suspicions were confirmed, the question remained: What to do next? Dare she confront Jack with her findings? Maybe his involvement was limited. After all, he would never be a party to hurting children. Still, he might argue that if child endangerment served as a means toward accomplishing their mission, then so be it.

No, what was she thinking? Whatever his stance, Jack must not learn she was privy to their—the Brotherhood's?—evil pursuits. If he learned she'd sneaked behind his back to go through his private papers… She shuddered as she visualized the horrific scene that would ensue— Jack's expression of contempt, his menacing look. Or worse. Yet, if he were indeed a major player, he courted danger, disgrace, and the threat of prison.

Slowly she moved from the railing to take a seat. She could see his side of the picture, could relate to his concerns over deceitful, manipulative people who held high positions; over minorities who were gaining too much power. But he was taking it too far.

If she could approach him in a non-judgmental manner, speak softly but persuasively about the direction his life was taking. If, if, if.

Joanne thought about their children. To go to them about their father was unthinkable. God forbid, they might even turn him in.

She held her head in her hands and massaged her temples. Could she remain blind to his actions, stay loyal, knowing the carnage that was to take place?

Yes, because he was all she had. Jack and the two B's—booze and bridge. It was as simple as that.

Or was it? Slowly she straightened. There was a solution. Anonymously, she could warn the authorities, provide them with names and places. Jack would never be the wiser, would never suspect his meek ever-obliging wife of treacherous acts. Think of the lives she would save.

She stood. Her breathing was steadier, but her head pounded and she felt queasy. Tonight, she remembered, was formal. Would she make it? Maybe with a pick-me-up. Or two.

She was one foot into the cabin when she froze. Jack stood at the foot of the bed, his gaze fastened on her gloves. He looked up as she stepped into the room. "Joanne, you don't look so good."

"I thought fresh air would make me feel better. I was wrong." What was he doing back so soon? Why did he appear enthralled with her gloves? Oh God, her travel diary with its thick black cover lay square in the middle of the desk as if begging for attention.

"I decided to skip the beach party," he said, "so if you're up to it, we can have lunch on board." He had picked up her gloves as he spoke.

She reached out for them. "I'll put those away. I was checking to see if they were clean enough to wear tonight. That is if I feel all right by evening."

Now he was at the desk, emptying his pockets of loose change. He placed his hand on the diary. "I didn't know you were keeping a record of the cruise."

"I thought if I jotted down a few notes it would take my mind off myself." Her words, she thought, sounded breathy, fragmented. She gripped the back of the desk chair. "Jack, why don't you go to lunch? I may venture out later for a bowl of soup or call room service."

He nodded. "Let's call room service." He started for the phone, and then stopped. "I'd better freshen up first."

As soon as the bathroom door shut, Joanne grabbed the diary and tore out the pages she'd copied, leaving the diary in place on the desk. She was shoving the material beneath her undergarments when Jack left the bathroom. She seized her evening slip and held it up as if inspecting it for wrinkles. Jack gave her an encouraging smile and headed for the phone.

What if he asked her to read aloud what she'd recorded so far? She'd have to make up an excuse, like she'd tried to gather her thoughts but felt too ill to write.

Joanne sighed. The practice of deception was wearisome, at best. Mentally she berated herself, thinking of all the what-ifs that lay ahead, of how much simpler it would have been to stay out of Jack's business.

Except she had no choice.

The bus trip to Ixtapa, which included a walking tour of one of the area's newest resorts, rated a shrug in Shirley's opinion. Call it too pricey, too far from the action. In all, a waste of time when they could be partying on the beach, picking up on the men.

Now back on the bus, Shirley sat with Trudy, she of the copper top and harem pants. Today Trudy wore a sheer knee-length sleeveless black cover-up over a fuchsia one-piece bathing suit. On each arm, four gold bracelets etched with a pattern of crosses bit into her flesh. Gold earrings in the shape of crosses dangled from her ears, while on her chest a heavy onyx and gold cross pulsated with every breath.

Shirley thought the ensemble peculiar yet exotic, though she questioned the mixture of fuchsia with flame red hair. As for her jewelry, either Trudy was hung up on religion or in-step with a hot new fashion trend.

In any event, Shirley now regretted her choice of a sleeveless red and white striped top over white shorts—and not for the reason her shorts were binding and wrinkled from being too tight, but because her outfit lacked flair. She was a gnat among fireflies.

She and Trudy had connected in the ship's lounge where they discovered they were assigned to the same tender; it was then they decided to sit together on the bus.

"I hope you'll join us for the luncheon buffet," Trudy was saying. "You remember the two ladies with me at the Solos party?" Her voice was high pitched, like that of a sweet little girl, and Shirley had to strain to hear her. "Well, they decided to skip this part of the tour and go directly to the beach party. Anyway, I know they'd be pleased if you sat with us."

"Fantastic," Shirley said. She'd already explained how she'd lost her travel partner, and Trudy had been a sympathetic listener.

"Oh!" Trudy gave a little titter and her cornflower blue eyes gleamed with merriment. "The two single men at our dinner table will be joining us, as well as two men who played bridge with us the other day."

Shirley couldn't conceive of Roy as a bridge player, but she had to ask.

The earring crosses danced as Trudy responded in the negative. "The only Roy I know is our mailman at home."

What did Roy the Rat do for a living? Shirley wondered. Used car salesman? Nah. He didn't have the people skills. Maybe a termite inspector. Yeah, perfect.

Shirley was happy to have someone to chat with for the five-mile drive from Ixtapa to the fishing village. When they arrived at the beach, Trudy immediately spotted her friends. "I don't see the fellows," she said. "If you want to wait here, I'll check with the girls to find out where we'll be sitting, then be right back."

Based on where Trudy was headed, the 'girls' presumably were in the bar area. Shirley decided to set out in the same direction and found Trudy and her friends putting tables together and grabbing spare chairs. The buffet, adjacent to the bar, was set up on tables beneath a long, thatched roof.

After an exchange of greetings, Trudy said, "I was about to come get you. The men from our table are off somewhere, and the others haven't arrived yet, so I think we'll settle down in here out of the sun."

With the area crowded and noisy, Shirley could barely make out Trudy's words. She didn't fancy struggling to make conversation while they waited for the men. "If you don't mind, think I'll wander a bit or"— she pointed to her bag—"find a place to work on my tan."

"That's fine, sweetie. We're not ready to eat yet. We'll send someone to get you when it's time."

After wandering for a bit, Shirley found a place on the beach. She decided not to strip to her bathing suit since they'd be eating soon. Possibly later she'd go for a swim. She wasn't far from the bar and with a wave caught Trudy's eye so they'd know where to find her.

She spread her towel, and then lay down. Despite the heat, she was comfortable, even dozing a bit, but after fifteen minutes, she began to perspire, and the flies, a minor annoyance initially, became a major nuisance.

Something brushed at her ankle. Another pesky fly, Shirley thought. But when she opened her eyes, she discovered she'd been aroused by a thrust of sand. She also discovered a strange man gazing down at her. She raised herself to a sitting position. "Do I know you?"

"You don't now, but I'm counting on changing all that."

A big man with massive shoulders and too little neck, he appeared to be about her age. He was red in the face, either from exertion or the sun, and a strand of thinning blond hair fell over his forehead. He crouched down so they were eye to eye. "Trudy and the others sent me to tell you we're having cocktails before lunch. There's a place saved for you."

His forehead was beaded with sweat, and his breath smelled of cigarettes.

"Why don't you go on ahead? I need to shake out some of this sand." She smiled at him. "It'll take only a minute."

Now upright, he smiled back. "Sure thing."

As she shook out her towel, she watched him make his way to the bar. In high school, the guy would have been to die for, was her guess. But that was then.

For one wild moment she toyed with the idea of returning to the ship. She craned her neck in an attempt to check out the other men in their party but couldn't see past swarms of people crowding the beach. What the heck, she might as well have lunch. Besides, a margarita would really hit the spot.

That she was seated next to Garth, the blond heavyweight, came as no surprise to Shirley. Out of direct sunlight, he wasn't so bad. In fact, his eyes were a gorgeous turquoise, and he had a flirtatious smile. With introductions all around, Shirley was surprised to hear Garth identified as one of the bridge players. The other player, seated across from them, was Paul—a short, pale expressionless man who constantly fingered his thin, dark mustache.

She perked up when the two male dinner companions were introduced. Pete, a lanky blond, could be described as a Robert Redford lookalike. Carlos was of medium height and build with thick, dark hair and soulful, brown eyes. "You must have been a beautiful baby," Shirley sang to herself.

Her margarita tasted sinfully delicious, and she drank with relish while responding to Garth's inquiries—where was she from, what did she do for a living, family stuff. She also managed to keep an eye on Pete and Carlos. They appeared to be sharing travel experiences, trips they'd taken together, like to South America.

Someone ordered a second round of margaritas. In Shirley's experience, drinks served to a huge gathering were generally wimpy. These, however, were not only great-tasting but strong, and Garth looked better and better to her.

"Do you play bridge?" he asked.

She shook her head. "I guess I'm out of the loop, but I've never even tried the game."

He moved his chair closer so that their knees touched. "Would you like to learn?"

"Are you a good teacher?"

"The best." His voice was a caress.

She licked a bit of salt from the rim of her glass, all the while meeting his gaze. "I've been told I'm a fast learner, particularly when it comes to games."

He held her gaze. "I like that in a woman. Maybe we should give it a try."

She smiled. "Maybe." She raised her drink to her lips, sipping slowly, and then hastily set down her glass. Whoa. Where was this going? Maybe it was time out for both of them because Garth was lighting a cigarette.

Back to the basics, Shirley decided. "We've talked about me," she said. "Now tell me about you. What line of work are you in?" With his build, it had to be something heavy duty.

"I'm a mechanical engineer." He took a deep drag on his cigarette, and then expelled the smoke. "I'm also an expert on demolition explosives—buildings, bridges, and so forth."

"Wow." He didn't wear a wedding ring, but since he'd asked about her family background, turnabout was fair play. She opened her mouth, and then shut it as Trudy clapped her hands together. Now she stood. Whatever it was she said, Shirley could hear the word buffet. It was time to chow down.

The men held back as the ladies started into the line. Shirley maneuvered to be next to Trudy.

"Are you having a good time?" Trudy asked. "You and Garth seem to be hitting it off."

"He's, uh, very nice. Kinda grows on you." Shirley helped herself to servings of watermelon and cantaloupe, hoping the flies hadn't visited. The next offerings were tacos and burritos. "I'm impressed with Pete and Carlos." She gave Trudy a poke. "I wouldn't mind being fixed up with either one of them." She tried to sound offhand and made a show of filling her plate.

Out of the corner of her eye, Shirley observed Trudy finger her pendant cross, and then bow her head. Was she meditating? Praying, for God's sake?

Trudy raised her head as they moved on and began tackling tamales, beans, and rice.

"Did I say something out of line?" Shirley asked.

"Of course not. I was debating whether or not to venture an opinion—well, it's not really an opinion because it's obvious to us that—that Pete and Carlos are a couple."

98

"Oh."

"I'm sure you'd enjoy getting to know them, Shirley. They're fun to be with, and their travel stories are fascinating. We could always make a breakfast or lunch date."

Get real, was Shirley's thought, but she smiled and said yeah, maybe sometime.

When everyone was back at the table, Shirley decided to concentrate on Garth. He ordered another round of margaritas for the two of them, and she couldn't help but think what a genuinely nice guy he was.

Laughter erupted at the other end of the table in response to something one of the men said. Even Paul seemed more animated as he tilted his head in their direction. Garth, however, continued to focus on her.

"I like women to look like women," he said, his gaze dropping to her breasts.

Shirley felt the heat in her cheeks, like she was back in eighth grade, a blushing adolescent. Get a grip, Shirley. "That pretty much sums it up for me," she said. "I mean about men looking like men."

They were silent for a moment, attending to food and drink. Then Shirley said, "You have great eyes, Garth. Such a gorgeous blue." Whoops! Slow down, she told herself.

He smiled. "Thank you. Maybe it's my Scandinavian ancestry. You know, blond hair, blue eyes? Of course, my last name, Swenson, is a giveaway as to race. Speaking of names, Clearweather is unusual. Is it American Indian?"

Shirley giggled. "Close, but no cigar. The name is Goodweather, and it's not Indian. My first husband was Jewish. I know Goodweather doesn't *sound* Jewish, but there you go. Anyway, when my second husband and I got divorced, I took back Goodweather since my son kept his father's name."

They sat close, Garth leaning into her, his forearms resting on the table. Now, arms crossed, he shifted his bulk so that they were inches apart. "You follow the Hebrew faith?"

A strange way to put it, she thought. "When Steve was little, we celebrated Hanukkah and Christmas—I forget what else—but we seldom attended services."

"How'd you come to marry a Jew?"

His question, his look of contempt cut through the buzz she'd been enjoying, leaving her with a hollow feeling as if her insides had been gutted. "How about if we change the subject? Is that all right with you?"

"Sure. Let's get back to bridge. You still want to learn?"

"I guess so."

"I forgot I have a tournament coming up, but Paul's a good teacher. Right, Paul?" He reached across the table to give him a thump on the arm.

Paul jumped, his fork flipping out of his hand. "Bridge lessons?" His tone was distinctly nasal. He peered at Shirley, and then raised his hand to his mustache. "I've never taught bridge, but I suppose I could try. What about you, Garth? Didn't you tell me you'd taught your ex-wife?"

Before Garth could answer, Shirley reached for her bag, and then pushed back her chair. "You boys work it out," she said. "I have to make a stop."

She headed in the direction of the restroom but hurried on past it. In the distance she could see a tender tying up to the dock, people standing in line. Possibly she'd make it if she ran.

What stopped her was the sound of Mariachi music coming from the patio beyond their eating area. Should she wander over? She took a tentative step or two, and then came to a halt. She caught sight of Roy and he wasn't alone. He was arm in arm with a bikini-clad dame whose crinkly platinum hair reached to her waist. Shirley had seen this person on deck, in the bar, in the casino. It would be next to impossible to miss her.

She turned away from them, continuing toward the tender. For a second or two she felt a pang of jealousy. Okay. So she'd struck out twice. She was down but not out.

Looking back, it was clear where she and Garth were headed— and it was not to the bridge table. Blame it on the party atmosphere, the drinks, and the flirty man-woman connection. Especially the drinks.

In a way, it was good Garth had turned ugly because by getting

100

out, she'd been spared making another humongous, moronic mistake. Shirley picked up her pace and felt a sense of wonderment.

Jodie would have been proud of her.

❧ *Chapter Twelve* ❧

Zihuatanejo, Ixtapa

"Tracy, I'd love for you to meet the Carltons. They're such dear, dear people," Ann Bradshaw proclaimed. The firmness behind the sweet words lingered in Tracy's mind as she waited to board a tender, to be transported to an area where buses were stationed to take passengers to Ixtapa. Tracy, however, would search for a red jeep.

The jeep belonged to Clive and Irene Carlton who according to Ann, had recently purchased a condo in Ixtapa and divided their time between Mexico, Hawaii, and Palm Springs. More about the couple attested to their affluence, their philanthropic projects, and their support of the arts.

Ann's persistence in the matter, along with a message from the Carltons that they would delight in meeting Ann's daughter-in-law, precluded any question of refusal.

Now as Tracy stepped into the tender, her gaze fell on a man who preceded her aboard and was now seated. Because of his girth—he was a big man with powerful arms—he stood out. She would have given him a cursory glance and moved on but he'd made eye contact, his head cocked to the side as if scrutinizing her. She immediately looked away, uncomfortable with the intensity of his gaze.

It wasn't a flirtatious look; it was more—what? Appraising? At any rate, he was hard to miss, not only because of his size but also because his eyes were a vibrant blue-green, a color she could liken to the waters off the Florida Keys.

Had it ended there, she wouldn't have given him a second thought. However, as she left the tender, she saw he stood off to the side as passengers filed past him. She caught him eyeing her as he lit a cigarette.

Tracy hurried on by, intent on seeking out a red jeep but soon became aware of weighty footsteps bearing down on her. It could be anyone, she reasoned, a dock worker, another passenger from the ship.

Without slowing her pace, she glanced back. It was the man from the tender. He stared at her boldly, as if daring her to speak out.

Was he toying with her? Baiting her? She was tempted to confront him, then thought better of it. Why court trouble?

Soon the footsteps faded and Tracy figured the man had tired of his little game. When she'd found the Carltons and settled into the jeep, she couldn't resist. She had to look back. Easy to spot, he stood next to a bus, dwarfing the people around him. For one crazy moment, she thought he might wave, turn on his heel, and be done with it. Instead, he dropped his cigarette and made an elaborate show of crunching it with his shoe, all the while holding her gaze.

Obviously, the creep had been watching her. Worse, he now appeared to be walking toward the jeep. To her relief, Clive started up the engine, and they were on their way.

As it turned out, Tracy was so taken with the Carltons, she was able, for the most part, to block out the incident. Their condo, tastefully furnished, displayed a combination of cream and beige hues, accented by apricot tones in wall hangings and pillows. Much of the structure was of glass so that the outside deck was merely an extension of breathtaking water views.

Though it was too early for lunch, Irene insisted on serving a snack on the deck when they returned from looking over the resorts and the marina.

Conversation flowed over wine, cheese, and a platter of apple slices and red grapes. Tracy felt quite at home with her gracious host and hostess, except for one jarring moment. She sighted a broad-shouldered blond man across the way from them on the walkway that paralleled the ocean.

He stood close to the passenger side of a parked car, thereby blocking out most of his body, and shaded his eyes with his hand as he looked up in their direction. Irene noticed him too. "We get a lot of tourists or potential buyers cruising the neighborhood," she said to Tracy, "but they seldom get out of their cars. Oops, now he's back in the car."

Irene dropped the matter, switching to another subject. Tracy, while contributing to the conversation, kept an eye on the car. Why hadn't they moved on? The man in the driver's seat—a Mexican?—now peered out the window, squinting into the light.

She couldn't tell if he was focusing on the Carlton's place nor, at this distance, could she identify his passenger.

Mentally, she gave herself a slap on the wrist. She would not add paranoia to her list of mounting concerns.

It was when Tracy was on the tender back to the ship—she had seen enough of Zihuatanejo from the jeep—that she replayed the events that transpired earlier. The nagging feeling persisted that the big blond man had not singled her out on a whim. She felt in her gut he was up to no good. What eluded her was the motive behind his actions.

Still, she doubted she'd cross paths with him again. He was simply a pathetic jerk who enjoyed playing the bad guy. Or so she wanted to believe.

In the ship's lobby, she ran into the Redfords. Apparently, they, too, had decided to skip the beach party. Patty explained she had a hair appointment—after all, tonight was formal—and that Ben looked forward to some quiet time.

As did Tracy. Her plan was to jot down story ideas over a solitary lunch. However, counter to her intentions, she joined Ben at a window table in the Veranda Café. She reasoned it would have been rude not to accept his invitation. Besides, he was good company.

He was also curious about the notebook she'd brought to the table.

She frowned. "I thought I'd have filled these pages by now."

"Ah, so you're a writer."

"Aspiring. I'd like to write fiction."

"You've picked the right venue for plot ideas and people-watching."

She started to say, "More than you know," then stopped herself as a waitress appeared at their table.

Ben smiled at Tracy. "If we're going to engage in a serious discussion, it better be over a glass of wine. Okay with you?"

"Definitely." When the order had been given, Tracy explained that the urge to write competed with the question of whether she might return to her music. "I doubt I could take on both challenges. It's hard enough to succeed in either profession."

"Both are tough fields, but good lord, if you have the talent, what's to stop you?"

"Ha!" Their wine had arrived and Tracy paused to take a sip. "It's not as if I'd be locked away in the attic if I attempted to pursue the arts, but life at home falls into a pattern." Suddenly she was opening up to a man she knew only casually, expounding on aspects of her volunteer work, her social obligations at home, the fact she was beginning to feel stifled by the predictability of her lifestyle, by a routine she found monotonous.

Finally, she pushed her salad, half-eaten, aside and shook her head. "I can't believe I've gone on and on about myself. I'm probably making you uncomfortable, ranting on about personal issues."

"No, not at all, Tracy." He looked pensive for a moment, and then said, "There's a part of me that wants to stray from my calling. What it boils down to is that I'd like to engage in something more risky, more exciting."

"Really!"

"I've worked as a consultant with the FBI, based on my research into fringe groups and hate organizations. I'm tempted to give up teaching and work full-time in that capacity. I think Patty suspects as much, though I haven't come right out with it." He smiled. "There now. I've confided something of my personal life with you. So we're even."

"Isn't it interesting how people so often open up to acquaintances, rather than to people close to them?" And how comfortable it was to talk to this man.

Ben finished his lasagna and now turned to his wine. "I heard from Patty," he said between sips, "that the two of you discussed Jack Watkins's… shall we say, *unique* way of looking at life?"

"Ah, yes. You know, Ben, this man came on to me like gangbusters at the beginning of the trip. He was almost unctuous in his flattery, his admiration. Then he began to probe into my family background, and guess what? There was a major shift in his attitude."

"How so?"

"It's hard to pin down. 'Contempt' is too strong a word. My feeling is that he no longer has a high opinion of me. Suddenly I'm day-old bread." She raised her hands. "Which seems a bit extreme. After all, I'm only half-Jewish." She said this in a mocking tone, but Ben's expression remained somber. She thought it time to lighten up and drop the subject, but something in Ben's demeanor spurred her on. "You've written about hate groups," she said. "Do you think he fits the profile of one of those fascist bullies?"

Ben seemed surprised, even startled by her question. He removed his glasses and examined the lenses as if searching for a flaw. "I'd have to know more about the man to venture an opinion."

Glasses back in place, he gave her a direct look. "I must confess I have an academic interest in Watkins. Would you let me know if he bugs you again about your family or if there's anything suspect in his conduct toward you?"

"I can certainly do that." With only a sip or two of wine left, Tracy finished her drink and set down her glass.

"You know, Ben," she kept her voice low so that he had to lean in toward her, "it's really ironic, this whole matter about being Jewish. My mother was practically anti-Semitic. Maybe she practiced her religion as a youngster, but from the time I can remember, she didn't want anything to do with the Jewish community—culture-wise, religion-wise, nada. She even suggested I not reveal I'm half-Jewish. Once I did question her attitude, but she cut me off and changed the subject."

"Hmm. You have to wonder why."

Tracy shrugged. "Possibly her family objected to her marrying a Gentile."

"Did your father promote this sort of mindset?"

"Oh, no. He was very open-minded and suggested a number of times we visit Mom's relatives in London and Poland. To no avail. We did have an occasional visitor from overseas. They were treated warmly, but I don't recall they were encouraged to return. So in a sense, the joke's on Jack Watkins." She cut herself off, aware that Ben's attention shifted from her to something beyond her shoulder.

Tracy turned to see Patty approach them. She did not look happy.

When Patty left the hair salon, she ran into Shirley who had returned from the beach party moments before. Patty was eager to find Ben, hoping he might be in the café and that they could have lunch together. Shirley, however, was bound and determined to have a chat, and Patty suspected from Shirley's manner a good deal of that determination was fueled by alcohol.

At any rate, she was subjected to a blow-by-blow account of Shirley's disappointment over two hunks who turned out to be gay and her disillusionment over some man who came on to her, then dumped her.

When Patty finally managed to break away, she was smiling. Shirley had seemed more indignant than upset and, in fact, had been entertaining with her recital of her misadventures. Though she'd included a darker side. In any event, she looked forward to sharing Shirley's travails with her husband.

The café was practically empty, with no sign of Ben. Perhaps he had come and gone. Then Patty spotted him. And Tracy. The two were close enough to be kissing, and as she neared them, she saw the empty wine glasses.

Tracy turned in her direction, greeting her with a smile, while Ben called out, "Hi, hon. Come join us."

Come join *us,* as if *they* were the couple? She managed to smile as she sauntered over to the table. "My, my, you two were certainly deep in conversation. What have I interrupted?"

Ben's gesture was vague. "Nothing of any consequence."

Tracy rose. "Here, Patty, take my chair. I was just about to leave." She paused a beat, and then said, "I was bending your husband's ear over some concerns about Jack Watkins. Ben's a good listener, as I'm sure you know." She smiled at them and made a hasty exit.

Patty took the proffered chair but remained silent as a waiter appeared to clear the table. When he was gone, she spoke. "Did you have an enjoyable luncheon with Tracy?"

Ben chuckled. "You make it sound as if lunch was planned. As it happened, I was already seated when Tracy arrived, so I suggested she join me."

"I see."

"Patty, have you eaten? No? Why don't you help yourself to the buffet or better yet, I'll do the honors for you."

Patty pushed back her chair. "I seem to have lost my appetite.

I'm going to the cabin."

Ben rose and followed her.

When they were back in the cabin, Patty busied herself at the closet, inspecting her formals, then opened and closed drawers, slamming them in the process. She poked around in her jewelry case and finally selected earrings and a necklace for the evening. She took more time to choose a matching dinner ring, and then set out her evening bag and dress shoes.

She observed Ben as he sat on the sofa, his long legs stretched out, taking up entirely too much space. She had to step around him as she flitted from closet to dresser drawers and back. He was reading a book he'd brought on Mexico, presumably focusing at this point on Puerto Vallarta, their next stop. Leave it to Ben to be INFORMED.

He put down his book and smiled at her. "Your hair looks lovely. They did a really great job."

"Thank you. It's nice you've noticed."

He drew in his legs and gave her a hard look. "Patty, for God's sake. What is going on? Why am I being likened to a pile of shit?"

"Ben!"

"You've said hardly a word to me. What is your message? There must be a message."

She felt her mouth quiver. Damn it, she would not break down. "All right, Ben. Let's talk." She paused to gather her thoughts. "You're not the man I married. That doesn't mean I don't love you, but I'm confused and disheartened."

"What in the hell are you talking about?"

"I didn't know you had a gift for vulgarity, Ben."

"You're not answering my question."

"What I'm saying is I can't believe—I simply cannot believe you've toadied up to Jack Watkins, this sick excuse for a man. It doesn't seem to bother you at all that he's a racist and, excuse me, a pile of shit." She felt a burning in her cheeks, appalled at what she'd said, but it had to come out, and she was glad she'd met his coarseness because now they were on common ground.

He glowered at her. "Why haven't you brought this up before?

108

We could have discussed this issue rationally. What's really ticking you off? Does it have to do with your coming upon Tracy and me in the café? Face it, Patty—since then there's been hell to pay."

Her legs felt wobbly and she took the chair opposite the sofa. "You're right. I should have brought up my distress over your permissive attitude toward Mr. Jack Bigot long before now. As for you and Tracy, what am I supposed to think when I find the two of you as cozy as lovebirds? Not to mention drinking wine together. It was a sickening display."

He shook his head as if in disbelief, and then got to his feet. "You smother a man, Patty. Sometimes I feel as if I can't breathe when I'm with you. I'm going for a walk."

She sat immobilized, unaware of the passage of time. Had Ben been gone five, ten, fifteen minutes? He said she'd choked the life out of him. Now she couldn't breathe.

The light in the room seemed to dim and a roaring sound like a miniature tornado filled her ears. She touched her arms, her face, and found her skin to be clammy, and because her heart now marched to a jagged, lurching beat, she wondered if she might be having a heart attack.

If so, the symptoms brought on a sense of relief because now she could concentrate on survival and not on her world shattering into a thousand splinters.

She forced herself to stand. *Call for help. Get to the phone.* She glanced up at the mirror over the dresser, and all she could see were her eyes as darkness closed in.

When she came to, Ben was on his knees, hovering over her. "Thank God, you're conscious. Can you turn your head, can you see me clearly? I don't want to move you if you have a head or neck injury."

It seemed such an effort to answer him. She closed her eyes for a moment, and then opened wide. "I see you just fine. There's no double vision, and I don't think I'm hurting anywhere."

Gingerly, he lifted her onto the bed, and then went to the phone.

When he'd hung up, he sat on the edge of the bed. "They're bringing a gurney to transport you to the infirmary." He took her hand. "Tell me what happened."

"When you stormed out of the room..." She couldn't continue, and what began as a wetness on her cheeks escalated into sobs she couldn't contain.

"Patty, my God, I'm so sorry. I should never have spoken to you as I did. You know I love you, that you're my whole life."

But you can't take back what you said, and that hurts. Oh, how it hurts.

❧

"I could keep you overnight for observation." Patty was seated across from the doctor in his office while Ben waited outside. "However, you might be more comfortable in your cabin."

"Oh, yes, I'd much prefer that."

"You're doing well. Your blood pressure, pulse, and heartbeat appear normal. Since you've experienced no pain or shortness of breath, I think we can rule out a heart attack."

"Thank goodness."

"Anxiety attack covers a broad spectrum, but something triggered the symptoms you've described."

Patty fiddled with the top button of her blouse, and then clasped her hands. "My husband and I never argue, but today we exchanged some harsh words." She drew her hands apart in a gesture of futility.

The doctor rolled back his chair to reach into a cabinet drawer. Now he held out two small packets. "These are mild tranquilizers." He continued with his instructions and Patty nodded obediently, agreeing also to return in the morning for a follow-up exam.

On their way back to the cabin, Ben held her arm as if she were a fragile little old lady. Once inside, he insisted she change into her robe and get into bed.

"We'll have dinner sent in," he said.

She shook her head. "There's no reason for you to pen yourself in. Go join the others."

He sat next to the bed, with his head bowed. "I'd be miserable without you." At her silence, he jumped up. Could he plump up her pillows? Would she like a glass of water? Were the lights too bright? Was she warm enough, cool enough?

She wanted to scream, *You're smothering me; let me be!* Which gave her pause. Oh, no, she wasn't like this with Ben. Or was she?

She didn't want to think about it. Not now. "Ben?"

"Yes, my darling."

"I'd like to take a little nap. Then, since you insist, we'll have dinner here. And"—she hesitated—"may we talk?"

"Of course."

The rest worked its magic and when Patty awakened, she felt renewed, invigorated. "I'm not staying in bed," she said.

"Patty…"

"No, no, no." She glided out of bed and before room service arrived, she'd added earrings and the previously selected dinner ring. "I'm fine now. Since we're not attending formal night, let's make the best of it. Did you order champagne?"

He looked at her as if she were out of her mind. "Do you really think that's wise?"

At her chin-up, defiant smile, he answered his own question. "Why not?" He grabbed the phone.

Patty was determined to put on a good face. The last thing she wanted was for Ben to regard her as a clinging, doe-like creature. Dinner had been exquisite, and she'd been surprised at how much she'd consumed. But of course, she had skipped lunch. The champagne added a festive air, as if they hadn't a care in the world. But now that they'd finished the meal, she felt rootless, an alien in what no longer was a familiar world, and her hand trembled as she set down her glass. She noted that Ben watched her closely.

"It looks as if we have a little leftover champagne," he said," maybe a glass apiece. We could take it out on the balcony. While we talk."

Outside, Ben made sure she was warm enough, that it wasn't too windy for her. Cloud cover obscured the stars and moon, but darkness, the hiss of the sea, and the steady rhythm of the ship plowing its way onward, provided comfort.

They clinked glasses and each took a sip. Patty remained silent. Let Ben start the discussion. Perhaps he found it a relief that she'd refrained from her usual chatter. In any event, light cast from within the cabin revealed Ben's solemn expression. Apparently he was giving careful thought to what he had to say.

Finally he turned to her. "I've sensed all along you've been upset over my seeming lack of concern—my indifference over Watkins's conduct."

"True. But it did finally occur to me you might have a reason for being nice to him for, well, for research purposes. She shook her head. "Obviously, I didn't take that into consideration when we were up in arms."

"I know I made light of Jack's behavior the night you danced with him. But, you see, I didn't want to alienate him. By remaining friendly, I hoped he might give something away, drop a clue—at the risk of sounding melodramatic—as to what despicable deeds might be in the works."

"Good heavens, you make him sound downright evil. How do you know so much about this man?"

"Let me start at the beginning. John O'Conner, one of my FBI friends, happened to call on an unrelated matter about the time we planned this cruise. He mentioned a meeting made up of neo-Nazi types and the like that was to take place in Acapulco. A snitch in the group informed them that some of these people preferred to use a cruise as a cover."

Patty nodded. "So you chose a date to coincide with the Acapulco meeting."

"John suggested I nose around a bit, keep my eyes and ears open."

"Sounds as if you were in cahoots with whoever makes the table assignments."

"Not at all. Chalk it up to a crazy coincidence. Believe me, I had no advance information about Watkins. However, the more I looked at the man, the more I thought something was familiar about him."

He went on to explain the FBI keeps tabs on a number of men and women they consider to be extremists. It was a long shot, but he thought he'd seen Jack's picture in an FBI file. Then, as now, his wide smile had set him apart. He was also in uniform.

"At our stop in Mazatlan I was able to get back to John's assistant in DC." He paused. "To cut through all this, he suggested I meet with Tom Mallory, a member of the investigative team. If you'll excuse the pun, we were on a fishing expedition."

"You mean the day you went deep sea fishing?"

"Yes. Tom and I used that trip as a cover to exchange information. I learned the FBI had a mole infiltrate the group that met in Acapulco."

"And?"

"That Jack Watkins was front and center at that meeting. I'll expect to hear more from Tom when we arrive in Puerto Vallarta. Mind you, I'm not directly involved, but at least I can keep an eye on Watkins."

"I wish you had confided in me."

"I didn't handle this very well, did I? I do trust you, Patty, but I thought by keeping my own counsel, I was protecting you."

"I certainly won't blab any of what you've told me, but Ben, it is an intriguing situation."

He reached for her hand. "It might go beyond that. Jack Watkins could be a dangerous man."

"Do you suppose Joanne is part of this group?"

"Highly unlikely. At least from the information I've garnered."

Patty nodded. "I can't picture Joanne setting burning crosses on peoples' lawns, or whatever it is they do. Oh! Shirley Goodweather and I had a little chat when I came out of the hair salon."

She related Shirley's experience with someone named Garth at the beach party, noting that Ben held on to her every word.

When she'd finished her story, she gently withdrew her hand from his on the pretext of taking a sip of champagne. *Where did they go from here?* She wondered. She wanted to believe she was 'his whole life,' but wasn't that the problem, that she was close to him, to the point he felt suffocated?

Ben was saying something, but she'd tuned him out, so absorbed was she in her thoughts. Something about their having this talk.

"I'm glad we've cleared the air," he said. "I'll keep you up to date, and it will be just between us. We'll be a team. Okay? Patty, are you listening?"

"Yes, yes, I am."

"Maybe you can elicit some more information from Shirley about this Garth character. Also help me keep track of Watkins. A deal?"

"Of course. It's good we have this understanding."

It was time to go inside, with Ben insisting she go straight to bed. He was pleased she was doing so well, but a good night's sleep would ensure a complete recovery.

"We still need to talk," she said.

He reached for her and held her close. "We will soon. Just know I love you very much."

"And I love you. I always will."

Once in bed, she doubted sleep would come soon, even with the help of a tranquilizer. Ben's belligerence, the words he'd used still stung.

Worse, she felt in her gut he was attracted to Tracy. And that hurt worst of all.

❧ *Chapter Thirteen* ☙

Puerto Vallarta

"So all it takes is a phone call to cheer you up?" Jack and Joanne strolled along the Malecon, Puerto Vallarta's waterfront walkway.

"I'm not sure what you're talking about," Joanne said, her attempt at laughter sounding hollow to her ears.

They stopped now to study one of the oversized modern sculptures that dominated the walkway but drew the eye beyond to the bay. "The last couple of days you've seemed edgy, preoccupied," he said.

Joanne fidgeted with her bag. She was never good at masking her feelings, but the last thing she needed was for Jack to question her behavior. "If you say so," she said, making her tone light.

"Who was on the phone?"

"Patty. She invited me to play bridge this evening before the ship sails, or possibly tomorrow when we're at sea. Ben may join us."

Jack took her arm, and they continued their walk. "I can tell how pleased you are. There, you see? You were wrong when you thought Patty tried to avoid you."

She started to respond but was distracted by the sudden appearance of a band of small children who blocked their path. They held up miniature wooden statues of religious figures, their pleas more aggressive than plaintive, with one child tugging at Jack's sleeve.

"No los quiero. Vayasé!" Jack thrust his hands downward in a negative gesture, and the children reluctantly moved on, though several cast soulful glances backward, as if testing his resolve.

Joanne widened her eyes in surprise. "I didn't know you spoke any Spanish."

"There may be other things you don't know about me." His statement was delivered in a teasing manner, accompanied by the quirk of an eyebrow, but Joanne felt her breathing accelerate, her throat close off.

At her silence, Jack looked at her with a hint of something in his expression she couldn't fathom. Was it curiosity? Suspicion?

The moment was dispelled as across the street from them, the doors of Guadalupe Church swung open to reveal a bridal party exiting the church. The Watkinses stepped to the curb for a closer look, and as the bride, outfitted in a voluminous white gown complete with veil and train, glided down the steps, Joanne felt the tension drain from her body. Ugly thoughts vanished as she focused on the purity and beauty of new beginnings.

Minutes later they continued on their way, intent on finding one of the restaurants they'd viewed on their morning tour of the town and outlying areas.

They chose Mogambo, an African-themed bar-restaurant, and decided on an open-window table that provided them a view of the promenaders and the Bay of Banderos.

As Joanne sipped her vodka martini, she felt cheered, her thoughts centering on the impending bridge date. "Patty said it would be nice if you rounded out the bridge foursome."

"Really? I haven't played for a while, but who knows, it might be fun. Interesting thing is, I ran into Ben this morning, and he was very cordial, very warm to me. Incidentally, he said the reason they didn't show for dinner last night was because Patty had suffered a stomach upset."

Joanne nodded. "That's what Patty told me."

Jack rolled his eyes. "It certainly was a dud of an evening without the Redfords."

"I know. I'm getting pretty good at tuning out Shirley, but Tracy surprised me. She seemed so withdrawn. Though maybe she was simply bored." Joanne started to raise her drink to her lips, then set it down. "I don't mean to criticize Tracy. I know what a nice person she can be."

Jack had been about to taste his margarita. Now he set his glass down hard. "Don't even think of giving her the time of day. She's not our kind. As for Shirley Goodweather, you can write her off, too."

His vehemence surprised her. "I'm no fan of Shirley's, but why are you on her case?"

"She blabbed to a mutual acquaintance that she was married to a

116

Jew, had a Jew baby. As for Tracy, her mother was Jewish. The mother! That makes Tracy a Jew."

"Jack, calm down. We still have tonight and two days at sea. We can't avoid these women or be rude."

"There are alternate dining choices."

"Eat in the café or Pizza Parlor? You can't be serious."

"You're right. Why should we make the sacrifice?"

As they continued to sip their drinks, Joanne tried to be content with people-watching, but she found herself stealing glances at her husband.

From Jack's brooding expression, it was apparent he'd lost interest in his surroundings. She stirred restlessly and looked back to see if their lunch order was on its way.

Finally, she couldn't stand his silence. "What are you thinking?"

"I'm thinking that at least Ms. Goodweather is no longer married to her Jew husband and besides, she's not worth a second thought. Tracy is another matter. She's educated, rich, well-traveled, and has access to influential people. Her kind needs to be put down."

"Jack, where is this going?"

He gave her a scathing look. "This is not the place to discuss problems and solutions."

"Solutions to what? To bringing down Tracy? What has she done to you?"

"Maybe you weren't paying attention."

"I am now."

"I've already explained that people of her ilk are a detriment to society."

"Because she's Jewish."

"Her people control the banks, the entertainment industry, the media, and the big corporations. You know that. That's where the power is. Contrast that to you and me. Our families were blue collar workers, unable to provide beyond our daily needs. So we did without, worked our tails off to achieve a college education.

No one handed us a damn thing, no sports convertibles, study programs in Spain, summers at the lake, the beach—wherever."

"But that applies to a majority of people."

"Don't you believe in change?"

"Of course, but not through violence."

"Who said anything about violence?"

Joanne's mouth went dry. She gave a small cough, then said, "The other day you mentioned something about having work to do in Phoenix, and I surmised—well, I don't know what I assumed. However, you seem a lot more outspoken and angry about Jews and blacks now than before you retired."

"You'd be surprised how many like-minded people I met in the service. Of course, we had to be discreet to protect our careers, our pensions."

Joanne waited for him to continue, but he sat there stony-faced, his mouth puckered as if he'd ingested something spoiled.

She knew she should drop the subject, steer the conversation elsewhere, but she had to know more. "You speak as if Tracy poses a threat."

"Oh, don't be naive, Joanne."

"I asked you before. Where is this headed?"

He looked at her as if she were brain impaired. "People like her need to be eliminated. She will be eliminated. Maybe sooner than you think."

Joanne stared at her husband. The picture was skewed, as if a thin gray curtain had descended to set them apart, blurring Jack's features, muting sound so that his words were muffled. Something about Tracy, about eliminating her?

She shut her eyes hard, and then opened wide. The grayness had dissipated and everything appeared normal.

She had to clear her throat. "We were talking about Tracy."

"What more is there to say?" His smile was broad. "Come on, Joanne, lighten up. We're on vacation. Wouldn't you like another drink?" He signaled the waiter.

The clock in the small waiting room outside the doctor's office read 2:15. For once, Patty had been prompt in arriving for her 2:00 appointment. Now she tapped her foot in double time to a fragment of a song that ran through her head. She'd been late for her morning follow-up exam and was told she'd have to re-schedule anyway, because the doctor had been called to the infirmary on an emergency.

The delay worked to her advantage because it opened up the morning for her and Ben to explore the town before his afternoon meeting with the FBI agent.

They lunched on the terrace at The River Café located on the Rio Cuale, and enjoyed its laid-back atmosphere. Though Ben had been sweetly attentive, talk had been desultory, with no mention of their falling out. But she knew that eventually they would have to address their problems. Perhaps when the wounds were less raw.

She sighed and looked up at the clock, then jumped as the door to the waiting room burst open. For heaven's sake, it was Shirley Goodweather.

"Patty, my Gawd, I heard you were sick, I mean *sick* sick. Are you still feeling bad? Is that why you're here?"

"It was nothing serious, simply a stomach upset, though I did have to see the doctor. He wanted me to return today for a quick follow-up exam because I'd experienced some, uh, dizziness." Patty gave a short laugh. "I've been waiting twenty minutes. Just like at home, eh?"

"Tell me about it. I work in a doctor's office."

Patty couldn't tell from the face Shirley made if she were on the side of the doctor or the patient, but she decided not to pursue the subject. She was not up to a long, rambling discourse on doctor-patient etiquette. "I hope you're not under the weather," she said to Shirley.

"Gosh, no. I ran out of a medication I take at home. It's no big deal if I skip a few days, but I kind of hate to be without it. Also," she gave Patty a little poke, "the doctor is really cute. I didn't see a wedding band when I talked to him about Jodie. Can't hurt to check him out, right?"

"I suppose not, particularly after your experience with Garth. Did you happen to run into him today?"

"No sign of the jerk anywhere. Oh, but what a great day it was. Of everything we saw on the tour, Gringo Gulch was my favorite place. You remember *The Night of the Iguana* with Richard Burton? Well, when he made the movie near Puerto Vallarta, Elizabeth Taylor came to visit him. He bought her a house in Gringo Gulch for her thirty-second birthday. Because his own home was located across the gulch, he added a connecting bridge so they could visit each other. Isn't that neat?"

"I do know the story. My goodness, how romantic. Now. Back to this man you met at the beach party. One of my bridge partners said she'd heard about someone named Garth who is quite an expert at the game. She wanted to reach him. Would you happen to know his last name?"

Shirley punched her forehead. "That's when everything fell apart, when we started discussing names. He thought my name was Clearweather, an Indian name. Then when I said Goodweather—"

"Shirley, dear, you did tell me about that." Patty looked up as the door to the doctor's office opened. In the doorway stood a nurse or assistant, chart in hand.

"Mrs. Redford? Dr. Rowlin will see you now."

"Thank you." Patty looked inquiringly at Shirley.

"I know it's something Swedish." She raised both hands. "But what?"

Patty rose. "Please let me know if you get a brainstorm."

She was about to enter the office when Shirley called out to her. "Patty! I've got it. It's Swenson. Garth Swenson."

What she didn't hear was Shirley mutter under her breath, "Friggin' racist, that's what he is."

"Did you say your name is Gracie?"

Tracy turned from staring out the bus window to nod at her seatmate, a plump, auburn-haired, middle-aged woman who was dressed in a billowy print maxi-length dress, her tiny feet encased in high-heel sandals with rhinestone buckles.

Tracy wondered if the woman boarded the wrong bus. They were on their way to have lunch at Chico's Paradise, an outdoor so-called jungle restaurant that also invited exploration of its many scenic features. It was not the Ritz, for God's sake.

Nor could it be likened to Bogart's, an elegant establishment where she and Marc would dine this evening. As usual, Tracy questioned the wisdom of their getting together, and then decided the hell with it. She had enjoyed the opulent surroundings and entrée choices when she was last in Puerto Vallarta and hoped she might return someday. But it was not the place to go unescorted.

Tracy rested her head on the back of the seat and closed her eyes. The setting at Bogart's was ravishingly romantic, a perfect backdrop for seduction. Not that she had any intention of ending up in bed with Marc. Still...

An urgent tapping on her arm brought her to an upright position. Lou... Lou... Louella—she couldn't remember the name—was making an announcement. "Gracie, I think we're getting close. The brochure said exotic, but darn it all, the landscape looks rustic to me. Yuck!"

The woman yammered the entire way, mostly with complaints about the food, service and entertainment on the ship. Now she was upset because they were not entering the Vegas strip?

"Lou Lou? Oh, Yolanda. Sorry. The brochure did describe a jungle atmosphere. You know: foliage, cliffs, caves, waterfalls, rock formations?"

"It also said exotic, like I said."

Tracy wondered at the woman's definition of exotic: A sheik on horseback invading her tent? "It will be cooler than in town," she said, using her perky voice.

"That's a blessing. Oh, look, Gracie, we're turning into a parking area. Oh, my, *all* those buses."

"I guess we're not the only tour, but as I recall, the restaurant is described as having five dining terraces, so obviously they can accommodate a number of people."

"Let's you and I hunt out the most scenic table."

They were coming to a stop now, and Tracy made a show of looking out the window. "Mmm, I don't see my friends, which means I shouldn't settle down to lunch just yet. I'd better try to find them."

"That's all right. I'll save you a place, as well as save places for your friends. How many would that be?"

They were stopped now, and Tracy rose with the rest of the passengers. "We'll see how it goes," Tracy said as Yolanda struggled to her feet. Thankfully, her seatmate would not be hanging out with her on a hiking trail. Not with those shoes.

When they were off the bus, Tracy gave Yolanda a big smile and said she'd look for her 'later', conveying to Tracy a vaguely distant time.

The lush surroundings conformed to the jungle concept, with rock formations providing shade against the punishing humidity. Tracy wandered a bit, and then decided to look for a table at the highest elevation.

The smallest table she could find seated four and overlooked the river. On the terrace below, Mariachis entertained, their renderings subdued in keeping with the soothing cadence of water splashing into pools, and the gentle drift of the river.

Tracy was perusing the menu when she sensed a presence at her back, confirmed as a shadow fell across the chair to her left. She looked up, and then tried to conceal her astonishment. How had Yolanda managed to negotiate the many steps that led to the top terrace?

"Here you are, Gracie. What happened to your friends?"

Tracy raised her arms in a gesture of helplessness. "I don't know what happened. I was sure they'd decided on taking this tour."

Yolanda plopped down in the chair opposite Tracy. "You certainly picked out a nice table for us, and thankfully away from those noise makers." Disdainfully, she indicated the singers who now sang a medley of familiar Mexican folk songs.

Just my luck, Tracy thought, but she might as well make the best of it. The waiter was approaching and Tracy decided she'd order one of the specialty rum drinks. Yolanda might very well take flight. She'd mentioned she was from Utah, and Tracy could only hope she was a devout Mormon who had no tolerance for users of alcohol.

After Tracy had given her order, the waiter turned expectantly to Yolanda who, Tracy observed, had shoved aside the drinks menu without looking at it.

"*Señora?*" he asked.

"Make it a double bourbon on the rocks."

Gulp, was Tracy's silent reaction.

Yolanda now studied the food selections. "Good grief, have you looked at this?"

"I've glanced at the menu."

Yolanda shook her head, rolling her eyes at the same time. "They specialize in black bean soup, crawfish, and ye Gods, spareribs! What is this, some sort of greasy spoon?"

"I understand their coconut pie is delicious."

Yolanda sighed. "After all those rich desserts on the ship, I'm not about to indulge in pie, let alone one of those mushy Mexican custard dishes."

When their drinks were served, Tracy, after debating between crawfish and swordfish, ordered the latter. Yolanda opted for carne asada.

The Mariachis had made their way up to their terrace and now serenaded individual tables. Tracy was grateful for the distraction and when the men circled their table, she kept them playing with several requests. Never mind her grouchy table partner. Tracy's focus was on the singers who deserved and received a generous tip.

When the men departed, Tracy steeled herself for an outburst of criticism, but instead, Yolanda gave her a quizzical look. "I'm surprised you, of all people, would find this kind of music entertaining," she said.

What did she mean by that? There was no way Yolanda could know about her musical background. "I don't understand your statement," Tracy said.

Yolanda fished in her bag for a tissue and dabbed at her nostrils. "What I mean," she said with a nervous laugh, "is that you're so glamorous and sophisticated, I'm surprised you'd find enjoyment in that kind of crappy music."

Tracy felt the heat in her cheeks but was spared having to respond as their waiter placed their luncheon orders before them.

Yolanda's expression was dubious as she surveyed her plate, but then she smiled at the waiter. "Bring me another double bourbon over ice."

As lunch proceeded, Tracy checked her watch. They had close to an hour before they were due back on the bus. She was determined to enjoy her swordfish, which was delicious, and to ignore Yolanda's carping about her meat, that it wasn't like the steak she was accustomed to at home.

Tracy was also determined to make her escape as soon as possible and had already summoned their server for her check.

"I'm going to explore another area," Tracy said to Yolanda as she pushed back her chair.

"If you'll wait 'til I finish my drink, I'll join you."

"I don't think that's a good idea," Tracy said. "You wouldn't make it over the terrain I'm going to cover. You need hiking shoes."

"Where exactly are you going?"

"There's an area, Espinoza's Pass, that's off the main trail. I understand it's quite a challenge because of the jungle-like vegetation, but I've heard the scenery is spectacular."

"You've convinced me I'd better stay put. You can tell me about your adventure when we're back on the bus."

That was easy, Tracy thought.

With that, she was on her way, meandering past waterfalls and pools where youngsters splashed and played. What a great way to stay cool, she thought with a tinge of envy.

Minutes later she spotted the sign for the turn-off to Espinoza's Pass. Several people were coming out of the area, back onto the main trail. They smiled and waved as she entered the pass. Not many of us hardy souls, she thought with a sense of pride; in fact, it appeared she was pretty much on her own, though she might soon catch up with other hikers.

Once into the thicket, she had to watch her step over rocks and brush, but she soon came to a clearing. Tracy paused to catch her breath and to allow time to delight in the pristine beauty of her surroundings.

She imagined herself washed ashore into a wilderness where she existed alone among colorful creatures that nestled in branches of towering trees and communicated by way of intricate musical trills. On reflection, she'd need a male companion, preferably handsome and articulate, who was also strong and inventive—not to mention handy.

Enough romantic drivel. Tracy looked at her watch and decided she had time to hike a little farther in. She moved out of the clearing onto a narrow path. Here, the birds' cries were more intense and sunlight filtering through leafy trees created an eerie pattern of light and shadow. The heat was stifling and she slapped at a bug that lit on her arm. After trudging on a bit further, she decided it was time to head back.

Tracy had taken only a few steps in the opposite direction when she thought she caught a flash of movement ahead. What followed was a crunching sound as if something trod on the leaves along the side to her left. Her hands began to tingle; her breathing accelerated. The foliage was high along the trail, and she wondered what might lie in wait. God forbid it was a wild or rabid animal.

Wouldn't you know, not a soul was in sight from either direction. She stopped and placed a hand on her chest as if she could still her wildly beating heart. Why was she making herself crazy? After all, this area was not restricted, but open to visitors. If something prowled in the thicket, it could be a disabled bird or stray cat or dog that belonged to one of the staff at the restaurant.

Once again, a rustling in the leaves ahead convinced her something was moving parallel to the trail. Whatever it was, she couldn't remain frozen to the spot. Quietly, stealthily, she moved forward.

As she made her way, Tracy held her breath, expecting something to pounce, then exhaled with relief. Nothing stirred in the brush parallel to her path, and straight ahead the clearing beckoned.

And then something grabbed at her arm. She gasped, and then watched in shock as the big, blond man, her stalker, emerged from the bushes. He released her arm and now stood facing her. She sprinted to the right in an effort to go around him, but he blocked her move.

Whatever he was up to, she could try to reason with him or yell her head off.

"Don't even try to scream," he said, as if reading her thoughts, "or I'll shut you up quick."

"Who are you? What do you want with me?" Her words came out as if she'd run the marathon.

"So many questions. You don't know me; you don't want to know me because I'd like to wipe you off the face of the earth, send you straight to hell. And maybe I will."

Tracy moistened her lips. "I don't understand. You have to be confusing me with somebody else. Until yesterday, I'd never laid eyes on you."

He stepped in closer to her. "I could really have fun with you, fuck you good and have you begging for more. We'd play our little games and then"—he drew a finger across his throat— "no more Tracy." He cocked his head to the side as he had on the tender. "What's the matter? Why the look of revulsion?"

"Stop this! Who are you? How do you know my name?"

"I'm a person of pure blood who believes in the white race, in the need to purge your kind from our nation."

Oh, dear lord, now it was clear to her what he was about. He glanced over at the thicket, and she thought how easy it would be for him to drag her into the brush. Oh, God, what to do? Maybe keep him talking? She had to buy time, pray for someone to come along.

"Do you consider yourself a member of a so-called master race?"

"Sneer, if you like. Our country is defiled, plagued with rot because of the Jewish establishment, because of niggers looting and burning businesses, faggots demoralizing our country."

"While you consider yourself a moral, upright person? What are you, a born again Nazi? Do you practice goose stepping and shouting *Sieg Heil*?"

"You have a filthy mouth."

"*I* have a filthy mouth?" Her laughter was unrecognizable to her, escalating into hysterical gulping sounds.

He stood there, hands on hips in an arrogant stance, with that infuriating grin. Inside her head she screamed, *Bastard! Dirty rotten bastard!*

Tracy dug her nails into her palms. Stop that, she told herself. Do *not* work yourself into a frenzy of hysteria. Do *not* melt into a puddle of despair. *Buy time!*

"Okay." She took a deep breath. "Obviously, you're from the ship and obviously you were out to stalk me yesterday when we left the tender. How would you know who I am or anything about my background? How did you know where to find me today? Are you and Jack Watkins bigot buddies?"

"Jack Watkins? Never heard of the man."

"Look," she said, "I'm no threat to you. Whatever your agenda, you've no reason to hold me here. Besides, someone is bound to come along."

His grin widened, and he took a step closer. "I don't see anyone. Do you see anyone?"

"Yes!" She shouted the word as two men, seemingly from out of nowhere, advanced toward them. "Help me! Help me!" she screamed.

"Bitch!" He spewed out the word. "Enjoy what time you have left."

The next moments were a blur as the men came running and the blond man pawed his way back into the thicket.

"Oh, thank God," Tracy said as the men hurried to her side.

"Are you all right, miss?"

"I guess I am," she said to the older of the two men. She was gasping for breath. "I didn't see you coming—couldn't see beyond this awful man who was terrorizing me. I'm so thankful you're here."

"Jerry, go after the guy."

"I don't see him, Dad. Where'd he disappear to?"

"It doesn't matter. Please don't try to find him," Tracy said. "He's a menace, he's dangerous." She began to shake, her teeth chattering.

"Is he someone you know?" Jerry asked. "Can you identify him?"

"He stalked me in port yesterday." She stopped to take a shaky breath. "I don't know him, but apparently he's a neo-Nazi or white supremacist. He threatened to do terrible things to me—to kill me." She began to cry.

The older man gave her a sympathetic pat on the arm. "It's okay. You're safe now. Let's talk to security."

Flanked by the two men, Tracy described her ordeal to the officer in charge of security for the restaurant and grounds. After pouring out her thanks and appreciation to her life savers, Tracy, with assurances she was all right, left to find her bus.

She was among the first of the passengers to board and made her way to the rear of the bus, in hopes she might avoid Yolanda.

For a moment she wondered if she were on the right bus, and then recognized some of the people she'd noticed for one reason or another on the trip over. Where was Yolanda? She was a standout, hard to miss.

Tracy watched as the last of the passengers took their seats. Yolanda was among the missing, which struck her as odd. Then again, with four bourbons under her belt, the woman might very well have forgotten where the tour was to meet or, heaven forbid, she was on her third double bourbon.

The Yolanda situation had distracted her momentarily from thoughts of what she'd endured. Now she hugged her arms for control, remembering that Peter suggested she return home with him, remembering also her dismissal of such an idea. But Peter was not here for her now.

She knew what she must do. She would go to Ben.

ᘒ *Chapter Fourteen* ᘓ

Puerto Vallarta

As Ben entered their cabin, Patty tossed aside her paperback mystery and jumped up to greet him. "Finally, you're back. My goodness, Ben, I've been on pins and needles. I can't wait to hear about your meeting."

He gave her a hug, and then stepped back. "How long have I been gone? An hour?"

"It seemed so much longer." She took in her breath and twisted her wedding band in a repetitive left-to-right direction. Was this another instance of what he called smothering? "Oh, my, I guess what I'm trying to say is…" This time it was the ringing of their phone that silenced her. She darted past him to lift the receiver.

"Hello."

"Patty, it's Tracy. Is Ben there?"

"Uh, yes. He just walked in." She stood there dumbly, a sudden gagging sensation making it difficult for her to swallow.

"Patty? Patty, are you there?"

"Yes." The word floated above her, oddly tinny to her ear. Then she snapped to, curiosity overriding resentment. "You sound agitated, Tracy. Are you all right?"

"I need to talk to Ben, to both of you. Please, could you come to my cabin right away?"

"Well, I suppose so." She looked over at Ben. "It's Tracy. She sounds upset and is asking if we'll come to her cabin."

Ben nodded. "This could be about Jack Watkins."

Patty spoke into the phone. "We'll be right there."

When she'd broken the connection, Ben's smile was apologetic. "Tracy wouldn't know about the neo-Nazi meeting that took place in Acapulco or Jack's association with the group—I shared that information with you only —but I did tell her I had an academic interest in the man, and she agreed to let me know if he acted up in any way. Of course, I'm only assuming this is the problem."

Patty met his gaze, hoping her expression conveyed the proper solicitude. "Let me trade these slippers for sandals and then we'll go." She took her time, all the while monitoring Ben's demeanor. He didn't seem unduly concerned or in a rush to get going. Could it be an act? Was he holding back for her benefit?

She sighed. Ben had said they were a team, and she'd simply have to shove the hurt aside and accept his statement at face value.

She smiled up at her husband. "Let's see what that son-of-a-gun Watkins has done now."

❧

"I thought it was a wild animal," Tracy was saying. Her voice held a quiver and her makeup was streaked, with mascara smudged under her lower lids. "It was an animal, all right, in the form of a maniacal, perverted racist."

As she continued her story, Patty listened in horror, her eyes welling up as Tracy recounted the man's ugly assertions, his threats to rape and kill her. "Oh, my dear," she said, clasping her hands, "thank God those men came to your rescue."

In the sitting area of the stateroom, Ben and Patty occupied the sofa, while Tracy took a chair opposite them, her body tensed like an animal's, about to spring.

Ben supported his chin with the tips of his fingers, his expression thoughtful, yet edged with anger. "I don't like what I'm hearing," he said. "This man stalked you yesterday, and then blatantly terrorized you today. He has to be stopped."

"Do you suppose there's a link with Jack Watkins?" Tracy asked.

Ben gave Patty a meaningful look. "I'd bet on it," he said.

The meeting with the FBI agent, Patty guessed. Then straight out of the comic pages, it was as if a light bulb had switched on above Patty's head. She turned to Tracy. "You say he's big, blond, heavily muscled? Okay," she said, responding to Tracy's nod, "I think we need to talk to Shirley Goodweather." She addressed Ben. "This could be the man she met at the beach party. Garth. Oh, shucks, what's his last name? Shirley told me."

In the next few minutes, Ben was on the phone to contact Shirley while Patty related Shirley's disillusionment with Garth, who had turned ugly at the mention of Shirley's Jewish husband.

By the time Shirley had been tracked down and joined them, outrage and anguish had lifted, replaced by an almost heady sense of purposefulness.

Shirley, Patty observed, was goggle-eyed as she entered the stateroom. "Oh, my Gawd, this is *gorgeous*. This place is so cool. Could we party here? Yes!"

Ben, in an apparent attempt to staunch Shirley's outburst of awe-inspired rhetoric, ushered her to the companion chair that faced the sofa, then immediately launched into a factual account of Tracy's daunting experience.

Shirley paled, her expression registering shock as Tracy added to the tale, including a description of her tormentor.

"Does that sound like your Garth?" Patty asked.

"If that isn't Garth Swenson, it's his twin brother. Oh! His eyes. Tracy, were his eyes a standout blue, an aqua or turquoise shade?"

Tracy nodded. "His eyes were a vivid blue-green."

"I can't believe this." Shirley's cheeks reddened. "And to think he and I almost . . . Well, never mind. The man's a monster."

Ben produced a small notepad from his pants pocket. "Shirley, based on the time you spent with Garth, tell us everything you can about this man. Would you also describe the people who were in your group?"

Shirley settled back in her chair and as she spoke, it was apparent she relished taking center stage. Ben had his work cut out for him, Patty noted, as he guided Shirley through her narrative, disallowing her to deviate from the specifics.

Patty shifted her attention to Tracy. She looked weary and dispirited. She felt sorry for her, wanting—well, *almost* wanting—to give her a consoling hug. Because Tracy had talked to Ben about her experiences with Jack Watkins, because she and Tracy confided to one another their distaste of the man, wasn't it natural for Tracy to turn to her husband and herself on a related matter? Maybe.

"Patty?" Ben waved his hand in front of her face. "You still with us?"

She started. "Forgive me. Since I'd already heard Shirley's story, I was concentrating on some other aspects of the situation." She looked at Tracy. "Ben seems to think there's a tie-in with our Mr. Watkins, which would explain how this Garth character could identify you and know your background. As for our activities in port, the subject has come up at dinner, so I suppose those plans could have been relayed to Garth."

"Or," Ben said, "someone on staff could have passed on that information for a price or because they're in league with these people."

"All right," Patty said, "that could account for the stalking incident yesterday when Garth was warming up his act. But Tracy, you didn't see this man anywhere today until he surprised you in that remote area. How would he know where to find you?"

Tracy sat straighter, her eyes taking on luster. "I think I asked him that very same question, among other things. Not that he gave me any answers." She looked blank for a moment, and then said, "Yolanda! My seat partner on the bus. She was a thoroughly unpleasant woman, the type you can't wait to escape from."

"Unpleasant how?" Shirley asked.

"Complaining, bitching about the cruise, our tour, the food, the entertainment. She also clung to me like a leech." Tracy rose and paced the area behind the chairs, then stopped to place both hands on the back of her chair, spreading her fingers as if to form a chord. "I'm beginning to think it was a set-up," she said.

Patty nodded her encouragement. "Do go on."

"Let me think for a minute, get this straight in my mind." She paused, and then said, "Here's the scenario. Because Yolanda's so obnoxious, I can't wait to get away from her. Fortunately, she can't very well accompany me on a hiking trail because she's decked out in garden party finery, which I'm led to believe is a silly affectation.

"The reality is she's programmed to keep track of me only until we part company. But of course, she does make a point of asking where I'm headed, what trail I'm exploring. The leech then unglues herself, and as soon as I'm out of there, she reports to Garth who undoubtedly lurks nearby."

"You've convinced me," Shirley said.

"Do you have a last name for Yolanda?" Ben asked.

Tracy tucked in her fingers to give the chair a thump. "No, darn it." Slowly she took her seat, and then edged forward. "I have Shirley's vote. Ben, Patty, what do you think? Does my theory hold water?"

"I find it a reasonable explanation," Patty said. "Ben?"

"Whatever the explanation, we need to report the incident to the head purser."

Tracy settled back in her chair, an expression of doubt narrowing her features. "I agree," she said, "but if it comes to a confrontation, it would be my word against his."

Ben stood. "We don't sail until 11:00 p.m. It might be possible to get corroboration from the security officer at Chico's Paradise."

Following Ben's lead, they all rose, with Shirley at the head of the line. "Gotta run," she said. "They'll be closing the doctor's office any minute." She winked at Patty. "I just remembered another medication I'm out of." At the door, she paused. "Tracy, I'm so sorry about what happened. I'll talk to you at dinner."

"Oh." Tracy put a hand to her mouth. "I may or may not be there."

"Sure, hon, I understand." A quick smile and she was out the door.

"As for you two," Tracy said, "I can't thank you enough for coming to me." She shook her head. "I shouldn't have involved you, but I didn't know where else to turn."

"You did the right thing," Ben said. "Besides, as I mentioned at lunch, I have some FBI connections and that might help us in getting the goods on Swenson and the Yolanda woman. For now, though, we'd better be on our way to talk to the purser." He opened the door. "After you, ladies."

"Ben, wait." Patty placed a hand on his arm. "I'll walk with you part way, then you two can go about your business."

"Honey, are you sure?" Ben's expression reflected disbelief, like that of a parent reacting to his child's refusal of a lollipop.

No, I'm not sure, Patty wanted to cry out. Instead, she gave her husband a loving smile. "In this case, I think three's a crowd. I'll wait for you in the cabin."

As the minutes dragged on, Patty tried to get back into her mystery novel but could not concentrate. She studied her wardrobe, trying to decide what to wear for dinner. For that matter, they hadn't settled on whether to stay on board or go into town.

She did her nails, worked a crossword puzzle, and then forced herself to sit very still, close her eyes and meditate. *You made the right decision,* she chanted inwardly, making this her mantra. She had let go, loosened her hold on the man she loved. Was this a step in the right direction? Or was she fostering a bond between Ben and Tracy, pushing them closer?

It was no use. She sprang out of her chair to step onto the balcony, and then hustled back into the cabin to pace. She needed to do *something.* But what? Ah, maybe the art gallery was open or the shops. She remembered the attractive Mexican-style tops and skirts that were on display. Also, she had neglected to review the pictures that were posted after the last formal dance.

Now she was back in business. And if Ben returned while she was gone, so be it!

Ben was in the cabin when Patty let herself in, and now it was turn-about time as he rose to greet her.

"No packages," she said, raising her hands, palms up, "though I made a valiant effort." His look of relief at her breezy tone, her smile, gladdened her. Could be she was on the right track, though in the back of her head a little voice cautioned, *"Don't overdo it."*

As before, he gave her a hug, and then led her to the sofa. "I'm glad you're back," he said when they were seated.

"I can't wait. I've got goose bumps. Tell me what you found out."

Ben raised his eyebrows, and then gave a deep sigh. "The mystery deepens. For starters, there's no Garth Swenson listed on the passenger manifest."

"But this man had to be on the ship. He boarded the tender, he played bridge with the people Shirley described."

"I know, and for whatever reasons, Garth Swenson was the name he chose to give."

"Were you able to find Trudy? Could she shed any light on the situation?"

"We found her all right, and she, in turn, found Paul. Unfortunately, neither of them was much help. Trudy had been puzzled by Shirley's early departure from the beach party because she and Garth had seemed to hit it off. Other than that, she admired Garth's expertise at bridge. Also, he impressed her as intelligent and politically well-informed, but lacking in the social graces."

Patty snorted. "That's the understatement of the year."

"As for Paul, he and Garth got along at the bridge table but that was it, as far as socializing. Oh, Paul said he learned Garth spoke fluent Spanish. What else?" Ben drummed his fingers on the sofa cushion. "That's about it."

"What about Yolanda?"

Ben shrugged. "Makes it difficult to check without a last name. So far, they've come up with a Yolanda Greenberg, age seventy-eight, traveling with her granddaughter, and a Yolanda Travis, age twenty-five, neither of whom fit the description Tracy gave us. I think we can assume she was a plant with false credentials to enable her to take the ship's tour. I doubt Tracy's Yolanda was ever on the ship."

Patty nodded. "And I doubt this Garth character will chance returning to the ship."

Ben raised his hands to massage the back of his neck. "When the staff completes their passenger check late this evening, they'll be one person short. I'm sure they'll alert the local police, especially as they now have a description, but I suspect the guy will be long gone." He lowered his arms. "Possibly on his way to Phoenix, Arizona."

"But Ben, if Garth, for want of his real name, speaks fluent Spanish, wouldn't he be better off staying in Mexico?"

"It's not as if he's on anyone's most wanted list. Yet. Besides, he has a job to do in Phoenix. Let me tell you what I learned from Tom Mallory. You remember a mole penetrated the meeting that took place in Acapulco?"

As Ben outlined the purpose of that meeting, detailing their

135

agenda, Patty listened with mounting incredulity. To think these people were primed to take down prominent citizens, to maim or kill innocent children.

"It's almost too much to fathom," she said, fighting back tears.

Ben took her hand. "They'll be stopped. Now that the authorities are aware of their game plan, they'll tag the people involved and get them to incriminate themselves."

"I suppose Garth, with his knowledge of explosives, will be a major player."

"Would have been," Ben said. "As for Jack Watkins, his days are numbered."

"Thank God."

Ben looked at his watch. "I can still reach Tom at his hotel. He's not due to fly out until tomorrow afternoon. I'd like to brief him on Swenson." He thought for a moment. "Why don't we arrange to meet Tom for dinner in town? Would you like that?"

"Would I! Oh, Ben, what a wonderful idea to mix a bit of intrigue into our travels. You make the call, I'll survey my wardrobe. But first, a shower."

She felt giddy, pleased to be a part of Ben's FBI involvement. As for Tracy, Ben had not brought her into the conversation, nor had she given Tracy a second thought. Not since the two had sought out the head purser. Well, not since she fled the cabin, waiting for Ben to return.

Tracy was young, resilient, with a good head on her shoulders. She would recover from her excruciating experience—bounce back, so to speak.

Of course she would.

The meeting with the purser served as a tonic to Tracy, imbuing her with a sense of purpose, ratcheting up her energy level. Never mind, they had not made much progress. The consensus? The man they knew as Garth Swenson would not return to the ship. With Ben at her side, she might have gotten through a face-off with her pursuer, but it was also a relief to have him off the ship. Just so long as the authorities caught up with the bastard.

Now as Tracy entered her cabin, she caught sight of the flashing red of her message button. Could be additional information from the purser or Ben. Or a call from Marc.

The message was from Peter. Her husband would be at the pier when the ship docked in Los Angeles to welcome her home.

At the pier, in Los Angeles. Isn't that just dandy? Thank you very much, Peter, for a belated appearance. Just think, if only you'd been here with me for the entire cruise, I wouldn't have been stalked, terrorized, and almost killed. But no, you had other priorities.

She felt the trail of tears on her cheeks and slumped down into the chair she'd occupied earlier. She knew she was being unreasonable. After all, Peter had shown concern for her wellbeing, while she passed off Watkins's probing and change of attitude toward her as no cause for alarm. But she needed Peter now, needed his loving touch and comforting words. Where was her cell phone? Then she remembered. She forgot to bring it on the cruise.

Tracy dried her tears, blew her nose, and then settled in at her desk. She glanced toward the windows, noting it was still light outside as the hour approached 7:00. It would be 6:00 at home but less bright in the Los Angeles basin, with smog to shroud the landscape or even a May drizzle to cloud the atmosphere.

She hesitated, and then plunged ahead, muttering, "Damn the expense." She needed her husband now. This very minute. She would call him with the cruise line's ship-to-shore service. Damn, she couldn't remember his cell phone number which she had programmed into her phone's speed dial. She would have to call their home number and hope he was there.

When the connection came through, she held her breath, praying Peter would pick up. What she heard was the sound of her own voice: "No one can come to the phone right now…" She tuned out the rest, her thoughts zigzagging in a dozen directions. Suddenly, it all came together.

"Peter, it's Tracy. Sorry I missed your call. I do need to talk to you, if you can get back to me in the next couple of hours. If not, it's okay, nothing urgent. I'll explain when I see you. Love you. Bye." It was a Saturday evening, so he would not be at the office. At least not this late.

Now that she thought about it, why hadn't she insisted he call her back? Still, if Peter did not return her call this evening, surely she'd hear from him sometime tomorrow despite assurances that he needn't bother.

Slowly, she rose and walked toward her closet, gloom settling over her like a sullen cloudbank shutting out the sun. Tomorrow was after the fact, and her revelations would be dulled by the lack of immediacy.

She was debating whether to shower first or take the time now to select an outfit, when the phone rang.

Peter! God was good. In seconds she was at the phone.

"Hello!"

"Hello, yourself. You sound bright and cheerful." It was Marc. "I hope we're still on for tonight. I apologize for not calling earlier, but I was held up in a staff meeting."

If she wanted to cancel, now was the time. Decide, decide, she told herself. But why cancel? Bogart's and Marc were the perfect antidote to the toxins that pervaded her very being in the face of evil.

They agreed on a meeting place close to where the taxis lined up and decided that 8:15 would allow for a leisurely dinner, plus transportation to and from the restaurant.

As Tracy prepared for the evening ahead, she wondered somewhat idly where Peter might be on a Saturday evening. At his parents' house? She thought not. Out on a date? Unlikely. She had the grace to blush. But Marc was not really a date. He was a fantasy, a throwback to an exhilarating past of beginnings, of heightened feelings, when each hour, day, or week held promise, predicated on the certainty that the achievement of one's dreams was within reach.

More pragmatically, Marc was the perfect escort—handsome, knowledgeable, and attentive, with the arts as their common language. He would also be out of her life in a matter of days.

She waited until the last minute to choose her outfit for the evening. Peter had not called, so she might as well focus on what lay ahead. The sleeveless, gauzy white dress she'd worn in Acapulco was also appropriate for Bogart's.

When she was dressed, she studied her reflection. With her hair down, with amber beads and amber and gold drop earrings in place of turquoise and silver, she projected a different persona from when she'd been with Peter.

What hadn't changed was that this dress, out of her entire wardrobe, generated the most notice, be it envious stares from women or admiring glances from men.

She knew she looked good.

Tracy took a sip of her martini, and then set down her glass. "So you can understand why I almost canceled our evening."

Marc looked stricken, his eyes seeming to grow larger and darker, his expression registering dismay as she recounted her ordeal at the hands of Garth. "I'd like to break every bone in his body," he said.

Tracy gave a short laugh. "You'd need a sledgehammer. No, seriously, I hadn't intended to unload on you, but when you mentioned I seemed preoccupied—well, I thought it was only fair to clue you in.

"And now that we've covered the gory stuff," she continued, "I proclaim the subject closed." She raised her hands. "Look around us. I feel as if I've stepped into the pages of *The Arabian Nights*." They sat under a tent-like ceiling swathed in a silky material in high backed chairs upholstered in shades of jade and gold, with footstools placed with a flourish under m'lady's feet by costumed waiters. Soft lighting, piano music, a gentle cascade of water from a nearby fountain further enhanced the scene.

Marc smiled. "*The Arabian Nights, Casablanca*. Take your pick. You'd grace either place."

And so would you, she thought.

"What did your husband have to say about your ordeal? I assume you've talked with him today."

His question ripped through the patina of fairy tale magic, her journey into a fantasy world cut short.

"I tried to reach him this evening but with no success."

He took her hand. "Your ring is beautiful. It looks new, and because of the setting, I would guess you purchased it in Mexico."

"In Acapulco, when Peter surprised me with his visit."

"Was that a happy reunion?"

She removed her hand from his. "Yes, of course."

"I sense some hesitation."

Tracy took a sip of her drink and then another sip before setting down her glass. She talked openly to Ben about her lifestyle at home, her inner conflicts, without bringing Peter into the picture. Because of Marc's warmth and intensity, these issues seemed to invite discussion on a more personal level, breaking down barriers of restraint. At this moment he was irresistible, and she felt the need to speak out, to give voice to her frustrations and grievances. But without maligning Peter.

"Our reunion was marred by something of my own making—my lack of enthusiasm over my husband's political aspirations, and I suppose my inability to understand his point of view. I thought we'd agreed to discuss the pros and cons of such a venture before committing." She shrugged. "Apparently, it's a done deal."

"Not surprising. Once a man or woman steps into the gilded circle of power, there's no turning back. Stature, perks, recognition—it's a heady world and totally addictive."

"Peter isn't like that. He's not shallow or vain. He's intelligent, personable, dedicated."

"Where do you fit into the picture?"

She laughed. "Interesting you should ask, because I've asked myself that same question. I'm sure I'll be on call to attend or organize fundraisers, to entertain in our home, attend meetings, and travel for the cause. I'm already up to here"—she drew a line across her throat—"with other obligations, but so be it."

"Dump all that. Get out while you can."

"I beg your pardon?" She stared at him, marveling at his gall. "How can you presume I'm unwilling or unable to do my part?"

"I presume no such thing. Willing and able doesn't necessarily mean putting one's heart and soul into a project." He stared up at the ceiling for a moment as if seeking inspiration, then sought her gaze, his expression troubled yet earnest. "Tracy, you are a beautiful, accomplished woman. How can you settle for being a fixture, a smiling dutiful presence, a . . . a mere appendage to your husband?"

"As opposed to?"

"A woman in her own right, pursuing her heart's desire."

"What you suggest is straight out of fiction, a romance novel." She gestured around her. "*This* is make-believe. Home is the real world."

"It doesn't have to be. You're young, you have no children. I assume you have your own money, which you could strike out on your own with."

"I can't hurt Peter."

"But you've thought about it, haven't you?"

"Yes," she said in a whisper.

"When the time comes, you'll know what to do." He reached for the menu. "May I suggest Persian Crêpes as an appetizer?"

When they arrived back at the ship, Marc insisted on walking Tracy to her stateroom.

"Isn't there some taboo," Tracy asked, "against staff and passengers dating?"

"Hmm. I must have skipped that page of the rules manual. Besides," he winked at her, "you'd be surprised what goes on after hours."

At her door, Tracy said, "Marc, it was a beautiful evening. You've been kind, generous, and attentive. I could go on and on." She laughed softly. "I must say I prefer your company to being the object of someone's wrath."

He took her hand and raised it to his lips. "May I step inside with you for a moment?"

Tracy preceded him into the cabin, her heart skipping a beat as she glanced at the phone. There was no flashing red to signal a message.

She was about to move to the end table next to the sofa to switch on a light when she felt Marc's hands on her shoulders. As she turned to face him, he gathered her into his arms. He held her for a moment, then gently tilted her chin and brushed his lips against hers. She parted her lips, and his kiss was softly passionate, then more urgent as she responded in kind.

Her breathing ragged, she stepped back from him. "Marc, this isn't right."

"Oh, but this is so right," he murmured. "You're my beautiful, elegant dream girl come true. And I could go on and on. But I meant what I said, that I would stay only a moment. You've had a harrowing day." He looked beyond her, toward the balcony. "I think we're moving, on our way out to sea. I'll make a point of seeing you sometime during the day. Perhaps we can have lunch together."

"If being in public together is a no-no, there's always room service. I have plenty of space here, inside or outside, depending on the weather."

"However it goes, save some time for me in the evening, will you?"

"Yes, I promise."

He stepped to the door. "Until tomorrow. Goodnight, Tracy."

When he was gone, Tracy stood in place where they'd kissed. "Oh God, what am I doing?" She spoke the words aloud, giving credence to the thought. The physical contact had been exciting, delicious, leaving her wanting more. Was this one last fling before caving into what must be? Or was this a step forward toward emancipation? Emancipation, she conceded, that would leave a trail of heartbreak.

And where did Marc fit in?

Too many questions. She switched on the light, grateful for privacy as she approached her closet and began preparations for bed. Marc had been right that she needed time to recoup, to put this day behind her.

Bed. It felt heavenly, the gentle rocking of the ship lulling her into a half sleep. Images came to mind of silken curtains and incense, a belly dancer moving to pulsating rhythms, the bells on her fingers casting forth an alluring obbligato to the sensuous beat. She recognized Marc at the piano with its draped background of half-moons and stars. Now he alone accompanied the dancer, his playing conjuring up a Middle Eastern tonality that was starkly sexual in its rhythms.

She wanted the sights and sounds to go on forever, to embrace that exotic world to the exclusion of all others, but the music was fading, the images becoming a blur.

Now that the music stopped, she found her breathing labored as

142

she battled an upward climb. She was trying to reach her closet, but the path was slick from the aftermath of a downpour, and rocks and debris in the way caused her to stumble.

Despite these obstacles, she was making progress and now at last was within inches of the door. She reached for the doorknob, and then withdrew her hand. Something odd, like a shuffling movement came from within. She strained to hear a repetition of the sound but all was silent, leading her to wonder if the extraneous noise came from her own tortured breathing.

Why did she hold back? All was quiet and serene. Still, she hesitated. She counted one, two, three, took a deep breath and slowly opened the door. The light failed, leaving the interior pitch black. Something about the stillness was unnatural—no, obscene. She felt her body turn cold, total numbness incapacitating her as she stood riveted in place. She was trapped, an unspeakable abomination about to be forced upon her.

There it was again, the shuffling sound, followed by heavy breathing. One beat, two beats. Then a figure lurched forward. It was the hulking, grinning blond man, and she knew with a sickening certainty what was about to happen as he opened his arms to her.

"Oh, my God, no!" Tracy, in bed, sat straight up, clutching at the bed sheets. She remained very still, hardly daring to breathe, listening for any sign of movement.

Silence. It was okay, only a hideous dream. She thought about her closet, about checking it out and shuddered. Then she relaxed. There was no way anyone could have entered her room, much less squeezed into her closet. A nasty dream, she told herself as she slid down under the covers.

In moments she began to nod off, erasing the blond man from her mind. Then her eyes flew open. How could she have forgotten? The raspy tone, the menacing words as he fled the scene.

"Bitch! Enjoy what time you have left."

❧ *Chapter Fifteen* ❧

At Sea: Formal Night

Joanne turned from the mirror to face Jack. "What do you think? The silver loops"—she pointed to her right ear—"-or"—she indicated her left ear—"these blue teardrop earrings?"

"They're both lovely, as is your gown. I don't know. You'll have to choose."

She felt downright coquettish. How long had it been since they'd made love? Jack's overtures last night had come as a surprise, causing her at first to be tentative, unsure of how she would respond. But he had been unhurried, skillful, making all the right moves.

She wandered over to her jewelry case. The act had been fulfilling, yet—she set aside the silver bracelet she'd selected then rejected as too gaudy—now that she thought about it, something was lacking. Was it the absence of playfulness, the promise of more to come? Now what would lead her to think that? Their lovemaking had been tender and meaningful, if not truly passionate.

She froze, her fingers gripping the silver loop she'd removed, and for a moment she gave in to despair as Jack's Phoenix agenda came to mind. She shook her head in an effort to erase graphic images of destruction and concentrated on inserting the matching teardrop into her earlobe. Translucent and misty in tone, the earrings crowned pale blue chiffon, embellished by silver beading.

There. All done. A dab of perfume and she felt her spirits rise, overriding what had been a nagging sense of uncertainty. And why not look on the bright side? They'd taken an important step toward repairing the fissure created by family problems and, best of all, toward restoring intimacy.

She smiled inwardly. Maybe, just maybe, *she'd* initiate their next encounter. With that thought in mind, she turned in a half pivot toward her husband, feeling the softness of filmy material brush against her ankles. She pictured them on the dance floor—better yet, in bed.

For now, however, she would have to settle for joining him on the sofa. "What are you reading?" she asked.

"The ship's newsletter and schedule for tomorrow. They were slipped under the door while you were dressing."

"You certainly seemed engrossed."

"I was looking over the activities planned for our last full day at sea." When she didn't respond, he set the schedule aside. "Why such a forlorn look?"

"It seems we just started on the trip, and here we are..." She choked back a sob, and then swallowed hard. "Don't mind me. I'm being silly."

Jack shrugged. "You know the saying. All good things must come to an end."

He couldn't possibly understand. For Jack the end of the cruise signaled the start of a more powerful pursuit than mere pleasure. He had a mission, and for him the means, however terrible, whatever its toll, justified the end. While for her, it meant living with the awful knowledge of what was to take place. Worse, she must betray her husband.

One thing was certain, she dare not, she *must* not, arouse suspicion by brooding or by showing her distress. Jack had already commented that she'd seemed edgy, preoccupied.

"I'm over it now," she said, being purposely vague. "Let's enjoy every minute we have left."

"Absolutely." Jack looked at his watch. "I know we talked about journeying up to the Crow's Nest for cocktails, but it's a bit early for that."

"Since we'll be packing tomorrow night, we should make the most of this evening. Let's enjoy our balcony and have a drink outside."

"Suits me. I think we have enough ice left over from noontime."

Joanne watched as Jack prepared their drinks—vodka over ice. Up in the bar, he would order scotch. But in deference to her taste, they brought vodka aboard for drinks in their cabin.

He's not all bad, she thought. And suddenly, because the thought was so inane, she had to squelch the desire to explode into laughter. She suppressed a giggle then said, "I'll wait for you outside."

The breeze was brisk, the sea choppy but the air, rather than chilly, was bracing and invigorating, Joanne decided as she seated herself at the small table.

"We could have chosen a more balmy evening," Jack said as he stepped onto the balcony with their drinks.

"I'm fine with this. We'll relish the memory when we're back in Phoenix with 110 degree temperatures."

When he was seated, they clinked glasses. Joanne took a sip, nodded approvingly, and then said, "Shall we make it a date for tomorrow evening as well?"

"Why not? I like your spunk, Joanne. Some women would wrap themselves in blankets or complain about their hairdos."

Despite the coolness, she felt the flush of pleasure across her cheeks, and even in the waning light she could detect the warmth in Jack's expression, a break from when he projected coldness or indifference.

They fell into a companionable silence and as Joanne contemplated the sea and sipped her drink, she allowed herself to take pleasure in the here and now. "I'm so glad we've taken this cruise," she said. "I think it's brought us closer."

"I'm glad you're glad."

It wasn't quite what she wanted to hear, but he wasn't going to change his personality overnight, if ever. Still, she had to believe they were making progress.

She took a healthy swig of her drink and was rewarded as a sense of optimism took hold. How often had she sold herself short, bowing to others? All she got for it was a loss of respect. It was time she spoke up. Starting with her husband.

"Jack, I'd like to bring up a serious subject."

His silence, his wary expression gave her pause. "Do you mind?" she asked.

"That depends."

"I'm not talking super serious." She'd rushed her words as some of her confidence eroded. "I was thinking about the future. You weren't sure if you wanted to begin a second career, and I simply wondered if you had any thoughts on the subject. "

"What would you like me to do, go to dental school, become a

146

house painter, run for governor?"

Wasn't Adolph Hitler a house painter? Or was it a paper hanger? was her fleeting thought. "Now, Jack, there's no need for sarcasm. I merely wondered if you'd thought about what lies ahead. You're still young, and you have a fine mind."

"Joanne, where is this going?"

"What do you mean?"

"We've been over this before. I already have my work cut out for me. End of discussion."

"Oh. All right." What was a safe topic, she wondered. Maybe a little gossip? But first she needed a refill. She raised her glass. "Would you top this off? I'm not quite ready to go in, but I promise to take it easy once we're up in the bar."

Jack nodded pleasantly and entered their cabin. When he returned with her drink, she sensed that the tension between them had dissipated.

Stick to small talk, she told herself. And then she couldn't help it. She felt compelled to share a bit of gossip.

"What are you smiling about?" he asked.

She looked over to the partition that separated Tracy's balcony from theirs. "I didn't tell you that while you were getting a haircut after lunch, I sat out here to read and relax. There was one tiny distraction, though. Tracy was also out on her balcony."

"So?"

"She had a visitor. Male. I was able to catch the drift of their conversation." She pointed to the railing. "If you stand next to the partition, it's possible to eavesdrop." His silence, his face devoid of expression disconcerted her. "Do you want me to continue?"

"Sure."

It wasn't a reassuring 'sure'. She paused a beat, then resumed. "I'd say the tenor of their conversation was romantic or intimate. It seemed very, very personal. So what do you suppose was going on? And who do you think the man was?"

Jack drained his glass. "Maybe that faggot piano player. She seems to enjoy going into the piano bar at night."

"Am I missing something? I don't recall that we've been to the piano bar."

"We haven't, but I am aware of Tracy's comings and goings."

"You mean you're following her? Why?"

"I have my reasons."

"Jack, you're scaring me. Are you planning something that involves Tracy?" She remembered he'd used the word 'eliminated'.

"Let's hope her liaison, or whatever you care to call it, was a pleasurable experience because her cheating sluttish days are over."

Joanne drank deeply, and then set down her glass. "What do you intend to do?" She could hear the quaver in her voice.

"I intend to take you up to the Crow's Nest where we will view the sunset and have a pre-dinner dance." He smiled. "Okay?"

She downed the rest of her drink, and then shaped her lips into a smile before preceding Jack into the cabin. Because there'd been intermittent cloud cover, she could only hope for a blazing sky as a finale to the day or at least the spectacle of a bright red orb descending below the horizon. Best of all, they would dance—and have drinks.

Inside the cabin, Joanne felt a chill course through her very being. Somehow, in some discreet manner she had to take Tracy aside. Whatever might happen, at least she would be warned.

She crossed her arms over her chest. God only knew what was in store.

❧

"This seems to be the night for chiffon," Patty said to Ben as they exited the Poseidon Lounge. They made their way toward the dining room, albeit slowly as they were on the early side.

"A vision in green. That's my Patty."

"Emerald green, my darling." Spurred on by having downed several champagne cocktails, she felt light as a feather, as if she were floating, a graceful ballerina, escorted by an admiring patron of the dance to a glittering soirée beyond the castle gates.

Uh-oh, behold an obstacle in their path. Not a moat, mind you, but an all too familiar figure who hurried toward them. *Clad in a form-*

fitting creamy silk gown with one shoulder bared, Tracy Bradshaw took on goddess-like proportions, was Patty's grudging acknowledgement. Moreover, the upswept hair arrangement that drew attention to her high cheekbones and the dazzling earrings—lapis lazuli?—brought out the smoky-blue of her eyes, enhancing that depiction.

Ah, but a closer look, now that Tracy was upon them, revealed the tautness about her mouth, her grim expression. Scratch divine status for the more prosaic characterization of troubled young woman.

"I was hoping I'd find you before we went into dinner." Tracy spoke in a near whisper. "Could we step over there?" She pointed to a small waiting area near the entrance to the dining room. "There's something I forgot to tell you."

It was an offer hard to resist, Patty thought as they gathered in the designated spot like conspirators about to hatch a plot.

"I must have pushed this from my mind, or call it denial, but late last night I remembered Garth's last words to me. It was a direct threat. He said, 'Bitch! Enjoy what time you have left.'"

Patty shook her head. "That is simply horrible, but do you suppose it was an empty threat, that he was merely venting his frustration over your rescue?"

"I don't know, Patty. I'd like to think it was said out of spite. On the other hand, could he be privy to some sort of scheme to destroy me? I know that sounds melodramatic, but this man was not kidding around. What do you think, Ben?"

"Garth, along with others, is hell-bent on destroying anyone whose ethnic or religious background differs from his. In fact, I know of a group that's planning to take immediate action in an effort to—their words—purify the white race.

"The good news is that the authorities are one step ahead of these white supremacists. So if Garth alluded to an organized endeavor to seek you out, it simply won't happen."

"That's reassuring," Tracy said, though her tone implied otherwise.

Patty looked at her watch. "Okay, folks, we'd better skedaddle." She pressed Tracy's hand. "We can talk more about this after dinner."

"Thanks, but that won't be necessary. You've both been

wonderful, but I've taken up far too much of your time."

Patty craned her neck as they headed back to the dining room. "I see Joanne and Jack straight ahead of us. Not to be catty, but she does seem a little wobbly."

Tracy sighed. "It's going to take work to sustain a conversation with that man. As for Joanne, I'd be zonked out too if I had to start each and every day facing the Colonel at breakfast."

At the table, the five of them exchanged perfunctory smiles, and then focused on the menu. *Where was Shirley?* Patty wondered. Faking a heart attack down in the infirmary? She wouldn't put it past her.

Nothing like making an entrance, Shirley thought as Julio escorted her to the table. She'd dallied a bit, fooling with her hair, trying on combinations of jewelry, dead set on making herself ravishingly sexy, the better to attract Mr. Wonderful. She scrunched up her lips. Okay, so this late in the game she'd settle for Mr. Presentable.

Now as she was seated, the salad course, a yummy shrimp concoction, was being served. Be that as it may, *she* appeared to be the focus of attention. Could be she provided a welcome distraction based on what she'd picked up earlier about a Jack Watkins tie-in with Garth, for God's sake.

"You certainly look lovely," Patty said. "In fact, elegant."

Murmurs of assent brought forth a beam of pleasure. "I saved this formal for last," Shirley said, "though I always thought black was an old lady's shtick."

"Not with those sequins and that neckline," Tracy said.

Ben nodded. "The boys will be waiting in line tonight."

Forget about the boys or the Crow's Nest. Shirley figured she'd arrive early in the piano bar and beat Tracy, who shouldn't be there in the first place. Maybe, oh jeez, just maybe the doctor would show up? She felt a tingling sensation up and down her spine. They would take it from there. And for once, she would not screw up.

"Shirley." Patty's smile was arch. "Are we making progress with our friend the doctor?"

"As they say in the medical profession, I'm cautiously

150

optimistic." She thought a moment. "It depends what you mean by progress, Patty. Dr. Rowlin seems to like me. I mean, he hasn't come on to me, but he's joked around a little—oh Gawd, don't you love his smile? He's such a babe. Best of all, there's no wedding ring, no family pictures cluttering up his desk. And if he was married, why would he be off to sea by himself?"

"Well, dear," Patty seemed to ponder her question, "maybe he's hooked up with that cute assistant of his." She brought her hand to her mouth. "Goodness, I didn't really mean that. Blame it on the champagne cocktails. Besides, she's no match for you."

Joanne set down her wine glass hard, spilling a bit of liquid. "Can I say something? Shirley, don't you know there's a protocol about staff and passengers socializing?" It came out *shochilizing.* "It's against the uh . . . regulations."

Jack flicked a look in Tracy's direction. "Not that everyone heeds the rules."

Shirley noted that Tracy appeared to ignore his comment. The woman looked gorgeous as always, but like she was about to die an early death. And why not? Being almost throttled or whatever by Mr. Monster Man was no picnic in the park.

Joanne stared at her intently as if she expected her to respond to her know-it-all statement.

Well, hang on, Miss Uppity. "I don't know about protocol," she replied, "but gee, Joanne, we're talking about a *doctor?* The man has to have some sort of social life. What's he supposed to do? Hibernate? Close his office and turn into a mouse or a pumpkin and vegetate until his next appointment? The man's gotta eat, have recreation. Would you give him permission to see a movie, or a show, or enjoy some night life?"

Joanne gave her a snobby look. "I can just picture your contribution to his," she paused, "recreation?"

Oh, the bitch! Before she could muster a response, Ben raised his hand in a placating gesture. "You know, Shirley may have a point. I can't imagine a doctor spending all his free time reading medical journals."

"Or a priest," Patty added, "confining himself to the chapel. My goodness, what would a priest do for recreation on a ship?"

Shirley giggled. "Maybe hang out in a bar? I have a girlfriend in

Sacramento who's told me some wild tales about one of the priests in her parish. He carries a flask wherever he goes and when services are over, he's really into the communion wine." She shrugged. "Not that I'm anti-Catholic."

Tracy looked straight at Jack Watkins. "I would not want to denigrate any religion simply because of a few bad apples."

Patty raised her glass. "Here, here."

Ben ran his hand over his chin. "I can't agree with you completely. There are sects that call themselves religious groups. For example, Christian Identity. Has anyone heard of this group? Jack?"

"It doesn't ring a bell."

"Christian Identity is anything but Christian in its beliefs," Ben continued, "though the Bible is the cornerstone of their faith. What's deplorable is that they interpret the Bible in a very bizarre way to justify hate crimes against Jews and other minorities."

Joanne uttered a sound that was halfway between a cough and a choke, while Jack, Shirley observed, held Ben's gaze, his expression impassive.

There was a pause in the discussion as the waiters cleared their salad plates, then placed entrées before them. *Ooh, don't stop now,* Shirley wanted to implore Ben. *We're getting hot. Let's see Jack squirm.* She decided to enter the fray.

"Ben?" Shirley wiggled her fork at him. "Are we talking about freaked out fanatics?"

"There's certainly a lunatic fringe who believe whites are God's chosen people, beginning with Adam who, they maintain, was white. They take it a step further to declare all other races are subhuman."

Jack's smile was sardonic. "You're presenting a one-sided picture. Now that I think about it, I have read up on the movement. Racial purity is not a new idea but has its roots in Christian mainstream religions. As for the followers, they're not all fanatics, Shirley. It's true most are white, but they represent a broad spectrum of socioeconomic classes; and from what I understand, many of these members are educated and boast of a stable family life."

Joanne was nodding. "That means they're not so bad, right? What about World Church? And, and isn't there an Aryan Nation something or other?"

"I think you're confused, Joanne. I have no idea what you're talking about."

Icebergs, frost, glacial images, all conjured up by Jack's tone. Shirley suppressed a shudder.

Joanne looked sick, her features taking on a pinched look. "Maybe I'm thinking of something I read in *Time* magazine."

It did not sound convincing. They continued eating, mostly in silence until it was time to order dessert. *Oh, my.* Shirley looked about herself. Not a happy group for their last big blowout at sea. Somebody had to introduce a new subject, but damned if she could think of anything to bring up.

She made eye contact with Patty who after giving her a quick smile, turned to Ben and began speaking in a low tone, her head tilted toward him like she was trying to make out, for crying out loud.

She'd try Tracy. "Are you bringing back a lot of goodies?"

"Goodies?"

"Clothes, jewelry, stuff for the house."

She smiled at Shirley, and it was a kind of sad smile. "Actually not."

Shirley waited, but apparently Tracy had nothing more to say. Okay, desperation time. She'd try the Colonel. "Uh, Jack, I know I've picked your brain about Steve, and I will pass on the info you've given me. Anything else you can share with me? I'm just so darned eager for him to get into an officer training program. I know he feels the same way."

Jack gave her a pained look. "I don't know what else I can add," he said.

Joanne swooped up her glass, threw back her head and sucked up the dregs of her wine. When she'd steered the glass to a safe touchdown, she peered around Jack to wag her finger at Shirley. "Why don't you ask him about our son, Teddy?"

"Oh. Is he in the service too?"

Joanne gave a snort. "He could be in Timbuktu, for all I know. Seems he took flight after an altercation with Daddy-dear."

"Joanne, for God's sake."

Shirley held back a snicker. Whoa, there. Mr. Unflappable was about to lose his cool.

Joanne tapped her spoon against her wine glass. "Do I have everyone's attention?" Now she gestured about the table. "Would you like to know what the fuss was all about? And it was a doozy, folks. You want to tell them, Jack, or shall I?"

Shirley shut her mouth, aware it was agape. She quickly inspected the table. Patty looked down, as though embarrassed, while Tracy showed a flicker of a smile. The professor, she noted, seemed more involved than usual, his gaze riveted on the Watkinses.

Jack was shaking his head. "I apologize for my wife. Joanne," he placed his hand over hers, "these people are not interested in the details of a family dispute. And besides, here comes dessert."

"I'm not interested in dessert." Joanne wiped away a tear, pushed back her chair, then hanging onto the edge of the table, rose to her feet. "I'm excusing myself."

Shirley watched in awe as Joanne left the table. *Wow, head up, shoulders back, with only a trace of unsteadiness. Where do you suppose she was headed?*

"She'll be okay," Jack said. "Joanne gets upset over our son, especially when she, uh, overindulges." He started to taste his cheesecake, then set down his fork, his expression somber. "Unfortunately, these occurrences are becoming all too frequent."

Shirley caught the exchange of glances between Tracy and Patty.

What did they know that she didn't?

❧ *Chapter Sixteen* ❧

At Sea: Formal Night

Joanne decided to check out the piano bar, this mysterious place known to Jack and frequented by Tracy. To her delight, she found herself in an atmosphere that restored calm—that offered temporary asylum from an abyss into ugliness and heartbreak.

She enjoyed an after dinner drink—no, make that two—and took pleasure in the music, the camaraderie of sitting among fellow imbibers without having to account for her actions.

Now entrenched in the ladies room, Joanne clung to the edge of the counter and squinted into the mirror. Not bad. Nothing missing except her lipstick and her dignity. With a shaking hand, she took out her lipstick from her evening bag, applied the color, and then with an effort to steady her hand, dropped it into her bag.

As for her dignity, she'd salvaged what little was left by leaving the table and in so doing, saved herself from breaking up into little pieces. She fought to quell the sob that threatened to surface. Damn Jack anyway for alienating their son.

Jack. Oh, God, there'd be double hell to pay. He'd either lash out at her or freeze up. *The Iceman Cometh.* Hmm. Catchy title of something she'd read in college. And perfect for Jack.

This perception of him was a small triumph doomed to uncertainty because no doubt about it, she'd made a fool of herself. And of him, Jack would accuse her. She snickered. Mr. Iceman, or whatever the darn name, suited Jack to a T. And she might as well enjoy this moment because confrontation time was right around the corner.

She put the thought on hold as the door swung open to reveal a flash of sequins and canyon-like décolletage. Christ almighty, it was her nemesis, Shirley Goodweather. She lowered her head in an effort to become invisible. To no avail.

"Joanne?" Shirley inched toward her. "Are you all right?"

"Why wouldn't I be?"

"Gosh, you don't have to snap at me. It was obvious you were pretty darn upset. I mean about your son. I didn't even know you had a son."

"*Have* a son." Joanne stepped away from the counter to face Shirley. "It's all your fault."

"Whoa, woman. What are you talking about?"

"Your incessant carrying on about Steve. If you hadn't started in again, this whole fiasco would never have occurred."

"Well, pardon me. I thought someone had to steer the conversation away from your husband's support of demented skinheads and anti-Semitic bigots. Besides, I thought Jack might have some last minute advice about Steve's military career."

"Steve, Steve, Steve. Jack was bored beyond belief every time you brought up the subject." She stepped sideways to grip the edge of the counter. "As for my husband being bigoted, look at you. Not a pretty picture, my dear. Because you have no toleranche"—she paused—"*tolerance* for anyone whose political views differ from yours."

"Joanne, bag the booze and wake up. We're not talking about Democratic schleps versus Republican fat cats, knee-jerk liberals against right wing reactionaries. We're not talking about…"

Joanne raised her hands. "Oh, how you do go on. You're giving me a headache."

"We both know what's giving you a headache, dearie, and it ain't little old me. Listen up. I happen to know that a man in cahoots with your husband stalked and then almost killed Tracy in Puerto Vallarta. This same man turned nasty on me because I mentioned my first husband is Jewish."

"Jack has no interest in you."

"I didn't say he did."

"That's right. You know why? You're trailer trash, a nobody. He's going for the gold, for Tracy. It's her kind—rich Jews, money hungry plunderers—who need to be eliminated, who *will* be eliminated. Why? Because they control the banks, industry, the entertainment field…and, and, well, there's more. Anyway, because of their greed, they drag down the rest of society."

Shirley stared at her bug-eyed, with her mouth hanging open.

When she recovered, she said, "Well done, Joanne. Even when you're soused, you've managed to quote chapter and verse from your husband's bible of racist propaganda. I'm sure he frames every word in gold, but do you believe in that shit?"

"What? What are you talking about?"

"What you just said, for God's sake."

"I don't know what I said. Oh, about Tracy." She thought back to the night she'd huddled on deck. It was Tracy who had comforted her. "She's a nice woman, very kind." She nodded. "You tell her to stay alert, to be very, very careful."

There. Let Shirley be the one to warn Tracy of impending danger. Now she was off the hook, thank you God. Despite her good intentions, what would Jack do if he spotted her talking to Tracy? He'd, he'd...what? She'd lost the thought. She rubbed her brow, then snatched up her purse and started for the door.

"Joanne, wait. What's going on? Is Tracy in some sort of danger?"

She turned back to Shirley, surprised to feel tears forming. She hesitated, and then said "I think so."

Shirley grabbed her arm. "In what way? Tell me!"

Joanne shrugged out of her grasp. "I don't know. I honestly don't know." She paused a beat, and then said, "Tell her it could be bad."

At Shirley's incredulous look, she added, "For God's sake, I don't know any more. That's it!"

She made her escape.

It seemed an eternity to reach the cabin, but Joanne persisted in finding her way, figuring she had no other place to go. By now she was exhausted and didn't much care what lay in store. If she had the cabin to herself because Jack was attending a show or tailing Tracy or searching for his wife, she'd undress, douse the lights and slip into bed. She simply wasn't up to explaining her outburst or pleading for forgiveness.

At the door to their cabin, she managed on the second try to insert her key card, and then let herself in. The lights were on low, and she felt a cold draft as Jack stepped through the balcony doors and into the room. She narrowed her eyes the better to focus on him. He looked more anxious than angry as he moved toward her.

"Where have you been?" he asked, "And with whom?"

"I wasn't with anyone. I was by myself."

Disgust flattened his features and as he stood with his back to the light, the blue of his eyes took on a grayness that was bleak and forbidding. "You're a mess. You've got black dribbles under your eyes, and your lipstick is smeared." He came closer, causing her instinctively to step back. "You've also lost an earring."

"Oh, no." She raised both hands to her ears. Shit. The teardrop on the left side was missing. The set comprised one of her few good pieces of costume jewelry.

"You haven't told me where you've been."

"Could we sit down?" She edged her way toward the bed and positioned herself at its foot.

Jack remained standing. "I'm waiting," he said.

"I'm sorry I made a scene." She lowered her head. "When it comes to Teddy, I simply fall apart."

"He brought on the estrangement himself."

She looked up at him. "He called you a Nazi, a fascist pig..."

"Among other unprintable names."

"Couldn't you have relented a little? If you had been patient, explained your stance on the issues, maybe we'd still be a family."

"Highly unlikely. Now. Where were you?"

"I needed to be away from our dinner group, so I went to the piano bar."

Jack took the chair opposite the sofa. "Who'd you talk to?"

"Nobody. I was buying myself time before I faced you." She massaged her forehead, wishing the ache would go away. If only she could get some sleep. "Oh. I went to the ladies room. Spent a little time there fixing up." She pressed her lips together, her smile rueful. "Not that it did any good."

"So all this time you were alone."

"Sure, I guess so. Jack, I'm really beat. Maybe we can talk about this tomorrow?"

"What's to talk about? What's done is done."

Was she getting off this easy? "I'd better get out of these clothes. Do you mind if I undress first and use the bathroom?"

"Be my guest."

Once into her nightie and robe, she felt somewhat better. Onward now to the bathroom.

A look into the mirror confirmed Jack's findings. Ugh. She did look terrible. She was tired beyond tired but made it a rule never to go to bed without cleaning her face. When she'd removed her makeup, she forced herself onto the next chore and picked up her toothbrush. It was while the water was running that she thought she heard voices. Or had she reached the point of hearing voices in her head? The loopy smile she gave the mirror turned into a grimace.

When Joanne was through in the bathroom, she stepped down gingerly into the room. Jack was on his feet, his expression reflecting puzzlement. Now what? Then she saw he held something in his hand.

"We had a visitor," he said. "Shirley Goodweather." He handed her the missing earring. "She said she ran into you in the ladies room and that after you left, she discovered your earring on the floor."

Oh Lord, what had she let slip to Shirley? Think, think, think. She had warned her. No, she had asked her to warn Tracy. Joanne felt as if her body were encased in ice. "Is that all she said?"

"What more could she say? You said you spoke to no one, so obviously the two of you did not hold a conversation."

"I didn't mention Shirley because it was inconsequential—a, uh, brief encounter. In fact, I'd forgotten she'd been in there with me." She started for the bed, and then stopped. "All these questions about did I talk to anyone. Jack, I assure you I did not broadcast to the world what took place with Teddy." And that was the God's truth.

"But you almost did." He spoke softly, without a trace of anger. Strangely, what he did show in his expression, in his eyes was completely out of character for Jack. It was pity.

Oh, hell, enough was enough. They could thrash out their differences in the morning.

In bed, Joanne turned on her side, away from the light that illuminated the closet area where Jack prepared for bed.

She must have fallen asleep instantly because when she started awake, the light was still on and Jack wasn't in bed. Maybe he'd dropped something or the shutting of the bathroom door had aroused her. She raised up her head, bleary eyed, to look at the clock on the desk. She found it difficult to focus. Was the time 11:30? Was that all? She felt as if she'd been asleep for hours. And then her gaze fell on an object next to the clock, something small and black. Shoot. She'd forgotten to put her evening purse away.

She lay back down and as she felt her body relax, her breathing slow, the thought occurred that she would not have been carrying a black bag with pale blue chiffon. The shape, the color reminded her of the diary she'd shoved into the drawer where their souvenirs were stored. Out of sight would preclude Jack's quizzing her as to her use or non-use of the diary. Anything, she'd reasoned, to avert suspicion. But if it was the diary, what was it doing on the desk? Had Jack been searching through her things?

She struggled to stay awake, to lift her head to take another look, but she felt weighted down, crammed into a floating tomb.

Now she drifted in and out of consciousness, and soon she'd be asleep. But in these final seconds, she prayed to God. Please, *please* let this be a dream. A very bad dream.

The creep. Shirley flounced away from the Watkins's cabin, feeling soiled, as if she needed a bath. Why even bother with the stupid earring? Oh, well, chalk it up to being nosy. Who wouldn't be curious as to what must be going on with those two, in light of the show and tell extravaganza at the dinner table? Or maybe, just a teeny, tiny bit maybe, she felt sorry for Joanne, bitch that she was.

At any rate, the woman was obviously a mess, on the brink of self-destruction. So give her a break. Return the earring.

On the downside, it was now her responsibility to find Tracy and pass on Joanne's warnings. Crap. What a way to end the cruise. Still, she was worried out of her mind for Tracy and if she could help, God bless us all.

So, it was hippity hop to the piano bar. Where else would Tracy be, but snuggled up to Marc while he poured out his heart to her through his music? Unless, remembering her earlier resolve, she beat Tracy to it.

And why shouldn't she compete for Marc's attention? Tracy had her man and an ocean view home in the Palisades, for crying out loud. What more could she want?

Whatever—she wouldn't want to be in Tracy's shoes, not for a minute. Jeez, just thinking about Garth made her stomach turn.

The image of big, bad Garth dissolved as she approached the piano bar, as Marc's music—low-down, dirty-down blues—made her skin tingle, made her want to thrust out her pelvis and wiggle her butt. God, what rhythm. Yes!

She slapped her own wrist. *Down, girl.* Patty had said she looked elegant, so she'd can the burlesque Betty routine and go for subtle. Pretend she was Jodie.

Step number one. Easy does it. She paused at the entryway to check out the room. Wouldn't you know, the seats immediately adjacent to Marc were taken. The blond on his right was no Tracy, but she had a Barbie doll cuteness, a pert nose, fluttery lashes, and a hug-me kind of smile, none of which was lost on Marc who was giving her the eye.

As for the man on Marc's left, they'd probably have to carry him out. The old geezer's eyes were closed, his head droopy and bobbing about, though not in time to the music.

She took a seat on the old man's side of the bar but far enough away from him to avoid contact. She wanted a clear view of the entryway so she could watch for Tracy, stop her before she settled in for the evening. Joanne may have been drunk, but there was a sense of urgency in her garbled message.

The music changed from wild and wicked to dreamy and sweet. Shirley ordered a martini, and while she waited, fantasized Barbie whisked away by Ken or the old man hauled off by an irate wife. She'd grab a seat by Marc in a sprint.

Her martini before her, Shirley remembered her new look called for a more refined approach, with sprinting a definite no-no. She made a face. What nonsense. With Tracy in the picture, Marc was off limits.

Her drink tasted on the strong side, but so what? That's why she liked martinis. She focused on Marc who was singing *Our Love is Here to Stay*. Humming along under her breath, she visualized herself in Marc's arms, feeling a quickening in her breathing, a twinge in her crotch.

The image faded as she realized someone gently tapped her left shoulder. Distracted from the music, she turned. The seat to her left was no longer unoccupied. Oh m'God, it was Dr. Rowlin.

"Shirley? Hi, it's nice to see you away from a medical setting."

Her heart gave a thump. This wasn't a daydream. This was real. "Dr. Rowlin, for heaven's sake. I must say you look great in civvies." He had a clean cut, fresh appearance, a poster boy for safe-to-take-home-to-Mom.

He laughed. "Believe it or not, I don't sleep in a white coat with a stethoscope around my neck. *You* look lovely. Black becomes you."

Bye, bye, Marc. "Thank you very much, Dr. Rowlin. I thought I'd pull out all the stops for our last dressy night at sea."

"Let's drop the Dr. Rowlin for now. I think in a social setting you should call me Jim." He grinned, "Though we'll have to reinstate formalities if you return to the clinic tomorrow. Let's see. How many times have you been down there?"

She was saved from answering his query when the bartender arrived to take his drink order. She knew he was teasing, which endeared him to her even more. Oh, baby, would she love to play doctor with Jim. It was time to nail down the particulars.

She leaned into him, squeezing her boobs in from the sides to create a mega bust effect. "Uh, Jim, do you often sail as a ship's doctor?"

"Not really. I wouldn't want to make a steady practice of it, but it's a break from the usual routine, and I do enjoy travel."

"Isn't being away at sea hard on your family?"

"Since I don't have a wife or kids, it doesn't constitute a hardship."

Aha! Shirley sipped at her drink as the bartender placed something tall and frothy in front of the doc. Some sort of tropical concoction, she guessed.

As if it mattered. What counted, glory be, was that he was single. Still, she'd better take it slow, maybe even make him a little jealous.

"Excuse my back for a second," she said. "I was supposed to meet a friend here and I'd better check to see if he's shown." Barbie, she noted, was fawning over Marc (Where was Tracy?) and the old man was gone, leaving that seat vacant. Was she tempted? Nope, she'd stay right where she was.

"I don't see him," she said.

"If you need to search for your friend…"

"No, no, no. This is fine. I'm enjoying talking to you. Now where is home?"

"San Francisco."

"Really! I live in Sacramento. Also I happen to work for a doctor. So you see, we have at least two things in common. What is your specialty?"

"Internal medicine."

"Here we go again. I work for an internist. Maybe you know him. Dr. Frank Edlemann?"

Jim's expression turned as frosty as his drink. "No, I don't know him."

Hmm, maybe he did know him, and they were on the outs. She would not pursue that subject and anyway, look who was making her entrance. She waved and called out, "Tracy!" but she sailed on by.

"I guess she couldn't hear me over the music," she said to Jim. But now the music stopped as Marc greeted Tracy who had taken the seat on his left. From Barbie's pout of displeasure, it seemed unlikely she'd stick around much longer. Marc was being much too attentive to Tracy. And she was neglecting Jim. In fact, he was asking something about Tracy.

She turned back to him. "I'm sorry. What did you say?"

"I've seen the woman you call Tracy in here a number of times. Is she a friend of yours?"

"We're at the same dinner table, and yeah, I've gotten to know her."

"Has she told you much about her background?"

"Oh, sure. Mother was a concert pianist, husband is an attorney.

You know, the good life."

"Yet, she seems taken with the pianist." He smiled, "You think they're—as they say in Hollywood—an item?"

How would I know? Shirley thought. "You mean hanky-panky behind closed doors?" *And why is he so interested?*

"She hasn't, uh, confided in you?"

"We're not that close." Oh, ye gads, was he interested in Tracy? Was he nudging up to her to get the scoop on Tracy? Time to turn this around.

"So. Do you ever come up to Sacramento? Of course, it can't compare to San Francisco. I mean, how cosmopolitan can you get? The shops, the restaurants are to die for."

"Sacramento is not high on my list of favorite places, though it's a pretty city. I've attended some conferences there."

"If you're ever up there, I'd be happy to show you around." He pursed his lips as if pondering her statement. *Come on, Doc, you're supposed to say, 'Wouldn't it be great if we met in Frisco?'*

Maybe she'd gone too far. Heaven forbid she'd scared him off.

"I appreciate the invitation," he said. He lifted the cocktail napkin from under his drink and passed it her way. "Why don't you write down your phone number."

"Gladly." Oh, wow, was this heaven or what? Possibly he planned to stay over in L.A. before heading home. If so, she'd stay on, make like there was some confusion over the date she was to return to work.

She handed back the napkin. "Jim, after we dock, are you going straight home?"

"No." Slowly he lifted his glass and pressed the rim against his lips in the manner of a caress. "My partner will meet me at the dock. We'll stay in L.A. overnight, and then continue on to Phoenix."

It wouldn't hurt to make it a threesome. One time. "That sounds like a plan," she said. "So you guys are partners in your medical practice?"

He set down his drink, patted her hand, and then smiled the sunny smile she adored, the one that was like a day at the beach. "I don't think you understand. Brian and I are life partners."

Jesus, Joseph, and Mary. She took a deep breath. "I get your drift," she said. She'd made her tone cool, offhand, though her inner voice wailed in protest. Not fair, dammit, not fair!

"Well, Doc, I mean Jim, I really need to talk to Tracy. So if you'll excuse me…"

"It's been a pleasure, Shirley." His smile was now less than beatific. It was more of a smirk.

ᕙᗯ *Chapter Seventeen* ᗯᕲ

At Sea: Formal Night

It hadn't escaped Tracy's notice that Shirley was engaged in conversation with a nice looking man—possibly in his early forties?—who looked like a winner. *Hang on to this one,* she mentally challenged her. *Seduce him or play the innocent. Just don't talk him to death!*

"Better him than me," Marc whispered, following her gaze.

"You're being naughty," Tracy said.

He winked. "You want naughty? I can deliver." He brought the Cole Porter medley he was performing to a close, adding the necessary flourishes to signal break time. His efforts brought a smattering of applause from the bar patrons and, to Tracy's surprise, Shirley Goodweather to her side.

"I need to talk to you," Shirley said.

"Maybe it can wait." She nodded to where Shirley had been seated. "The man's not only attractive, but he seemed taken with you."

"He's also gay. Tracy, it's important we go somewhere private to talk."

Tracy could tell by the rigidity in Shirley's posture, the worried look in her eyes that she was dead serious. With a sinking heart, Tracy wondered if it were she or Shirley who might have cause for alarm. "All right," she said, "let's go to my cabin." She turned to Marc to explain where she would be and why.

He squeezed her hand. "Hurry back, my love."

"I promise."

Shirley's stride was swift and purposeful, her no-nonsense demeanor feeding Tracy's unease as they approached her cabin.

Once inside, Shirley took charge, directing them to the sofa. When they were settled, she twisted about, scanning the suite as if to ensure they were alone.

Enough theatrics, Tracy decided. "Shirley, for heaven's sake,

166

you've got me curious to the breaking point."

"Okay, I have to lead up to this. After dinner, I met up with Joanne in the ladies room. It wouldn't take a genius to figure out she'd been off to one of the bars to toss down a few. The woman could barely stand up. You could see she was hanging onto the furniture for dear life. Not that it stopped her from making ugly with me.

"She ranted on and on about how I always bring up Steve at the dinner table and one thing led to another to where I laid into her about Jack being tied in with Garth. I told her what the bastard did to you and how he'd turned nasty on me."

Tracy took in her breath. "I know you meant well, but by goading her you may have done more harm than good." She threw up her hands. "Or maybe not. How did she react?"

"She launched into a defense of her husband, then like she was reading from a script recited what had to be his racist ranting's. What's important, though, is that if I hadn't brought up Garth, we'd never be the wiser. Now hear me out." She went on to explain Jack's screwed-up philosophy as parroted by Joanne, and his evil intentions, most notably to do away with Tracy and her ilk.

Tracy shook her head. "I'm sure Jack carries on in that manner all the time. As for Joanne, obviously, she was intoxicated, and who knows, it's possible she fabricated the whole thing."

"I don't think so. It's true Joanne's statements were disjointed, but I'd swear she knew what she was talking about." Shirley twisted her ring, an oversized shiny green stone, studded with rhinestones. "You know, this is crazy, but out of the blue Joanne changed her tune, going on about what a kind and nice person you are."

Tracy nodded. "On the night she fell on stage, I found her on deck, distraught. I tried to comfort her."

"At any rate, she said you should be careful and stay alert. I asked if you were in some sort of danger. She said she thought so, but that's when she went vague on me. Anyway, she said to tell you 'it', whatever that means, could be bad. Tracy, she seemed to care. I'd swear she was using me to warn you."

"Whew. That's heavy. Can't say I'm thrilled with the message, but I do thank you, Shirley. I appreciate your concern."

"What are you going to do?"

She shrugged. "What can I do? All we have is the word of a drunken woman."

"Please don't take this lightly."

"I'm not. I'll talk to Ben in the morning." Tracy looked at her watch. "The evening's still young. Why don't you go back to your companion at the bar?"

"I told you, he's gay."

"Rotten luck."

"Tell me about it. Mind you, he's the ship's doctor, and I thought I'd hit the jackpot." She went on to explain their commonality of interests. "Though he froze up when I mentioned I work for Dr. Edlemann."

"That sounds like a Jewish name."

"What is this ship, the U.S.S. Bigot? Incidentally, he was asking questions about you. Your background, your interest in Marc. I thought, oh, oh, this guy has the hots for Tracy. I'm just the go-between."

"Now we know differently, don't we?" Tracy gnawed on her lower lip. "Why would he ask questions about me? It doesn't make sense. Something's out of kilter."

"He seems like an okay person. Certainly not neo-Nazi scum. But who knows?"

"At this point I wouldn't be surprised if my sweet, little cabin attendant was moonlighting as a spy. In any event, it can't hurt to pass on this information to Ben."

Shirley was on her feet. "I think I'll grab a nightcap in the Crow's Nest. Want to join me?" She put her hand to her mouth. "Oops, sorry. You've got that luscious Marc to return to."

"I think I'll stay put for a while." Tracy rose to escort Shirley to the door. "Again, thanks. Forewarned is forearmed, or however the saying goes."

As she stepped out into the corridor, Shirley made a show of looking left and right. "Not a soul in sight. Watch your back, honey." With that, she moved briskly to the elevators.

Tracy wanted to laugh at Shirley's histrionics, but nothing she'd related was a laughing matter. She shut the door, and then hastened to the veranda doors, making sure they were locked. If Jack wanted to get to her, he could easily remove a section of the partition that separated the balconies.

She thought about returning to the piano bar, and then rejected the idea. What if Jack or one of his cronies lurked in the hallway? Besides, she imagined Marc would find his way to her. It was now midnight, and he'd said he was closing down at 1:00.

She returned to the sofa, smoothing out her gown as she recalled her pleasure over Marc's admiring look, the words he'd whispered into her ear: 'exquisite, ravishing.'

In the afternoon on her balcony they talked freely and with passion about art, literature, and, of course, music. Marc's warmth, his expression of caring and absolute attentiveness, contrasted with his light teasing and infectious laugh, a combination of traits she found captivating.

The temptation to take him to bed was so strong that if he had initiated the idea and then persisted, she'd have given in. That they held back only intensified her desire. Marc, she felt, must have sensed there was a better time. And, in fact, their afternoon rendezvous was akin to foreplay.

She rationalized it was okay to live for the moment, to be with Marc in what should be a grand and glorious fling before having to make choices over what lay ahead.

Letting her imagination soar, she entertained the idea of a continuing liaison with Marc and, however unlikely, that they might carve out a future together. But she quickly dismissed the thought. She loved Peter and knew she could never hurt him by entering into another relationship. Unless she were a free woman.

What she hadn't told Marc was that she'd fully expected to hear from her husband in the morning or definitely by this afternoon (all the more reason not to give in to their impulses). At the latest, surely he'd call sometime this evening.

She looked at the phone, despising its presence. For an inanimate object, it did a damn fine job of mocking her. Why hadn't Peter called back? She couldn't imagine he could be so derelict in ignoring her call. Suddenly, the full magnitude of Shirley's revelations took hold.

She looked at her watch. It was far too late to call Peter. No, by

George, it was not too late. In fact, the later the better because at this hour Peter should be home. And if he were not?

She was on her feet. Only one way to find out.

In minutes she returned to the sofa. Once again, her efforts resulted in getting the answering machine, in hearing her own voice. Shit. What was going on? Where was her husband? Wasn't he aware or couldn't he somehow sense she needed him, that she feared for her life?

Or perhaps worse from his point of view, that she was about to commit adultery?

At one a.m. on the dot, a soft knock on the door caused Tracy to start, and then set aside the book she'd been trying to read. Marc must have shut down a little early, possibly concerned that she hadn't returned to the piano bar.

She hurried to the door, but then paused, opening it only a crack. Stunned, she stood face to face with a smiling Jack Watkins.

"I could tell your light was on," he said. "I couldn't sleep and thought I might chat with you a moment." He gave the door a nudge and peered beyond her shoulder.

"I have company," she said.

"I certainly won't detain you. I'm, uh, wondering if you happened to talk to Joanne after she left the dinner table? She's in the cabin now and out for the night, but in her state of mind, I can only assume the worst."

"I'm not sure I follow you."

"When she's under the influence, she tends to exaggerate, to make up wild tales."

"I've not seen Joanne since she left the dinner table. Now if you'll excuse me?"

Jack pushed in the door, causing her to stumble backwards. "Where's company? Hiding in the closet?"

"What do you think you're doing?" Before she could let out a scream, a voice in the hallway called out, "I repeat the question. What do you think you're doing?" It was Marc. Thank God.

Jack stepped back. "I was having a quiet chat with Tracy concerning my wife. But I certainly don't want to intrude. Have a nice time, you two." The mockery in his tone and expression revolted her.

Marc stepped into the cabin and closed the door. He reached for her hands and guided her to the sofa. "Your hands are like ice. Let me warm them."

She blinked back tears and shook her head. "I can hardly get my breath, my heart is racing so. I'm so grateful you arrived when you did."

"I kept waiting for you to return to me."

"I didn't dare venture out on my own. I was afraid I'd be stopped with no one to intervene, no witness."

"Witness to what?"

She told him about Shirley's confrontation with Joanne that led to the warning that Jack was out to destroy her. "Given Joanne's state of inebriation, this may not be as bad as it sounds. On the other hand, Jack and his racist pals would happily string me up and feed me to the vultures."

"Oh, *mi amor,* that's not going to happen." He drew her close. "Did he threaten you?"

"No, but because of Joanne's warning, I was shocked to see this man at my door. No, make that petrified. At any rate, I suspect he was concerned that his wife may have talked out of turn. If he's going to pounce, he needs me to be vulnerable and unsuspecting."

"You'll be safe. We'll see that you're safe. As for tonight, he knows you're not alone." He cupped her chin. "You're trembling. Let me hold you."

His caresses were gentle and soothing, followed by kisses that were soft and comforting. She felt a sense of peace and wellbeing, as if the dark, arctic tundra had melted, transformed into an oasis of light and warmth.

And then the light exploded into something beyond consoling and healing, inciting an urgency to remove clothes, and then cling together in bed. He was slender but well-muscled, his hands taking command on her now as they did at the keyboard.

But now, after an impassioned beginning, he slowed, held back, touching and caressing with all the delicacy of a lyrical symphonic poem—a sweet interlude that only heightened her desire for consummation.

"Yes, now you are ready." he murmured and their ardor increased, building to fever pitch until there was blissful release.

Spent, they lay in each other's arms.

"You're truly awesome," Tracy said, her tone hushed in deference to her statement. "You make love like the composer of a masterpiece."

He laughed softly. "I'm almost afraid to ask. Who did you have in mind?"

"Easy. Tchaikovsky all the way. Or let's start with him for an exalted beginning followed by the exquisiteness of a Chopin prelude. Concluding with?" She thought for a moment. "How about Wagner or Brahms?"

"How about Tracy? I don't need the old masters for inspiration when I'm in the company of a young and beautiful woman."

She drew a finger across his chest. "Are there many young and beautiful women?"

"Surely you don't picture me as celibate?"

"Hardly. But that's not what I asked."

He withdrew his arm from around her to raise himself on one elbow to look at her. "Do I sense some antagonism?"

"No, of course not. Come to think of it, though, I may feel a wee bit jealous of those who've come before me, not to mention the gobs of women you'll seek out after me."

"Querida." He slid down next to her. "All that matters is what we've meant to each other on this trip, the beauty of now."

"I see."

"Oh, my darling, I cherish you. I will always remember our encounter." He started to reach for her, but she raised herself to a sitting position, pulling the sheet up to cover her breasts. He remained motionless, as if uncertain of what to do next, and then pushed himself up as well. "Tracy, what do you expect of me?"

"I honestly don't know. I confess I've been overwhelmed by

your affection and warmth. We seem to have so much in common, such a strong connection."

He took her hand. "I'm not a Don Juan, out to seduce the ladies. I was attracted to you the minute I laid eyes on you. But it was not my intention to take you to bed."

Tracy gave a little snort. "The thought never occurred to you?"

He sighed. "What can I say? Never in my wildest dreams did I imagine we'd end up like this."

"But you decided to give it a try."

"Tracy, dearest, let's put our cards on the table. We come from two different worlds, and your world is out of reach for me. I'm not your long lost love from your student days. Unlike that man, I have minimal talent and even less ambition to succeed in a high profile musical career."

"You're skirting the issue."

"All right. Despite everything I've said, despite our differences, I longed to be with you."

"And now that you've achieved that aim?"

"I will treasure the memory of you forever and ever."

"What if we were to meet at some future time?"

"You don't need me. I have nothing to offer. Go back to your husband and work things out, or gain your independence. By all means, go back to your music or concentrate on your writing."

"What if I decided I did need you? *If* I were a free woman."

He leaned over to kiss her on the lips. "Who knows? Nothing is impossible. Now I must return to my quarters." He moved quickly and was soon into his clothes.

Tracy found her robe and covered herself. They stood together at the door. "Will I see you tomorrow?" she asked.

"Of course, though it would have to be during the day."

"I know. Bags outside the door by 11:00 p.m. I can't believe tomorrow is the last day."

He wrapped his arms around her. "And I can't believe I may

never see you again."

"Maybe it doesn't have to be that way."

"Perhaps not." He kissed her. "Goodnight, dearest Tracy."

When he was gone, Tracy tidied up, put her clothes away and checked once again that her balcony doors were locked.

Back in bed, she marveled over all that had occurred in one evening. First on tomorrow's agenda would be to talk to Ben. But she didn't want to think about that now.

Her thoughts were on Marc, on the exotic tide of their lovemaking. If she were to feel pangs of guilt over her actions, it would have to wait until tomorrow. For now she felt no shame or remorse, only that right or wrong, she had feelings for Marc. And somehow, despite her expression of cynicism over Marc's intentions, she felt in her gut that his feelings for her were genuine.

With that in mind, she decided to put everything on hold. It was time for sleep.

Ann Bradshaw looked on disapprovingly as Tracy and Marc embraced. Embarrassed, Tracy stepped away from Marc and bowed her head. When she looked up, Ann was gone, and it was Michael who now reached out for her. She started toward him, and then stopped. His smile was angelic, his head tilted slightly to the side as she remembered him, but his eyes were blank, totally void of expression.

"I can't be with you," she said. "What happened to Marc? Where is Peter?"

He dropped his arms. "Make up your mind, Tracy." His voice was flat; his posture reflected indifference.

"I have to find Peter, settle this once and for all."

"Maybe Peter has left you. Did you ever think of that?"

"He wouldn't simply walk out on me. I know he loves me."

"You don't think he senses your ambivalence, that you're not supporting him one hundred percent? You don't think it hurts that you're not cheering him on?"

"It's thrown me that he's running for office."

"Oh, come on, you questioned your marriage long before that."

"Not that long."

"But you admit..."

"Yes, yes. Go away. Leave me alone."

"It's not much fun to be alone, Tracy. Marc can't be a part of your world. Peter may have given up on you. He hasn't called."

She began to sob. *"Stop saying these things. I'm going to find Peter. I have to find him."* She raced for the door, but it wouldn't open. She was locked in, and now she was alone in the room.

The phone. She'd call for help. Call Peter. But she couldn't remember the number. Frantic, she searched through her purse and found her address book. But no entry existed for their home in Pacific Palisades.

She paced the room, willing herself to remember the number, growing more agitated as the numbers remained a blank.

Suddenly, the phone began to ring. She snatched up the receiver. *"Peter, where have you been? I've been trying and trying to reach you."*

"Tracy? I know this is Tracy, but you don't sound so good." It was a male voice, but it was not Peter.

"Who is this?"

"You don't recognize me? Not even in your nightmares? I'd know your voice anywhere. Of course, we met only once, but there'll be another time. You can bet on that." There was a pause. *"Still don't get who I am?"*

He spoke softly, but his words jabbed at her like needles pricking her skin. *"You're evil,"* she said. *"You're slime."*

"I'm Garth, pretty lady. Only you won't be so pretty when I'm done with you."

She slammed down the phone, only to jolt awake to find herself in bed. Disoriented, she placed a hand over her wildly beating heart. Had she been dreaming? She lay very still, trying to restore calm as she sorted things out. Of course, it had been a dream, the kind that stays with you in your waking hours as the images and words pound in your head.

The confrontation with Michael was unsettling, reflecting her uncertainties over Peter, and Marc's reluctance to contemplate any further contact. But it was the phone call from Garth that was most unnerving, because it was Garth down to the core.

Tracy yawned in spite of herself. "So tired, so tired," she muttered. She turned on her side and cradled the extra pillow, forcing her mind to shut out the ugliness of her dream. She would recreate her moments with Marc. His words, "Goodnight, dearest Tracy," were like a caress and his voice lingered in her head, generating warmth and contentment.

As her heart rate slowed and her muscles relaxed, she felt that delicious drowsiness that prods one to the brink of sleep.

Let it be a dreamless sleep, was her prayer.

Tracy fought arousal, but something jarring pulled her back into consciousness. Was it an alarm? She buried her head in her pillow, but it was of no help in muffling sound. She thought it might be her phone, but if this were part of a dream, she vowed to ignore its strident pitch, unwilling to be pulled back into a sickening repeat of the Garth call.

Persistent, the sound continued. It was her phone and now fully awake, she had no choice but to answer the damn thing. She turned on her bedside light and checked the time. Who would call her at 4:45 a.m.? Whoever or whatever it was, they would keep ringing until she answered.

Angry now, she jerked the receiver from its cradle. "Who is this?" Silence. Oh, swell—a hang-up call at this hour. Except she heard no dial tone to indicate the call had been terminated. "Hello. Is someone there?"

Still nothing. About to hang up, she thought she heard a faint clicking sound. She had to strain to hear it, but as it increased in volume, it sounded like the ticking of a clock. Then, it shut off completely.

She wondered if her phone had malfunctioned. Either that or someone was playing games with her. She froze as the ticking started up again in the background.

"Tracy?" It was a voice that sounded distant, yet had a hard edge. The voice, obviously disguised, could have been a man or a woman. She stood in place like a statue, afraid to move, even to breathe.

"I wanted you to know, Tracy, that the hours of your life are ticking away. Tick tock. Tick tock. Soon it will all be over." The voice crooned. "Bye-bye, bitch."

When the dial tone sounded, Tracy released her breath, and then placed the receiver in its cradle. She looked about her. Everything was in its place, neat and tidy, with the first light of dawn seeping in from under the drapes. In a few hours she would go to Ben, but for now she felt numb, unable or unwilling to fathom what might lie ahead.

She groped her way to the bed and lay down, assuming a fetal position, the extra pillow pressed hard to her chest. Somehow she knew she was okay for now. The enemy needed to grind her down to a quivering bundle of hysteria, too threatened, and too intimidated to be vigilant, on guard.

She vowed she would not let that happen. Her priorities had changed. Whatever the state of her personal life—her marriage, lifestyle, career options—what mattered now was to stay alive.

And by God, she would.

❧ *Chapter Eighteen* ☙

The Morning After

"I thought breathing in this fresh sea air might clear my sinuses." Patty reached to push her arms through the sleeves of the sweater she'd thrown over her shoulders.

"If it's too chilly for you, we can take breakfast inside," Ben said.

"I'm willing to give the balcony a try. My goodness, Ben, how often can we sit outside at home? Virginia is sweltering by now, and if it's not the heat, we can rely on thunderstorms to chase us into the house."

"Speaking of home..." Ben pushed aside his plate. His mouth was a thin line, his expression pensive.

Patty raised her coffee cup to her lips, but the cup seemed to take on a life of its own, and she had to use both hands to set it down. "Yes?"

"I confess I'm terribly conflicted."

"Oh? About what?" The sudden dryness in her mouth caused her to slur her words. The statement *'We need to talk'* churned through her mind. Since that terrible afternoon of Ben's cutting accusations and her collapse, they had moved on. But she knew it was not in either of their natures to sweep under the carpet something as devastating and potentially damaging as their set-to. They still needed to talk.

"Mind you," he said, "I'm not ascribing this to a midlife crisis."

Patty fiddled with her napkin. What was the 'this' he referred to?

"It's simply that I may be at a crossroads, and I need to contemplate my future. My professional future," he added quickly.

"You're not satisfied with your work? Ben, you're brilliant in your field, a gifted teacher as well."

He smiled. "I'll know whom to turn to if ever I need a recommendation."

"You're certainly respected and well thought of. Do you feel stymied in your career?" *Or is it me? Am I somehow a hindrance?*

"Not really." He rose and gripped the balcony railing, staring at the horizon. Then he turned to face her. "I'm considering the idea of quitting the university to work full time for the FBI. However, I would not make this move without your blessing."

"Oh, my dear." She could taste her relief as something palpable, like a warm, sweet substance soothing her throat. It was not she who was at the root of his distress. "Of course you would have my blessing. But think what you'd be giving up. You have tenure, the esteem of your students and superiors, the certainty of moving up in your field."

Ben gave the railing a thump, and then returned to his place at the table. "I think I really want to make this change. And it's not as if my interest outside of academia is fly-by-night. After all, I do have a degree in criminology.

"As for your arguments—and they do have merit—the prevailing idea is that of accomplishment. But! Predicated on what? The answer is certainty, security, a step-by-step pattern of mathematical progression so that point A leads to point B and so on.

"It's that very comfort zone I find stifling. Because it's so predictable. I seem to thrive, come alive when there's risk, the excitement of pursuing unmarked territory.

"So." He grinned. "Maybe I'm not as conflicted as I stated earlier?"

"I do recall that when you're consulting, you take on a sparkle, a buoyancy I find most attractive." She leaned over to kiss his cheek. "Go for it. Let's take the chance of testing the unknown."

He gave her a teasing smile. "Did I hear *let's*, as in *let us*?"

"I think you'd agree we performed well as a team here on the ship, aiding Tracy, I mean, and in working with your FBI connection. Might I lend a hand at times?"

"Absolutely. But nothing is set in stone, Patty. A lot has to be worked out, both with the university and the folks at FBI headquarters. One option would be to take a year's leave from the university to test the waters before making a final decision."

"Oh, gosh, Ben, now you're ruining everything by being practical. It was more fun when we were caught up in the excitement of the moment." She laughed. "Only teasing. Do you mind if we go inside? I feel a chill in the air." She picked up their empty plates to carry inside for the cabin steward to remove.

As soon as they entered the cabin, Ben claimed the sofa and proceeded to check their shipboard account, reconciling these figures—shore excursions, dining, lounge and miscellaneous expenses—with his record of the same. Patty thought about packing, then decided it was too early to empty drawers and drag shoes out from the closet. She'd save that onerous task for later.

Now as Patty observed her husband at work, she felt a rush of love, a positive sense of expectancy over what lay ahead. She was grateful they had cleared the air regarding Ben's clandestine activities both before and during the cruise. Still, there was a hitch.

Neither of them had explored the reasons behind Ben's outburst or what generated her possessiveness and dependency on him. They had to address these issues and not let them fester.

She sent a quick prayer heavenward and took a deep breath. "Ben, this may not be the best time for a discussion, but I don't know when is a good time. Could you set aside your paperwork for a little while? We've attacked one serious topic this morning, and I'd like to hone in on another matter."

"Sure." He patted a place beside him. "Let's talk."

"It's about our fight. Well, no," she fingered the buttons on her sweater, and then clasped her hands. "This is about us, our behavior that afternoon. I can tell you now that I was jealous. I sensed an intimacy between you and Tracy that disturbed me. I suppose my actions were childish and uncalled for, and I'm not proud of my behavior.

"But Ben, your reaction was brutal, so hurtful. It seemed so out of character."

He bowed his head and let out a deep sigh.

"Would you rather talk another time?" she asked.

"No, no. Putting off an explanation won't make either of us feel any better." His smile was rueful. "Now you know I have a dark side. As for what set me off... I suppose it was because I have a hard time dealing with rejection, both on a professional and personal level. I interpreted your conduct as rejection and unfortunately things got out of hand. It doesn't excuse how I acted, and I pray it never happens again."

"I'm sure it won't, my dearest. On my part, it's plain I need to step aside to give you breathing room."

"Patty, I was angry. I lashed out at you, getting back at you."

"Yes, but you also spoke the truth. I've given this matter some thought, and here's what I propose." She jumped at the sound of the phone. "Oh, no. Let's ignore it."

"Honey, I don't think that's wise." He strode to the phone.

Now what, she wondered. His face had lighted up upon greeting the caller, but as he listened, his smile faded and the lines in his forehead deepened. "Stay put," he said. "We'll be right there." End of conversation.

"Don't tell me; it's Tracy."

"She called about some new developments."

"You're suggesting its incumbent upon you or us to fly to her side? We were in the midst of a serious discussion, Ben."

"This shouldn't take long."

"That's not the point! You could have told her we were tied up for the moment." Patty was on her feet. "I don't like this. I don't like this at all."

"Do you want me to call her back and say we can't come?" His expression was stony.

"Yes! No, no, of course not." *One day, just this day and then they'd be done with Tracy.* "I'm sorry, Ben. I'm sure it's important or Tracy wouldn't have called. It's simply…bad timing."

He extended his arms, and she came to him for a hug. "I promise we'll get back to that serious discussion. For now think of it as a mission. We're a team, Patty, and together we'll try to make sense out of what's going on."

She managed a smile. "I did make noises to that effect, didn't I?"

His smile was warm and loving but as they prepared to leave the cabin, Patty wondered if his quest for change, for taking risks drew him to Tracy while she, on the other hand, represented—as he had phrased it—his comfort zone.

It was not a reassuring thought.

"Déjà vu," Tracy said as they took their places like actors on stage, Ben and herself on the sofa with Tracy in the chair opposite them. "I can't tell you how glad I'll be to see the end of this cruise. Well, it hasn't all been bad." She smiled. "However, wait 'til you hear the latest."

As she related the confrontation between Joanne and Shirley and the aftermath of that meeting, Patty was impressed with Tracy's spirit. Her color was good, her eyes were clear and she seemed pumped up rather than as in previous get-togethers, when she'd been a mere wisp of herself.

"If that wasn't enough," Tracy continued, "I received an early morning telephone call that was short and succinct: The clock was ticking away the hours of my life, and time was running out. He, she, whoever it was, included the sound effects of a ticking clock."

"How utterly bizarre," Patty said. "Not to mention awful. I would have been terror-stricken."

Ben rubbed his chin. "I gather you couldn't tell if it was a man or a woman?"

"The voice was definitely disguised. Oh. I should have mentioned that Jack Watkins knocked on my door at one a.m., ostensibly to ask if I had talked to Joanne after she left the dinner table. He was concerned she might have come up with some wild tales."

"He was making a social call at one a.m.?" Patty asked.

"It started off low key, but I could tell he was checking to see if I were alone. Then he really became brazen and tried to push his way in. Fortunately, someone came along at that moment, so he backed off."

Patty had to catch her breath. "Good heavens, girl, what a horrible night. Ben, what's your take on this?"

"I think Jack was playing cat and mouse, toying with you, Tracy. Had he made his way in, I doubt he'd have laid a hand on you. His intent, as I see it, would be to scare you silly by his menacing manner, I suppose in an effort to wear you down."

"For the kill?" Tracy's smile was sardonic.

"There's not going to be any kill," Ben said. "Remember, Jack doesn't know the authorities are on to him. He thinks the best is yet to come, so his idea of fun is acting out his racist garbage by tormenting you."

Patty nodded in agreement, and then grasped Ben's hand. "What about the phone call? Do you think it was Jack?"

"I doubt it. That mode of scare tactic doesn't appear to be his style."

"I thought of Garth," Tracy said.

Ben nodded. "Could be. I'm sure he's incensed you got away from him, so he may be getting in his digs."

Patty looked at her watch, then at Ben. "Hadn't we better start packing?"

"I should get busy too," Tracy said. "Oh! One more thing, and I'll make it short." She described the conversation between Shirley and the ship's doctor in reference to his questions and seeming interest in herself. "I felt sorry for Shirley. She was devastated when she learned he was gay."

Patty gasped. "Dr. Rowlin? That's hard to believe."

"His probing about me was obviously not based on romantic interest. So what was he up to?"

"Good heavens," Patty said, "do you suppose he's in league with the neo-Nazi gang?"

Ben shook his head. "If he is, there's a contradiction. White supremacists historically have had a low opinion—to put it mildly—of gays. Makes for an interesting scenario, right? I may nose around a bit and check this out.

"Well. We'd better go," he said to Patty. When they were standing, Ben addressed Tracy. "Thanks for sharing this information. I don't think there's going to be trouble. However, I am going to put in a call to my FBI contact, see if they have Garth under surveillance. Meanwhile, stay alert and scream like hell if you find yourself in a tight spot."

At the door, Patty took Tracy's hand. "I'm impressed with your courage and poise. If I'd gone through what you've experienced, I'd be a candidate for the loony bin."

"I suppose it's a matter of perspective, Patty. My focus had been on personal matters, including career options. Ben and I had talked about change, whether he might decide to work full time for the FBI, whether I should chuck what I do now to pursue a career in music or writing. Now all that counts is survival. I'm determined to get through this and if I do, the rest, God willing, will fall into place."

Patty released Tracy's hand. "Good for you," she said.

As they walked back to their cabin, Ben seemed caught up in thought, perhaps mulling over the latest turn of events. This was fine with Patty. She was up to her ears with Tracy and her problems and had no desire to delve into what might be construed as fact versus speculation.

One thing was clear. Ben and Tracy had discussed personal issues. Therefore, her assumption of an intimacy between them was bolstered. Being right, however, was a hollow victory, and darn it all, it rankled that Ben brought up the subject of a career change with Tracy before discussing it with his wife. Now she questioned her haste in supporting his arguments for change.

When they were back in the cabin, Patty found her sinus medication, and then moved lethargically to the closet.

Ben stood by the sofa. "Patty? Honey? I recall you were about to hit me with a proposal."

"I think I've had it with serious discussions for a while. Besides, I feel a sinus headache coming on."

"I'm sorry. Maybe you'll feel better by lunchtime. Or if you're not up to going out, we can order in."

Back in the investigative saddle again, he sounded so perky. "Sure, Ben, we'll see how it goes. Would you pull out one of the suitcases from under the bed?"

When he had done so, (she had eliminated 'please' and 'thanks' from her request), she expected him to return to his calculations. Instead, he remained standing. "I'm going to try to reach Tom. I think he's still at the San Diego office."

"Good idea," she said, trying to match his cheeriness.

It took a while to connect, and then Ben had to wait for Tom, who was not immediately available, to call back. In the meantime, Patty shook off her listlessness and plowed into packing.

Thirty minutes later the call came through. When Ben fell silent after giving his report, Patty wondered what Tom's response might be and felt a tingle of excitement, along with a boost in her energy level.

Now Ben was focusing on Dr. Rowlin, his lifestyle, his interest in Tracy. Ben placed his hand over the mouthpiece. "Tom's doing some checking. As for Tracy's early morning call, Tom thinks it was probably Garth. They've been monitoring his calls from a downtown Phoenix hotel, and it seems he's spewed out the party line to a number of prey."

"A busy boy, eh?"

"Hopefully, he'll soon be even busier making license plates or cleaning prison latrines." He removed his hand from the mouthpiece. "Yes, Tom."

Patty could sense from Ben's posture as he stood taller, and from the intensity of his gaze that Tom's 'checking' had produced results. Unfortunately, his nods and "uh-huh's"—except for one "I understand"—didn't furnish a clue as to what Tom had come up with.

"Tell me!" she said when Ben was off the phone.

He scratched his head. "There's not much to tell. Only that two doctors listed in the files practice medicine on cruise ships. One of the descriptions Tom gave me suggests it could be Dr. Rowlin."

"I'd say that's a good fit."

Ben shrugged. "It's all pretty vague. Our Dr. Rowlin was not spotted at the Acapulco meeting. Which may or may not be relevant."

"Does Tom think he's in cahoots with Jack Watkins?"

"It's a possibility." He looked toward the door. "I'm going to mosey on down to the clinic and take a look around."

His stance was far too casual, and when he'd sauntered out the door, Patty shook her head. Back to square one, darn it, with Ben holding back information. There had to be more, dammit. Why was he being evasive?

"Mine is not to reason why…" The stanza ran through her head. Crap. It might be a nifty refrain, a model for some people but not for her. Somehow, some way, she'd get him to open up.

She was the director, building the scene in her mind that would lead to Ben's revelations, starting from his entrance. She had taken the next step in creating dialogue, when the phone rang.

Shoot. "Hello."

"Patty, its Tracy."

"Ben's not here."

"That's okay. You'll do just fine. Shirley Goodweather called. She'd forgotten to mention Dr. Rowlin told her that his post cruise plans called for spending one night in L.A. then going to Phoenix. Another link with the bad guys, do you suppose?"

"Could be. I'll certainly pass on that information to Ben. Thanks, Tracy."

When they'd broken the connection, Patty grinned. Tit for tat, Ben.

The dialogue she'd created in her head was due for a re-write.

Joanne skipped breakfast, huddling under the covers until Jack returned from the Veranda Cafe. Only then did she drag herself from bed to move sluggishly about the cabin. "Do you want me to order you something from room service?" Jack asked.

"You'd do that for me? All right, maybe coffee, toast and melon slices."

When he'd finished placing the order, she said, "Jack, I'm sorry I created a scene. It must have been terribly embarrassing for you when I left the dinner table."

"Who am I trying to impress? Shirley? Tracy? As for Mr. know-it-all and his dopey wife, I couldn't care less."

"You're not furious with me over my actions?"

"While I don't support your standing up for our son, I understand the grief he's caused you."

You've caused us, she amended. But my God, Jack being conciliatory? "I think I'm feeling better already."

"Good. Let's enjoy our last day at sea. You know, we don't have to join the others at the dinner table this evening. We can order in, have a delicious dinner, just the two of us."

"I'd like that. And remember, we did talk about having cocktails on our balcony."

"I haven't forgotten. I'm sure it will be a memorable evening."

She did feel so much better. "Maybe I'd better start packing, get that out of the way."

"I'll do my part in a bit. First, I need to do some shopping. We're low on vodka and I'm out of shaving lotion."

When he'd left the cabin, Joanne felt suddenly downcast. Though Jack's surprisingly forgiving attitude had given her a lift, now she felt merely weary. The effects of her overindulgences were settling in, along with a gnawing sense of shame.

Still, she could count her blessings. That Jack had not chastised her or retreated from her was enough to make her day and the next week, as well.

Now to business. Where to start? The closets? Maybe the drawers. *The drawers.* Oh, God, what about the diary. Reluctantly, she turned her gaze to the desk. The black object she had seen or imagined she'd seen was not there. Now sober, she realized her concern about the diary should have been of little consequence. It was what else Jack might have found had he rummaged through her things that stopped her in her tracks.

All at once, she had trouble breathing, the air around her weighty and stale, as if she were drowning in dust.

It took only a few steps to reach the dresser, but she could have been crossing a vast desert. If the diary was not in its designated place, then something was amiss. Worse, if the information she'd copied turned up missing… She felt faint and clutched the back of a chair, her gaze traveling to the door. Jack could return any minute, and she had to know one way or another. She forced herself to move.

Ah. The diary was where she had placed it. Had she been delusional, creating a worst case scenario as a form of self-punishment?

She reached for the bottom drawer, and then paused as she felt a sudden overwhelming sense of panic. With shaking hands she gripped the drawer knob, but nothing moved. She tried again, and the drawer slid open to reveal everything in its place, a tiny edge of paper peeking out from under her evening slip.

She glanced toward the door, and then got down on her knees to hover protectively over the drawer's contents. She'd come this far, she had to be sure nothing was missing. Hurriedly, she retrieved the pages she'd copied, and then breathed a sigh of relief. Everything was in order, thank God. All of it. And then she noticed a smear at the bottom of the last page. In her hurry, had she made the smear?

Or had Jack?

"Good. You're back from the clinic," Patty said as Ben entered the cabin.

He gave her an expectant look. "What's up?"

"You tell me."

He looked confused. "What? Tell you what?"

"Ben! Stop playing games."

"*I'm* playing games?"

"All right. We're both playing games. I want to know about Dr. Rowlin and your visit to the clinic. In exchange, I'll tell you about Tracy's phone call." There, she had him. She could tell he'd switched gears.

He took her hand. "Patty, come sit down with me." He led her to the sofa. "I can't be completely honest with you for reasons that will become clear later. But I can confirm a definite tie-in with Watkins and Dr. Rowlin."

"And I can tell you Dr. Rowlin is off to Phoenix with the rest of the thugs." She related the phone call from Tracy. "How about that?"

He did not seem surprised; in fact his reaction to her news was a blank stare. Then he studied his shoes, before he said, "Here's a tidbit for you. Watkins didn't see me, but I spotted him leaving the clinic, carrying a small paper sack. I presume that whatever it contained was furnished by the good doctor."

"You think something sinister is afoot, that Jack obtained some sort of caustic substance or lethal ingredients to poison someone's drink?" She chuckled at the outlandishness of the idea, but she could see Ben was not amused. "On the other hand, Jack could have visited the clinic to pick up a medication for himself or Joanne."

"Your first hypothesis is a distinct possibility." He grinned. "So is your second suggestion." He patted her arm. "Okay. Let's continue with packing. You want me to start on the wardrobe suitcase or," he nodded toward the drawers, "gather my stuff together?"

"Ben, did you get in to see Dr. Rowlin?"

"Uh, he wasn't available. Maybe I'll try later."

He wasn't available, she thought, because except for emergencies, the clinic was closed at this hour. Jack got in, but Ben couldn't? If that wasn't an ominous sign, what was?

Ben started for the dresser, and then stopped. "Incidentally, I hope you weren't upset over Tracy's remarks about both of us wanting to make changes in the status quo. I wouldn't have said anything, but one comment led to another. It simply came out."

"You don't have to explain. I understand."

It was obvious he was relieved by her reaction. But she had let him off the hook for what essentially was not a big deal. Or so she tried to convince herself. That he brought it up at all was more of a diversionary tactic than an apology, she thought. Because he didn't want to talk about the Rowlin-Watkins alliance. Ah, but her curiosity was stretched to the limit. She could press him for details or wait it out.

So it was back to the script to draft Scene II. She would formulate it both ways and see what she came up with. It might be fun to try to outwit her husband.

It also was frustrating as hell.

❧ *Chapter Nineteen* ❧

Afternoon at Sea

Tracy viewed herself in the mirror. Was the strain of interrupted sleep and assorted terror tactics taking its toll? She'd felt spirited and fearless this morning when talking to Ben and Patty. Or had it simply been a matter of her adrenaline sprinting off the map?

Whatever was going on, she didn't want to run out of steam, nor did she want to appear panicked or fearful. What counted was to look her best for Marc.

All the more reason, she thought, to adopt a dapper, sporty look. Her navy blue and white top set off by gold buttons and worn over navy blue slacks was suitably nautical and appropriately casual for first and last night at sea.

She thought back to that first night on the ship and shook her head as she recalled how she'd questioned the wisdom of being on her own, how she'd fretted over the makeup of her assigned table. In retrospect, those concerns were so innocuous, indeed almost laughable in light of her present troubles.

As on that first night, champagne cooled in an ice bucket. In addition, Maria delivered a tray of hors d'oeuvres and a platter of mixed cheeses with crackers that Tracy placed on the coffee table.

She supposed Marc would be pleased with her impromptu party. Also a little food and drink would help to dispel any awkwardness between them. Who knows how they would view each other in the light of day? In fact, she would welcome a show of indifference from Marc, as it would make it easier to sever ties.

Yeah, really. She sat for a moment, and then jumped up to pace the room. How *would* he act toward her? Lovingly? Solemnly, in view of their having to part? With sophisticated nonchalance, a la Noel Coward? How about merely cordial or polite? Oh, no, scratch that one. She'd settle for lovingly.

Would he show up at all? What if he failed to appear?

Then all of this agonizing would be for naught.

At 2:00, the agreed upon time, she heard a soft rap on her door. Brushing aside her qualms, Tracy stepped briskly to the door, only to pause. "Who is it?" she called out.

"It's Marc."

It was his voice, yet she hesitated, opening the door only slightly. Then, breathing a sigh of relief, she ushered him into the stateroom.

He gave her a hug, and then held her at arm's length. "You look adorable. No, let's make that smashing."

She laughed. "Make up your mind."

"You want words or action?" He folded her into his arms.

"Whoa," she said, still laughing. "Slow down. Look. We have a celebration at hand."

He released her from his embrace. "How very, very nice." When they were seated, he turned to her. "May I ask what it is we're celebrating?"

"The moment," she said, remembering his words from last night.

Marc gave her a bemused look, and then nodded. "Let me pour the champagne."

When he had done so, they raised glasses, clinked, and then took a sip. "You look wondrously alive, so beautiful," he murmured.

"Good for me," she said softly.

He gave her a searching look. "Do I sense something is a little off?"

"Possibly, if you consider my night of nights, featuring the bad, the wonderful, and the horrible."

"At the risk of sounding conceited, I hope I was part of the wonderful."

With just the hint of a smile, she said, "I think I made that clear."

"If I follow you, then something happened after we parted."

"Yes, indeed." She told him about the threatening phone call and her subsequent conversation with Ben.

Marc looked grim, the corners of his mouth turned down, but then he pressed her hand. "I'll make it a point to escort you to and from dinner."

"Oh, Marc, that's sweet of you, but I doubt it's necessary."

"I insist. In the morning, the corridors will be full of passengers and crew. But we don't want to take any chances for tonight."

"Let's compromise. I'll go on my own to dinner. People will be everywhere at that time. Then, if you still insist, I'd welcome an escort after dinner."

"And I would welcome a moment alone with you."

"To say goodbye? I can't believe we're nearing that time." Good grief, her eyes were tearing. Quickly she busied herself with spreading cheese on crackers.

In the next hour as they passed the time sampling the goodies and drinking champagne, their conversation touched on shipboard life, travel, and the arts.

"Where will you go next?" Tracy asked.

"I'll need to confer with my agent. With the *Sea Star* line adding South America to their calendar, there's a strong possibility I'll be assigned that itinerary since I'm bilingual."

"It all sounds so romantic, so appealing. I can picture you at the piano, hear your music. I'll miss that."

He reached for her hand. "Despite what I said, that your world is out of reach for me, I'm fighting one hell of a battle not to give in to my feelings. Tracy, you have to know what happened between us was anything but a casual fling. I haven't stopped thinking about you."

"I'd say we're on the same wavelength." She thought for a moment. "I brought up the idea of a possible future connection if I were free." She shrugged. "Marc, I still don't know the answer to that. I seem to have pushed that issue aside."

"The marriage issue."

"Yes. It's almost funny. One of the reasons I came on this cruise was to sort out my priorities—in particular to examine my relationship with my husband. Then I get caught up with you. And the neo-Nazi creeps."

"Unforeseen circumstances, eh? Will you tell him about us?"

"I may." For a moment she fought tears, and then brightened. "If I survive this ordeal, which I have every intention of doing, I'll most certainly muster the strength to bring everything out in the open with Peter." She frowned as another thought intruded.

"What is it, Tracy?"

"The more I think about it, the more I have to ask myself—what if you hadn't been in the picture? What if Jack Watkins didn't exist? Would I know beyond the shadow of a doubt the direction my life should take? I don't think so. I don't think it's a matter of being flummoxed by events beyond my control.

"If you can stand a bit more philosophizing, let me add I've learned that while I can *ponder* my fate from a deck chair on a cruise ship, I can't *execute* decisions that will affect the rest of my life. Not without going to the source. Peter and I simply have to thrash things out."

"I can't argue to the contrary." Marc looked at his watch. "I need to get going, but first let me give you something." He reached into his pocket for his billfold and removed a card. "This," he said as he handed it to her, "is my permanent address in San Diego. I'll be home for several weeks before I head out to sea again. I'm affiliated with the Spanish Village Art Center in Balboa Park, so that should keep me busy."

"I've heard of that organization. Is this a language-related activity?"

"I'd say my Spanish comes in handy when I assume managerial duties. But I've also displayed my own work in ceramics and pottery."

"Why Marc, I had no idea. It seems you're multi-talented."

He winked. "I didn't want you to think I spend all my free time on the beach." He spread his hands. "I know I've worked hard to convince you I have nothing to offer, that I could never be a part of your life. Maybe I was trying to convince myself rather than you. At any rate, I wanted you to have this information in case…well, in case you wanted to contact me."

She took his hand and met his gaze, holding it. "We'll see, won't we?" she whispered.

"Yes." His voice was husky, and he had to clear his throat. He reached over to kiss her gently on the lips, and then was on his feet. "I'll see you later. Count on it."

All she could do was nod. And follow him with her gaze.

At the door, he turned back to smile at her, and then let himself out.

She thought of Peter, of their farewell in Acapulco when he looked as if he were memorizing her features. Marc had given her that same look.

She examined his card. He lived on Valencia Drive, a romantic name that befitted the man. Somehow she couldn't picture Marc residing on Horn Avenue or Sinkhole Place.

Later she'd see that Marc had a copy of her address. Her reasoning wasn't clear to her, but it seemed right for him to have this information.

If only she could fast forward the time, skip the evening and overnight hours. She wanted to be with Peter now to unravel the mystery of his whereabouts since Acapulco, to decide once and for all if they had a future together.

Chalk up an even more pressing reason for expediting her exit from the ship. How could she have forgotten for even an instant that her very survival was at stake?"

&

"I can't believe how fast the time is going," Joanne said to Jack. "I wish we could just keep on sailing."

"Think of the memories you'll have of Mexico and the ship. Have you been using the travel diary?"

"I really meant to keep a record, but somehow I never got around to it."

"Too bad. Well," he checked the time, "the meeting for disembarkation procedures starts in ten minutes. Are you coming with me?"

"No, I still have a little packing to do."

"I'm also going to stop at the purser's desk. I think they made an error on our account." He started for the door. "See you later."

When he was gone, Joanne tucked some miscellaneous items in along the sides of her suitcase, including the diary. That damn diary. It troubled her that Jack had brought up the subject. Still, it was possible she made too much out of his remark.

The diary had served its purpose, with the missing pages now concealed inside the book covers of two novels she'd placed at the bottom of the suitcase.

Joanne had to remind herself her act of betrayal was justified if it led to sparing the lives of innocent people. But in so doing, she had also bought her ticket to hell by placing her husband's life in jeopardy.

Of course, she could up the ante by making two anonymous phone calls—one to the authorities and another call to someone within the party to tip them off that the FBI was closing in. Either way she would save lives.

And either way she risked God knows what. No wonder she felt time closing in on her, pushing her to a place she'd rather not be. Too bad she couldn't stay on the ship forever.

She wished now she'd gone to the meeting with Jack. Sitting, standing, walking—nothing offered relief from her growing agitation. Would she ever be at peace? The answer was a qualified yes. The cocktail hour soon would be upon them.

She sighed. 'Soon' was the operative word, but it was so nebulous, so out of reach, yet full of promise. Of course, with Jack out of the cabin, she could easily sneak a shot of vodka.

She approached the cabinet where they stored their liquor and stared at the closed door. It would be so simple to satisfy her craving with one shot only. 'Soon' could very well be 'now'.

She blinked and stood back from the cabinet. What if she failed to stop at one shot, two shots? Her fall from grace would be obvious to Jack and demeaning to herself. Besides, she had a lovely evening to look forward to. She smiled. Maybe there was hope for her yet.

So, onward to something constructive. Her nails were a mess, in need of buffing, with the polish beginning to chip. She hunted in her carry-on bag, found her polish and brought it into the bathroom.

Whoops. Joanne grabbed onto the basin. They were experiencing some swells, a rolling motion, the kind that invited queasiness. She set the polish on the counter above the basin, and then carefully turned the top. Nuts. It was stuck. She brought the bottle to her chest, holding it firmly with her left hand, while with her right hand she twisted the top as hard as possible.

Too hard. It had opened all right, only to fly out of her hands, spilling the contents. Red blobs appeared everywhere, on the basin, the floor, around the bottom of the toilet.

She grabbed tissues to wipe up the mess and though she succeeded in mopping up most of it, a number of red stains remained. She needed a cleaning solvent. Maybe under the sink she'd find a cleanser or spray cleaner.

Hanging onto the counter as she felt another sustained rolling motion, Joanne squinted inside the cupboard and spotted toilet brush and extra toilet tissue. No help, so far. Then she noticed something in the far left corner. With some effort, she reached all the way in and brought out a small, white paper sack inscribed with SS, the ship's logo. Curious, she peeked inside to find a bottle about the size of the miniature liquor containers stored in hotel mini bars. She held it up to the light.

Good heavens, a warning label was posted, with the words Lethal-Poisonous. Could be it was a bug or weed killer, but it didn't make sense this deadly little package would randomly show up in their bathroom. Or did it make perfect sense? Dear God, what if Jack intended to spike Tracy's water, wine, or coffee with the contents of the bottle? Contents? Probably a drop or two would suffice.

Joanne thought of Jack's malice toward Tracy, how the mere mention of her name turned her relatively easygoing husband into a Jekyll--or was it Hyde?—mentality. At any rate, he changed, his features becoming pinched, his eyes more granite than blue, his face a bleak, icy mask. She hated that side of Jack, particularly when the words *Tracy* and *eliminate* appeared in the same sentence.

Still clutching the bottle, she dragged her gaze from it to her reflection in the mirror. Her face was chalky white, her expression registering horror.

For one crazy moment, Joanne thought of calling Tracy. What would she say? Don't come to dinner; you're about to be eliminated?

Then she remembered they had elected to dine in their cabin. And, glory be, it had been Jack's suggestion.

The color returned to her face, and she smiled at her image in the mirror. *Nice going, toots, getting worked up over nothing.* However, there still existed the mystery over the bottle. She placed it back in the sack and returned the package to the exact spot where she'd found it. She'd point it out to Jack later in the evening.

When Jack returned, he seemed energized. No, more than that. He seemed wired, she thought, as if girding up for whatever his role might be in the coming weeks, months or, however unlikely, even years.

The churning in her stomach was compounded by beads of sweat on her face as if she were experiencing a hot flash. Throw in motion sickness and she would be a total wreck. She had to pull herself together. Damn it, she owed herself an enjoyable final night at sea.

"I take it all is well with our account?"

"You bet. And it turns out disembarkation will be a snap. I'll go over the details with you later."

"We can talk about that on our balcony over cocktails."

"Good idea."

"In fact, we're getting close to that time. Maybe we'd better study the room service menu." She waited, but now he seemed preoccupied. "Jack?" She reached for the cabin directory. "If you like, I can read the dinner selections to you."

"I've changed my mind. I think we should join the others at dinner."

"I thought you were fed up with each and every one of them."

"I am. But why should we make way for them? We have every right to be served at that table."

"But Jack, we talked about a quiet dinner for two."

"Why do you sound so anxious?"

"I'm not *anxious*. It's simply that I'm…well, I'm embarrassed to have to face those people."

"Don't be. You're worth more than all of them put together."

Loving words, but the thrust of his chin, the narrowing of his eyes belied the sentiment. No question about it, they would join the others.

Lord help her, but she knew what she had to do.

"Ben, I swear you're going to wear a hole in the floor and we'll drop into the sea. Besides, I don't know how you can keep your balance with all this rocking. Sit, my darling."

"Sorry, Patty. How are you feeling?"

"Come sit down, and I'll tell you. There. That's better. How am I feeling? So-so. My darn sinuses are acting up again, which I guess is why I'm so grumpy. Now what's your story? Why are you acting like a caged animal?"

"Just thinking about the bad guys."

"The bad guys, huh? And Tracy?"

"Honey, you have to admit she's at risk."

"Maybe we're all at risk. I doubt Jack views any of us favorably."

"Patty, you're being unrealistic. Think of what Tracy's been through."

"I'm sick and tired of what Tracy's been through. *And* of Tracy. Oh, don't look at me like that. Don't shake your head!"

"Patty, calm down."

"I don't want to calm down. I'm feeling perfectly awful and at this moment, I don't like you very much. So why don't you go out for a drink and then on to dinner? I'll stay here and order something light."

"Okay. Whatever suits you."

The cabin seemed to sway, and she had to hang on to the furniture as she moved past him into the bathroom and shut the door hard. When she looked into the mirror, she saw her cheeks were flooded with tears.

❦ *Chapter Twenty* ❦

Last Night Out

Tracy ventured onto her balcony with low expectations. Could she tolerate wind, spray, and the roughness of an overactive sea? What she discovered was a relatively calm ocean. Moreover, though it was a bit of a stretch, she could downgrade the wind from turbulent to invigorating.

She stood now at the railing, enjoying in the waning light ripples of water in playful interaction, the accompanying whooshing sound like voices emerging from the deep to engage with the elements in a robust cocktail party.

Whimsy aside, her thoughts now centered on her own little party with Marc. That he acted toward her with warmth and affection had set the tone for a comfortable encounter, free of tension or awkwardness. The surprise of surprises was that he backed down from his adamant stand regarding their differences. And by giving her his card, he met her challenge with one of his own, a reality check that countered her ifs and maybes. Would she contact him? Only if she were separated from Peter.

The thought saddened her. Other variables loomed as well. Whether on her own or with Marc, did she have the guts to tumble out of her sunny environment? Could she embrace a lifestyle that differed from her upbringing, take a step down into a lower socioeconomic class? Not that it would necessarily result in that. After all, she had her own money. However, with or without Marc, as a single woman her life would change dramatically. Perhaps for the better. Perhaps.

Tracy shivered as the wind picked up, and now she clutched the railing as they hit a rough spot. Despite her earlier longing for the voyage to end, she would welcome entering into a state of limbo if it weren't for the threats on her life. Truth be told, she dreaded the showdown with Peter. More to the point, would she confess she had been unfaithful?

She started at the sound of her buzzer. Someone was at her cabin door.

Her pulse began to race as she approached the entryway. It could be perfectly innocent…Maria bringing fresh towels…a delivery meant for another cabin. Or it could mean trouble. Why take a chance? She decided to ignore the summons.

She turned her back on the door when the buzzer sounded again. Oh, what the hell. "Who is it?"

"Tracy, its Ben."

As before, she opened the door a mere crack, then all the way, and she invited Ben to enter. She could tell from his somber expression, the taut lines around his mouth that this was no social call. "Something's up. I can tell."

He nodded. "Could we sit for a moment?"

"Of course." She raised her hands, palms upward in a gesture of frustration. "Right now I'm so paranoid, I'm even forgetting my manners. I'm surprised Patty's not with you," Tracy continued when they were seated.

"Patty isn't feeling well. Her sinuses are bothering her, and she's a bit on edge."

Maybe more than a bit, Tracy thought, as she observed Ben's scowl. "Ha! That makes two of us. The edge part I mean." *Oh, my, how to put this diplomatically?* "Ben, I hope Patty's not upset over your stopping by. I suspect she feels I've leaned on both of you far too much. And she's right."

"Patty doesn't know I'm here because when I left our cabin, I had no expectation of seeing you." He went on to explain the change in their dinner arrangements, and that he'd been on his way to one of the lounges for a pre-dinner drink when he decided instead to try to find Dr. Rowlin.

"To cut this short," Ben said, "and without going into detail, I had been informed by an FBI friend of a connection between Jack Watkins and Dr. Rowlin."

"Aha. That explains his going on to Phoenix."

"I understand that's what he told Shirley. As for Watkins, earlier in the day I observed him leave the doctor's office within a time frame not generally available to patients. He carried a little white sack."

"Again, pardon my paranoia, but this little white sack business makes me nervous, particularly if he's in cahoots with the doctor. For me, Jack Watkins and sinister intentions go hand in hand." She paused a beat. "Okay, my friend, where do I fit into this scenario?"

"I was coming to that."

Tracy nodded for him to continue, but now he fell silent. Why did she feel a sudden chill? Probably because he looked so solemn, like the bearer of dire tidings. "Ben, talk to me. Please. I'm not about to kill the messenger. What about Dr. Rowlin? You said you wanted to find him?"

"I did come across him and as it turns out, he needs to speak with you. He's asked me to bring you to his office."

"Are you serious? I wouldn't be on the same deck with the man, let alone be in spitting distance."

"I think you'll change your mind if you'll only hear me out. What I'm about to reveal is extremely sensitive. It's essential you keep this information to yourself because if it were leaked, lives could be endangered. What you don't know, Tracy, is that Jim Rowlin is on our side. He's been working undercover for the FBI." Ben stood and gestured toward the door. "Shall we?"

As they made their way to deck 3, Tracy's head was spinning. How might reality fuse into illusion or vice versa? She remembered examining a surrealistic painting, a montage of masks denoting good and evil. Viewed at a certain angle, these traits appeared to intermingle, the focus on shared characteristics blurring the original intent.

And what about Ben? Could she trust him? Was he what he made himself out to be? Or was he leading her into a trap?

Ben must have sensed her hesitancy, if not her fears. "Tracy, I'm sorry if I've seemed overbearing. No one is forcing you to do anything against your will. We can always turn back. But I'm convinced it would be to your benefit to meet with Jim Rowlin. I think you know I care about your safety, that I care about you."

Was he trying to tell her his actions were not entirely altruistic? For a moment their eyes met and she could discern a warmth that in another time and place she might respond to.

She dropped her gaze. "You're very perceptive. I was having second thoughts about going through with this." She forced a smile. "I'm okay now. Let's proceed."

Dr. Rowlin greeted them in a courteous but businesslike manner, his expression devoid of even a hint of a smile. Tracy felt like a patient awaiting test results with the potential to yield devastating news.

"Please sit down," he said as they entered his office. "I thank you both for coming."

As he took his place behind his desk, Tracy stole a look at Ben. Had the doctor confided his purpose for asking to see her?

"Mrs. Bradshaw, I take it Ben has informed you I'm working undercover for the FBI?" At her nod, he continued, "As you can imagine, this is a very hush-hush situation. It's imperative we keep this information under wraps."

"I understand. My lips are sealed."

"Good. To explain my role—and I'll keep this brief—for the last eight months I've worked with the FBI and with infiltrators into white supremacist groups to build a false identity. Jack Watkins thinks I'm one of his kind and trusts me implicitly. Over the duration of the cruise, we've engaged in several discussions, and he's been open with me as to what he calls his mission. However, unbeknownst to him, I've taped every conversation. I'd like to play one of those tapes for you now."

While he set up the equipment, Tracy turned to Ben. "Do you have any idea what this is all about?"

"To a certain extent, yes." Ben shifted in his chair and looked away from her to gaze into space. When he turned back to her, his smile was apologetic. He started to say something, but then Dr. Rowlin signaled he was ready to begin.

Tracy recoiled as she heard Jack's voice. Past the so-called pleasantries, his tone changed from affable to serious.

And now his voice became strident as he spewed the party line. Why were they subjecting her to this garbage?

Then she heard her name. In seconds as she listened with mounting horror, the reasons for her presence became increasingly clear.

On the tape was a message: Tracy Bradshaw was marked for extinction.

Jack stood at their balcony railing peering out at the water. "It's definitely calmed down. At least for the moment." He turned and took his place next to Joanne. "I'd say it's quite pleasant out here. Wouldn't you agree?"

Joanne studied her drink. While Jack had been generous with the vodka, what remained now was mostly ice water. It was time for a refill.

"Joanne? You're certainly quiet this evening."

"Oh? You think so?"

"Maybe preoccupied is more descriptive."

"I was hoping you'd change your mind about going to the dining room."

"I don't understand why it means so much to you to dine in our cabin."

"I told you…"

"Oh, Joanne, no one's going to give you the evil eye because of your outburst. People can be very forgiving."

All right. He'd had his chance. She held up her glass. "Would you fix me another?"

"Gladly." He picked up his glass. "Seems I'm out, too."

"Before you go in, there's something I meant to tell you." She described her mishap with the nail polish, her discovery of the small package, her concern over its contents. "Do you know anything about this?"

He shook his head. "Very odd indeed. I'll take a look."

She almost believed him. With one drink under her belt, she'd mustered the courage to tell him about the bottle. Now she could only hope that disclosure of its lethal contents might deter him from taking action against Tracy.

When he returned with their drinks, it crossed her mind that Jack usually held off with his own refill until she was well into her second drink. He also seemed more chatty than usual, more willing to please. That she could consider any of this a bad sign mystified her. Still, she felt uneasy over these changes of behavior.

She waited, but he had not yet volunteered an opinion about the package. Instead, he seemed engrossed in the weather.

"Uh-oh. I think we're in for a change. That wind is suddenly up to no good. And will you look at those swells, Joanne. Can you feel the motion now?"

"Yes, but I'm fine. I did feel queasy earlier inside the cabin. Being outside does seem to help me. Jack, did you examine the bottle?"

"Yes, I did."

"Well?"

He shrugged. "Tis a mystery."

"It didn't simply walk in there by itself."

"I'll go along with that."

Oh, he was being insufferable, playing with her. Now if only she had the strength to carry out her intentions.

As they moved on to other subjects, Joanne waited for the second drink to imbue her with a sense of wellbeing, to make everything right with her world. So far these desired effects had not materialized, but maybe it was just as well. She needed to stay alert.

She'd give him one more chance to come up with a plausible explanation about the bottle, a convincing argument that he meant no harm, or she had no choice but to move forward with her plan.

"Jack, I want to talk to you about that bottle."

"What's there to discuss?"

"I think you're up to no damn good."

"*What* are you talking about?"

"I don't know how that bottle came into your possession, but I think you want to use it for evil purposes. Namely, to destroy Tracy. That's why you insist on going to dinner."

He threw up his hands. "This is ludicrous. You think I'm going to sit down at the dinner table, take out a bottle of poison and do away with Tracy?"

"What else can I think? How many times have you declared Tracy will be eliminated? And no, I don't picture the scene you just described. Of course not. But I think you have a plan."

"If that's the case, I wish you'd let me in on it. Your ideas might have merit."

"Now you're making fun of me."

"Joanne, you're way out of line. How about I fix you one more drink before we go to dinner."

It took every ounce of determination to respond lightheartedly. "Yes, I'd like that."

He'd hardly touched his second drink, which was all to the good because the pills would dissolve more quickly, or at least it would be less obvious his drink had been tampered with.

It was now or never. She glanced into the cabin, then withdrew two tiny sleeping pills from her skirt pocket and dropped them into his drink. Small but powerful, she mused. One tablet alone worked for her. But two mixed with liquor? It would knock him out, and then she would grab that little sucker from under the sink and toss it into the ocean.

Jack was back, and with a flourish set her drink on the table. "Let's toast our last night at sea," he said.

They raised glasses, and Joanne was glad to see Jack drink deeply. She wondered if the effects from the pills would be immediate. Possibly it would take a little time.

Once again, they engaged in small talk. She purposely avoided any mention of Tracy, concentrating instead on mundane matters, like catching up on the mail once they were home, the necessity of filling their pantry, of setting up dental appointments, and the like.

From under hooded eyes he watched her. "How are you feeling?" he asked.

"Not very well, but if I go inside, I'll feel the motion more."

"Let me take your glass. There's a drop or two left, and then we can dispose of the bottle."

In seconds he was back. He handed her the glass, then sank down heavily into his chair.

"Cheers again," he said.

He closed his eyes, and then opened wide. "Strong stuff," he muttered as he tasted his drink.

The water was becoming increasingly choppy, and Joanne shut her eyes against wind that brought droplets of water to her face and arms. Raindrops now spattered the railing and deck.

"I don't know why I feel so groggy," Jack said. His words were slurred and his eyelids were at half-mast.

He was almost under, praise God. She had pulled it off and felt the gratification over mission accomplished, over taking matters into her own hands for once in her life. This boded well for future successes. As for owning up to her misdeeds, she'd simply have to tell her husband there had been no other choice.

"I think we're heading into a storm," Joanne said, raising her voice. She waited for a response, but Jack's chin now rested on his chest.

She almost fell as she maneuvered around Jack's outstretched legs to enter the cabin. The drinks were getting to her, she thought. Between the booze and trying to maintain her balance against the roll of the ship, it was rough going. But she had to get to that bottle, especially as she didn't know how long Jack would be out.

Once inside, she started for the bathroom, only to stop midway. The bottle, out of its sack, rested on Jack's nightstand. How brazen. What was he thinking?

Her heart thumped in her chest, competing with the rasp of her breathing as she snatched up the bottle, and then made her way outside.

The rain was moderate, but driven by the wind, it soaked her as she stood at the railing. She raised her arm, bottle in hand, and then hesitated as she heard something like the scraping of a chair against wood.

Joanne gasped as she felt Jack's hand bring down her arm with an iron grip and seize the bottle. Good God, despite the pills, determination or desperation, abetted by the wetness and a bracing wind, had kicked in to restore partial consciousness.

She grasped at his hand. "You can't kill Tracy," she shouted.

On his feet, Jack staggered toward her and shoved the bottle into her face. "You need…little more. Yes, little bit more."

She fell to her knees and covered her face with her hands.

"Thas good . . . going under . . . enjoy last cocktail, Joanne."

She could barely make out his words. Something about going under? A last cocktail?

He hovered over her, and then lost his footing so that he was on his knees at her side.

The bottle seemed to take on a purpose of its own, first dangling from Jack's fingers, then dropping onto the deck where it rolled in the direction of the balcony railing. Instinctively, Joanne reached out and retrieved it, but Jack slapped it out of her hand.

With a lurch of the ship, he placed his hands on the deck to steady himself. Now on all fours, he thrust back his head, taking in great gulps of air.

Joanne whimpered, calling on God to protect her. It didn't matter anymore about the bottle. She wanted out of the wet and cold. She wanted the warmth and safety of the cabin. She tried to get to her feet, and then froze as part of the balcony railing gave away.

She yelled out a warning and once again attempted to stand, but Jack, moving sluggishly, pushed her down, pinning her to the deck.

In the limited space, they now were a tangle of bodies. "Get off of me, Jack. Let's go inside. Can you hear me? Are you awake? Move, damn it; the railing's broken."

He grunted something she couldn't understand. What was he doing? His hands were at her throat, only to slip to her shoulders. Oh, my God, he was shoving her toward the edge of the deck where the railing had come apart.

She had a sense of water everywhere—dripping on her from above, a vast bottomless cavern awaiting her below. She grabbed a table leg, resisting Jack, fighting against the pitch of the ship, and screamed with all her might.

Then darkness enveloped her.

ᶜ᷍ᵔᵕ *Chapter Twenty-One* ᶜᶠᵕ

Last Night Out

Patty was in a hurry. She'd dallied over her hair, rearranging the sides and back and had spent too much time erasing tears and covering blotchy skin with fresh makeup. Despite her efforts, her hair remained limp, but she'd brought a semblance of the old Patty to her mirror.

Given the circumstances, Ben might not care that she'd taken pains with her appearance, but looking smart made her feel a heck of a lot better.

Not that she was free of discomfort, but to languish in the cabin while Ben dined with the others—all right, with Tracy—was untenable. Besides, showing up for dinner would serve as a bridge to later in the evening where in the privacy of their cabin she was determined to swallow her pride and apologize for her behavior.

The lime green pantsuit she wore was a favorite of Ben's, but it nagged her that something about the outfit was incomplete. Ah, what it needed was the Bustamente sunburst design she'd bought in Cabo San Lucas.

Shoot, had she packed it away? Probably, but she made a frenzied search through her carry-on luggage, her closet and drawers, to no avail. Was this a foreshadowing of disaster in the making? Images flashed through her mind of standing before the mirror, holding the piece of jewelry to her chest, of Ben coming up behind her to kiss her neck, and for a moment she felt a welling of frustration over events that led to her present sorry state.

Whoa! She clutched the back of a chair to maintain her balance. Wearing high heels when the ship performed its own version of rock and roll was probably a no-no, but darned if she'd play dwarf to Tracy's model-like stature.

A quick check in the mirror, and Patty charged out of the cabin. With the aid of corridor railings, she headed for the elevators, granting no leeway for a change of heart.

Ben would be forgiving. He had to forgive her. The words

echoed in her mind, an incantation that by its urgency and repetition would make this so.

Now as Patty neared the ship's dining room, she braced herself for the usual crush of passengers lined up for dinner. Except there was no line-up. Where was everyone?

Once inside, she noted waiters standing in small groups, seemingly oblivious to the few people who occupied tables.

She stretched her neck to search for Ben but didn't see him. Surely he'd show up for dinner. Possibly, he'd stopped at the cabin to check on her. She made a face and muttered, "Wishful thinking."

At least she wouldn't be alone. She spotted Shirley Goodweather seated at her usual place. As Patty approached, Shirley raised her hand in a half-hearted greeting. She looked as if she'd downed one too many margaritas or martinis, whatever it was she drank.

Patty smiled brightly at Shirley as she took her place. "Just the two of us, eh? So far, that is. I'm sure Ben will be along any minute."

Shirley looked puzzled. "I passed Ben in the passageway on my way here. I don't know where he was headed, but it was away from the dining room." She gave Patty a speculative look. "Maybe I shouldn't say this, but he looked like he'd lost his best friend."

Patty's hands flew to her neck, fingers prodding in search of the missing sunburst pendant. Was he that upset with her? Had she compromised her marriage?

She rested her hands in her lap, fingers entwined, a bit of stage business to signal composure. "As far as I know, Ben planned to come to dinner. In fact, I urged him to go ahead even though I'd decided not to venture out of the cabin." She explained about feeling unwell, but that she'd perked up enough to change her mind, this about-face occurring after Ben had left.

However convoluted her explanation, it was the best she could do. Shirley, for her part, seemed distracted, her gaze traveling here and there about the room. "I don't think we're moving," she said finally.

"We've stopped?" Patty looked about her. "I think you're right. But why?"

At once, Shirley became more animated. "You haven't heard the rumors? My Gawd, girl, they say a lot of passengers are sick, that the ship may be quarantined. But then I ran into Trudy, and she told me a police boat brought criminal investigators on board."

"Good heavens." Patty scanned the entryway. No sign of Ben, but more people entered the dining room, so maybe Shirley's information was erroneous. Still, there had to be an explanation as to why the ship had come to a standstill. "If I can catch Julio's eye, it's possible he knows something. Oh, good, he's coming our way."

"Señora Redford, Señora Goodweather, will it be just the two of you this evening?"

Shirley shrugged.

"Your guess is as good as mine."

"Oh, I shouldn't think so," Patty said. "Surely the others will be coming soon. Let's wait a bit longer. Uh, Julio, we're wondering, is there some sort of emergency?" She lowered her voice. "We're not moving and we've heard some pretty wild rumors." She gave him an encouraging if apologetic smile. "I don't mean to put you on the spot."

"It's okay, ma'am." He moved closer to them and spoke softly. "We've been told a woman fell overboard, that they couldn't rescue her. It's not, how do you say, official, but that's what the staff has heard. Now, if you'll excuse me."

"Holy cow!" Shirley's eyes widened, her mouth agape.

Patty stared at Julio's retreating figure. "Good lord, I hope it's not anyone we know—not that it matters whether we know or don't know this poor soul. It's just that…" She was babbling and not making any sense. And then it hit her. "Oh, my God, what if it's Tracy?" And if it were? Patty felt the deep flush of shame suffuse her face. Ben might never forgive her petty jealousy.

Shirley grabbed her hand. "Patty, you look terrible. What is it? Don't have a stroke, for God's sake. I know Tracy's been threatened, but it could be anyone. Besides, Julio said the woman *fell* overboard, not that she was pushed or thrown. This person could have been drunk or on drugs, maybe LSD. Some of these wacked-out druggies think they can fly." She made a swooping gesture with her arm.

"So I've heard. Whatever the case, we need reliable information." Now as more people entered the dining room, Patty half rose to see if Ben was among the arrivals. If not, she would search for him.

There! She'd spotted him. He stood in the doorway and as he caught her eye, he motioned for her to join him. "Shirley, I see Ben, but I don't think he's coming to the table. I hate to leave you alone, but I don't know what he has in mind."

"Go, for goodness sakes. If you're not back and no one else shows up, I'll head over to the Veranda Café." She winked. "Could be I'll hook up with Super Hunk or a prince in disguise." She laughed. "Yeah, in my dreams."

Patty was already out of her chair and on her way. When she was close enough to judge Ben's demeanor, her heart sank. He looked grim— or was it anger that made him glower?

She rushed to his side. "I can't tell you how terrible I feel about the way I acted. I don't know what came over me. Can you ever, ever forgive me?"

"Honey, it's okay. You're still my girl." His expression softened, but his tone was anything but lighthearted. "Let's step away from the door."

She followed him to the area where they'd stood in conference with Tracy.

Patty blinked back tears. "I came to dinner with the idea of trying to soften you up, so that you might accept my apology."

"Sweetheart, I told you its okay. There are more serious matters at hand."

"Oh my, yes. Something strange is going on. We've heard some ugly rumors." She repeated what Shirley had told her, which in turn led them to question Julio. "He said his staff had been informed a woman fell overboard to her death. Ben, is it true?" She sucked in her breath. "Please don't tell me it's Tracy." When he didn't answer, she persisted. "Is it Tracy?"

He shook his head.

"Then who? You obviously know more than you're letting on."

He nodded, and then placed a hand on her shoulder. "Why don't you come with me?"

Dr. Rowlin looks tired, Tracy thought, as tired as she felt. He'd brought in an extra chair so that now the three of them—she, a bewildered looking Patty, and a solemn-appearing Ben—faced him as he presided over their little group from behind his desk.

"I think we'll be more comfortable if we proceed on a first name basis. That okay with you, Patty?"

"Yes, yes, of course, Dr. Rowlin."

He smiled briefly, then continued, "Your husband wanted to include you in what I'll call our post-crisis discussion. Has he explained I've been wearing two hats, one as the ship's doctor and the other as an undercover agent for the FBI?"

"I filled her in on the way here," Ben said. "I also told her about the meeting Tracy and I had with you earlier."

Patty's expression registered consternation, though edged with compassion. "Good Lord, Tracy, it simply boggles the mind that this man had set out to...to take your life."

"As you can imagine, what I heard on the tape put me in a state of shock. It's bad enough to talk in the abstract about the act of killing, but when the discussion centered on Jack's plan to poison me, I freaked out."

"Oh, my dear, I can't even find the words..." Patty did indeed seem speechless. Tracy gave her a sympathetic smile—it was almost as if Patty was the victim—and then focused on Jim. These past hours must have been extremely stressful, yet as he straightened, then leaned in toward them, his fatigue seemed to lift. It was his show, by golly, and he would wield command over a rapt audience that included herself, even though she knew the outcome of today's events.

"My relationship with Jack," Jim began, "was predicated on mutual trust, which meant I had to pretend to espouse his ideology, however repugnant to me. And toward that end, we agreed to take whatever action was necessary to further the cause." He waved his hand in a gesture of dismissal. "You know the background, so I don't have to lecture you on the kind of irrational reasoning that justifies killing and maiming.

"Anyway, the demented can be clever. Jack led me to believe that Tracy was in imminent peril, while all along it was his wife he intended to do in."

Patty gasped. "But why?"

212

"What we've gathered is that Joanne had become a liability. She was emotionally unstable, and because she drank too much, he probably feared she would spill his dirty secrets to the wrong people. Because she could not be trusted, his only recourse was to get rid of her.

"I suppose he figured that while I'd provide him with the means to kill Tracy, I might draw the line at doing away with his wife, hence the charade.

"At any rate, what we've pieced together is that from the outset of the trip, Jack had established a plan. He made sure they booked a balcony cabin and encouraged Joanne to drink so that family wounds surfaced, leading to public outbursts that showcased her unsteadiness, her instability.

"His plan was to poison her drink, and when she was lifeless, shove her overboard—all this made easier by a broken railing. In this scenario, he would report her missing amid claims he had not been with her when she disappeared. And when questioned, he would attest to her progressive deterioration in body and mind, as witnessed by others.

"However, a fierce struggle took place between the two of them."

Patty looked confused. "If she was poisoned, how could she put up a fight?"

Ben turned to his wife. "She wasn't poisoned. What Jim mixed in that bottle was a harmless concoction of water mixed with a mild mouthwash to give it a little color."

Jim nodded. "A drop or two was supposed to do the trick, so that any change of color in Joanne's drink would be minuscule."

Patty shuddered. "So she knew what was going on."

"Indeed," Tracy said. "I'm next door to them, and I heard her screams."

"The bastard," Patty said. "At least he'll get his due." She wiped away tears. "I feel so bad about poor Joanne."

Jim's expression turned grave. "She's in for a rough go."

Patty looked at Ben, then back at Jim. "Wait a minute. What do you mean?"

"The woman-overboard story was a false assumption based on

213

rumor. Joanne is sedated and resting in the infirmary. Remember I said there was a violent struggle? Jack is the one who went overboard."

No one spoke, and then Ben stirred. "Jim, you stated earlier the balcony railing was broken?"

"Right. Jack apparently had an accomplice—a crew member, we think—who cleaned the outside windows and deck, and in the course of his duties, disabled the railing. I suppose after the deed was done, Jack planned to contact this person to repair the damage."

"Sounds feasible," Ben said, "but I'm not clear as to how Joanne could have survived over Jack."

Tracy felt a boost in her energy level. "My turn," she said. "I talked with Joanne before she was sedated." She explained how Joanne, out of desperation, had doctored Jack's drink with sleeping pills and her motive for doing so. "Unfortunately, the pills were only partially effective. At the height of their fight, Joanne remembers hanging on to a table leg, kicking at Jack, screaming. She's vague about the rest but thinks at the time he was trying to push her overboard. She hit her head and blacked out for a few seconds. She has a fuzzy recollection of Jack losing his balance and letting go of her when the ship pitched sharply."

"And in his drugged state," Jim continued, "he could have become disoriented, grabbing onto thin air where the railing had broken."

"In any case," Tracy said, "I called the emergency number when I heard the screams."

Jim looked at his watch. "At this point, the search and rescue operation is in its search phase only. Let's see, we've all, with the exception of Patty, been interviewed by the authorities. I turned over my tapes to them, and they have Jack's briefcase. That, my friends, yielded a gold mine of information relating to people and properties earmarked for annihilation in Phoenix. So I'd say everything is under control, though we'll be delayed in arriving in L.A. tomorrow. And Tracy, I think you can rest easy now that Jack is no longer in the picture."

"Amen to that," Patty said. She turned to Tracy. "You talked with Joanne. What in the world will she do when the ship docks?"

"When I was with her, she was so shaken..." Tracy paused a moment to steady herself. "Sorry, but when I think how she tried to protect me—" She took a deep breath. "To answer your question, she'll be with family. I stayed with her while the purser assisted her in reaching her daughter, who in turn admitted she knows the whereabouts of her brother. The daughter and her husband will be at the dock to meet Joanne. Whether or not her son shows up, at least he'll be informed of the situation before he reads about it in the newspaper."

"She'll need the support of her family," Ben said. "I assume she'll be detained for questioning, have to make a statement, and so forth."

Jim rotated his shoulders, and then leaned back in his chair. "All of the above," he said.

Ben raised his eyebrows at Jim. "It's been quite a run for you. Are you tempted to make a full time career out of chasing down the baddies?"

Jim laughed. "Hell no. After tomorrow I'm going back to practicing medicine full time. When I take a cruise, it'll be for fun, just like for you folks." As they laughed, he rose. "I'm going to check on Joanne, then get a bite to eat. I suggest you do the same."

Ben looked at his watch, and then turned to Patty. "I think we're still okay for the dining room. Want to chance it?"

"By all means. Tracy? Will you join us?"

She was in no mood for making conversation or rehashing today's events. She smiled. "Thank you, but no. I'm going to call room service, then curl up with my journal." She raised her hand to cover her yawn. "I'm sure I'll relish a good night's rest."

"Won't we all?" Ben agreed, and with that, they went their separate ways.

In the Veranda Café, Shirley sat at one of the coveted window tables, though it was too dark outside to enjoy the view. She sat alone, but felt okay about that. The cafeteria-like setting didn't exactly rattle her romance antenna. Besides, the men going through the buffet line were too old or too young, and scruffy to boot.

The captain's announcement that a man had gone overboard relieved her of any concerns about Tracy, but she still didn't know who the victim was or the circumstances surrounding the tragedy. However, she was determined to get the skinny on what really happened, because once home, people would line up to hear her version of events.

Boy, would it ever be good to get back with friends and acquaintances and also to return to work. She imagined another conversation with Jodie:

"So, Shirley, did you meet Mr. Right?"

"No, Jodie, I met two Mr. Wrongs which, as we all know, do not make a Right."

"Too bad. I know you had high expectations."

"Yeah, but you know? I'm heads above the jerks I got involved with. And I've learned something. I don't have to settle for just anyone. Where is it written you have to have a man in your life? Oh, sure, it would be nice, and God knows I miss the sex, but I'm going to hold out for someone decent, a person who will respect me, value my opinions, love me for who I am…"

She looked up, aware now that someone stood over her.

"May I join you?"

It was Dr. Rowlin. He held a tray with a main entrée dish, salad, and coffee.

"Of course." Damn, but he was so nifty looking, so clean cut.

"I see you're about finished with dinner."

She pushed her plate aside. "I haven't had dessert yet, and I'd enjoy some company." As he took a place opposite her, she said, "Gosh, it's been quite an evening. I'll bet you've been up to your ears in whatever it is that's going on."

He nodded. "It's a big story, all right, but for now I've had enough high drama. I just want to relax." He tasted his meat, and then looked up. "Tell me about you. Have you been happy with the cruise? Did you like Mexico?"

He appeared to enjoy her recital of events, laughing at her exaggerations. Of course, she edited out her misadventures.

"I must say, Shirley, you're a breath of fresh air. I like your vitality and," he paused, "other things about you."

He couldn't mean physical? Oh, well, gay men could be fantastic company, even if it stopped short of a romp in the hay.

When he'd finished his meal, they went together to the buffet to select their desserts, and then returned to the table. He was so attentive, so darling, she hated to see it all end.

"Jim..."

At her hesitation, he grinned. "That's what my parents named me."

"Okay. I wanted to say that, uh, regardless of circumstances, I'd be delighted for you and your partner to contact me when you're in Sacramento. It would be my pleasure to show you both around."

"That's very generous of you. When you brought up Dr. Edlemann, I appeared, for reasons I don't care to explain now, not to have heard of him. That couldn't be farther from the truth. I supervised his residency at Los Angeles General Hospital, and I have great respect for his abilities.

"As for having a partner, I used that as a ruse to avoid any entanglements. I think I owe you an explanation, but I'd like to save that for when we get together in Sacramento. A deal? Shirley?"

She swallowed hard, and then had to clear her throat. "Doctor, I mean Jim, any time. Yes, it's a deal."

"I'm due up your way next month. See you then?" He rose. "I have to check on a patient." He paused, and then said, "I'm sorry I misled you, but I'd like to think it was for the greater good."

All she could do was nod as he made his way out of the café.

She'd tone down her voice, her gabbiness, lose weight, and learn to be classy.

And then the frantic voice within her head subsided into a seductive whisper. Maybe, just maybe, Jim Rowlin liked her exactly the way she was.

Julio had been extra-accommodating, Patty thought, providing her and Ben with a full meal, wine included. Throughout dinner, they discussed the events that led to Jack's death, as well as Joanne's terrible ordeal, her dubious future.

Now as they sipped their wine while waiting for dessert, it was time to get personal. "I'm glad we're alone," Patty said. "With all that's been going on, I haven't made you a decent apology. I'm truly ashamed of myself, and I'm asking for your forgiveness."

Ben smiled at her with the old warmth. "You felt lousy, and I was anything but attentive to you, so the score is about even. I'll accept your apology if you'll accept mine."

"That goes without saying." She leaned over to kiss his cheek.

He thought for a moment. "Remember when you stated you had a proposal for me? Did we ever finish that conversation?"

How could we, with Tracy in constant distress? "No," she said, "but I suppose now is as good a time as any." She took a sip of wine, then held up her hands and stretched out her fingers. "I'd like to start with a little background, so let's count. I'm active in little theater, a member of Symphony League, in an art guild, belong to a bridge and book club, and am a Red Cross volunteer."

"Impressive."

"Maybe, but I've spread myself thin, flitting here and there, and I suspect I come across as capricious, a butterfly, even shallow. But through all this, I've worked hard to foster the arts."

Ben pressed her hand. "What you're doing is commendable. Don't sell yourself short."

"Thank you, my darling, but I'd like to take this a step farther." She took a deep breath. "As you know, before we married I was an administrator at George Washington University. What I propose is to return to the work force. I want to secure a paid position in one of the arts fields as a professional fundraiser." She peered questioningly at her husband, but his expression reflected neither approval nor disapproval. "I have the energy, the contacts, I'm knowledgeable, people-oriented, and I know my way around Washington, DC. Well? What do you think?"

"I think you've just stated what should be included in your résumé. And I think you'd do a terrific job." He raised his glass. "Let's drink to your success."

And to independence, she added silently. She would have Ben's respect as well as his love.

Thank the Lord, they were back in step again. She could sense Ben's devotion to her, feel his love. But deep down, she understood that his obsession over Tracy's welfare went beyond the risk factor. There existed an underlying attraction, at least on Ben's part.

She smiled as desserts were placed before them, but her good cheer was occasioned not by food, but by thoughts of the future. Ben would start a provocative new career, and she would venture into a world of meaningful pursuits, pay included. She knew better than to expect immediate results in her quest, but her love of music and the arts would ease the rocky path toward attaining her goals.

Best of all, Tracy would be out of their lives for good.

Maria provided room service, bringing Tracy's dinner, and then removing the dishes. Now Tracy felt not only comfortably full but blissfully safe for the first time in days.

As for tomorrow, let the chips fall where they may. Oh, my, such brave words, but at least she had gained some insight into her situation; namely, that the complexities called for more than reflection on whether she should start a new life. She had to be open with Peter regarding her dissatisfactions and frustrations. And that was only for starters.

She yawned and glanced at her watch, then thought, *why rush to turn in?* The delay in reaching port would provide for a leisurely morning. She picked up her journal, and then set it down. Were they moving? Finally? She started for her balcony to investigate, and then stopped. She thought she heard a knock on her door.

Slowly, she approached the entryway. Maybe it was her imagination. No, the silence was now broken by a soft rapping sound. Instinctively, she drew back. The danger was past, and yet—

She opened the door a fraction, then all the way. "Marc! Come in."

There was a sense of urgency about him. When the door was shut, he grabbed her hands. "Tracy, I had to see you."

She nodded. "Come, let's sit down." When they were settled, she said, "I'm sorry if you were looking for me in the dining room, but I didn't make it to dinner. I just wasn't up to it."

He drew his fingers through his hair. "It wouldn't have worked out anyway. I've been tied up in staff meetings, and then we musicians were instructed to be at our posts to provide a sense of normalcy." He smiled for the first time. "But that's beside the point. When I heard the rumor of a woman overboard, I practically went into cardiac arrest. I was beside myself. I looked for you everywhere."

"I was with Joanne Watkins after she was rescued and then with Dr. Rowlin and others at a meeting in his office." She explained how Joanne sought to protect her, and without giving away too much, the doctor's role in keeping her out of harm's way.

Marc took her hand, gently this time. "When we learned what really happened, I almost broke down, I was so relieved you were safe."

She felt tears forming. "Thank you for caring."

"There, you see? I do care." His tone was light and his eyes twinkled, but then he gathered her into his arms. "I need to hold you for a moment." Slowly he released her, and then kissed her softly on the lips. "I don't want to leave, but I must."

"You're on break?" she asked.

"Unfortunately, time is about up."

"Wait a minute." Tracy moved swiftly to the desk and wrote out her address and phone number. She handed him the slip of paper as he got to his feet.

At the door he said, "I'm grateful we've had these few moments alone."

"I am too, Marc." She raised her arms. "A hug goodbye?"

As they embraced, he drew her tightly to him. "I don't know if this goodbye is for now only or forever." He drew back and placed his hands on her shoulders, holding her gaze. "What I do know with every certainty, Tracy, is that I've fallen deeply in love with you."

He didn't wait for a response but was out the door.

❦ *Chapter Twenty-Two* ❦

Late Tuesday Morning: In Port

"I'm glad you called first," Joanne said as she opened her cabin door to Tracy. "Obviously, I'm not ready to face my public." The raw sound that escaped from her throat stopped short of a laugh. "Please come in. I do want to thank you for being with me when I was trying to reach my family. "

Tracy's response was a sympathetic smile, coupled with a gesture of dismissal, but as she entered the cabin, Joanne noted her visitor's pallor, the shadows beneath her eyes. Still, there could be no comparison to what a fright she must look.

Joanne motioned for Tracy to take the sofa, while she sat on the chair opposite. How strange, she thought, not to see Jack in his usual place, the briefcase with its sinister contents at his feet.

Tracy reached into her purse. "I've written out my address and phone number. I'd like for us to stay in touch."

Joanne accepted Tracy's offering, and then pulled a card from her bag that she handed to Tracy. "It's all there, though you'll have to scratch out the Lt. Col. part. And yes, I would like to stay in touch."

Tracy's eyes widened, containing her tears. "I can only imagine what you're going through."

"I'm not sure what it is I'm going through. I suppose I should be thankful I'm alive." She pressed the back of her hand to her forehead. "Beyond that, I can't seem to think very clearly"

"You spent the night in the infirmary?"

"Yes and Dr. Rowlin checked me out this morning. I don't have a concussion or broken bones. I'm sore, though. You can see the bruises." She held out her arms. "Oh. Dr. Rowlin told me someone snitched on the crew member who assisted Jack, so he's been turned over to the police."

"Accessory to attempted murder? I should hope so."

"If there's a bright spot, it's that the authorities have Jack's briefcase. Now they know about the carnage that was supposed to be

221

carried out in Phoenix." She went on to explain how she'd hoped to thwart their actions. "I'd like to think I'd have had the courage to follow through with my plan."

"Good heavens, Joanne, I marvel at the measures you took to protect me from Jack. Talk about courage."

"What I *thought* were his murderous intentions toward you, yes, while all along…" She couldn't articulate the words. It was like drawing a shade to block out ugly, vile scenes that defied description. But the shade was beginning to inch up, light eclipsing shadow, to reveal acts of deceit and cunning.

"I tried to be so careful, but I think Jack discovered the pages I'd copied out of his briefcase. Not that he would have let on, but I suppose that could have been the deciding factor in…in determining my fate."

The shade snapped all the way to the top. "How could I have been so clueless? There were signs of trouble I simply ignored. Implied threats, for one." She bowed her head, and then looked Tracy in the eye. "I know I have a drinking problem. Jack knew it too, but he encouraged me to drink, always ready to fix me one more. If I overindulged, he didn't try to stop me. Instead, he advertised the fact I'd had one too many or that I was under the weather—how I hate that phrase—pretending in front of others how concerned or disturbed he was over my condition.

"He set me up!" The words ripped through protective layers of numbness induced by shock, exposing her to the glare of hard core reality. Her husband was a monster, a man so obsessed with his cause that he would turn on his own wife.

"All those years we had together." Her voice softened in remembrance. "Don't you think that should have meant something to him?"

"To a normal man, yes."

"God knows *I* wasn't perfect. Military life was hard for me. But I was a good wife, Tracy, a good mother."

She clenched her fists and bit down hard on her lower lip, but nothing staunched the sudden flow of tears, her racking sobs.

Tracy was at her side, bending over her, a consoling arm around her shoulders. "It's good you're letting it out. Grief is part of the healing process."

Grief? For a fiend? For a man who would poison her, then throw her to the sharks? Shudders coursed through her upper body. God help her, but she had to get a grip on herself. She forced herself to take shallow breaths, and soon her sobs gave way to a spasm of hiccupping.

Tracy stood back from her, looking sad and teary eyed. "I hate to leave you, but I should get over to the showroom." She held up a green ticket. "Can't leave the ship without presenting this, and I don't know when they'll call my color. On the other hand, if you're ready to move out of the cabin, I'll stay with you for as long as possible."

Joanne left her chair to hunt for a tissue, dabbed at her eyes and blew her nose. "That's kind of you, Tracy, but I'm to be personally escorted off the ship. I'm told I'll be interviewed by the port authorities, sign a statement, and whatever else is necessary. Thankfully, my daughter and her husband can be with me."

Joanne accompanied Tracy to the door, and then reached to squeeze her hand. "You're a very dear person."

Tracy gave her a chin-up kind of smile. "Joanne, we're survivors. We're both alive, and that counts for one hell of a lot."

Joanne could only nod as she felt her throat close off, her vision become blurred by tears.

When Tracy closed the door behind her, Joanne wiped away her tears as Tracy's words echoed in her mind. True, they both had survived. But if she hadn't set out to protect Tracy by attempting to incapacitate Jack, she would have died, unable to fend off her husband.

This realization caught her off guard, and she had to sit down as she contemplated cause and effect in the grand scheme of things. For these few moments she was lifted out of her misery as the full implications of her good deed set in.

Minutes later, a sharp knocking on her door brought her to her feet. It was time to go, and she quickly gathered up her things.

Now, as she moved down the corridor with her escort, Joanne thought again of Tracy. How was it that some people had it all—beauty, wealth, intelligence, a loving husband?

No doubt about it, Tracy was blessed, for she led the perfect life.

In the showroom, Tracy secured a chair away from chattering groups and other waiting passengers as Joanne's anguish played out in her mind.

Despite the heartbreaking circumstances, Tracy benefited from their visit, as it served as a distraction from her own problems—oh Lord, make that *added* problems. Though she'd sensed Marc had feelings for her, she'd been caught by surprise over his admission that he was in love with her. And sleep had not come easily.

So what to do now? Write Dear Abby? Run, hide? Take another cruise? Hardly. In minutes she would be with Peter, and they would take it from there.

She looked up as she heard the words "ticket holders" over the microphone. Alas, the announcement was for orange, not green. She reached for the paperback novel she carried in her bag, and then rejected the idea, figuring her level of concentration was on a par with the preschool set.

Back to people-watching, she spied the Redfords coming down the aisle. She was seated several chairs back from where they walked, but Ben had spotted her. He stopped, smiled, and bent down to say something to Patty. She turned to look at Tracy, gave a jaunty wave, and kept going. Ben hesitated a moment, then followed his wife.

Okey dokey. They'd undoubtedly had their fill of the trials and tribulations of Tracy, girl victim. She watched as they stationed themselves on the other side of the room. She envied them. How was it that some people led such neat and tidy lives?

Well, not all people. You couldn't miss the green and yellow sundress, with accompanying klutzy jewelry, nor mistake the wearer barreling down on her. Oh, shit, she was not in the mood for this.

"Tracy!" Shirley called out. "I missed you last night. I didn't get to say goodbye."

Tracy waved a greeting, her smile perfunctory, and then took a second look. Shirley had risen above the florid design of her dress and her gaudy accessories. She looked radiant. "Don't you look terrific?" Tracy said.

Shirley was all smiles. "I feel pretty terrific, too. Oh." She assumed a solemn expression. "I heard it was Jack Watkins who went overboard after this humongous struggle with Joanne. God, I feel so sorry for her, even though I never liked her. I thought she was snippy, had as much style as a toad, and made this big deal about being an officer's wife. And in case you've forgotten, *she* played bridge. Let me tell you, we went head to head a couple of times. But, you know, I was beginning to see her as a pathetic, downtrodden creature, trapped in a miserable life with that SOB excuse for a husband. I have to confess my heart went out to her."

"Let's hope she makes it," Tracy said. "In my book she deserves the best. She fought Jack to keep me out of harm's way." At Shirley's bewildered look, she explained the bottle episode. "And you cared enough to come to me with a warning."

"Oh, that's right. That was the night I was so upset. Remember I told you Dr. Rowlin was gay?" Her pause could be construed as dramatic. "It turns out he's straight. Furthermore, I'm going to see him in Sacramento next month. At any rate," Shirley added, "I'm walking on air. Oops, they're calling red ticket holders. That's me. Quick, write down your address, and I'll give you mine."

When they'd exchanged that information, Shirley gave her a wistful smile. "Maybe in my next life, I'll come back as someone like you."

Oh, my dear, haven't you heard? Appearances can be deceiving.

Inside the baggage terminal, porters with carts scrambled among passengers, vying with one another to procure business. Tracy was about to accept one annoyingly persistent handler when she caught sight of Peter hurrying toward her.

With an apologetic smile, she waved off the porter and opened her arms to her husband.

"Tracy!" Peter hugged her to him.

"Home at last."

"Thank God you're safe. It's been on the news about the man who went overboard, amid all kinds of speculation." He drew back from her, giving her a searching look, his expression troubled. "The report also mentioned a neo-Nazi connection. Was this the bigot who gave you a hard time?"

"None other. I must say, it's quite a story."

225

"I should have insisted you leave the ship."

She shrugged. "It didn't seem much of an issue at that time."

Again, he gave her a probing look. "Honey, you must be exhausted. Let's find the car."

Whatever her condition or emotional state, first on the agenda was to get to the bottom of Peter's mysterious disappearance these past several days. But this was not the place to bring up that very important matter.

However, in the privacy of their car, Tracy could hold back no longer. "Unfortunately, Peter, it wasn't all fun and frivolity aboard ship. Things got pretty messy."

"Incidents that involved you?"

"Yes."

Peter had taken streets that paralleled the freeway as a more direct approach from the airport to Pacific Palisades. Now as they stopped at a red light, he turned to her, obviously distressed.

"Tell me about this."

The light changed to green and the honk from the car behind set them in motion.

"I can't compete with traffic or concentrate on details when we're driving. When we're home, I'll fill you in. However, I do need to bring up something that can't wait." Peter was no fool, and she could tell from his guarded expression and stiffening of his body that he sensed trouble.

"I received your message about meeting me in L.A. when we were in Puerto Vallarta. I called back and left you a message."

He nodded.

"You said nothing was urgent."

"But I thought you'd try to reach me, regardless. If not that night, then the next day. In fact, I did put in a call to you very late the next evening, and still no answer. You weren't home Saturday evening, nor the following night. I couldn't imagine what happened to you."

"I didn't get back to you because I was up at Lake Tahoe, attending a weekend conference with my advisors. Doug Atkinson, the head honcho, has a beautiful home overlooking the lake on the north shore."

"I see. No hard-backed chairs in a stuffy room with day-old coffee for you. Substitute gourmet food served on a deck overlooking one of the most beautiful lakes in the world. Nice."

"We weren't meeting there for the food or scenery. In fact, we managed to accomplish a hell of a lot." At her silence, he continued, "I can tell you're upset with me." He reached over to press her hand. "This is not how I pictured your homecoming."

Tracy felt a dull throbbing in her head, a pall settle over her. "Peter, I needed you. I needed you desperately. If only you'd gotten back to me."

"I'm disturbed more and more by what I'm hearing." He looked at his watch. "I'm scheduled to check into the office this p.m. to sign off on a case and attend to some other matters, but I suppose that could wait until tomorrow."

"Don't put off your duties on my account."

He didn't respond, but she sensed something was going on as she noted the tightening of his jaw, his hard grip on the steering wheel.

Tracy had been too self-absorbed to pay much attention to their whereabouts. The streets and landmarks were familiar and not of any particular interest. She was aware of dazzling sunshine and rare smogless vistas, all of which did little to lift her spirits.

Suddenly, she began to observe their surroundings. Peter had turned off into an attractive commercial area, replete with boutique hotels and luxury condominiums spread out among restaurants that rated from casual to elegant, the more desirable properties fronting waterways and marinas. They were entering the aptly named Marina del Rey.

Tracy turned to her husband. "What's going on? Are we taking a detour?"

"I'm kidnapping you, whisking you away to a picturesque place where I can ply you with food and drink and tell you how beautiful you are and how much I've missed you."

She laughed, feeling a lessening of rigidity across her shoulders. "What brought this on?"

"I don't want to put off hearing about what happened to you on that ship. If we go home now, you'll want to examine your phone messages, unpack, check on Janet's housecleaning, and examine the pantry—"

"Stop. You're tiring me out. Let's go back to how beautiful I am, how much you've missed me."

"With pleasure," he said as he maneuvered into a parking space at one of their favorite restaurants.

Tracy never tired of the entrance that boasted an elaborate walkway, bordered by waterfalls and exotic flora and fauna. The ponds were stocked with koi and goldfish; their colors—vibrant scarlets, oranges, greens, and golds—shimmered below the surface of the water. The decor might be decried as ersatz Hawaiian, but it set the tone for mellowness and a journey of sensuous delights.

They opted to dine outside on the terrace that overlooked an expanse of green that led down to a small marina. The waterway beyond was quiet except for an occasional speedboat making a splash or pulling a water-skier. A few sailboats bobbed gracefully about, providing contrast to more aggressive watercraft.

Peter looked about him. "Not too many patrons on a weekday, which means we'll have privacy."

"The setting is all wrong," Tracy said. "Harrowing experiences need to be related in an atmosphere of darkness and chill with accompanying thunderbolts and lightning strikes."

"Afraid I can't provide a dark and stormy night scenario. You'll have to settle for sunny and warm. And a libation," he added, acknowledging the waitress who was now at their side. "What would you like to drink?"

When Tracy chose a gin martini, Peter seemed surprised. She seldom ordered hard liquor at lunch, preferring wine instead.

Peter ordered a scotch and water. *It would appear from our choice of drinks we both need fortification,* was Tracy's wry thought.

When their cocktails were before them, Peter toasted her return home, and then set down his drink. "Tell me everything. I want all the details."

She began by reviewing her steadily declining relationship with Jack Watkins, and then segued into a verbal portrait of her stalker in

Ixtapa, followed by a description of her brutal encounter with this same man in Puerto Vallarta.

Peter looked sick, his skin turning the color of paste, his eyes tearing. He rubbed his forehead as if attempting to erase the aforementioned graphic images, then reached for her hand. "The bastard. If I could get to him, I'd kill him. Tracy, I could have lost you. Thank God those two men came along."

"Yes. Thank God."

He let go of her hand, made a fist and hit the table. "I blame myself. I should have—"

"Peter, stop! You had no way of knowing what a jam I was in. As for the aftermath, people were helpful and protective, Ben especially."

"You had a strong man at your side. But not your husband."

Was he more upset over her ordeal or over the fact he'd been out of the picture? No, that wasn't fair. Peter was obviously shaken and horrified by what she'd told him.

He took a sip of his drink. "At some level you must have felt resentment toward me."

"Yes, I did." She broke the silence. "I think we should move on. I want to tell you about Watkins's post-midnight visit and my pre-dawn phone call. Then I suggest we take a break and order lunch."

With all of that accomplished, she then apprised him of the happenings leading up to Jack's death. He appeared riveted by her recital of events that culminated with the struggle between Joanne and Jack.

"Good riddance to Jack Watkins," he said when she'd finished her tale. "Justice can prevail. But what an astonishing story." Peter shook his head. "My God, what you went through. I can't believe how things turned out. This cruise was supposed to coax you out of the doldrums, revitalize you."

"We can talk about that later. Bring me up to date on you."

She caught something in Peter's expression, a twitch in his cheek muscle that signaled concern. But then he began an accounting of his days' activities both at the office and at home. He was part way into summarizing his Lake Tahoe weekend when their luncheon salads were served.

"Enough about business," he said. "Let's enjoy each other. Oh. I did want to mention my parents are giving a small dinner party Friday evening, mostly in your honor. You know, to welcome you home?"

"How nice of them. I'll look forward to that."

"Care to read that line again?"

"Sorry if I sounded blah. I am pretty tired." *Make that exhausted, wasted, and guilt-ridden, for starters.* She cracked a smile. "Maybe it's the martini. Maybe I'm not cut out to be plied with drink."

Glib words, but his comment about the purpose of the trip brought her down. *God help us both,* she thought.

Once home, Tracy found herself engaged in a flurry of activity, with phone messages to return, mail to sort through, plus the chores Peter had already outlined.

"Go back to the office," she insisted. "I appreciate your wanting to help, but it's easier for me to handle these things in my own way and at my own speed."

After a brief hesitation, he seemed to accept her line of reasoning and made his escape.

They proceeded through dinner without any interruptions, but later in the evening Peter took several phone calls in his study—a follow-up to the Lake Tahoe conference, he explained.

In bed, Peter reached for her. "It's good to have you back, to feel you in my arms."

She stiffened. "Peter, I can't."

"I know you're tired. Let me just hold you a bit."

"It's true I'm beat, but there's more. We need to have a serious talk. The sooner, the better."

Gently, he withdrew his arms, and then turned on his side, away from her.

"Peter?" She drew in her breath, clasped her hands tightly together, and then let out her breath in a long sigh. "Good night."

"Good night, Tracy." His words were muffled. "Get a good

night's sleep."

Sure. But only if you believed in miracles.

❧ *Chapter Twenty-Three* ❧

The Next Day

W hen Tracy awoke, she expected her bedside clock to read two, three, or four a.m. To her surprise, a perky 8:30 declared that it was time to rise and greet the day.

She groaned and turned over. The room was dark, with no evidence of sunlight seeping through the bottom or sides of the closed drapes. It had to be five-ish or six-ish. She looked again. It was 8:32, and Peter was gone, undoubtedly on his way to the office.

Tracy struggled out of bed, feeling anything but refreshed after almost ten hours of sleep. "Let there be light," she muttered as she opened the drapes, then questioned why she had bothered. She yearned to crawl back into bed and assign her jolly little clock the task of waking her when the marine layer dissipated and June gloom retreated to make room for afternoon sunshine. Instead, she moved sluggishly into the bathroom.

She avoided her reflection until she'd rinsed her face and brushed her teeth. Feeling better, she ran a comb through her hair. *Go for simple,* Tracy told the somber face in the mirror as she pulled her hair back into a ponytail. Before Peter returned home, she'd style her hair and apply makeup—she grimaced—in readiness for the big scene.

After slipping a robe over her pajamas, Tracy stepped out onto the deck to get a feel for the day. The grayness and stillness seemed to dictate a suspension in time, allowing one to pause for reflection.

On a day like this, she and Sophia brought coffee onto the patio outside their kitchen in defiance of the weather. What had they talked about? Probably something personal, something that touched their lives.

She blinked back tears, feeling her loss all over again. She needed her mother, needed her solace and support as she poured out her heart. Tracy drew her robe more tightly to her against the dampness and morning mist. Sophia loved and respected Peter, so maybe she would tout their continuing relationship as best for Tracy. And maybe not.

She could hear her mother's voice: "Be open and honest about your feelings and desires. If Peter still can't accept your need for change, if he can't perceive the seriousness with which you view this issue, then move on and do what you have to do." In simpler terms, "Dump all that."

She smiled in spite of herself as she reentered her bedroom. Was it her mother's voice she heard or Marc's?

Whatever the unfolding drama, the housekeeper they employed three days a week was off on Wednesdays, so it behooved her to get going and attend to practical matters—like putting on the coffee.

At the bottom of the stairs, she raised her head and sniffed the air. Something smelled good. It was the aroma of coffee, now wafting stronger as she neared the kitchen. Had Janet changed her schedule?

When Tracy entered the kitchen, her gaze fell on a table set with their good informal china placed on blue and yellow cloth placemats that matched the cheery design of their kitchen curtains. Yellow roses provided the centerpiece.

But it wasn't Janet who stood with her back to her at the stove; it was Peter. He appeared to be laboring over an elaborate egg concoction, with sausage frying on the side.

Her astonishment was such that she simply stood there, speechless.

Peter must have sensed her presence. He looked over his shoulder and gave her a big smile. "I thought I heard you stirring." He placed a lid over what he was cooking, lowered the heat, and then turned to give her his full attention. "Wow, look at you. Like a teenager, so fresh and youthful."

"Peter, for goodness's sake. I feel like plain Jane in her skivvies, attending the ball. But thank you for being so generous." She took her regular place at the table. "I'm surprised you're not at the office."

"With Janet off, I thought it might be depressing to face an empty house your first morning at home. So I'm here to keep you company and see to it you have a good breakfast."

"I always have a good breakfast, but that's beside the point. This is all very lovely. I'm impressed, to say the least."

Her mind raced, posing questions. *What was going on? Was Peter in denial?* Whatever the case, in no way could she blurt out her concerns under these circumstances. For now she was spared the anguish of confronting him. But only for now.

"A choice for m'lady. Orange juice or V-8?" He placed glasses by their plates.

"Uh, Peter, no. I really don't want any juice." In fact, she had little appetite. "Why don't I pour us some coffee?"

"No, no, stay seated. This is my party."

As he moved swiftly to remove the glasses, then pour their coffee, Tracy tried to ignore the voice from within that questioned his motives. Everything he did was right, an act of devotion. Yet she felt uncomfortable. *Overkill* was the word that popped into her head.

Either way, she felt removed, as if she were watching an attractive, youngish couple within the frame of a sitcom or movie. The good husband serves their breakfast and then they deliver their lines, making pleasant conversation—in all, touching on the mundane while avoiding any mention of life in the run-for-office lane.

At one point, Peter jumped up to bring blueberry muffins to the table.

She had to protest. "Here I am fresh from a cruise, and you're feeding me as if I'd been denied food? Not that I'm complaining. It's all delicious." He'd been creative with the eggs, adding peppers, onion, mushrooms, and cheese, along with various seasonings.

"I'm glad you're pleased. Why not allow me to take over some of the cooking chores, play chef every now and then?"

"I'll grant you're good in the kitchen." Inwardly she winced. How noncommittal could she be? Whatever Peter's thoughts, either her response bounced off of him, which she thought unlikely, or he was determined not to blunder into risky territory.

He looked at his watch. "I'll need to get going soon. I don't want to rush us, but I hate to leave you with the dishes."

"Not to worry. I have all day. Not a thing on tap, for a change."

"In that case, I'll have a little more coffee. Honey?"

"Half a cup is fine."

No sooner had he filled their cups, when the phone rang. He was up before she could move. From his side of the conversation, she gathered it was Ann.

"No, you're not interrupting anything; in fact, your timing is perfect because I'm practically out the door." He beckoned to Tracy. "Mother would like to talk to you, so I'll say goodbye now."

Before he handed her the phone, Tracy said, "Thank you for being so thoughtful."

"It was fun. I enjoyed playing chef." He paused. "I'll be home around five. And then, we'll talk."

He looked so vulnerable, she looked away for a moment, fighting tears as he handed her the phone. "See you later," she said. "Oh. And don't forget your briefcase."

It was their private joke, referring to a time Peter had been so preoccupied with a recalcitrant client that he'd left home three times in one week without his briefcase. His smile was wide and genuine, and he gave her a thumbs-up as he left the breakfast room, and Tracy greeted her mother-in-law.

"I hesitated to call yesterday," Ann was saying, "because I thought you needed time to settle in. Also, I wasn't sure when the boat was supposed to dock. I understand you had quite an adventure."

"Let's just say I'm glad to be home."

"Oh, my dear, we can't leave it at that. After all, you have first-hand knowledge as to what happened on that boat."

"It's a long, complicated story. I'd hardly know where to begin."

"At the beginning?"

Tracy felt her energy level slog down to subzero. She felt mired in mud, unable to find that beginning.

Apparently, her mother-in-law had interpreted her silence as a pause to marshal her thoughts. "Wait. Don't start. I have an idea. Let's do this in a leisurely manner. At lunch. It will be my treat as a celebration of your homecoming."

"That's sweet of you, but you're already going to the trouble of giving a dinner party in my honor."

"At dinner we wouldn't be able to chat, just the two of us, or have you feed me all the juicy details. I have in mind a seafood restaurant I know you'll enjoy. I'll make the reservation for twelve noon and pick you up at 11:45 on the dot."

And Tracy knew Ann would arrive on that dot, not a minute before, not a minute after.

So much for 'not a thing on tap'. After clean-up in the kitchen, the first order of business would be: lose the ponytail.

The restaurant, set close to the pier in Santa Monica, was sleek and elegant, its abundance of glass enabling diners to view the giant Ferris wheel that rose above an expanse of Pacific Ocean. Today, the ocean brought forth for Tracy an image of the chilly pearl-gray waters of Mendocino on the Northern California coast. It was a fitting backdrop for another round of playacting where she would mouth lines that she hoped were appropriate. Make that coherent, as well.

They each ordered a glass of Chardonnay and the combination shrimp and crab salad. Now as they waited for their salads, Ann's gaze shifted to her daughter-in-law in the manner of a captain viewing the troops. "You look tired, Tracy. Lovely as always but not as bursting to go, as I'd hoped."

"I'm not sure I follow you. Bursting to go?"

"Ready to move in stride with Peter's campaign. We have a lot of work to do before the November elections. I'm sure Peter will fill you in as to what's been accomplished, but even more importantly discuss with you the *Blueprint for Betterment* and where you fit into the plan."

"Now you've lost me."

"Oh? That's our clarion call for victory through action. It's brilliantly conceived, Tracy, and I'm so excited I've already scheduled a fundraiser that we'll hold at the club. You and I will co-hostess the event." She raised her glass in a gesture of triumph.

Our clarion call? *Blueprint for Betterment? Egad.* Tracy raised her glass to her lips and stared out at the ocean, watching the sea gulls circle and swoop over the misty waters. Ann was giving her an expectant look. She had to respond.

"It seems a lot has happened while I was away. I'm glad there's been progress."

"Oh, my, yes. And here's a bit of nifty news I wanted to bring up." Tracy could almost hear the purr that accompanied Ann's smug smile.

"State Senators John Cage and Dan Pearson and their wives will be attending my Friday evening dinner party."

"That's a real coup, Ann. Congratulations."

"Just wanted to let you know so you'll look your best. As you always do. Now. Do tell me what happened on that boat."

Ship! Not boat, Tracy wanted to bellow. Instead, she embarked upon an abbreviated account of what had taken place, including her role in the events that led to Jack's death. Ann's horrified reaction, particularly to Tracy's travails, was no act.

"You poor thing." She squeezed Tracy's hand. "What a shocking story. I had no idea you were at the center of that ghastly situation. Given what you've been through, I'd say you're doing remarkably well." Now it was Ann's turn to stare out at the ocean, her expression bleak. "I doubt I'd have coped as well." Then she brightened. "I predict our plunge into politics will be therapeutic—a sure way to erase all the nasty stuff."

Their salads arrived and Ann picked up her fork, only to set it down. "Peter's run for state assemblyman is just the beginning. We both know he has everything going for him. He's smart, personable, and attractive."

Tracy nodded. "I agree. He projects the right image."

"But that image has to be showcased. He'll need to attend public functions, work the fundraising circuit, and solicit votes by dropping in at lunchrooms, union halls, senior centers, schools and the like." She resumed eating, and then set down her fork once again. "So much hard work. But the rewards are endless. This first step could evolve into so much more. Think state senator, even governor. Tracy, imagine yourself as first lady of California!"

Tracy choked on a piece of shrimp. What next? First lady of the United States?

When Tracy walked into her house, the phone was ringing. She hurried into the family room in time to catch the tail end of a message: "You can imagine how concerned I've been. Please call me." It was her father.

She called him immediately, and for the second time that day, gave the chilling details of what had occurred both on and off the *Sea Star*.

His reaction was much the same as Ann's: horror, shock, and relief that she was home safe. "Don't be surprised if you experience some rough periods," he said. "I'm glad you have Peter to help you through this difficult time."

"Well, yes…" Suddenly, she burst into tears.

"Tracy, what's wrong? Are you and Peter having problems?"

"It's complicated, Dad." She paused to gain control of herself, took a deep breath, and then muttered, "Here we go."

Her father listened without comment as she struggled to verbalize her dissatisfactions, the urgency to take up her music or writing, plus the complicating factors of Peter's political aspirations.

"I know you think I could never measure up to Mom."

"Oh, honey, that's not true. When I walked in on you at the piano, I thought of your mother playing the Rachmaninoff *Second*. It was almost as if she were there. But I couldn't discuss the two of you in terms of comparisons, and I suppose I gave the impression I felt you could never become the artist she was. I've always thought you were immensely talented.

"Having said that, it's a long, hard road to the concert stage, and it would take tremendous dedication and perseverance to achieve that status." He paused. "Do you still love Peter?"

"Yes, but I fell into a situation—that is, I became involved with a man on the ship. He understands music, the arts, the pressures I'm under to conform to a lifestyle I often find stifling."

"I see. And now you have the additional stumbling block of supporting Peter in his run for office."

She could picture her father in his problem-solving mode, leaning back in his chair, knuckles kneading his chin.

"This is a tough one," he said. "I'm tempted to say don't move too hastily, but I'm sure that's crossed your mind. Why don't you come over to Rancho Mirage and spend a few days or a week with your dad? I'd enjoy your company, and a change of pace and scene might put things in perspective."

She laughed. "Didn't I try that? And look what it got me, almost killed. If I came to Rancho Mirage, I'd probably get bonked by a golf ball and require brain surgery."

He laughed, then sobered. "Let's keep in close touch. Remember, I'm here for you."

"I know you are. Peter and I are set to have a serious talk this afternoon. I'll let you know how that turns out."

They said their goodbyes, and Tracy felt better than when she had departed from Ann. Why hadn't she clarified the issues relating to her music years ago?

☙

Afternoon sunshine spilled between tree branches onto a carpet of green, while roses and delphiniums stood taller, their colors teased into brighter and bolder hues. Tracy, unmindful of pastoral pleasures, nursed a gin and tonic on their patio.

"That bad?" Peter asked as he joined her. His tone was light, but his manner reflected seriousness of purpose in no nonsense contrast to his amiable morning persona.

"5:00 is considered the cocktail hour in most places," Tracy said.

His smile was brief. "Well, why not?"

He returned soon with a scotch and water. He'd loosened his tie and removed his jacket. Now, as he seated himself beside her at the table, he said, "I understand you and my mother got together for lunch."

"Ann treated me to a very nice meal at Oceans at the Pier in Santa Monica. She was very disturbed over my ordeal, very sympathetic." Tracy paused to sip her drink. "She also had a lot to say about your run for office. She practically has us ensconced in the presidential box, come sixteen years from now."

Peter gave her a sidelong look. "Mother can get carried away."

"I appreciate her enthusiasm. I only wish I could respond in the same manner."

Peter set down his drink. Hard. "You never wanted me to run for office. Right?"

"You sound so angry."

239

"I am angry. What's wrong with wanting to be a part of the power structure? What's wrong with wanting to make a difference and working hard toward that aim? What's wrong with you, that you can't grasp what it's all about?"

"We should have thrashed this out at the very beginning." She gave him a meaningful look, and then shrugged. "Maybe I don't fit the mold."

"What mold?"

"I don't have to explain it. You know what I'm talking about."

"Refresh my memory."

"Oh, for God's sake. We've been over this. It's like we'd be starting a whole new life, with demands upon both of us. Life in a fishbowl."

"Think about the rewards."

She'd heard that same argument from Ann. "Rewards for whom? Us, you, me? Mainly for you. Where would I fit in?"

"You would be the perfect adjunct to reach the voting public. You're sharp, classy, and elegant."

"Peter, listen to me. This isn't only about your run for office. There are other factors involved."

His expression changed from glowering to wary. "There's another man in the picture?"

"Please, let me talk. Let me have my say."

"Sure."

Sure as in, 'I really want to hear what you have to say'? Or *sure* as in 'I'll listen, but that's as far as it goes'? She'd bet on the latter.

"Both you and Ann have commented that I've seemed restless, preoccupied. It's not that I haven't had enough to keep me busy. It's just that I feel I could sleepwalk my way through luncheon A, fundraiser B, volunteer group C. I'm not stimulated any more by these activities. Granted, these are worthwhile endeavors, attended to by hundreds of well-qualified women who thrive on being involved in community services. But I want out! Peter, I'm bored beyond belief."

He looked at her as if she'd spoken in foreign tongues, and then gave her a sardonic smile. "You're pretty young to be going through a mid-life crisis." He waved his hand in a gesture of dismissal. "I'm sorry if that sounded glib. What is it that you truly want to do?"

She breathed in, then out. "Okay. I'd like to return to my music or take up writing as a serious occupation." When he failed to comment, electing to stare into his drink, she said, "I know you consider these career goals as flawed."

"Not flawed, simply unrealistic."

"You have that little faith in me?"

He shook his head. "I didn't mean it to sound personal. I'm talking percentages in terms of success and failure."

"And I'm talking about my dreams."

He sipped his drink in silence, and then said, "Maybe we can work out a compromise. Stick with me through November. Then, whether I'm elected or not, the campaign activities will cease, and you can drop your club and volunteer work."

He thought for a moment. "Why haven't we discussed this before?"

"I have broached the subject with you, only to be frustrated by your lack of understanding."

"Tracy, that's not fair."

"You're right. I gave up too easily. I went along with conforming to a lifestyle that screamed in capital letters *Suitability With Our Status in Life*. For a while, it was okay. Then gradually something began to gnaw at me. I sensed I was out of step, that I wanted something more out of life than the club circuit and ladies' groups. And," she sighed, "I have to factor in my fear of failure."

"Fear of failure." He drew out the words. "And yet you want to make a career out of music or writing?"

"I've come to realize I can't shut down because of concerns I won't succeed. It's not making the effort that's a cop out."

"That philosophy could extend to my present situation."

"At least you're having your chance."

"And you can, too. But I need you by my side now."

241

"We're talking about six months? Okay, fine. But if you are elected—and I can't imagine you would not be—I can only picture more demands upon our time and energy. Then, too, as Ann pointed out, there's always the next step up the ladder."

"If I hadn't decided to run for office, would we still be having this talk?"

"Yes, because my defection from our current lifestyle could hamper our social life and, in the long run, be detrimental to your career."

"If I acceded to your demands, what then?"

"We'd move forward in our chosen paths—I would hope harmoniously."

"And if I strongly objected to these changes?"

"I need to take the risk. Peter, I can't stumble back into the same old patterns. I need to try my wings, take chances while I'm still relatively young."

"So what you're saying indirectly is that my say is not worth shit."

She flinched. "What I'm saying is this. If what I want out of life is unacceptable to you, morally wrong—whatever you choose to call it— then I suppose we'd have to go our separate ways."

He tipped back his head and closed his eyes, then opened, his gaze directed upward. "I can't believe I'm hearing this," he murmured. He straightened and turned to her. "Our marriage means so little to you? You'd walk out on me, ruin our lives, our reputations, and nail me to the cross? I offered you a compromise, damn it!"

"One minute you're saying we can negotiate our differences, and then in the next breath you're bringing up what-ifs—what if you gave in to my requirements, what if you strongly opposed my demands, as you call them." She threw up her hands. "I'm not out to crucify you. Don't be so dramatic."

"What is this, a casual day at the beach? Since when is ending a marriage a call for apathy and indifference? You might as well say piss off, and be done with it. How can you be so cold-hearted?"

"I'm not cold-hearted, I'm simply determined. I've vacillated so long over this decision that I need to stand firm. It doesn't have to mean the end of our marriage."

He stood now with his back to her, his hands jammed into his pockets. Then he turned to face her. "You're talking out of both sides of your mouth."

"Whatever you think, I had to get this out in the open. You've sensed something was wrong and to go on pretending everything was hunky-dory wouldn't be doing either of us a favor."

"What about my run for office?"

"I can't ask you to give that up. But we'd need an understanding as to my role in the campaign. And afterwards."

"I see."

But he didn't see. This talk, that she had counted on to be a breakthrough and clear the air, was not going at all well. Mentally, she felt disheartened and confused. Physically, she was beginning to feel queasy.

Slowly Peter took his seat at the table. His expression was grim. "I asked before, is there another man in the picture?"

Oh, God. "Yes and no. I became acquainted with the ship's pianist."

Peter nodded. "A man in tune with the arts. And he encouraged you, I presume, to pursue your dreams, to betray your husband?"

She felt as if she were on the witness stand. "We talked about my need for a change in my life."

"And what else went on?"

"Peter, you came to Acapulco ostensibly to be with me. But let's factor in the all-important political connection, the fact that your run for office was a done deal—never mind talking it over with your wife. And then when I needed you desperately, you were conferring with your advisors at Lake Tahoe. I had no idea as to your whereabouts. I couldn't imagine why I was unable to reach you."

"I repeat! What else went on?" he shouted.

"I…we…"

"Never mind. I don't want to hear this. I don't want to hear your excuses or lies." His tone was clipped and tight as if he were forcing each syllable into an utterance. Worse, his expression was flat, his eyes lusterless.

Peter's detachment was punishing. She would have preferred him to call her a tramp, a slut, to raise his voice, to rail at her.

He was on his feet. "I can't stay in this house with you. I'm going to pack a few things and check into a hotel."

She rose, too, and gripped the back of her chair, feeling faint. "There's no need to leave. We can work this out."

"I have to get away to be by myself for a while." He spoke to the ground.

"What about Friday, the dinner party?"

"If I'm not back sometime tomorrow, I'll talk to you Friday morning." Still no eye contact.

"Oh, Peter, I hate this." Tears streamed down her face.

He finally looked at her. His expression was stern, but his eyes had filled with tears. "How do you think I feel?" He started to turn away, and then hesitated, giving her a second look. "You're deathly pale. What is it?"

Tracy placed a hand over her mouth. "I'm going to be sick." She barely got the words out, and then made a dash for the house, Peter following.

She threw up in the downstairs bathroom, and then threw up again and again. Finally, with shaking hands she rinsed her face and mouth and came out of the bathroom.

Peter waited outside. "Are you all right?" he asked.

"I think I can blame this on a bad piece of shrimp." Her voice was hoarse, and she grabbed his arm. "Help me upstairs, and then you can be on your way."

When they reached their bedroom, Tracy fled to the bathroom, once again throwing up, followed by the dry heaves.

"This could be serious," Peter said when she came out. "I can take you to the emergency room or stop at a pharmacy and ask for something."

She shook her head. "I think I'm a little better. I need to be in bed."

He nodded and left the room, leaving Tracy to prepare for bed. She was dozing off when she felt a tap on her shoulder. Her eyes refused to open but a fraction—enough, though, to see Peter place something on her nightstand, and to note he had on his jacket.

"I called downstairs to make arrangements for tonight. I've provided you the name of the hotel and phone number in case you need to reach me."

"Thanks," she whispered. She squinted to look up at him and could see how tired and drawn he appeared. She stifled a sob and turned her back to him.

In seconds she heard the bedroom door close behind him, and then slow, measured steps taking the stairs. She held her breath and strained to hear if Peter had left the house. Had the front door been opened? She couldn't tell.

She released her breath in a sob as her question was answered. There was no mistaking the thwack of a door firmly closed.

❦ *Chapter Twenty-Four* ❦

The Following Day

The morning sunshine was like a downy comforter, wrapping Tracy in its gentle folds as she sat once more on her patio, nibbling on toast and sipping the tea Janet insisted on preparing for her.

How ironic, she thought, that yesterday's morning mist and chill had served as prelude and opening act to a lavish breakfast orchestrated by her husband, while today, on a golden morning, she breakfasted on invalid's fare, her husband missing—perhaps for good.

She closed her eyes to concentrate on the song and chatter of the birds, and to allow the accompanying soft breezes to invade that blanket of warmth to boost her out of her lethargy.

It was only momentary, but as clouds masked the sun, it suddenly turned cool. Tracy shivered, and as she opened her eyes to the dimming light, her thoughts turned to Peter.

Had he slept well? Had he slept at all? As though drugged, she drifted in and out of consciousness in a dreamless state, exhausted from her ordeal. And when morning came, along with remembrance, the thought of facing the consequences of yesterday's showdown plunged her deeper into a state of inertia. She simply was not ready to forge into battle.

Nor was she ready to handle company, but there it was, the sound of voices in the kitchen, a door opening, Ann's emphatic, "No, no, nothing for me, Janet. Thank you, but I've had breakfast. I just want to check on Tracy."

A moment later, Ann glided up to the table. "Here you are," she said. "Isn't it pleasant out this morning?" She took the seat her son had occupied the afternoon before, and then cast her gaze on Tracy, her expression of concern deepening the creases between her eyes. "How are you feeling?"

"Gutted, tired. But better."

"Better is good. Peter called this morning to say you'd become ill with what you assumed was food poisoning. He wondered if I'd been affected as well."

"I wondered, too, but you seem fine, thank goodness."

"After all you've been through," Ann looked heavenward, "and then to have *this* happen. It's simply not fair. However, with all this rotten luck, you're due for a break, for everything wonderful to come."

Tracy smiled and murmured her thanks for Ann's positive statements, but she was thinking her mother-in-law would disavow those sentiments in the flip of a switch if she knew what was going on between herself and Peter. Apparently, her husband had not broken the news he was out of the house. Nor why.

Ann pushed back her chair. "I'm off to the florist's. Johnson's is displaying a beautiful floral centerpiece that I want to snatch up for the dinner party. Oh." She hesitated. "About the dinner. I hope you can make it, but we'll understand if you're not up to it."

Tracy shook her head. "The thought of food has lost its appeal, plus I'd be a drag. I doubt I could hold up my end of a conversation."

"It could take a week or more to recover your appetite and strength. I agree, you shouldn't push it." Ann was on her feet. She kissed Tracy on the forehead. "Take care. Peter will simply have to make do without his bride by his side. This time." A smile, a wave, and she made her exit.

Tracy's tea was cold, her toast soggy, but she felt a glint of cheer. At least her illness provided an out for Friday's dinner party. Thank God for small favors.

Carrying her cup and plate, Tracy entered the kitchen and found it unoccupied. She could hear activity in the laundry room and made a brief stop to inform Janet she would be resting upstairs.

The rest turned into a long nap, and by noon, Tracy felt well enough to slip into jeans and a white cotton shirt, embellished across the front by a band of navy blue stripes that gave way in the center to a depiction of a ship's steering wheel in shades of light blue and silver. It was a nautical look that suggested a sail out to sea or a walk along the waterfront, neither of which were of any interest.

Lunch consisted of a cup of soup and toast. By dinnertime, she'd graduated to a bowl of soup, a cottage cheese and pineapple salad, with ice cream for dessert. Not a word from Peter.

At 8:30, Tracy curled up onto the couch in the family room and tuned into a rerun of *Murder, She Wrote*. Halfway through the story, she felt herself nodding off, fought it, then apparently dozed because when she opened her eyes, the TV was off, and Peter stood before her.

"How are you doing?" he asked.

She lay there for a few moments, taking in his presence, struggling to become alert, and then raised herself to a sitting position, feet on the floor, back straight, in an effort to match his formality. His question could have been addressed to an underling he tolerated, just barely.

"I'm better, but still recovering. Your mother stopped by this morning to check on me. She was very understanding that because of my condition, I won't be attending her dinner party." When he didn't respond, she added, "Buys us some time, don't you think?"

"I guess you could put it that way. At any rate, I'm glad you're better."

"Have you had dinner?"

"Oh, yes." He paused and loosened his tie. "I'll be settling into the guest room. So I'll say goodnight."

As he turned from her, she called out, "Peter, wait."

With obvious reluctance, he faced her. "What is it?"

"We both talked about compromise. Have you given some thought to that possibility?"

"I haven't sorted it all out yet. But that's not our only problem. There's that small matter of adultery."

His sarcasm implied huge over small, and she couldn't fault him for that. "Peter, you have every right to feel outrage, bitterness, condemnation, whatever. But you have to understand..."

"I told you I don't want to listen to your lies or excuses."

She leaned in toward him, trapping him in place by the intensity of her gaze. "You're a fine person, and you've been a good husband. I'm deeply, deeply sorry for the hurt I've caused you."

"Hurt. What an insipid word. It's meaningless. It's crap."

"I'm still too feeble to grovel, but if it'll help, I will."

He stared at her blankly. "I wasn't being flippant. I'm sorry it came out that way. I'm sorry, sorry, sorry. What more can I say?" She stifled a sob.

"It's getting late, and I still have work to do before bed." He strode from the room.

With Peter gone, with the TV off, the room seemed to close in on her, censorious in its silence. She shifted her gaze from shadowy inanimate objects to her left hand, moving her fingers so that the diamonds caught the light. Finally, it came to her what she must do.

She rose and left the room. She had a call to make, and she would place that call from their—from *her* bedroom.

The next morning, Tracy sat at the kitchen table, her breakfast consisting of a soft-boiled egg and an English muffin, light fare she could tolerate. She had risen at 7:00 to dress, and it was now almost 8:00, she realized, as she checked the time. She'd heard Peter shaving in the guest bathroom and wondered if he intended to have breakfast at home or eat out.

She didn't have to wonder long. She heard his steps—he sounded in a hurry—and observed his entrance. He appeared perplexed, even shaken.

"What are your suitcases doing at the front door?" No preamble, no "Good morning."

Tracy rose and carried her dishes to the sink. "A cab will be here in ten minutes." She turned to him. "I'm booked on a10:30 flight to Palm Springs. I've decided to stay with my father in Rancho Mirage for a while."

"Okay, fine, whatever suits you."

She could almost taste his anger, but so be it. She had her own welfare to consider, and it was not possible to mend fences or plan a future separate from Peter's in this poisonous atmosphere.

He made an abrupt turn, as if to leave, and then remained in place. Hands in pockets, he contemplated the floor. "We can't let this go on indefinitely."

"I know." She waited until he finally made eye contact. "We won't, Peter. But you need time. God help us, but we both need time."

June in the desert can be blisteringly hot, or as a sweet reprieve drop into double digits before giving way to July's and August's searing temperatures. On this seventh day of Tracy's stay in Rancho Mirage, the local news predicted a daunting 112 degrees.

Responding to Tracy's expression of dismay, her father winked and said, "Not to worry. By the end of the week, we expect a cooling trend, maybe 105 degrees or even 103."

Her response had been on the sarcastic side. Still, she found it a pleasant change to wake up every morning to sunshine and warmth, to view palm trees standing sentinel over greens, while the mountains beyond granted character and grandeur to the picture perfect landscape.

John McDermott lived in a gated, country club community, frequented mainly by wealthy part-time residents. His home on the golf course featured a sweeping view of the fairway and mountains. Lagoons and ponds that beautified the greens as well as serving as repositories for errant golf balls, were home to ducks, egrets, and several swans that waddled from pond to pond, imperiously taking up residence where it suited them for the moment.

Tracy enjoyed watching the wildlife, especially the duck couples with their babies marching in single file as they followed Mama into the water. On the patio, brilliantly banded hummingbirds hovered over the feeder, tiny creatures that darted at one another, engaged in aerial warfare, the victor taking nourishment at the trough.

Nature's realm. The pristine beauty of Tracy's surroundings calmed her. The antics of the birds and fowl—their innocence, their mischief—amused her and offered distraction from her woes. She was also regaining her strength.

But she couldn't remain in this quiescent state. Already she felt restless and started to think seriously about returning home.

Peter hadn't been in touch, which she could justify, given the circumstances of her departure. But his silence weighed on her, and she could only hope their time-out would be productive, that at the very least they might come to a truce.

Marc had been in her thoughts as well, but she could not bring herself to call him, not when the situation with Peter was so ugly. *One step at a time*. That was her mantra, a phrase she repeated to herself when she tossed and turned in the night.

During those sleepless hours, she sometimes played the how-what-if game. How had Peter known another man was in the picture? What if she had proclaimed her innocence on all counts? What if he'd never brought up the subject? Would she then have confessed to adultery? Or hugged her secret to her for the rest of her life?

In her dreams, she could edit the scene between them to her satisfaction. But when she awoke, it was to depressing reality.

Her music helped her get through the day. When Tracy first arrived, the piano in the living room loomed like a rapacious animal ready to devour her. But Brahms, Schubert, and Beethoven had mollified the beast, and in time, harmony prevailed.

Usually, she turned to her music when her father was out, like now, when he'd left for a luncheon engagement. Her routine called for practicing scales and exercises designed to enhance technique before she delved into the classics. Today she felt the urge to shoot discipline to the wind. She wanted to let go, to submerse herself in music that was showy but romantic, music that conjured up a spectrum of emotional diversity.

The Rachmaninoff *Piano Concerto No. 2* lay at the bottom of the pile of music stacked in a case next to the piano. Until now, she'd avoided the piece, unwilling to recapture the sadness from her past.

Now she seized the music, and began to play with a sense of empowerment. This time, her approach was not tentative. If her playing lacked the polish that comes with practice, an edge, a raw vitality and forcefulness, enhanced her treatment of the opening chords and passages that led into soaring lyricism.

The music flowed, and she hummed along out of sheer gladness, bringing in the symphonic parts where the piano paused.

Then she faltered, aware of a noise in the background that sounded like a door closing. Damn. Her father had probably popped in to retrieve the glasses he had a habit of forgetting. She flexed her fingers but was reluctant to proceed, afraid of any residual emotional fallout.

"Please don't stop. That was beautiful."

That was not her father's voice. Tracy looked beyond the raised lid of the baby grand, and then slowly rose from the bench.

Peter stood just beyond the piano.

"Oh, my God," she muttered.

"I stayed outside for a while, listening to you play," he said, "then I knocked softly, not wanting to disturb you. Apparently, John's not around?"

"He's at lunch." She grasped for something more to say, but words failed her. Finally she came around from the bench to greet her husband, noting he looked good—clear-eyed and rested, though thinner. In deference to the desert heat, Peter had traded his office uniform for a short-sleeved multicolored sports shirt worn over white pants.

She led the way to the sofa where they sat at a respectable distance from one another.

"Are you here for the day only?"

"For today and overnight. I've checked into a hotel here in Rancho Mirage."

She nodded. "Thank God for air conditioning. Have you heard what the predicted high is?"

"Tracy, let's cut the small talk."

"Okay, fine. Your move."

"I'm sorry if that sounded sharp. I'm not here to antagonize you."

"Then why are you here?"

"Why don't we talk over lunch? I have a place in mind," he said, responding to her raised eyebrows.

She almost said no, that they should stay put, talk now, and then thought better of it. Whatever the purpose of his proposed talk, whatever the outcome, it would be easier to maintain composure in a public place.

"Give me five minutes," she said, getting to her feet. "I'm going to change out of these shorts into something more formal, like jeans or capris."

He smiled absently, acknowledging her remark, but clearly, fashion was not on his mind.

This is it, Tracy thought as she entered her bedroom. Act III, the denouement. No more sorting things out, putting decisions on hold.

What will be, will be.

Peter had requested and been provided a booth in a quiet section of his hotel dining room. Now that they'd each been served a glass of Merlot, he gave Tracy a wry smile. "I guess I'd better call the meeting to order.

"So. Let me start off by saying it's been a very long week." He emphasized the very. "I admit at first I was angry and upset that you'd taken off. But it was the right decision."

She nodded. "I figured if we were going to resolve our situation, we both needed a time-out."

He did not respond but appeared to be lost in thought. Had he even heard her? She had absolutely no clue as to what was coming.

Peter sipped his wine for a moment, and then set down his glass. "You stated I've been a good husband. Would a good husband encourage his wife to go off by herself, knowing something wasn't right between them?"

"You had other priorities."

"Good for me. The point is, Tracy, had I been with you, those bastards would have left you alone."

"Come on, Peter, how were we supposed to know I'd be caught up in a neo-Nazi nightmare? As for what was going on between us, I should have tried harder to make myself heard."

"But just how responsive would I have been?"

It was a question she chose not to answer. She tasted her wine, and then said, "You've obviously been doing a lot of thinking."

"Not at first. When this all ignited, I was a walking wound. I was furious. I was crushed. And, of course, the fact you were with another man was a blow to my pride. And then I began to assess my role in the breakdown of our marriage, and I could understand why you would turn to someone else, particularly when you were so vulnerable." He swallowed hard. "Having said that, I can't snap my fingers and make it all go away. There are times when I hurt like hell, when I feel like throwing a major tantrum."

She took a shaky breath. "What I did was wrong, so wrong."

"I'm not going to stop you from beating yourself up over this, but as I said, I'm beginning to see your side of this too."

"Are you saying you can forgive me?"

His smile was on the tepid side. "I'm getting there."

"Good." Tracy reached to squeeze his hand. "I've missed you." It was true. She didn't want Peter out of her life. She knew that now and could only hope they could reach an accord. As for Marc, it now seemed dreamlike, their flirtation, their delight in a commonality of interests, and their night of love. No, it was more than that. She had felt exuberant, so intensely alive with him, though she had to wonder if part of that feeling derived from the seductive nature of their relationship, the excitement of the forbidden. Could one maintain that heightened sense of ardor over the long haul? Hardly. She knew better than that. And yet, perhaps with Marc…

She grimaced inwardly and dropped the thought. Peter was telling her about the Friday night dinner party.

"Everything was perfect. My parents were the perfect hosts, the table was perfection, the guests, the food—need I go on?

"It was all drivel, meaningless. I played my part, of course, working hard to impress the senators and charm their wives, but I felt empty, Tracy, all hollow inside. As angry as I was with you, the evening just wasn't the same without you. Nor the day after, nor the day after that. I began then to stop nursing my wounds and look at the total picture.

"Tracy, I don't want another failed marriage. If running for office is too much an intrusion into our lives, if it will make you happy, I'll gladly quit the race. And I would never throw it up to you I was denied my chance and all that crap. Also, if getting out of the race resulted in life becoming uncomfortable at the firm, I'd quit that too. We could go away, start over."

"Peter, my goodness, slow down! I told you I would never ask you to back out of the race. I've been doing some thinking too, and I do believe you could make a difference. You have it all, plus the perseverance to get a job done."

"But where would that leave us?"

"I can't go back to being who I was, so let's talk about a compromise. What if I were to take a semi-active part in the campaign?

For example, attend evening functions with you, be there for you for any special situation that arises. Would that be enough?"

"Hey, I told you I was willing to drop the campaign. I still am, but if you insist…" He laughed. "Honey, it's up to you to call the shots."

"Peter, are you sure?"

"Tell me what I can do to convince you."

She weighed his statement, and then shook her head. "You seem different somehow."

"I've come to realize I'll do whatever it takes to keep you in my life." He smiled. "I suppose as a lawyer, I should stipulate 'within reason.'"

"I promise I won't demand sables, diamonds from Cartier, or round-the-world trips. Not at first, anyway." She laughed, then sobered. "I like where this is going. You know, I think we just might make it to the next anniversary and way beyond that."

"I'd bet on it." He paused and gave her a speculative look. "Not to press you, but we seem to be moving in a positive direction. Why don't we whip up to Santa Barbara next weekend for a getaway?"

She looked at him closely. He'd loosened up, and she liked the new Peter. She also liked the idea of a weekend in Santa Barbara and what that implied. She told him so.

He stared at her for a long moment. "I'm feeling a little overwhelmed, but a hell of a lot happier than I've been in a long time."

"I couldn't have said it better." She blinked away a tear, and then drew in her breath. "Oh dear. I forgot about Ann. She'll certainly be upset with me for substituting occasional time for full time in the campaign."

"It doesn't matter. I'll deal with her and my father."

"Was she surprised I left town?"

"At first. But then she reasoned you were worn out physically and emotionally and needed some quiet time."

"Good. I'm glad you didn't tell her about us."

He leaned forward and took her hand. "Now I don't have to, thank God. Oh." He drew back. "About this man on the ship. I'm not sure I'm ready to hear this, but I have to ask. Do you still have—feelings for him?"

"No," she lied. "What happened…happened. End of story. I love you." And that was not a lie.

"And so they lived happily ever after?" He laughed softly. "I'm sure we'll have our ups and downs, but right now I feel closer to you than I ever have." He signaled the waiter and indicated they'd have a refill. "How can we possibly order lunch without a toast?"

"Will you look at us? I can't believe how this has turned out." She hesitated, and then said, "I wasn't planning to stay on in Rancho Mirage much longer."

"We could drive back home together tomorrow."

"I'd like that." Again, she hesitated. "Earlier you indicated you were close to forgiveness, but not quite."

"I've stepped up the process—by a lot. I have a lovely room on the fifth floor that would be graced by your presence."

"I'm a married woman. Why would I want to spend the night alone in my father's home?"

"Then it's settled," Peter said as their drinks were placed before them. He raised his glass. "To you, my darling. I love you, Tracy. I always will."

The tears that sprang to her eyes were of joy and contrition. And for loss.

❧ *Epilogue* ❧

The hotel, located in downtown Sacramento, was the city's largest and most luxurious, catering to state political figures and the occasional visiting celebrity.

"Plus governors past and present," Peter whispered in Tracy's ear earlier as they and the senior Bradshaws moved through the receiving line in the Comstock Ballroom where guests were gathered to honor newly elected legislators.

"Can you feel the energy in this room?" Tracy whispered back. "It's like a night at the theater. I'm loving this."

"Maybe so, but I can tell you're taking mental notes, sizing up the bad guys and the really awful jerks for that first novel."

She laughed at his comment, but for now she'd set aside her jottings and notes to concentrate on the piano, spurred on by her teacher's encouragement and Peter's approval. He even sat in on a few practice sessions, cheering her on.

Now having disengaged himself from a jolly foursome—*from his side of the aisle?* She wondered—Peter was back by her side. Before he could raise the question, she said, "I'm doing fine, but it is a little close in here."

"Why don't we take a breather?" He indicated the doors that opened onto the mezzanine.

"Why don't *I* take a break? You need to mix and chat with your colleagues."

"If you're sure you're okay?"

"I'm more than okay, Peter." She turned from him before he could question her further, and then called over her shoulder, "Be back soon."

The spacious balcony, furnished with strategically placed overstuffed chairs and sofas, offered intimacy or breathing space. And a comfortable place to sit down, was Tracy's thought. But now what caught her eye was fall foliage framed by the wall of windows across from the balcony.

She moved to the railing for a closer look at November's rich palette of lemony yellows melting into leafy golds, of intense orange shades blending into softer russets.

Darkness would soon obliterate color, stubbing out autumn's warm glow, and in days to come, daylight would reveal naked branches bowing to winter's frost under ashen skies.

Cycles. For some, change signified a quickening of the senses, a boost in energy with the pledge to begin afresh or the promise to complete what was started. Not so for others for whom the seasonal shift represented only a continuum of futility or a deepening of despair.

Case in point. Friday a week ago had been a memorable day, both sad and bittersweet, occasioned by a phone call and the arrival of a package.

The phone call came when she was at the piano, struggling over a particularly difficult passage in a Bach partita. For once, she welcomed the interruption and hurried to the phone.

"Mrs. Bradshaw?"

"Yes?" The voice was male and unfamiliar.

"This is Ted Watkins."

"Ted Watkins? Oh. You must be Joanne's son."

"Yes."

She felt her heart skip a beat at the silence on the other end. "I've talked with your mother several times by phone since we returned home. I hope she's all right."

"My mom mentioned how much your conversations meant to her. She said she always felt better after talking with you."

Once again there was silence. "Ted, is something wrong?"

His response was a shaky intake of breath. Then, "Tracy? Can I call you Tracy?"

"Of course."

"It's about my mom. She was on top of things for a while, doing okay. Then she started drinking again and—she drove drunk, hit a light pole, and"—once again he took in his breath—"she didn't make it."

"Oh, no." Tracy fell silent, jolted by his news. "I'm so sorry. I can't tell you how sorry I am." She blinked back tears. "Joanne was special to me, Ted. A lot happened on board ship, and she was there for me, big time."

"She told me everything. The whole shitty story." He paused. "Sorry about that."

"I understand. Ted, if there's anything I can do?"

"No. My sister and I are taking care of everything. I just wanted you to know."

"I can tell you your mother cared about her children. Please know she loved you very much." Tracy started at the ringing of her doorbell. It rang again, insistent, piercing. "Someone's at my door. Can you hang on for a moment?"

"I'd better not. I have more calls to make."

"Thank you, Ted. Call again. Let me know how you're doing."

As they rang off, there was a pounding on her door. Good grief, what was going on?

It was special delivery for Tracy Bradshaw, a large package that required a signature.

Puzzled, because she had not ordered anything, Tracy immediately checked the return address, then felt her heart race. The delivery was from San Diego, the Art Center in Balboa Park. It had to be something from Marc.

She had not talked with him after her reconciliation with Peter, but had written him a letter. Tracy, the writer. Ha! It took her half a day to compose the damn thing. He had not written back, which she supposed was for the best. And now this.

She felt flushed, and her palms tingled as she carried the package into the kitchen where she would dispose of the wrappings. Slowly, carefully, she cut through the tape and removed the paper that concealed a plain while box. Probing through the packing material that filled the box, she found an exquisitely fashioned gold-rimmed ceramic bowl in shades of blue, ranging from pastels to smoky hues.

The accompanying note read:

Dearest Tracy,

> *All things happen for a reason, and alas, we were not destined to be together. Still, what we had was precious and unique to us. I hope you will accept this bowl that I made for you as a gift from my heart.*

> *You have enriched my life, and I will hold you in my memory forever.*

It was then she'd broken down to weep for Joanne and for what would never be.

Now as Tracy relived that day, she struggled against tears, then took a deep breath. There, all was well. It was as if a gigantic smile beamed from the very core of her being to embrace her with light. It was a light that flooded her with joy as she pictured the child that would enter their lives in May.

She turned from the railing, mindful of one very overprotective father-to-be. If she tarried much longer, Peter would be sending out a search and rescue team.

What stopped her was the sight of a woman approaching her at a half run. Good heavens, it was Shirley Goodweather.

"Oh, m'Gawd, Tracy! I thought I recognized you, even from the back."

During the exchange of greetings, Tracy noted Shirley looked terrific, for Shirley, though overdressed for the occasion. Sequins, cleavage, drop earrings, and an up-do hairstyle (much like her own) made Shirley a stand-out.

"I was determined," Shirley was saying, "to see you, come hell or high water. I mean, it's in the newspaper about Peter Bradshaw representing Pacific Palisades. Bingo! It all connects. I know his gorgeous wife, we've been through the pits together, and here she'll be in my bailiwick, by God." She gave her a conspiratorial wink. "I was about to sneak into the reception when I spotted you."

"No need for sneaking. We'll walk in there together, with you as my guest."

Shirley was beaming. "I always said you had class."

Tracy hesitated, and then said, "Dare I ask about you and Jim Rowlin?"

"Ask away. We've been seeing each other most weekends, and I'll be spending the Christmas holidays with him in San Francisco." She gave Tracy a little poke. "I wonder what Santa will leave for me under the tree. Maybe a ring?"

"Sounds promising."

They were nearing the entrance to the ballroom when Shirley asked if Tracy had talked to Joanne or heard from the Redfords.

Tracy placed a restraining hand on Shirley's arm. "I'm afraid the Redfords are a lost cause. My guess is Patty was annoyed that I called on Ben way too much when I was in trouble."

"Well, Jeez Louise, how small can you be? Little Petty Patty."

Tracy smiled. "You do have a way with words." Then she sobered. "I have news about Joanne." She related her conversation with Ted Watkins.

Her demeanor appropriately solemn, Shirley shook her head in mournful respect. Then she brightened.

"Is that your husband coming our way? He's certainly eying you." She made a low humming sound. "I'd take him anytime over Marc. Whoops. Insert foot into mouth."

Tracy laughed. "It's okay. All's well in the house of Bradshaw." She looked up. "Hi, sweetheart. I'd like you to meet Shirley Goodweather."

With introductions completed, they entered the ballroom to encounter Ann hastening to Tracy's side.

"I just talked to a woman from our area who owns a baby furniture shop. She's also an interior designer and has some terrific ideas for decorating a nursery." She pursed her lips. "Uh-oh. I see someone I need to talk to. A *very* important lady. At least in her eyes. Catch you later."

Shirley looked from Tracy to Peter, then back to Tracy, eyes bulging, mount agape. "You're expecting?" The words gushed out, sentences forming paragraphs.

Tracy wondered if Peter would find some excuse to retreat, but he appeared fascinated by Shirley's enthusiastic, if rambling, discourse on the joys of parenthood, later confiding that Tracy's verbal portrait of Shirley was on the mark.

As for Ann, she was thrilled by the news of her pregnancy and thus far had not imposed her views of motherhood or child rearing. Whatever Peter said to his parents, they had unconditionally accepted the new direction her life was taking. In fact, Peter reported overhearing his mother brag to a friend about her daughter-in-law, the concert pianist, who was brilliant, beautiful, and talented – in all, an asset to the family.

Given recent past events, Tracy could only marvel at this incredible outcome.

As for the future, she would opt for a smoother ride over her collision-course past. High drama, danger, illicit love. Why would anyone choose a path so fraught with risk?

She smiled. It wasn't always a matter of choice.

 *THE END*

At Risk – Jackie Ullerich

About The Author

A native Californian, Jackie Ullerich was born in Los Angeles, grew up in San Diego and attended UCLA, where she graduated with honors, earning a secondary teaching credential in theater arts and English. She also attained Master Teacher status, which qualified her to train and supervise student teachers at the high school level.

In a major change of venue, Jackie left the classroom for the world stage to travel and live in a variety of places, both in the U.S. and overseas, with her Air Force husband.

Her years of living in Turkey and Greece coincided with changes in government, including tanks in the streets. But hostile environments were offset by exploration of ancient cultures and the colorful tapestries of contemporary life.

Of her many experiences, teaching English as a foreign language at the Turkish War College in Ankara, was an adventure in itself. While her novels reflect first-hand knowledge of exotic and historic locals, California provides a backdrop for most of her writing.

Presently, Jackie and her retired Air Force JAG husband reside in Palm Desert, California where her husband golfs while Jackie writes.

CPSIA information can be obtained at www.ICGtesting.com
Printed in the USA
LVOW032231131211

259294LV00005B/41/P